PENGUIN BOOKS

SHIKARI

Yashwant Chittal is one of the most significant voices of modern Kannada literature.

Pratibha Umashankar-Nadiger straddles two disciplines—academics and journalism. She was, till recently, the associate editor of *Climate Control Middle East*, and was formerly consulting editor of *Books & More*. As special feature writer for *Weekend* magazine, *Khaleej Times*, she received the best feature writer award for 2008 and 2009 from the government of Dubai. Apart from cover stories, edit pieces, interviews and essays in literary journals, her published works include two coffee table books on eminent Zoroastrians (which she edited), a biography in Kannada and a set of English textbooks (co-authored). She is presently working on her doctoral thesis on Partition writing by women.

shikari

the hunt

YASHWANT
CHITTAL

TRANSLATED FROM THE KANNADA BY
PRATIBHA UMASHANKAR-NADIGER

PENGUIN BOOKS
An imprint of Penguin Random House

PENGUIN BOOKS

USA | Canada | UK | Ireland | Australia
New Zealand | India | South Africa | China | Singapore

Penguin Books is part of the Penguin Random House group of companies
whose addresses can be found at global.penguinrandomhouse.com

Published by Penguin Random House India Pvt. Ltd
4th Floor, Capital Tower 1, MG Road,
Gurugram 122 002, Haryana, India

First published in Kannada as *Shikari* by Manohara Granthamaala, Dharawad 1979
First published in English in Penguin Books by Penguin Random House India 2017

ISBN 9780143428480

Typeset in Dante MT Std by Manipal Digital Systems, Manipal
Printed at Repro India Limited

www.penguin.co.in

MIX
Paper from
responsible sources
FSC® C047271

Translator's note

When I first began to read *Shikari* with a translator's eye, it became immediately clear to me that rendering Yashwant Chittal's complex world to the English reader would be a daunting task.

Hunting is the leitmotif that runs through *Shikari*, as Nagappa, the protagonist, unwittingly finds himself at the centre of ferociously fought modern jungle warfare, where professional and societal forces collude against him. He is also prey to his own past, both hunted and haunted by it. This results in a narrative that is at once seamless and fractured, shifting back and forth from a barely present, non-intrusive narrator to Nagappa's relentless inner monologue—the thinker and intellectual, constantly introspecting, analysing, theorizing and chronicling events past and present—creating, in the process, a palimpsest of memories and broken images through which Nagappa's life emerges. Nagappa speaks in several voices and registers, the cadence of his voice, often changing mid-thought, moving from the obscene to the colloquial, and from the lyrical to the erudite, interspersed with philosophical and scientific musings. It takes the readers' knowledge for granted, making the narrative dense, and often literary, imbued with irony—dark, raw and unmitigated.

The narrative complexity of *Shikari* notwithstanding, entering Nagappa's mind and translating his persona was perhaps the most challenging aspect of the book to navigate. Though Nagappa elicits immense empathy and compassion, he is no tragic hero, even in his own eyes. Chittal unravels, through Nagappa's inner conflicts, layers of his troubled psyche, which makes us wonder if he is the victim of his own paranoia. Thus, our attitude towards him remains ambivalent.

I also, of course, was faced with the question that all translators encounter when grappling with the nuts and bolts of two distinct languages: How does one translate the untranslatable? Indian languages are rich in onomatopoeic words. For instance, a word like *dhutt*, which, in Kannada, is an auditory metaphor for something occurring suddenly, defies translation. A non-auditory word does not carry the same valency. But to retain these onomatopoeic words, would be to risk provincializing or exoticizing the language.

For all these reasons, and more, translating Chittal's masterpiece, *Shikari*, has been an immensely challenging experience, and an equally gratifying one. I hope that if something has been lost in translation, perhaps, something has been gained in the process.

As *Shikari: The Hunt* emerges from the formidable shadow of Chittal's creative genius to embark upon a journey of its own towards a wider readership, I acknowledge with profound gratitude all those who made this possible: Malathi Chittal for giving permission to translate this work into English; Penguin Random House India for trusting me with this book; Premanka Goswami, commissioning editor, for seeing this project through; copy editors Jyotsna Raman and Shatarupa Ghoshal, and the team that proofread the manuscript; Gunjan Ahlawat, head-creative, and his team for the beautiful cover design, and all those who have worked behind the scenes; my friends for life, Narayan, Sujata, Charanjeet, Meeta, Lalita, Naina and Saraswati, and my family for their unstinting support. I am especially grateful to my daughter, Rachana, who has always stood by me. What would I have done without you?

I am deeply indebted to writers Jayant Kaikini, my translation of whose story started it all; to Vivek Shanbhag for having faith in me and suggesting my name to Penguin Random House India; and to M.S. Sriram for reading the manuscript and sharing his feedback, despite his many commitments.

I fondly remember my parents, whose abiding grace has been upon me.

10 September 2017   Pratibha Umashankar-Nadiger
Bengaluru

PART 1

1

As the situation he found himself in began to make some sense to Nagappa, he recalled K, the hero of Kafka's novel *The Trial* that he had read years ago. Just like it had happened with K, somebody must be spreading false rumours about him. Or why would this bizarre order from the personnel and administration manager come yesterday morning, when he was getting ready to go to work? The thought unnerved him.

You have been suspended with immediate effect due to serious charges against you. You will be informed of the charges at the earliest. You have been ordered not to attend the office till such time that we inform you about them.

The order was very clear. And it had come with a piece of advice: *With the view that you are not adversely affected in any way in the event of the charges being proved false, it is in your interest to apply for a month's leave immediately.*

Nagappa had sent in his leave application. But he now faced the predicament of having to hide from others the real reason for his forced leave. He wracked his brains for a plausible explanation he could give, but couldn't think of any. And then there were these 'charges'. The more he tried to think what they could possibly be, the more intriguing the whole thing appeared to him.

For a moment, he wondered if it was all a terrible mistake. He couldn't somehow bring himself to believe this was really happening to him, because he was to leave for America in a couple of months for higher training—something he had dreamt of for years. And now this, when he was eagerly waiting for the day.

A thought occurred to him: Was being selected for the training the very reason for this sudden turn of events? As time passed, he became convinced that was the case. What had started as a vague suspicion began to appear like the truth. This meant Phiroz still harboured that old hatred towards him. This's surely part of some vicious plot hatched by that Machiavellian manipulator . . . that evil politicking bastard . . . the son of a bitch Number One! Nagappa thought. Things would become clearer if he could somehow find out what the charges framed against him were. Now he could do nothing but wait for further information from the personnel and administration manager.

He found the wait unbearable. He became suddenly and acutely aware that he had nothing to do. He shuddered. The question of what to do with his time had never bothered him before. But now, empty hours stretched before him, directionless. He recalled reading in a book on psychology that one of the greatest problems the human mind finds difficult to grapple with is the structuring of time.

Suppressing the waves of amorphous panic that threatened to engulf him, he tried to define it and give it some shape. But the more he tried, the more it seemed to gain an upper hand. He shook inwardly, uncontrollably. He spent the day analysing each passing mood and thought and recording it. And his chronicling continued:

Comment 1: This is the second day of my forced leave. The thought that came to me as I woke up: If I keep thinking about this problem, I might either end up in a mental asylum or committing suicide. Both are ways of running away from the situation—attempts at alienating myself from the world. Is the constant act of analysing the meaning of life a sign of a profound inner search or of losing faith in life—in one's very existence? Isn't embracing life with enthusiasm and living with a sense of commitment a natural instinct? Isn't it the very wellspring of life's process?

Why does this question, that doesn't seem to bother millions of other living beings, constantly trouble me? Maybe it's not because of my philosophical bent of mind, which I secretly take pride in, but because I have no zest for life. I think the very wellspring that energizes my being has run dry. Maybe it's meaningless to search for the meaning of life. How can you search for something that doesn't exist? This so-called 'meaning' is something we've invented. And then, how is creativity possible when there is no zest for life? How can the creative impulse spring in this arid desert?

Comment 2: This is something that struck me when I was resting in my easy chair after breakfast: What energizes the life force within us, what spurs us on even more than our sexual drive is our territorial instinct . . . a sense of belonging—the need for a strong geographical connect to a place. According to recent research, it seems this's the most powerful driving force in all animals—humans, beasts, birds and even aquatic creatures. Experts think that perhaps this basic territorial instinct is expressed through our attachment to our property, our land, our region. Could be true. But based on my own experience, I think the most powerful driving force—more potent than our love for our property and place—is achievements in our chosen profession, our careers. Achieving success in this arena of 'action', no matter how small, is what motivates us the most. Since professional success is the outward, visible sign of our ability and the measure of our self-worth, our desire to outshine others and rise to the top is the motivating force behind all human actions, our fundamental source of inspiration—the prime mover.

Comment 3: After my post-lunch siesta, when I was about to have my tea, another thought struck me: Maybe I wouldn't be in this predicament today, if I hadn't channelized all my creative energies towards building this company I'm working for, or if I hadn't been under the illusion that I have contributed greatly to its present position of eminence. But I guess there's no end to such useless conjectures and 'what ifs'.

When Man stands at life's crossroads and thinks he has the freedom to choose any of the several paths before him, he finally chooses, and can really choose only *one* path. So, in reality, the possibilities narrow down to just one. And the very act of choosing the path determines our entire personality, not the other way round: Our choice is not a response to an outside 'stimulus' based on our innate nature, but the way we respond to the options decides and shapes our personality. I'm reminded of Tolstoy's story *Death of Ivan Ilych*. Here, Ilych, dying of cancer, reflects on his entire life and feels he could have lived it differently. Tolstoy, perhaps, suggests that this deep and futile sense of regret at the end of Ilych's life is more poignant than his imminent death itself.

Comment 4: What I realized when my eyes became moist with Amma's memory as dusk gathered: We walk through life knowing we'll never be able to retract our steps. Is this path then always unidirectional? There are times when I have felt that the path that has accepted us as its wayfarers waits for us long before we arrive there. What if I had worked for another company instead of this? Or if I had not entered the corporate world at all, and worked in a college, or if I had quit this job and gone into teaching? (There was a possibility of that.) What if I hadn't been born in this country at all? What if I had married and had children, instead of remaining single? Or what if my parents hadn't got married, or if I had been born to someone else, or if my parents had married other people? It's strange, even ridiculous, that not just being born to these particular people, but even if the time of my conception had been different, or the sperm and egg during the moment of conception had been different, a totally different person would've come to life. This very thought shakes my belief in the freedom of choice and makes me realize its suffocating limits. One single sperm among millions and millions of sperms from millions and millions of males fuses miraculously with a female egg cell from among millions and millions of egg cells from millions and millions of women at one divine moment to decide the birth of a being. Isn't it a manifestation of nature's infinite evolutionary experiments? And does me being chosen to be born make me a representative of such ceaseless experiments? Is that why I, Nagappa, the second son of Santayya Sharma, the firstborn of Krishna Sharma of the Kaundinya *gotra*, was decreed and destined to take this life form?

Hey, Nagappa, you erudite thinker, well done! Well done, indeed! You should be proud of yourself for being a student of science! Hail to your brilliant theory of evolution! Long live evolution! And when you are in this self-congratulatory mood for coming up with such a brilliant theory, learn to lighten up a bit, you SOB! Learn to smile. Laugh. Don't sit like this, brooding, as if the skies have fallen. And remember, Mother Nature—that mother of all mothers—sometimes fails in her experiments. Even she goes horribly wrong.

Comment 5: The thought that came to my mind before I dozed off: Why did Appa, who chanted Vishnu Sahasranaama every day, confer *this* particular name upon me, when he had a thousand names of Vishnu to choose from? And what about *his* name? And when I think of the part it has played in the saga of my painful past . . .

It's amazing how even the most trivial incidents have led to major events in my life. A decade ago, I casually mentioned to a friend that I had decided to quit my company and join a college as a professor. His wife, cutting me short, asked, 'Why? Did you lose the chance to become a manager?' That question, and more than the question, the way she asked it, changed the course of my life. But I think I got stuck with the nickname 'Professor' from that day.

I now wonder what had really decided everything: Was it her question? More than that, was it the way she asked it? Was it the tone? More than the tone, was it the sneering curve of her lips, the crooked angle of her neck and, more than anything, what that angle implied—that indecipherable 'something' which seemed to taunt me—that had prompted my decision? Or had I already decided not to quit my job, whose echo I heard in my friend's wife's question? Was my mind already made up, and I merely interpreted it in that turn of her neck? We seek deeper, inner meaning for our actions that are prompted by some random reasons, and try to verbalize it. Is that what we call by the grandiose name our 'philosophy of life'? Maybe it's our civilized way of supporting our actions . . . Take a bow, Professor Nagnath! Great! Amazing how you twist everything to give it an intellectual veneer! How you justify your circuitous logic by making it sound scholarly, even noble! Ha!

Oh, I forgot to mention: When I joined the company, the MD's secretary, Mary, seemed to have made up her mind to lure me with her infectious laughter, her sparkling eyes and swaying hips. It was she who advised me to change my name from Nagappa to Nagnath. And it got shortened to Prof. Nag. Strange, isn't it, that when my life is falling apart, this is what my mind chooses to think of?

Comment 6: If I have to pronounce my name the way Parama Master in my primary school used to during attendance, it is Nagappaaa Santayyaaa.

I was born in a small village called Hanehalli in Uttara Kannada district nearly forty years ago. I grew up in Koligiriyanna's neighbourhood. Over half a dozen swear words that roll off my tongue effortlessly were learnt from Koligiriyanna. Of these, son of a bitch and son of a whore are my favourites. When I'm really angry, I might even say, son of a whoring widow or ill-begotten bastard, but not loudly; only in my mind. These days, since a lot of things make me angry, I've created my own numerical code for these obscenities—SOB 1, SOB 2, going up to the power of SOB 10, representing son of a bitch, son of a whoring widow, etc. I even call it 'numerical aphorisms'. Of course, the code breaks down, revealing some very colourful language when I'm really provoked and unable to control my rage.

Apart from my work, what I really love is literature. In fact it's my first love. But I'm an ardent student of science, that too, chemistry. Ideologically, I lean towards Darwin's Theory of Evolution, Freud and Jung's Psychoanalysis and Marx and M.N. Roy's writings. These days, I also find myself intellectually moving towards Konrad Lorenz and Eric Berne.

I've never aspired for too much in life, nor do I fear too many things. In fact, I fear just three things—the law, the police and fire accidents—and more than them, what they symbolize and a kind of mysterious, nameless dread attached to them. I don't know why I fear them. No, actually, I do.

I become emotional when I think of Amma, and also my village: The scent of its soil when I breathe in its dusty air, when I visualize its green fields and hedges and its turmeric dawn and dusk, and when the evening clamour of crows near the banyan tree and at the edge of the fields echoes in my ears, and whenever I imagine that my long-lost brother and sister have come back and are knocking at the door. When I think of my elder brother, whom I've never seen, and my younger sister, who got lost in a crowd, I unconsciously bite my lower lip hard to control my suppressed anger till blood oozes out. What *really* makes me angry is Appa's cowardice . . .

Nagappa, why did you stop, you SOB 1? You still don't have the guts to admit even to yourself that Appa was a coward, do you? Are you falling asleep, Nagappa? Sleep well. Your real guts will be tested tomorrow, when you see the personnel and administration manager's letter. Just wait.

2

It was in his childhood friend and sworn enemy Shrinivasa's house that Nagappa was writing all this. Shrinivasa, who had changed his name to a more stylish Shrinivas Rao, owned a spacious four-bedroom seafront apartment in upmarket Shivaji Park. And one of the rooms had been got ready for Nagappa, who sat thinking these thoughts and recording them.

Nagappa read what he had written the night before, as soon as he woke up. He was in a self-deprecating mood. It seems, this SOB 1 doesn't fear too many things in life, he mocked at himself, closing the notebook with a sneer.

He walked to the window and stood gazing at the sea. His eyes fell on the greenery bordering the compound wall. Flowering shrubs of marigold, betel saplings, *basale* creepers entwining bamboo frames, a copse of banana plants and tall trees swayed in the morning breeze. It reminded him of home. This SOB 2 manages to recreate his village wherever he goes, Nagappa thought with envy. It seems he still drinks the humble gruel before going to his press every morning. He keeps broadcasting this with great pride and show of humility to whoever cares to listen.

Why Shrinivasa of all people, Nagappa wondered. Why am I staying in Shrinivasa's house! This SOB 1, whom I've hated for the last twenty years with the kind of hatred bordering on revulsion, why did I accept *his* invitation?

'Forget about your office and its problems. You're anyway on leave for a month. Come, relax at my place, away from it all. It seems you're writing a novel . . . about me. Great. Don't hesitate. Write everything. I've read what you've written about my mother, though you've tried to hide the fact. You're a writer. We're mere mortals. Unrefined. My only connection with words is to print them in my press. If my press had the facility to print Kannada books, I would've printed yours. Allow me to at least get the jacket done. Let's print it in four colours if you want.'

Nagappa wondered how much of what Shrinivasa had said was sincere and how much was just to bait him. He had heard from Sitaram that Shrinivasa was extremely angry and upset when he read the story about his mother. Maybe Sitaram has told Shrinivasa that I'm now writing a novel about him, Nagappa thought. Trust Sitaram to say something like this.

Nagappa suspected that the interest Shrinivasa had shown in the so-called 'book' he was supposed to be writing, and his fake encouragement was an attempt to stop him from writing it. But the constant worry about what awaited him in the office and the unbearable uncertainty of its outcome had corroded Nagappa's creativity and his ability to think rationally. He felt he had to go somewhere away from it all to decide the moral stand he needed to take about his present predicament and the company politics that had led to it. So, when Shrinivasa invited him home, he agreed willingly, without analysing the real motives behind Shrinivasa's gesture and his own surprisingly spontaneous decision to go with him. For once, he had not subjected the motives to his usual scrutiny, which had become second nature to him.

What he now wanted to write was about his office politics—the evil forces working behind the scenes to destroy him—and not a novel on Shrinivasa, rather, his troubled relationship with Shrinivasa. Yes, he had been planning to write such a novel for long, but he had not got down to writing it.

What I need to do now is to focus on myself, he thought. Why am I being framed? Why is this dirty politics causing me so much anguish? I need to go to the root cause of both—the real motives of those working against me and my needless suffering, as I have done no wrong. I need to analyse my relationship with my colleagues, especially, Phiroz Bandookwala: Do the events that have shaped my personality keep resurfacing and interfering in all my interpersonal relationships? Of late, I've begun to have a strong suspicion that this could be the case, especially after reading Eric Berne's theory of Transactional Analysis.

Hey, Eric, don't get too conceited. It's the professor in me talking. I'm merely articulating my personal experiences in your words. That's all. I know I'm speaking as if we know each other, but blame it on this surging sea that makes all suffering appear trivial in its presence. Blame it on its joyous, triumphant roar. It has momentarily broken my usual reserve.

Soon, thoughts of Phiroz surreptitiously began to invade Nagappa's mind, and he was struck by the resemblance between Shrinivasa and Phiroz. No, it wasn't obvious. It was something one realized suddenly, instinctively, at an unexpected moment, like the face of a murderer in a movie or a play seen long ago, flashing unbidden before one's eyes. The epiphanic revelation left him numb. He didn't know what had caused it. Maybe I'm obsessed with Phiroz, he thought, trying to soothe his nerves. I must focus on the task at hand—writing. Yes, I must write. I must write every day. Write not to blame anyone but to understand my relationship with others around me—its inner workings—and thereby understand myself.

Comment 7: Something funny happened yesterday . . .

Though Nagappa had decided to chronicle the history of his interpersonal relationships in an attempt to understand himself, he realized he had veered away from it only when he started writing about yesterday's incident. Maybe it's futile to divide one's experiences into strict timeframes, he thought. Or maybe the present experience will help throw light on the way I've come to accept and internalize my experiences all my life, and thereby the path I'm going to tread. It's cowardice to turn my back on life. I will not, and cannot allow the evolutionary experiment nature is conducting through me to fail. God! Why am I trembling? Is it because of the fear that we alone are responsible for this life, bracketed between our unsought for birth and death?

Coming back to the incident, I got tired of reading and writing the whole day, and walked to the seashore. As I sat gazing at the sea, my mind was full of the Konrad Lorenz I'd been reading: We do not know of a single animal which is capable of personal friendship, and which lacks aggression. I remembered my irritation as thoughts of Phiroz and

Shrinivasa kept interfering with my reading. I'd no idea Shrinivasa's wife was so beautiful. Lucky bastard! I tried to brush aside the thought.

If I have to sum up Shrinivasa's life, it's the story of his constant struggle against childhood poverty and humiliation and the fierce war he waged against them—a stupendous tale of grit and courage. He lures me towards him in some unknown way.

I'm meandering again. Anyway, coming back to yesterday, as I was sitting, looking at the sea, my attention was drawn to an old man. Maybe he just looked old. What stood out were his wrinkled cotton jacket and black cap. Though I couldn't see it, I thought his head was tonsured, with a tuft at the back. He was staring at me, but suddenly looked flustered because I think I smiled without realizing it. I turned away. I felt I'd seen him somewhere, but couldn't recall where. Was it in Shrinivasa's house? Earlier, when I walked to the beach, I had a feeling someone was following me. When I looked back, the figure slunk away. Was it him? I'm too immersed in my own thoughts to notice things. I must come out of it.

For no reason, I remembered Vomu: He didn't have much of a personality, but his face glowed with good health. He was a born rebel. One day, he said, 'Sir, it looks like you're always thinking about yourself. It's not a healthy thing to do.'

Not bad, you SOB 1, I'd thought. We'd only known each other for about ten days. I liked what he said. One day, I asked him, maybe a bit impertinently, 'Vomu, why don't you change your name?'

'Why, what's wrong with it?' he demanded, sounding more self-confident than angry. Maybe his confidence had the backing of a historical reality—he was a Dalit boy. I must call him tomorrow.

I looked for the old man, but he had disappeared. Yes, I was sure now. I'd seen him in Shrinivasa's house. Not really 'seen', but maybe had a glimpse of him. I think he had been following me.

The sun was setting. The sight thrilled me. I looked at it as if for the first time. But the next moment, the old man's face clouded my mind. I felt uneasy. Despite the cool evening breeze, I was sweating under my collar. I got up. Have I lost the natural ability to enjoy something? I thought. Can't I ever spontaneously experience anything? Why is it that every new thing, every unfamiliar person evokes in me this nameless fear? I wiped my sweaty neck and face. The bristles felt rough. I hadn't shaved for four days. I was aware of my sleepless, sunken eyes behind the glasses.

I must find out about the old man. Must ask Shrinivasa. I began to walk briskly towards his apartment building. Was the old man following me? I quickened my pace. My heart was thudding. I looked around at the seashore and the road leading to Shrinivasa's building, but he was nowhere in sight. I felt I saw a figure turning the corner. That must be him. I thought I saw him disappearing into a narrow lane next to the building. I was pretty sure. I gave up all pretence and began to run, but couldn't catch up with him. Suddenly, I felt several eyes on me. People were staring at me from the balconies of Shrinivasa's six-storey building. Like a thief caught red-handed, I quietly walked towards the entrance with downcast eyes.

I was dripping with sweat when I reached my room. As I lay exhausted on the bed, the question that rose in my mind like a pot resurfacing noisily from the depths of a well was: What am I running from? What am I trying to escape? Can I sum up my entire history in a couple of sentences, the way I had summed up Shrinivasa's life? Why don't I have the courage to face it?

Someone was knocking at the door. I got up, switched on the light and opened the door. Shrinivasa's second daughter, Chetana, stood flashing a warm smile. I felt joy wash over me. Shrugging off my despondency, 'Come in,' I invited her. I quickly splashed some cold water on my face, wiped it and sat in front of her. She smiled again. Her cheeks dimpled. I felt rejuvenated.

I realized then that the all-important question Phiroz had asked me years ago, which had provoked me, which constantly troubled me, which had a stranglehold on me, had loosened momentarily. I had turned from Nagappa of Koligiriyanna's ghetto into Professor Nagnath now. 'I must tell you what just happened,' I said casually, and narrated the incident. She began to laugh, and I had an inkling she already knew about it. It seems she had seen the whole thing from the balcony. I joined in her laughter. 'Kaka, he's our cook,' she said. 'He got back from his village last evening.'

Nagappa had sat down to write about the incident. The notebook was open in front of him, but the page was blank, except for the sentence that had set off his train of thought.

Comment 7: Something funny happened yesterday.

When did I write this, Nagappa wondered. He picked up his pen and began:

Comment 8: Damn these terrible memories! The more I try to run away from them, the more they suck me into their vortex. The soft footfalls I hear following me everywhere provoke a thousand tales, summon a thousand demons from my past. Am I running because I'm scared, or am I scared because I'm running? Must read William James again.

3

Despite the constant, unfounded, indefinable feeling of guilt resembling self-flagellation that cast its dark shadow on Nagappa's mind, there were luminous moments in his life that shone once in a while, radiating deep inner warmth. He woke up with memories of his mother:

It has been nearly thirty years since Amma's death. Why then am I remembering this particular day after a long time? I can see her before me: It looked like grandfather's house. Beyond the front yard was a ten-foot compound wall with waist-high wrought iron bars at the front entrance. She was holding a platter in one hand with a coconut, a garland of jasmine flowers, betel leaves and a wick for the lamp, and my hand in the other. I must've been four then. She crossed the threshold. This image of hers resurfaced, mingled with the scent of jasmine from the garland. I took a deep breath and inhaled the fragrance of the flowers once again. She must have been on her way to the temple. I could still see the beautifully sculpted idols of Rama and Sita in the inner sanctum under the glow of oil lamps hanging from chains. It was probably the first time that I was seeing the pitch-black idols along with Amma's image.

I lay awake, holding on to the image. I felt languorous and happy. My mind wandered in search of the wellspring of my happiness—my birthplace. I felt like writing about it. Yes, I must begin from there—from the roots that went deep under its soil, and those who had nurtured me—Koligiriyanna and my childhood friends: Honnappa, Sheikh Farid, Uttami, Paru, Damu, Enku Murkundi, Dinni, Bastyanv, Kaanee Gowda . . . I must write about all of them. I must begin from my dusty, old, ramshackle village neighbourhood, far away from Phiroz and Shrinivasa. I must write here, sitting in Shrinivasa's house . . .

It struck me that though I've been here for two days, I haven't spoken to anyone except Shrinivasa and Chetana. I don't even know who all live here. I came to know only yesterday that Shrinivasa has three children. Chetana told me. It seems the eldest daughter and the youngest son have gone to their aunt's house in Kumta for the summer. Shrinivasa had never spoken about his children, and I had never been curious enough to ask. Is Shrinivasa's mother still alive? Where does she live? In Gokarna?

Shrinivasa had insisted I come and stay in his house for a month. Though I'd finally given in, I'd no intention staying here for more than a week. That's why I brought a small suitcase with only a few clothes and books. I wonder why the neighbours gave me curious glances when I came in the other day.

Maybe because it's just for a week, I don't feel like getting to know anybody, thought Nagappa, trying to support his aloofness. He knew it was an excuse for his innate hesitation—

his discomfort bordering on fear—that always stopped him from interacting with strangers. In fact, though his present job wasn't suited to his nature, he had stuck to it because he instinctively shied away from a new environment.

When what had started as nostalgia and then a casual observation about Shrinivasa's household threatened to invariably stray into his workplace, Nagappa sat up.

He had not seen the cook ever since last evening's disaster. Poor man, Nagappa thought. If he realized I was chasing him, or got to know of it from Chetana, I wonder what he'll think of me. Shrinivasa's wife has not yet spoken to me, but I suspect Shrinivasa has told her a great deal about me. I wonder what he has told her. Maybe even Chetana, gauging from that knowing glint in her eyes. What do they think of this lonely, ageing bachelor with a Nepali keep? Is there a hint of disdain in their curious glances? As usual, I'm back to thinking about myself . . .

Nagappa got out of bed and stood near the window. It was not yet daybreak. Everything was shrouded in grey. He could hear the waves crashing, but could not see them. As things began to take shape, the sandy shore and the green patch reminded him of his village once again. He heard a soft knock on the door and opened it. The cook quietly placed a cup of tea on the table and left, closing the door behind him.

When Nagappa sat down to write about his village, what came to his mind was his first meeting with Phiroz. If he were to search for the reason behind the unwarranted and unrelenting hatred Phiroz had harboured against him these last eighteen years—the way he had hounded him, his casual cruelty, his dismissive look—it could all be traced back to their very first meeting.

Have I started writing about all this because I want to go to the root of this troubled relationship? Nagappa asked himself. Does Man become introspective when he goes deep in search of something, or does he go deep in search of something only when he begins to introspect? Does he become an introvert when he becomes analytical, or does he become analytical when he becomes an introvert? There's William James again!

Comment 9: Am I deriving some kind of consolation in the thought that Phiroz is the root cause of all my pain and hurt? I don't know why, but whenever I start thinking of Phiroz, I invariably reach the conclusion that it's all somehow my fault. Phiroz has that knack—one of the many weapons in his armoury. The others are even more lethal: He can get you to talk and pretend to listen attentively, and yet show his indifference. He can provoke you to get agitated, yet remain calm and aloof. He'll let you blabber on, without uttering a word. And when he does speak, he puts on this demeanour of the utmost dignity. His words sound like rare gems of wisdom, refined by his profound knowledge and vast experience, scattered judiciously. He denies what he has just said the very next moment, confusing everyone around him, while always remaining an enigma.

Another thing: He's always holding a pipe even if he isn't smoking. This is to create an aura of urbane sophistication around him. He deploys this potent weapon masterfully to make you think he's open and frank, while revealing nothing. This SOB 1 is an absolutely phony character. To watch him smoke is like watching a magic show he puts on for you. He begins with the elaborate ritual of cleaning his pipe, like setting the stage: He pokes a thin little stick, specially meant for the purpose, into the pipe to shake the residue loose and empties it into an ornate glass ashtray. He now holds the pipe to his lips (the low-life two-faced bastard!) and blows into it with flared nostrils and taps it gently on the rim of the ashtray. He then squints into the pipe to make sure no caked-up tobacco is stuck to the sides. Tilting his head slightly to express satisfaction that it's now clean, he proceeds to fill it with fresh tobacco.

Oh, the suaveness of opening the tobacco tin! The subtle manner in which he shows off the expensive brand of Three Nuns he smokes! The ostentation with which he presses the tobacco with his thumb and pushes it into the pipe! And when all this is going on, we're supposed to keep gawking at him, admiring his Greek-god face and his long, aristocratic fingers. He wordlessly nods at you, as if to say, 'You talk, I'm listening.' By the time he lights the pipe and smoke starts swirling from it, you're totally mesmerized by his personality and have forgotten what you've come to say. Aware of the effect he's having on you, he glances at you from the corner of his eye. I *hate* this civilized beast from the very depth of my being. This man, who doesn't speak, somehow scares me.

Even that day, Phiroz had triggered a wave of stomach-churning panic in me. He had regarded me with his cold, piercing gaze, like sizing up an adversary before a fight. He had looked me in the eye like a hunter intimidating his quarry, forcing it to make a false move. He had then casually thrown that question at me—about my father . . . about my father's profession. When I look back on that day, I realize that the question had decided my future in this company.

Don't thrust your dirty hands into my origins, you scumbag! The company has appointed me because of my qualifications, my ability, not because of my father's pedigree. If I were to delve into your past, it might involve both history and geography, you sisterfucker! Come to the present. If you want to wrestle with me, let's do it right here, right now, in the open, not in the dark caves of the past . . .

Why am I challenging Phiroz to this imaginary duel? Why am I squandering my life away, trying to second-guess his every move?

Nagappa had no answers. He rose from his chair, feeling drained.

As he paced the floor, as usual, the simmering hatred gave way to a spiral of guilt: Is my innate cowardice the real reason for this hatred? Is this cowardice, in reality, my lack of courage to challenge Appa? Was it Appa's memory that was ignited when I saw Shrinivasa's cook? Was it my father I saw in his eyes?

I remembered what I had read years ago: A person enters society, honed by millions of years of evolution, the process of gestation and childhood experiences. Whether he blossoms as a human being or withers away depends entirely upon the situation he finds himself in. It depends upon which of the two fundamental forces embedded in human nature he comes face-to-face with—life-nurturing love or destructive powers of hatred. It is possible to study the social history of Man from this perspective.

But, for now, what I need to understand is, why do Shrinivasa and Phiroz hate me so much? I must search for the reasons. I must find out.

4

Nagappa got out of the building through the back gate, walked towards Cadel Road and stood waiting to cross to the other side. Though the traffic seemed ceaseless, he looked unmindful of it.

There was a brief lull, and he was about to step on to the pedestrian crossing, when he heard someone call out, 'Hello, hello, how come in Bombay? Weren't you working in Hyderabad or somewhere?' Nagappa looked up. Before he could respond, the man walked up to him and said, 'I saw you coming out of Advocate Kamath's compound, but wasn't sure it was you.'

By the time Nagappa tried to place the vaguely familiar face, they had crossed the road.

'I'm Doshi,' the man introduced himself. 'We've met at Honnavar's place in Wadala when you used to come there to give tuitions . . .'

'Oh, yes, Doshi . . . income tax officer. You've changed a lot,' Nagappa said, remembering.

'I know. I've put on a lot of weight. Side effect of marriage. I've just joined yoga classes at Chowpatty's Kaivalya Dham.

And I've quit my government job . . . am now income tax practitioner. My family is not in town. So I'm a bit free. Thought of taking a walk on the beach for some fresh air. If you have no other plans, we could walk together . . .'

'Yes, why not?' Nagappa replied. Doshi's warm friendliness made him momentarily shed his usual reserve.

They walked along the tree-lined shore, which invariably reminded him of his village.

'So, how's your company? Your job?' Doshi casually asked. Nagappa did not reply. Doshi sensed the sudden silence and felt uneasy. He knew Nagappa worked for a well-known multinational company, and was considered brilliant in his field, which had prompted the question. Nagappa felt bad he couldn't answer it. 'If all had gone according to plan, I was to go to America next month for higher training. But one of our directors played politics . . .' Nagappa finally managed to say, breaking the stifling silence.

The sun was setting and the sky looked bloodshot. The breeze had died and the sea appeared waveless.

'I'm a victim of dirty politics . . .' Nagappa said in a barely audible voice, after a long pause.

'I understand. My sympathies,' Doshi said. 'This's nothing new to me. Wherever there are people, there's politics. I quit my job for the same reason. Be strong. Don't lose hope. Everything will be all right. I'm there if you want to talk about it.'

'Thanks,' Nagappa said, overcome with emotion. 'You've given me courage. If you don't mind, could I visit you one of these days to share my . . . problems?'

Doshi gave him his card.

Without intending to, Nagappa told Doshi that he had taken a couple of months off to write a book, and was staying at a friend's house nearby for a week. When he mentioned Shrinivasa's name, 'Oh, Shrinivas! I know him well . . .' Doshi drawled, as if to imply, why him of all people.

'So is it fiction you're writing? In your language? Good! Good!' he said after a pause. 'You're lucky you have this god-given gift. We need such hobbies to escape from the daily grind, from this . . . this cut-throat competition. Look around you, and you only see savages wearing civilized masks ready to pounce on you. What our ancestors did on four legs in forests, we're doing on two.'

Doshi, too, appeared eager to unburden himself. Both felt this accidental meeting after years had brought them close, and decided to meet again the next evening at the same place.

As Doshi walked away, Nagappa regretted lying to him. He had seemed genuinely friendly. It was true he was on leave, but not for writing a book. And he had not taken leave. The leave had been forced upon him. The thought brought a lump in his throat. He felt dispirited.

The other day, when he had run into Shrinivasa at Santosh Bhavan, the lie had slipped out. At that moment, he couldn't think of any other excuse for not being at work. And he had now repeated it.

'What our ancestors did on four legs in forests, we're doing on two.' Had Doshi been reading Konrad Lorenz? Or was he speaking from personal experience? It conjured up the image of Phiroz standing on four legs, bristling and snarling. Bile rose up to Nagappa's throat. Forgetting he was still on the main road, he spat out, 'You dirty pig!'

He immediately felt ashamed of himself, and walked briskly towards Shrinivasa's house.

Should I tell Doshi the truth, he wondered, as he sat on the bed. But how much can I trust him? After all, I really don't know him. Just because he appeared friendly doesn't mean I can confide in him. What if behind my back . . . No, I mustn't overthink everything. I mustn't curb the spontaneous feeling of warmth I felt towards him. And now I need people like him more than ever.

He remembered the supreme confidence with which Doshi spoke English, mixed with Gujarati in his thick accent, and smiled. Just then, Chetana came in, flashing her radiant smile. 'Kaka, it seems you're writing a novel on Appa. Is it true?' Seeing the look on Nagappa's face, 'Amma told me,' she added in a low voice.

Was it mere curiosity? Or was there a shadow of adult anxiety in her innocent question?

Nagappa did not reply. He just smiled weakly.

5

Comment 10: God, is there no end to this torture? Why is pain inflicted upon me again and again where it hurts the most? Is the path that Appa took the only way out? No, I shouldn't lose courage so easily. As Doshi said, I shouldn't lose hope. But why on the same wound . . .?

The reference to wound had unconsciously stopped Nagappa from going on. His mind instinctively tried to think of something else. He remembered how Doshi's metaphor of wild animals had conjured up the image of Phiroz. He now felt he had been unfair to innocent beasts. Poor things, he thought, they live as nature has intended them to. Do they have the ability or courage to transgress the laws of nature? But Man? Can he ever live within the confines of what we call 'human nature'? And even if our traits can be traced back to animal instincts, and we feel their constant tug, aren't there certain qualities distinct and inherent to human nature that have got embedded in the process of evolution over millennia? What about what we call 'human emotions' or even 'humane emotions' like love, respect, compassion, concern for others, selflessness? Don't they have any meaning? What about rationality? Sense of justice and fair play?

If Gilbert D'Souza was here, he would've laughed them off as pompous words—mere sounds without meaning. He would've shut me up with, 'Cut that silly sentimentality out!'

Nagappa suddenly felt like listing nuggets of wisdom that Gilbert freely dispensed. It seemed to suit his present mood. What came to his mind first when he tried to recall his friend's face was his thick, well-groomed moustache, the impish smile hovering at the corners of his mouth and the glint in his eyes that reflected it.

Comment 11: Thus spake Gilbert: 1) You have nurtured a host of unrealistic misconceptions about the potential of this animal called Man. You have not really been singed by the fierce struggle for survival. Things have fallen into your lap at the right time all through life. If your pen had the power to portray human nature filtered through the raw experiences of this Gilbert D'Souza, by now you would have grown stronger in the very act of writing about it.

You don't have the courage to look at the true face of human nature. And even if you do, you don't have the guts to accept it for what it is, let alone confront it.

2)   Selfishness is the only driving force underlying all our interactions with others—unadulterated selfishness, which does not hesitate to sacrifice others at its altar.

3)   Social inequalities that you see are not merely created by the inequitable distribution of wealth and the means to earn a livelihood, as your Marxists believe. It controls even fame and position in society, and who is important and who isn't.

It influences the distribution of power. It decides who wields it and who doesn't.

Think about it. Is the surplus that society generates limited only to wealth? Is its importance limited only to the economic sphere? Is disparity in the distribution of wealth the only fundamental reason for oppression and social injustice?

4) Hey, brother, beware: to imagine that my suffering is greater than anyone else's and that my pain is the most acute is also a kind of malady. Let's not, for heaven's sake, take some kind of morbid pride even in our suffering.

5) If you want to ease the suffering of others, come, I'll take you to an organization which is quietly doing such work in this vast, anonymous city. If you have the courage to face what you see there—how they battle with their ordeals and try to rise above them—if you have the stomach to portray their lives, then write about them. Tell me when you're ready, and I'll take you there. Write those stories, not to become famous in the annals of literature, but to let others know of their courageous fight against death, their struggles, trials and triumphs. Nagappa, remember, the attitude of those who opt for life is quite different from those who turn their backs on it.

If only Gilbert was in Bombay now, I could've poured out all my troubles before him, Nagappa thought, as he lay on the bed, feeling friendless and lonely. I had felt the same way the day I got the call from office. Though I know many people, not one of them is close to me. I thought I shared an intellectual bond with Sitaram. But even he seems to have drifted away. In fact, all those I could share my thoughts with have grown aloof after I stopped writing. No, I stopped writing because they moved away.

Gilbert never tried to get too friendly with anyone. Everyone liked him in spite of this, or maybe because of this. He was very different from Nagappa in many ways. As a Roman Catholic, prayer was the source of his inner strength. He was a reporter with the *Times*, and though Nagappa had got to know him through Sitaram, Gilbert had grown closer to him than Sitaram. He spent all his free time helping the physically challenged at Cheshire Home in Andheri. He had recently been posted to Kathmandu—Rani's city.

When Nagappa was suddenly removed from the post of R&D manager at the Hyderabad factory and transferred to the Bombay office a few months back, he had spoken to Gilbert about how deeply it had affected him. Gilbert had shut him up with a stern, 'Stop that immature nonsense. Act your age.' Nagappa felt a bit ashamed of himself now.

I must visit Cheshire Home, Nagappa thought. I could ask Doshi to come along, if he's interested. I'm sure he has a car. We could drive there. I must ask him tomorrow.

6

Comment 12: Since I came awake at four in the morning, I started writing. Are motives behind human actions as simple as Gilbert makes them out to be? I think even his opinion about me is rather simplistic. I could have blamed Appa for all my problems and escaped responsibility. I tried. But what did I gain by it? Only escape from my past. This constant running away from it. Was Appa entirely responsible for how he treated me? How much of it was preordained and how much depended on his own free will?

If only I knew how to free myself from this searing torment which I have been clutching to my chest and running all my life, unable to share it with anyone . . . Is there no deliverance from this gnawing suspicion, this terrible secret that kills my will to live every moment—this secret that has not let me be? If only I had the supreme courage to conquer my childhood trauma that sealed my fate! It decided how I resonate with the world around me . . . how I react to my experiences. It's not that I lack the courage to face true human nature, as Gilbert thinks. I'm crippled by my inability to confront the truth about my birth and my inner demons.

What Gilbert had told me long ago has been troubling me these days: It's ridiculous to think my pain is more unbearable than anyone else's. Maybe it's unnatural to look at suffering from this perspective.

I don't know why, today, as soon as I woke up in the morning, I was convinced of it more than ever before, or, perhaps, had gathered the courage to unhesitatingly accept what I had been convinced of long ago: My shirt catching fire that night when I was in deep sleep was certainly not an accident. Appa wanted to burn me alive. He had deliberately torched me. Ten days later, Appa tried to commit suicide by jumping into a well. I was only eight then. Why did he want to kill me? What could have been the compelling reason for wanting to kill me and kill himself? Was it also the reason behind my younger sister Kalyani's disappearance? She disappeared without a trace amidst the milling crowd in this city. She was just a year younger than me. Was it all part of the same plan? A suicide pact of sorts? I'm still not sure of this. Maybe I'll never know. Maybe I'll never be able to know. Will my elder brother know?

The thing that confronts me suddenly between sleep and wakefulness, that which torments me, is my deep-seated fear, of which I cannot speak to anyone. All my writing . . . my stories have been my attempts to give shape to these fears. I don't have any great ambition to become famous. I never wanted to be known. I needed to escape from the path Appa took. I needed to stay alive. That was the most important thing at the time.

The editor of an obscure journal from Hubli had written in his editorial: *Such half-baked pseudo-philosophical stories with no social message and societal concerns should be banned, or else, we may have to raise awareness among readers to start a revolution to ban magazines that print such banal stuff,* forgetting that many of my stories had appeared in his journals. He had printed my name in bold letters in his editorial. Earlier, two other editors of two separate magazines had sent back my stories, giving no reason for rejecting them.

The one thing I cannot bring myself to do, though I've really been meaning to, is burn my stories. I think you can sing even if there are no listeners. You can tear up a painting you've spent months to create, without showing it to anyone. But why do we feel this great need to seek out a reader for what we write? Why do we feel the process of writing is complete only when it is read by someone?

I know no other way to communicate with others, except through my writing. I feel suffocated when I'm gagged like this. I don't even know why I was gagged. I'm unable to deal with it. I've kept a few of my stories locked in a box, hoping that someday, someone will read them. I can say this much with confidence: The 'death wish' reflected in my stories cannot be attributed to my Brahmanical birth, as that foolish editor seems to think. If truth were so simple, Appa wouldn't have perhaps committed suicide. It's probably only in this country that the cause of our birth is the cause of our death.

Looking at the direction my writing has taken, Gilbert would probably dismiss it as either 'silly sentimentality' or 'immature nonsense'. My hand automatically stops when I realize this . . .

Irritated and impatient with himself, Nagappa got up and stood near the window and, banging the window sill with his fists, screamed, 'Yes, that's what I am—immature and sentimental! And I don't give a damn!'

The next moment, he realized that his sudden outburst was actually directed at Phiroz, who constantly lurked somewhere in his mind. He must have now surfaced. He has got under my skin, Nagappa thought, with disgust. 'Damn you, you leech!' he cursed. He closed his eyes to calm himself and let the sea breeze waft over him as the day broke.

Many things about his parents were still a mystery to Nagappa. All he knew were fragments of information he had stumbled upon at various points in his life. Each time he found something new, it added to his hurt.

He had felt the same way when Phiroz had casually asked him about his father. It was only later he realized that it was a deliberate ploy. At the time, the question had touched a raw nerve. But it had not triggered the usual anguish. It was just that he was unable to grasp the relevance of the question to the context. Deliberately misinterpreting Nagappa's fluster, 'It's okay. Don't answer if you find it difficult to. It was a casual query,' Phiroz had said dismissively, and got engrossed in lighting his pipe.

'He had a small tea shop in our village,' Nagappa's belated reply had come out, provoked by Phiroz's show of indifference. 'Oh,' Phiroz had said, briefly glancing at Nagappa, and placed his pipe back between his lips. That sneering curve of his lips, the momentary pretence of interest and that studied disdain had enraged Nagappa. 'My father didn't live on your charity or the charity of your community, you son of a whore! He was a self-made man. Appa may have been poor, but he had great self-respect. He never stooped in front of anyone. And whatever I am today is because of my own hard work!' Nagappa said. But the words wouldn't come out. They remained stuck in his throat. All he could do was grit his teeth and quietly swallow his anger.

The anger seemed to be tied to some other old humiliation: It reminded him of his close friend who had ganged up with those who had gagged his writing, after first encouraging him to write. The sheer cruelty of the act had left him speechless. He couldn't bring himself to utter either the name of the journal or its editor. He wanted to scream abuses at him, but the right words failed him.

Probably, writing was to him what prayers were to Gilbert—it sustained him.

Suddenly, the wind seemed to have been sucked out of the grey seascape before him. Nagappa moved away from the window.

7

'Appa may have been poor, but he had great self-respect.' The more Nagappa mulled over this statement, the more he began to doubt if it was true.

He had heard that his ancestors were originally from Goa. His father had left Goa and come to live in Hanehalli. What made him leave Goa? Nagappa wondered. Are there any other relatives still living in Goa? The owner of our house in Hanehalli was also from Goa. Were my father and he related? In what way? Nagappa realized he didn't have answers to even the most basic questions about his roots. More than a lack of interest, it was an unconscious reluctance to delve deep that had stopped him from finding out. He had often thought of his past as an unsolved riddle.

Hanehalli was a small village where almost everyone knew everyone. But his family stayed away from the upper-class people. Nagappa had grown up with the feeling that they looked down upon his family. He had vaguely sensed that Appa, Amma and Appa's widowed sister lived in fear of something. Whenever Nagappa looked back, the image that came to his mind was of a huge pair of frightened eyes staring

at him. That was why he had never been able to establish
a bond with his past. But it had now metamorphosed into
a savage beast hounding him—a deep, dark force. He was
aware of the transformation, but had not confronted it.
The half-sensed, half-remembered fragments of his past had
woven themselves into a vague and unsubstantial series of
disjointed images—like something seen in a dream. When
Phiroz asked him that seemingly innocuous question, he
was unable to deal with it. He had no idea it could inflict so
much pain.

The pride he had once taken in the struggles his parents
had gone through had given way to shame. The thought of
the brother he had never seen but only heard of and his lost
sister deeply perturbed him.

Nagappa had felt proud of his moral courage when he
told Phiroz in a moment of righteous indignation that his
father was a tea seller. But now, he was angry with himself
for giving Phiroz the opportunity to humiliate him. He was
angry with Phiroz for using it.

Questions about his ancestry and the attitude of the
people of Hanehalli towards his parents had begun to trouble
Nagappa for the first time only after he left the village and
went to Kumta to study.

There was no high school in Hanehalli then. He studied
in an English medium school up to the third form in the
neighbouring Bankeekodla village. Though he lived in
constant fear of Datta Master's cane, those were the happiest
days of his life.

But a dark shadow was cast on this at the high school
hostel in Kumta, where Shrinivasa's brother Madhava and
his friend Gajanana mercilessly ragged him. It started with

the very first question they asked. In fact, it was similar to what Phiroz had asked—about his caste. They were the ones who put it in his head that his mother was not a Brahmin but from the Kalavanta community of temple dancers. It was five years since his mother's death. More than the revelation about her caste, what caused Nagappa great anguish was the obvious pleasure they took in tormenting him about it and the way they tormented him: They would make suggestive gestures and obscene noises mimicking the sexual act, with vulgar smirks on their faces. They would laugh at Nagappa's stunned face. Even now, the memory of those days left him feeling numb.

They were three years his senior. Gajanana was the son of a wealthy zamindar from Manaki. His every word, every gesture exuded arrogance. Madhava was his evil sidekick. Nagappa was an easy target for their cruel jokes. Everyone wondered how Gajanana had become friendly with Madhava, who came from an extremely poor family. Nagappa suspected that their friendship was based on their hatred towards him and the sadistic pleasure they derived from tormenting him. The way I learnt to accept and process my experiences was decided during those days, Nagappa thought. It disturbed him, and he sat up in bed.

That day, when I got a call asking me to go on leave, why did I blindly obey the order, he wondered. Was this a conspiracy Phiroz had planned against me?

Though he had been told they would let him know in writing about the reason for the charges, he had not yet received anything. He had gone to his Khetwadi chawl to check yesterday afternoon. All the men had gone to work. The women in the neighbouring houses had given him a strange look, but not asked him anything. I was away for three days. They must be wondering where I'd been to, thought Nagappa. I hardly take a day off. Usually, I don't even take my annual leave. And now this forced vacation for a workaholic!

His mind was constantly on edge. What started as a mere suspicion had now grown into an irrefutable fact: I have foolishly walked into the trap set by Phiroz and his cohorts. How could I have been so gullible? How could I have taken the personnel manager's order at face value? I've not even called the MD. Actually, he's my boss, not Phiroz. All sorts of rumours must be circulating about me in the office. Wonder what my colleagues are saying . . .

Nagappa decided to call the office after breakfast.

There was a knock on the door. Nagappa quickly buttoned his shirt and opened the door, expecting the cook with his morning cup of tea. But Shrinivasa stood before him in his shorts, exposing his loose, hairless chest, his massive stomach hanging over his shorts, and bulging belly button. He walked into the room with a stupid grin and gave Nagappa the cup of tea he was holding. 'How can you wear your shirt in this muggy weather?' he asked. Nagappa's heart didn't skip a beat. He didn't instinctively go pale, as he once used to. The sinking feeling that Shrinivasa perhaps knew the burning secret he had been holding close to his heart, didn't automatically cross his mind. By now, he had got used to the question. He calmly gave the reply he always gave: 'It's something I've been born with—congenital bronchial trouble. I get congestion if my chest gets exposed even for a few minutes.' He paused and asked, 'How come you've brought my tea today?'

'Oh, that's a long story. I'll tell you later,' Shrinivasa said with a strange smile. Nagappa didn't particularly like the way he had smiled. He knew Shrinivasa had come rehearsed to say something, and he waited as he drank his tea. 'What about your trip to America? How's the preparation going?' Shrinivasa asked glibly. Nagappa couldn't hide his surprise. I've never asked for much from life. But this's something I want more than anything in the world. Oh god, please don't snatch away this one thing from me, he prayed. Let my dream of going to America not be shattered. Don't make me face the humiliation of failure in front of everyone. But how did Shrinivasa know?

'You're wondering how I know about it, right?' Shrinivasa smiled again. 'I went to your office yesterday. It was a big order, so I had to personally handle it. Anyway, what I came to tell you was the press is closed today for Maharashtra Day. Give your writing a break. Let's go to Thane. Our new building for manufacturing printing machinery is almost complete. I'll show you around. Get ready and come to the living room.'

Shrinivasa left without waiting for Nagappa's response, but just as he was closing the door behind him, as if it was an afterthought, he said, 'Oh, by the way, don't leave your notebook on the table. Keep your novel locked in the table drawer. The key's there.' Nagappa went cold.

He tried to steady himself. My mind is growing morbid, he thought. Because I'm holed up here all day without talking to anyone, I'm beginning to read meanings into everything. No, I mustn't interpret even the smallest things as signs of some impending catastrophe. But has someone in the office told Shrinivasa about why I'm on leave? And does he know something I don't know yet? Should I ask him?

Nagappa knew he didn't have the courage to find out.

A thought struck him as he was locking his notebook in his suitcase: Maybe this SOB is lying about going to my office. Maybe Sitaram has told him about my trip to America. Shrinivasa seems to be convinced I'm writing a novel. Sitaram must've told him I'm writing something, and this dimwit seems to be convinced it's a novel. But what if he isn't bluffing? What if he has found out about my US trip from the office? No, I'm getting too self-absorbed. I mustn't keep thinking about myself all the time. I must go out. When I meet Doshi in the evening, I should tell him about all my problems. I haven't met Vomu for a long time. I must write about him in my journal tonight. Should get Gilbert's address and write to him. Should try to visit that Cheshire Home he talks so much about.

Nagappa suddenly realized that Rani had not figured in all this. Ever since the call had come from his office, he hadn't been able to think of anything else. He felt bad for Rani. But the next moment, he shrugged off the feeling, telling himself that it was a purely physical relationship and there was no room for emotions.

The MD's secretary, Mary, had shown a lot of interest in him. But he had held himself back. His instinctive inhibitions and fear had stopped him from making a move. Getting close to a person meant opening yourself to someone. And I always withdraw into my shell the moment someone tries to get close to me, Nagappa thought. It frightens me even to think that Mary has any feelings for me. What if I call her? I'll come to know all that's going on behind the scene. But what if she misunderstands me . . . misinterprets my call? So what! Let her think whatever she wants to. Why do I live in constant fear? And how many things do I keep fearing? And why do I fear so many things? Yes, instead of calling the MD, I should call Mary.

When he stood under the shower, he wondered why Mary had a soft corner for him, of all people. Did she love him? He dismissed it as a silly thought. But it brought a smile to his face.

As usual, he looked away when he soaped himself. His fingers felt the knots of the burn scars on his chest and stomach. He shrank inwardly. He tried to visualize Mary's lovely face, but his eyes filled with tears. He stood under the shower for a long time, letting the water course down his face.

8

When Nagappa went to the living room, Shrinivasa, his wife, Chetana and the cook were dressed and ready. When Shrinivasa had said that he would take Nagappa to see the factory, he had assumed it would be just the two of them. The thought of going out with so many people made him nervous. He shrugged off the sneaking feeling that Shrinivasa's wife's ravishing beauty also had something to do with his nervousness. He wasn't sure he could go through the ordeal in his present state of mind, and wanted to wriggle out of it. Shrinivasa pre-empted this: 'Sharada had this sudden whim to go on a picnic. It was her idea to pack the idli-chutney made for breakfast and eat it at the factory. We've even got coffee in the thermos. Look, even our Achyuta is in such a good mood,' Shrinivasa said with fake enthusiasm, and almost dragged Nagappa out of the house.

So Shrinivasa's wife's name is Sharada and Achyuta is the cook, Nagappa thought, as he got into the car. The picnic hamper was already in the boot. Achyuta had placed the huge thermos between his feet. Sharada, Chetana and Achyuta sat behind, and Nagappa was forced to sit next to

Shrinivasa. Suddenly, he thought of his lost brother as he glanced covertly at Achyuta. It sent a chill down his spine.

The car crossed Tilak Bridge, Dadar TT, King's Circle, Sion and hit the Poona highway. As the car sped along, images flashed past Nagappa, disappearing even before they were formed: the Sion Hill, the ruins of the fort at the top, the khadi with its reeking stench, the mountain range lining its edge, and then the symbols of prowess in chemical technology—the petroleum refinery and fertilizers and petrochemical factories with their ugly mass of twisted pipes stretching skywards, competing with the peaks and blanketing the sky. And suddenly, rising above the black and brown heap was the tallest one a chimney spitting fire, with each burst turning into puffs of black smoke. The air was thick with the odour of chemicals. As they passed the salt pans reflecting fragments of the landscape around, Nagappa remembered his village.

He was uneasy. The awareness that had quietly been gnawing at him grew stronger: This isn't just an ordinary outing. Shrinivasa has some insidious game plan. It seems his wife had this sudden 'whim' to go on a picnic! A likely story! And this SOB 1 has been talking non-stop. And it's all 'I me and myself'—his press, his plans for expansion, his business acumen . . . And look at his supreme self-confidence! It seems he has made pots of money. The Shrinivasa I knew years ago, and today's Shrinivas Rao are like two different people. Since his own self-confidence was at its lowest ebb, Nagappa felt it was the most valuable asset one could possess. Everything else seemed to stem from this one quality.

Speaking about Dalits, Gilbert had once said, 'The cruellest thing we did to these people with centuries of oppression is breaking their self-confidence. Breaking their spirit.' Nagappa couldn't remember the context, but the words hit him hard.

He recalled the first time he met Shrinivasa in Bombay. With it came other memories that deeply disturbed him: Nagappa was thirteen when his father finally committed suicide. He had just finished the first year of high school in Kumta. There were three more years for Matriculation. He was a class topper. The headmaster and teachers had dreams for him that he himself didn't have—that he would get the first rank in the board exams and bring laurels to the school.

Though he knew he didn't stand out in any way, his brilliance gave him some confidence. He was neither very good-looking nor did he have a strong physique. The scar on his chest and stomach made him cringe inwardly in a crowd. What if someone found out? What if they asked what had happened? And the more he tried to hide it, the more frightening it became. His eyes always looked guarded. He was wary of everything and everyone. This had a lasting impact on the way he interacted with others. He knew he would always be a loner. He became an introvert. That was when he started daydreaming—what he couldn't do in reality was possible in his daydreams. Another habit which started then that he hadn't been able to shake off was reading. When his classmates finished their homework and went to the playground, he would cover himself with a blanket and lie on his bed with a book.

Babbooti Pai would win the first prize in elocution contests, mugging up speeches Nagappa wrote for him. He could face a large crowd. Ramesh Shetty, who had no stage fright, was always the hero in school plays. Vasudeva Kini with his strong physique was the champion in all sports. The talkative Anthony Fernandes . . . How easily they could mingle with others! And how they could impress girls! The coquettish Sumana Kumtekar from Bangarapatte fell for Gajanana for the way he charmed girls, and the brazenness with which he did it. He had heard that she was also from a Kalavanta family. She exuded sensuality. Nagappa could never muster enough courage to speak to her or to any other girls in school. This symbolized for Nagappa all that was beyond his reach.

His diffidence became a deep-rooted affliction. Gradually, the debilitating affliction remained, while what had caused it became nebulous, turning into an unnamed, amorphous fear. He increasingly took refuge in the world of daydreams, as it was not as intimidating as the real one— the world that threatened to devour him if he tried to reach out to it. That was probably why he started writing. Writing became an extension of his daydreams, just as reading was. It was an attempt to enact my unrequited dreams in stories, to capture within words what I couldn't in real life: impossible dreams, improbable relationships, Nagappa thought. That's probably why I can never understand young critics (or those who call themselves critics), who declaim that writing should have a higher goal—of reflecting the aspirations of a society, bringing about social change, starting a revolution. My writing has no social message. I haven't set out to correct all that ails society. I don't seek to preach. What I'm probably trying to do through my writing is to find out my own relevance in a world, in a society that has turned its back on me—that is indifferent to whether I'm dead or alive. More than any social relevance, I'm trying to establish to myself my relevance.

This line of thinking surprised Nagappa. His mind had long ago reached the conclusion that his existence had no meaning. But his body, which carried this mind, somehow adamantly refused to accept it. It asserted its presence. It probably goes back to the day I was set on fire, Nagappa thought. Even when my body was writhing in pain, the instinct of self-preservation embedded in it over millions of years had asserted itself. 'I mustn't die' was the only thought. The deeper philosophical question of 'Why should I live?' is a more recent one. What haunts me is not the physical pain I suffered then, but the fundamental question: What made Appa want to burn me alive? Why did he want to wipe me out of existence? What could have been the inexorable circumstances behind his heinous act? I've begun to think that the constant search for his motive has been the driving force behind my writing. That's what is reflected in all that I write.

Hey, Nagappa, you SOB 1, you're back to square one, aren't you? Back to where it all begins and ends. Nagappa, you coward bastard, fighting against the memory of Appa's cruel order: 'Die! Die! Die!' you've come back to the 'Original Question'. And having arrived there, you're now running away from it as usual! Why? Because you don't have the guts to go beyond it. Look at you trembling, spineless wimp! And you're running away from Phiroz's cruel teeth-gnashing. His claws are out and you're running scared!

'Yesterday, when I was at your office, I was introduced to your deputy managing director. He has come from Hyderabad, I was told. Parsi, right? A gem of a fellow! Such high position, but not an iota of arrogance . . .' Nagappa heard Shrinivasa saying.

'Aye, aye to that!' Nagappa felt like shouting. 'Amen!' But what struck him was the uncanny coincidence. Did Shrinivasa read my mind? Did he know I was thinking of Phiroz? What was even more disturbing was the news of Phiroz being in the Bombay office. Is there a connection between his coming here and my forced leave? Nagappa broke into a sweat.

Shrinivasa chose that moment to show off his driving skills and went at breakneck speed. When they finally reached the fork where they had to take a turn towards Thane, he overshot and braked suddenly. Everyone in the backseat fell forward. Shrinivasa's wife clutched Nagappa's shoulders to avoid banging her head against the front seat. It lasted a moment, but Nagappa's body tensed. He couldn't bear to look in her direction.

Steadying herself from the jolt, Chetana burst out laughing. Others joined her. Nagappa couldn't. He was mulling over what Shrinivasa had just said. The sisterfucker Phiroz always manages to impress everyone, he thought, seething with anger.

Shrinivasa, leaning towards Nagappa, said in a conspiratorial whisper, 'Yesterday, I came to know why you're on leave. Why didn't you *tell* me? I think you need a better lawyer than Kamath.'

Nagappa stared at Shrinivasa dumbfounded.

'I know what you're going through,' Shrinivasa said with fake sympathy. 'That's why I planned this outing.'

Nagappa was too shocked to respond. He struggled to grasp the import of what he had just heard. When he tried to clasp the seat cushion to control his trembling, he saw Achyuta staring at him. He froze.

9

Doshi didn't turn up as promised the next day. Nagappa waited for him for a long time near the clump of trees where they had parted. He grew anxious. He wanted to tell someone all that had happened in the last few days. Shrinivasa had continued to chatter all through the Thane trip. He seemed to have more money and clout than Nagappa had imagined. It looked like he knew many higher-ups in his company and had some kind of a hold over them. In fact, he had insinuated this. Am I being unnecessarily paranoid? Nagappa wondered. Can I take all that Shrinivasa tells me at face value? Shrinivasa had asked me to keep the notebook locked. Was he worried someone might read it? But who? Chetana couldn't read Kannada. The same with Sharada. Also, why would she enter my room, rather, the guest room? Achyuta? Does he know how to read? Or has Shrinivasa read it? Not likely. If he had, he would've known it's not a novel I'm writing. Oh, I know! He *suspects* I'm writing a novel about him, and it has given him the scare. This mighty Shrinivasa—the eldest progeny of Nadoo Mhaaskeri Padmanabha Keni—with his hairless chest, smooth, bloated baby face and hideous paunch, about whom I know so much, is scared of my notebook. He's scared of its very sight! He's scared even to open it! That's why he's playing mind games with me. You cowardly bastard! I can play games, too. I can *really* scare you! Boo! And how long am I going to be a captive in his house? I think I should go back to Khetwadi. Yes, I've felt a sense of security these last three days here. And Chetana's cheerful presence has calmed me a bit. But Achyuta's behaviour has become intriguing. He looks at me as though he's trying to, waiting to tell me something. That has added to my uneasiness. And I haven't yet gathered the courage to speak to Sharada. Maybe that has made her even more attractive. I've been trying to write about my brother and sister. But my mind has gone blank. The notebook lies open with the blank page staring at me.

There's a shed next to Shrinivasa's building. It's an unauthorized makeshift structure for repairing cars and trucks, standing on illegal land. Though it's been there for a long time, it has an air of transitoriness, as if it's going to be demolished any day now. Adjacent to it is a cluster of squalid huts where the garage workers live with their families. I've heard they brew illicit liquor there. That's why, perhaps, along with the shadow of poverty, their eyes have a furtive look— the look of those on the run. I often see a girl of about twelve near the garage. She looks at me intently whenever I pass by. Belying her uncombed grimy hair, the grease-smeared face and tattered clothes, and despite the shadow of fear and anxiety in them, her large, hope-filled eyes have a strange brilliance. Maybe they use her to sell their illicit hooch.

As I was coming back from the beach, I bought a packet of Cadbury chocolate for her. I asked her name when I gave it to her. 'Saraswati,' she said, and stood staring at me with her big, brilliant eyes, without a trace of joy, gratitude, greed, eagerness or hurry to eat the chocolate. When I looked into those eyes, I began to believe in rebirth and laughed to myself. Perhaps, this was why I wanted to write about my sister. Is my sister living a life of squalor in some dump like this, or is she in some wretched whorehouse? It's a gut-wrenching thought. It has been haunting me for years. How could Appa do such a terrible thing? What was it that made him loosen his hold on her finger in a crowd? What made him abandon his own child and leave her at the mercy of the city streets? What was the compelling reason for this dastardly act? The questions remain unanswered. And the truth remains—the indigestible, unbearable truth—beyond the reach of my imagination.

Kalyani was a much-loved child—Appa's favourite—beautiful like Amma. I'm like Appa. And how often have I not contemplated suicide like him! Yet, some powerful force beyond my understanding, beyond any reasoning, breaks my resolve again and again and pushes me back towards life.

Is it the memory of my sister that draws me to Saraswati? Or is it the immense, nameless sadness that lies beyond the brilliance in Saraswati's eyes that has made me remember my sister? Why am I regurgitating all this? How often in these last so many years have I not roamed the filthy, narrow lanes of Girgaum, with their dingy tenements, in search of her! What if I suddenly find her? But how can I find someone lost thirty years ago? Even if I were to come face-to-face with her, will I be able to recognize her? I may have already seen her and not recognized her, though there's nothing to prove this. But I must concede that I secretly nurture a foolish hope that

I might find her one day. Shall I admit one thing? At times, I imagine that Achyuta, who looks at me intently, could be my long-lost brother. But I laugh at my own wild imagination. Though I know it's too far-fetched for it to happen even in Indian movies, I've often been tempted to ask Saraswati, 'Where's your mother?' But I've held myself back, fearing it might be misunderstood. I know there's not a shred of evidence to tell me my brother and sister are alive, and that I'll ever find them. But my intense yearning to see them at least once makes me think I will. Perhaps, such things don't need any evidence. That's why I have this irrational urge to find them—to live if only to find them.

If my sister is still alive, I've a strong feeling she's somewhere in the Girgaum area, because that's where Appa and she got separated in the crowd . . . where he loosened his grip over her finger. I don't know why, but I always imagine her living in abject poverty. Just like he hardened himself to set me on fire, why didn't Appa have the heart to kill Kalyani? Why couldn't he bring himself to do it? Was it because she was his favourite child? Was it because she looked like Amma? He never loved anyone as much as he loved Amma. Something in him snapped when Amma died.

Now when I look at all these things, so many hidden truths come to light: After Amma's death, though outwardly Appa seemed the same, he had become a different person. I realize that now.

Yes, I didn't die when he set my shirt on fire, but were the ugly scars on my chest and stomach the only ones the incident left on me? Were they the only disfigurement I was left to deal with? I must visit the institution Gilbert so often spoke about. He had great sympathy and respect for the way the inmates there coped with their physical deformities. But I must ask him: Is deformity only physical? Just because a person looks physically healthy, does it mean he has no other handicaps? What about our inner hurts? Don't they make us different from others? Are we abnormal or less normal?

Like it had so often happened, Nagappa had not written a word of all that he had been wanting to write. In fact, he hadn't even taken the notebook out. He realized this only later.

10

Finally, one night, Shrinivasa himself brought the letter Nagappa had been waiting for. He said the personnel and administration manager gave it to him when he had gone to Nagappa's office on some work. And this SOB 1 obediently offered to deliver it to me! Nagappa thought, seething with anger. So there's no doubt that this SOB 2 has a hand in the conspiracy the company is hatching against me. He mentally showered on Shrinivasa the choicest abuses he had learnt at Koligiriyanna's feet, like some religious chant, as he took the envelope to his room and bolted the door.

He read the letter. But it didn't make any sense:

A departmental inquiry has been instituted to investigate a complaint insinuating your role in a recent accident at the factory in which three workers lost their lives. The DMD will personally conduct the inquiry. Please get ready to proceed to Hyderabad as soon as you get the flight ticket, which is being arranged.

He read the note again and again, and by the time he realized its implications, he knew its contents by heart. In all this, he had forgotten to break into a sweat in instinctive anxiety. Instead, he stood absolutely erect, still, with the hair on his skin bristling. Animal courage, which had sprung from some unknown depths, had taken over. This trap that Phiroz has laid out for me isn't something new. I know it well. I know how it works. I know all its pitfalls, as if from a previous birth, he thought, surprisingly unperturbed by anger, fear or hatred. It no longer scares me. This is the decisive moment—the moment when I'll have to choose between life and death. The arena has been set. Let everything be thrashed out between us once and for all. Look, I'm standing, ready and waiting for the final confrontation. Phiroz, the poison you've been spewing at me from the beginning, the needless cruelty, the contempt, the enmity . . . let everything be finally resolved. I'm prepared for the endgame. I know your evil designs behind this so-called 'departmental inquiry'. For you, it may be a mere game. But for me, it's the question of my career, my professional integrity, and that's why a question of my existence and annihilation. I know I might lose. But I won't go down without a fight. It might spell my end, but I'll expose you, your malicious intent and the web of deceit behind your victory. You sisterfucker, be ready for it! I have the courage to face you, fight you!

Nagappa's chest swelled. From where did I get all this courage? he asked himself. And why this sudden surge of joy? This rush of strange emotions? Some brute strength passed on from generations, flowing through my veins, must've found a momentary spurt, priming me for the final face-off.

His spirit rose. His mind was clear, free of anxiety, as if a cloud had been lifted. He was once again in possession of his razor-sharp intellect. It thrilled him. He had to decide his next move: 'I'm enjoying this, Phiroz, I'm enjoying this thoroughly,' he said, smacking his thigh in exhilaration. His words echoed in the closed room, and he realized where he was. The thought of

Shrinivasa being part of the conspiracy momentarily unnerved him—not because he was frightened, but because he was aware that he was gullible. Shit! Why do I trust people so easily? he cursed himself. Of all the people, why did I seek refuge in this slimy creature's house, forgetting all that has happened in the past? I'm sure there was nothing noble in his invitation. It must all be a carefully planned ruse. Why must be. It *is*! Or else, how come I bumped into him at Santosh Bhavan after such a long time? I had gone there for coffee, and he sauntered in. It was the day I'd got the call from the personnel and administration manager! Why *that* day of all days? It can't be a coincidence. He had come there to lure me home. How could I have walked into this trap? It was an ambush, and I walked straight into it! How could I have not seen through it right away? Why didn't I make the connection between the call from the office and the 'accidental' meeting with Shrinivasa? How could I stupidly accept his invitation? Never mind, Shrinivasa of Nadoo Mhaaskeri, I know you haven't forgotten that incident twenty years ago. Nor have I. And I haven't forgotten the hatred you have nurtured towards me since then—this king cobra of Koligiriyanna's ghetto with a soft hiss hasn't forgotten. It's good that we both know it. It's good that it has all come out in the open.

Shrinivasa had inherited his vindictive nature from his mother. The story Nagappa had written about her had portrayed this trait in her, and the extent she could go to destroy those who had incurred her wrath, waiting for the right moment for years.

In a moment of epiphany, something suddenly struck Nagappa: Shrinivasa fears me. Shrinivasa, with his immense wealth and his power and prestige among the members of his community in Bombay, fears me because, I, the mild-mannered Nagappa, know of Shrinivasa's past, his poverty, the battle he has waged against it and the means he has used to win it. And every moment he enjoys his wealth and position, he fears me. And his decades of hatred towards me is based on nothing but fear. And it goes back to Netravati's suicide—the events that led to it and the evidence I had given in the coroner's court. I've always known of his fears and his bravado. I know why he reads all my stories. He's frightened. Could it be the same kind of fear and deep-rooted insecurity that's behind Phiroz's hatred towards me? I know what he fears—his own ignorance—his appalling ignorance of technical matters. And I alone in the entire company know about it. And he knows I know. And despite his ignorance, he was the technical director of the company for several years! And now he's the deputy managing director! Ignoramus, empty-headed SOB 2! He has risen to the top only through his cunning manipulations . . . by playing politics . . . camouflaging his ignorance behind his swagger, his carefully cultivated image. But how come these two villains, who have gone through life hiding their mediocrity, come together, that too at the exact time when I'm about to go to America? Why now, when my true merit has at last been recognized? Or is this the very reason why they have decided to join hands to conspire against me?

Nagappa couldn't shake off the suspicion. However, it didn't change his resolve to stand up to them and fight them to the end. This new-found courage made him tell Shrinivasa that he would be going back to his Khetwadi house the next morning after breakfast. It also nudged him to call the company's personnel and administration manager, Noshir

Khambata, on his home number from Shrinivasa's phone. 'I look forward to coming to Hyderabad. Please send my flight ticket to my Khetwadi residence,' he said, and realized his voice sounded loud and overconfident. 'And thanks for everything!' he added, sarcastically. Sensing Khambata's confusion, he deliberately repeated, 'Noshir, I look forward to the trip. I think I'll enjoy it!' He cut the call before Khambata could respond, and was surprised by his own nonchalance.

The next morning, Nagappa briefly looked at Shrinivasa's wife and said, 'I'm leaving.' When he was on his way home, he realized they were the first words he had ever spoken to her. The tinge of sadness in her eyes, the playfulness in Chetana's when he pinched her cheek and Achyuta's strange, silent gaze followed him for a long time.

As he climbed the wooden stairs to his third-floor house in Khemraj Bhavan, he found himself nodding at a few people he met on the way, instead of avoiding their eyes as usual. He was thrilled by his self-confidence. He turned the key and pushed the door open with the kind of joy he had not experienced in a long time.

PART II

11

He looked at the room as if for the first time. Everything about it appeared dear to him. He glanced at the people moving about in the chawl across the street with a new-found interest. He was vaguely aware that something happening within him had caused his present mood, he controlled his instinct to analyse it. Instead, he sat staring at his bookshelf. His mind was empty and refused to focus on anything. Remembering something, he took out his notebook from the suitcase. I must finish writing the things I've been planning to, before going to Hyderabad, he thought. I must write about the plot Phiroz and Shrinivasa are hatching against me, its inner workings, their secret motives—all that I've been able to gather so far, and the things that have struck me. Only then will I be able to decide on a game plan to counter theirs. I need to think clearly so that I have a strategy ready. What occurred to me at that epiphanic moment—that Phiroz and Shrinivasa are afraid of me—appears to be true, though I'm not entirely sure why. There could be reasons other than the obvious ones . . .

It gave Nagappa a sense of satisfaction that, for a change, he was trying to go to the root of their fears, instead of focusing on his own.

I must wake up early tomorrow morning and start writing, he told himself. That's the best time. I must go and see Rani tonight. It's been over a week since I visited her. Poor girl, she must be worried. He felt warm inside at the thought of Rani—her slightly flat nose, soft cheeks that dimpled when she smiled (just like Chetana's!), the small mouth with thin lips, her full breasts and supple thighs that drove him crazy. This was not why he had been drawn to the Nepali girl, though. The real reason, which he was aware of, but had not allowed himself to think about, was the feeling that his sister too, must be living the life of a prostitute. The vague feeling had, over the days, begun to show symptoms of a disease.

Nagappa became restless. The earlier sense of calm had disappeared. He rose from his chair and stood near the grille-less window, looking down at the street below. Just as he became aware of a distant memory beginning to resurface, Arjunrao from the corner house on the same floor pushed the unbolted door and walked in.

Arjunrao was the editor of *Vajradhari*, a weekly whose circulation depended solely on Pandit Mapankar's astrology column. Arjunrao fancied himself to be an intellectual, but was a windbag. Given a chance, he could hold forth on social inequality, M.N. Roy and radical humanism, like a card-holding communist. But scratch the surface, and he was an unadulterated right-winger—a staunch Hindu Mahasabha fanatic. Nagappa was in no mood to listen to one of his political tirades. 'Not going to your press today?' he asked.

'I've taken the day off. We're having Satyanarayana pooja at my place. If you have no other plans, please come home for lunch.'

Nagappa accepted the invitation but couldn't help smiling.

'Actually, I don't believe in all this nonsense. But I'm going along with it for the sake of my wife,' Arjunrao said defensively, as he pulled a chair and sat down. 'Looks like you're on long leave . . .' he drawled, making it sound like an off-hand remark. Nagappa realized that inviting him for lunch was an excuse. Arjunrao had come to pry.

'Yes, I'm on a month's leave,' he replied testily.

'It seems you're writing a novel . . .'

Nagappa was caught off-guard.

'Shrinivas Rao had come to our press the other day. It seems you're doing your writing at his place . . . He said he had offered you a room in his house.'

Nagappa could no longer hide his irritation. 'Yes, I was there for the last few days. But I've now decided to do my writing here. Pity you don't understand Kannada, otherwise I would've read excerpts for you. You would've recognized some of the characters. In fact, even you're one of them. The story revolves around a real-life incident—Netravati's suicide, which happened right here in this place. I'm writing everything as it happened. I've not even changed the names. That's the uniqueness of this novel. Shrinivasa appears as Shrinivasa. And you as Arjunrao, the editor of *Vajradhari*, residing at no. 53, third floor, Khemraj Bhavan, Khetwadi. It's a new experiment in the portrayal of realism in fiction. I realized Shrinivasa's house was not the right place to work on it. So I decided to come back here—where it all happened.'

Arjunrao looked flustered. Nagappa's words had hit the target. He relished the moment.

'W-w-w . . . why me of all people . . . in the book?' Arjunrao stuttered and grinned stupidly. But quickly regained his composure. 'So it looks like you haven't still forgotten the tragedy. Twenty years is a long time. But how can anyone forget? But Shrinivas Rao's different. Tough guy! Look how he has shrugged off everything, got married, had kids and settled down. It seems he has made tonnes of money and is planning to stand for municipal elections. He had come to our press to get posters printed. Said his press is too busy for such things . . . handles only big orders. Smart chap. Look at his luck! When he was staying with you here, he was just a clerk at a government press in Charni Road. And now . . .?'

The conversation had taken a totally different turn, and Nagappa felt his resolve to remain strong weakening. He had lost his earlier bravado and wanted Arjunrao to leave him alone. 'You must be busy with the pooja preparations . . .' he mumbled.

'Not at all. My younger brothers and their wives are taking care of everything. The priest's coming only in the afternoon. I'm anyway on leave. I was looking for someone to chat with. If you haven't had your breakfast . . .'

'I had it at Shrinivasa's place.'

'Then how about a cup of tea? It'll give me an excuse to have another cup.'

He yelled out his daughter's name. Instead, his brother's wife appeared at the door. He asked her to bring two cups of tea. As she turned to leave, she threw Nagappa a glance, which he didn't bother to interpret.

Arjunrao was in no hurry to leave. Nagappa wanted to wriggle out of the situation, but knew making an excuse that he had to go out wouldn't work. He resigned himself to listening to Arjunrao rant about everything and everyone. Fortunately, I don't have to really pay attention to this SOB 3's pointless chatter. He's quite shallow, but basically a harmless creature, Nagappa thought. Maybe his company will do me good. He felt his tense nerves relax, as tea arrived.

When Arjunrao finally left, Nagappa changed and settled down to write. As he opened the notebook, he was amused that this was what everyone had assumed to be his 'magnum opus'—the tell-all novel. 'You SOB 9! You ill-begotten bastard!' he said to his notebook in mock anger, and smiled.

Comment 13: I think, of the many fears that eat us alive, the possibility of losing what we have is one of the greatest fears. I shudder when I think of the valiant and determined battles I fought to escape from my fate—of being born into an extremely poor family in a small village. My aim then was to come up in life. And today, I dread losing it all—a fall from the position I have attained. Isn't this fear the reason why we gradually lose the fire in our belly . . . our revolutionary spirit? We fight all odds when we have nothing to lose. But what happens to us when the stakes are high? I don't fear losing my job. I know I can somehow earn a living. I'm not a shirker and have never shied away from hard work. Then why do my innards churn at the thought of losing my professional reputation? Is it the fear of falling in the eyes of others—of society, of peers? Isn't social acceptance, a position in society and our profession, the things we unconsciously crave for the most? Don't they contribute to our personal well-being?

A surprising thing: At an individual level, if I think of my colleagues or those in this chawl, or those from my community, for example, Arjunrao and Shrinivasa, I can confidently say that I couldn't care less about what they think of me. But the inescapable truth is some unknown power that rises above these people as individuals frightens me. I think this is what lies at the heart of Phiroz's and Shrinivasa's fears, too. Yes, they must fear the same thing. And I must be the root cause of it. And ergo, their conspiracy to eliminate me!

Prof. Nagnath, simply brilliant! Zindabad! Three cheers to you! Nagappa, you SOB 1, how elegantly you have arrived at the proof! QED. How beautifully you have tried to find excuses for your cowardice! Where did you learn these cerebral manoeuvres? It reveals nothing but your typical bourgeoisie mentality. Fear of losing, indeed! You're nothing but a lily-livered intellectual who's looking for some place to hide. How long will you keep running? There's an end even to an escape route. Instead of fleeing, have the courage to come back to reality . . . to where you really belong. Don't break in the morning the resolutions you make at night. Hold on to them tight. Stay firm. Be strong. Shake off your defences. Shed your armour. Come out of the shell you've created around you. Open up . . .

12

Nagappa got up at the crack of dawn and started writing. He liked to write early in the morning, before the world invaded his privacy and aroused the usual morass of emotions of fear, anger and anxiety. He knew from personal experience—and not just from reading Carl Jung, as he told himself—that the part of the mind that is involved in creative pursuits is quite different from the one that deals with the workaday world. For him, reading was as much a creative activity as writing. And he wanted to keep this part of his brain active for the sake of his own sanity—for his mental, and thereby his physical, well-being.

Comment 14: The brain centre where the instincts of self-preservation, survival and the ability to deal with predators have been encrypted in animals, honed by millennia of evolution, is the same place from where creativity and what we call morality and ethics, distinct to human beings, spring. I believe that we have lost our connection with this original wellspring. I blame this disconnect for the erosion of our spontaneous creative instinct and our moral rectitude—our basic integrity. Our present-day politicians are a good example of this tragedy. And if we are to find the main source of corruption in public life, we need only go to the root of our large-scale modern industrialization that has destroyed our inborn inventiveness and our morals. I think I should write a long essay about this. It could perhaps be the fitting reply to the small-minded editor of the small-time journal from Hubli.

The view from the bare window was all too familiar to Nagappa. But it looked different each day, in the serenity of dawn. 'Does this newness lie only in the scene outside? he asked himself. Right in front of him was a four-storey chawl, with two-room pigeonhole tenements like the one he lived in. In fact, there were pigeons, too. When Nagappa stood near the window, as he did now, he could hear their coded conversation of grunting and cooing on the window sill, as the strong smell of pigeon poop assaulted him. There were hordes of people living huddled in the chawl. Once in a while, a familiar face looked up, flashed a smile and was gone. Sometimes, there was a sudden glint in a pair of female eyes.

The dairy downstairs, encroaching on the pavement, came to life when the *bhaiyya* blew on the embers heaped on the coal stove and boiled fresh milk in a huge pan, stirring as the cream rose to the top. The sugarcane juice shop next to it signalled its presence a little later, with the tinkling of bells tied to the handle, as the Maratha owner turned the wheel, sweating and singing, as he pushed the canes under the crusher. Beyond all this was a smithy that invariably drew him, as if with a spell. He watched fascinated the forge spewing tongues of crimson flame with sparks flying from the red-hot iron rod as it was beaten into shape. It elicited in Nagappa a surge of emotions beyond the reach of words.

Amidst the soulless chaos of a city waking to yet another grimy day, the solitary banyan tree in the middle of the lane stood as a symbol of life, rising above the man-made mayhem and monotony. Nagappa loved looking at it.

As he now stood staring at its dark silence, waiting for the magical moment when the rising sun would light up its leafy green canopy, he thought of something and decided to write it down later: It's foolish to write a poem on a rose bush when the entire village is burning. (Perhaps, writing poetry itself is foolish.) But if we were to question why the village was burning, we would realize that it was because mankind forgot to love the rose bush. Writing a poem about its beauty could have, perhaps, averted the conflagration. Because we have started exploiting nature for our own selfish needs, our way of perceiving nature itself has changed in the last few centuries. In a sprawling city like this, one hardly sees nature's creation in its pure form, amidst the throng of lifeless, man-made objects standing on the foundation of our arrogance. And we have reached a point where we have started using even living things as if they were lifeless objects . . .

Nagappa realized that while he stood looking out of the window to get into the mood to write, an unknown part of his mind was unconsciously thinking of the inquiry Phiroz had set up and was going to conduct. What connection can I possibly have with the fire accident at the Hyderabad factory? he wondered. I wasn't even in Hyderabad then. It had been over three months since I had been transferred to the Bombay office. He smiled at the absurdity of the situation, but realized that while his fist remained unclenched, his body was still rigid with tension. There isn't a shred of evidence against me, he assured himself. How can Phiroz even think of framing me? And why? And why *now*? Why when the families of those who died in the accident have received compensation from our company and the insurance money? The underwriters themselves had issued a statement to the press that the fire had not been caused by either arson or due to negligence on the company's part.

But Nagappa knew the fire was caused due to negligence. And a few people knew that he knew.

The industrial disaster took place in the division manufacturing peroxide from methyl ethyl ketone. Let alone manufacturing it, even its storing and transportation was considered hazardous, as it is a highly flammable substance that could explode at the slightest impact or friction. As a precaution, peroxide was mixed with phthalates and plasticizers to make it less hazardous and combustible, and filled in carboys and polyethylene bottles and stored in concrete bunkers, away from the main building. Customers' orders were dispatched directly from the bunkers. The factory manager and the technical manager had taken the necessary precautions in this regard. However, the measures were directed more at saving company property, rather than taking care of the safety and health hazards faced by the workers. The workers had not been adequately trained about the precautions to be taken.

Nagappa had expressed his concern and dissatisfaction about the safety measures several times in front of a few of his colleagues. Instead of paying attention to him, the authorities had tried to brush aside his warnings. When the matter had gone up to Phiroz, as the DMD, he had strictly warned Nagappa not to interfere in matters that didn't concern him.

Though it was well-known that Nagappa's technical expertise was unmatched in the entire organization, the top management thought he could easily be swayed by emotions, and wasn't very pragmatic by nature. They were worried about the repercussions if his fears about the hazards posed by chemicals to the workers reached the office bearers of the workers' union. That was the reason why they resented his 'stupid interference'. But Nagappa thought the workers were needlessly being exposed to a dangerous working environment, not out of necessity, but because of the slack attitude of Phiroz and his minions.

Nagappa had taken it upon himself to write to reputed companies in the UK, the United States and Germany, which manufactured peroxide, and got manuals on the standard precautionary measures to be taken. He had sent those to both the MD and the DMD, along with memos specifically stating for the record that he had sent them the manuals. The DMD couldn't contain his anger when he received them. Nagappa shook, remembering how he had been summoned to the DMD's cabin and given a dressing down. More than anything, Phiroz was angry that Nagappa had addressed the memo directly to the MD. 'Don't try to bypass my authority. Remember, you report to *me* and *not* to the MD!' he had thundered.

But the matter had not ended there. The news of Nagappa's humiliation had spread across the factory—from supervisors to office boys and watchmen. He came to know rather late that the smear campaign was a part of a carefully planned conspiracy hatched by the factory manager. He felt mortified and couldn't speak to anyone for days. As the R&D manager with an excellent reputation, being scolded like an errant child was a loss of face for Nagappa. The worst blow to his sensitive and withdrawing nature came when the girls in the administration department who thought highly of him—or at least he thought they did—gave him strange glances and laughed among themselves whenever he passed by. The telephone operator, Reena, was an exception. She had called him on his intercom one morning and said, 'Don't worry. Keep calm and keep your cool. Everything will be all right.' Nagappa's eyes had moistened at this reassurance and kindness from such an unexpected quarter. Though he was aware that Jalal Husain had just entered his cabin, Nagappa had said in a shaky voice, 'Thank you, Reena. Thank you so much! It's so sweet of you. I need your . . . I need your . . .' He was about to say, 'your good wishes', but the line got cut. Probably, the DMD must have walked into her office or she must have got a call.

Though Nagappa felt bad that the words remained unspoken, there was relief on his face. But the lewd remark Jalal made erased it: 'So someone's eager to serve you sweets first thing in the morning . . .'

'Jalal, please,' Nagappa had begged. 'Don't deliberately misinterpret everything. Only I know what I've been going through these last few days. Reena is the first person to say something nice to me in a long time . . .'

Nagappa was disgusted by the pleading tone in his voice. But Jalal was not in a mood to back down. 'But you must admit it, Reena is a sweet girl,' he had teased. There was a tinge of jealousy in Jalal's words. But Nagappa ignored it and walked to the window. The sight of the red hibiscus flowers in the garden outside was comforting.

He looked up when he heard the office boy come in with the day's mail. He grinned and saluted Nagappa, probably for the first time, and deliberately placed a bulging envelope right on top of the heap. Jalal leaned forward and exclaimed, 'Oh, from the MD . . . from the head office!' It was well-known in the company that the MD had great regard for Nagappa. This had made others jealous, especially Phiroz.

Nagappa wondered what the letter contained. The news of being reprimanded by the DMD must have reached the MD, and he has sent a salvo, he thought, and couldn't bring himself to open it. But Jalal was staring intently at it, waiting for Nagappa to open it.

Finally, Nagappa tore open the envelope with shaking fingers and read the letter. When he finished reading it, unable to contain his joy, he held Jalal's hand and said emotionally, 'My friend, the news I'd been waiting for has come at last. I'm being sent to America for training . . . and I'm selected to represent the company at a technology conference in Hawaii.'

'Wonderful! Let me see . . .' Jalal stretched out his hand.

From that moment began Nagappa's saga of torment. Overwhelmed by the news, Nagappa unthinkingly gave the letter to Jalal before he knew what he was doing, though 'PERSONAL AND CONFIDENTIAL,' was printed on it in big bold letters. The sleight of hand had happened quickly and casually.

A few weeks later, Nagappa was suddenly transferred to the Bombay office, and removed from the R&D department he loved working in. The designation of 'manager, special assignment' had been created for him. Nagappa wasn't sure what the post entailed. He took solace in the fact that it gave him an opportunity to work directly under the MD. But he sensed that the MD had been deliberately sidelining him ever since he had come to the head office. Was that the reason why his US trip kept getting postponed?

13

The Khetwadi neighbourhood was already up and about. Milkmen with huge aluminium cans and newspaper boys were on their rounds. The Udupi Brahmin's Restaurant below Khemraj Bhavan and the Communist Party office at the entrance of the lane were buzzing, while the old man in the opposite chawl was getting ready for his bhajan singing, which was loud enough to wake the dead—the familiar sights and sounds of early morning.

Nagappa was still thinking about how he had unwittingly given the letter to Jalal. I never did learn to be street smart, he rued. What good is my intelligence if I don't know how to survive in this rat race? You should know how to manoeuvre your way around and deal with people tactfully. And I know neither. People with less ability than me have raced ahead and are sitting in top positions in the organization, while I'm trailing behind.

He had the habit of impulsively sharing any new R&D idea he got with colleagues, without officially sending it for approval. On quite a few occasions, it had reached the DMD's office as a proposal for a 'brilliant concept' even before

Nagappa could put it across to him. Phiroz had accused him of plagiarism a few times when he presented his own idea. The humiliation and anger he had experienced at such moments was still raw. What hurt Nagappa more was the obvious and irrational pleasure Phiroz derived from hurting him. He was unable to understand the magnitude of Phiroz's hatred for him. At such times, Nagappa would turn to his writing for solace. He had become aware again and again that creativity was his only source of pure joy. He was also aware that only when he finally put his name on the work he had created was he truly free of the original source of inspiration.

Of late, in his search for the meaning of life, he had begun to wonder what his place was in the larger scheme of things and, more than that, what was his relevance in the process of creation itself. He felt if such a question, or even a quest was, indeed, significant, then, perhaps, his own stamp of identity was equally important in the quest. But when he was denied the identity and authorship of his work—the distinctive signature of his 'self', his individuality, or what could simply be called his due credit, Nagappa knew that he perhaps chose to remain silent. He knew this was not because he was indifferent to fame, but because he possibly lacked the moral courage to raise his voice against such injustice. But he had not bothered to delve deep into such a possibility.

Khetwadi was now wide awake, and the babel of sounds emanating from the busy streets below and the prayer song of the old man had reached an unbearable crescendo. But Nagappa had blotted out these sounds. His mind focused on one thing—the blunder of giving the confidential letter from the MD to Jalal. It suddenly struck Nagappa that he had failed to see through Jalal. Jalal had all along managed to hide his professional jealousy towards Nagappa behind his charming smile and an easy-going nature. When Nagappa now looked at the chain of events that had followed Jalal reading the letter, he felt defeated. Oh, god, if I can't even trust someone like Jalal, then whom *can* I trust? he thought. And if mistrusting everyone around you is expediency and a survival skill, then what kind of life are we living? And how can you go on if your emotions are bereft of any inner impulse? Are all our emotions and actions tied to some or the other ulterior motive? This was one of the reasons why he hadn't acted against those who plagiarized his original R&D ideas, or pretended to be indifferent even when he had proof of others plagiarizing them, realizing the utter futility of taking any action. But when he shut himself off from all the noise around him and turned inwards, the question that nagged him was: Does Jalal's professional jealousy have something to do with Phiroz's hatred towards me, and for the unfolding of this drama? The thought unnerved him.

Not that a mild suspicion about Jalal hadn't crossed his mind before. But Jalal exuded such warmth that the very thought had made him cringe with self-disgust. But now it was important to find out Jalal's role in the conspiracy Phiroz had hatched against him. He knew that Jalal pretending to be his close friend, while secretly working against him, was nothing but basic self-preservation. For the first time, he felt revulsion towards Jalal. Everyone is scurrying around like animals to save their own skins, he thought. Yes, I was devastated when I was uprooted without warning from the R&D department and the work I loved so much, just when I was reaching a high point in my career. I was tossed to the Bombay office overnight. But within six months, I proved myself with my technological acumen and commitment to work, and earned the respect of my colleagues, the directors and customers. This must have upset Phiroz's plans. That's why he pretends to be dismissive of my work and my contribution to the company. But I don't understand his mindless cruelty. And now Shrinivasa has joined the pack of hunters surrounding me. If people like Phiroz, Jalal and Shrinivasa have ganged up against a harmless person like me, then I must have inadvertently come in the way of some sinister plot of this cabal. Something is brewing. I must find out about it before I go to Hyderabad. Would Mary know? What if I invite her for a movie . . . for dinner? Mary has treated me with respect and affection, and even made veiled suggestions for a 'date' a few times. But I've held myself back. Once I'd even pretended not to understand her suggestion. She had mischievously winked at me and smiled, 'How sweet and innocent!'

The very thought of indulging in a guiltless social activity like dating seemed like an adventure to Nagappa. He felt his ears turning red. He gave up the idea.

He realized he was hungry and decided to go to Santosh Bhavan on Benham Hall Lane for breakfast. He thought of calling Mary from one of the public kiosks to find out if she had any information about his trip to Hyderabad. Though Arjunrao's house had a phone, he had never used it to make a call. Occasionally, his office called him on that number if the matter was urgent. In fact, he had received the order from the personnel and administration manager on Arjunrao's phone the other day. The memory of it made him quickly step out of the house and lock the door in a great hurry.

14

Nagappa felt uneasy for no reason as he walked towards Santosh Bhavan. Though he usually took the 6th Lane towards the Khetwadi main road leading to Prarthana Samaj, today he took the 7th Lane. At its entrance stood the Communist Party press that brought out its mouthpiece, *People's Age*, and the Girgaum branch of the party office, which also controlled labour unions. He had once thought of bringing to their notice the health hazards faced by the workers at the Hyderabad factory. He had later given it up as a foolhardy idea. It now resurfaced. He was surprised by his quickening heartbeat as he crossed the party office. He walked fast and reached the main road and turned towards Prarthana Samaj. He told himself that he was excited at the thought of calling Mary. There was a telephone kiosk outside the party office. He had walked past it. He now wondered if he was using Mary for his own selfish purpose to get some inside information, especially since he had ignored her advances all along. He finally gave up the idea of calling her, but not for the reason he had given himself earlier. He suddenly thought of Rani when he saw a bus going towards

Nana Chowk. But the desire to meet her quickly gave way to a nameless anxiety. I'm still afraid . . . I'm afraid of something I'm not able to define yet, he thought. As he reached the Prarthana Samaj junction, he stood stock-still at the traffic island, unable to take another step forward. His mind was empty of thoughts, but the turmoil within persisted. He was only a few minutes away from Benham Hall Lane. The prospect of a sumptuous breakfast didn't seem inviting any more. He had lost his appetite.

He bought a copy of the *Times of India* at the corner newspaper stall. It was part of his daily routine when he went to Santosh Bhavan for breakfast. 'Have not seen sir for the last few days. Hope all's well?' inquired the boy at the stall. Nagappa was deeply touched by the unexpected words of concern. He tried to say something when handing him the change, but couldn't. 'Wasn't well,' was all he could finally mumble.

If I lose my job, I'll open a newspaper stall like this one or an old paper mart, Nagappa said to himself. Though said in jest, as he walked, he felt he hadn't meant it as a joke. In fact, he felt they were not his words at all, but a command issued by someone. His smile disappeared. He walked along Benham Hall Lane with a downcast face.

The lane was lined with women selling vegetables and fruit and men with red caps hawking all kinds of odds and ends. They were shouting out the price of their wares and calling out to passers-by. A little girl in a long skirt selling strings of jasmine followed him, 'Dada, dada, buy one . . .' He remembered Saraswati and impulsively bought one. When he breathed in the intoxicating fragrance of the flowers wrapped in fresh leaves, he smiled to himself, as if he had

just realized the real reason for buying it. He put it in his
pocket and walked towards Santosh Bhavan. His appetite
had returned.

Nagappa knew Appa Nayak, the owner of Santosh
Bhavan. They were from the same district back home. As
soon as he saw Nagappa, he grinned, showing his betel juice-
stained teeth, adjusted his white cap as a preamble, and
began: 'Haven't come this way for a few days? Yesterday I
happened to meet Shrinivasa. He told me you were supposed
to spend a month at his place, but have to go to Hyderabad
suddenly . . .'

Seeing the colour drain from Nagappa's face, he stuttered,
'He mentioned it casually when your name came up . . . You
go ahead and order your breakfast, I'll join you. And, oh, a
boy had come asking for you yesterday evening and today.
He left this for you.' He gave Nagappa a sealed envelope.

Nagappa wanted to be left alone. Though there were
vacant tables downstairs, he climbed up to the family section.
They began service there only in the evening. Since he knew
the waiters, no one objected.

It looks like Shrinivasa is going around telling his friends
about what's happened at the office, Nagappa thought. Why
is he spreading news about the worst calamity of my career?
The thought shook his inner resolve to take on Phiroz and
his gang.

He ordered *uttappa* and coffee. When the waiter left, he
opened the envelope and pulled out a strip of paper with a
typed message: *This is from a friend and well-wisher. Please call
today after 8 p.m. on no. 54879 for an important message.*

It looked like a Bandra number. Could it be from Mary?
Nagappa wondered. He didn't know where she lived, but

had heard that she was staying as a paying guest in Bandra or Khar with a family. How can I possibly know where she lives? he thought. I've hardly known her these past seven or eight months.

Before that, Mary and Nagappa exchanged pleasantries whenever he came from Hyderabad to meet the MD at the Bombay head office. He had complimented her on her excellent manners and dress sense a couple of times. And once, probably, a few weeks after joining the Bombay office, he had told her she had a beautiful pair of eyes. It was a spontaneous remark, and not meant as a pickup line. She had smiled with her full lips, (which he didn't have the courage to compliment), and said, 'You flatterer,' and winked at him. The memory of it lifted Nagappa's spirits.

The waiter brought the uttappa and chutney. 'Your favourite vadas are ready. Shall I get you a plate, sir?' he asked, seeing Nagappa in a good mood.

'Yes, and bring the coffee with it,' Nagappa smiled.

But when the waiter left, a terrible suspicion began to nag him: What if the note is not from Mary? Who would want to send me a cryptic, anonymous note? Is this also part of the conspiracy . . . a trap? And if it's from Mary, what could be the urgent message she wants to give me? And why all this secrecy? Mary, or whoever it is, probably wants to help me, but doesn't want to be dragged into the mess. The person wants to be careful. This means the conspiracy being hatched against me is sinister. Oh, god! Can anyone trust anyone? Why have we all got caught in this terrible state of such deep mutual suspicion? Even when expressing concern about a fellow human being, we want to be cautious . . . stay out of trouble. We're losing our natural, spontaneous compassion towards others. We constantly watch our step, our backs. And if it's Mary who has sent it, what consequences . . . what terrible retribution does she fear? Why not send the note to my house? Why leave it in a restaurant? The reason for specifying the time to call could be to make sure she's at home to receive it . . .

The waiter brought the plate of vadas and coffee. Appa Nayak came upstairs and sat in front of Nagappa. The strong scent of attar wafting from him drowned the aroma of coffee. Colourful character! Nagappa thought, irritably. This decadent old SOB 2 has no other work but to sit at the counter, collect cash from customers and think of ways of spending it on himself and his lavish lifestyle. He sits there gathering gossip about everyone . . .

'I don't think the boy who gave the note is from this area,' Appa Nayak began. 'Looked like a Christian. When I asked him who had sent it, he just said, "A friend", that's all. In fact, he didn't want to give it to me. He waited for a long time for you. I don't think he knows you. Whenever someone came in, he asked if it was you. When I asked why he wanted to give a note to someone he didn't know, he said, "The person who has sent it knows him well."'

Nagappa wanted to hit Appa Nayak with something heavy. His rage had reached a breaking point. You SOB 1! Why are you stretching this one bit of information into some kind of a cheap thriller? Nagappa wanted to scream. Someone gave you an envelope to give it to me, and you've given it. Now just shut up and leave!

'It seems you're writing a novel about Shrinivasa . . . Your friend Sitaram is going around telling everyone about it. Of course, Shrinivasa knows it, too. But I don't think he's worried too much about it, from what he told me: "Let him write, and let him write everything! In fact, I've invited him to write it in *my* house,"' Appa Nayak said, with red betel juice flowing from the corners of his mouth.

By the time he spat the juice in the washbasin and came back, Nagappa was filled with uncontrollable rage, but wasn't sure who its target was—whether it was Sitaram, who had been spreading rumours about the novel, or Shrinivasa, who went around trying to hide his panic with false bravado. Or was it this pot-bellied gossipmonger, who salivated at the whiff of a scandal?

Purged of the betel juice, Nayak's loose tongue was itching to speak: 'Don't get on the wrong side of Shrinivasa. Enmity with him isn't good. You know his nature. He won't hesitate to go to any extent to destroy anyone who's against him.' After a pause, feigning a lack of interest in the whole affair, he whispered, 'You know I personally don't believe in getting involved in such things, but I'm saying this out of affection for you—he has a lot of clout among the Saraswat Brahmin community in Bombay. Agreed, it's all based on money power, but he's a very powerful person in the community . . . occupies a high position . . . has a lot of influence over important people like the head priest of the *matha*. He has taken the entire responsibility of the Wadala Ganesh festival this year. There're all sorts of rumours about the caste of your ancestors among the community elders, which has caused some suspicion. It seems . . .' Though he saw Nagappa had turned livid with rage, he continued with some kind of wicked obstinacy, 'It seems, they're saying your father and mother weren't from our community at all . . .'

Nagappa got up mid-sentence, leaving his coffee untouched. Appa Nayak was taken aback at this impudence, and barked,

'I'm telling you all this for your own good. Shrinivasa has sworn to expose your entire family background in front of our community with solid proof. He's going to Goa to find out things about your family. I'm only trying to warn you . . .'

'Nayaka, listen, and listen carefully! I don't want to have anything to do with you or your disgusting community! I'm not particularly proud I belong to it. That's why I've not taken part in any of its activities. Let Shrinivasa go and conduct research about my family history. I'm not scared. Actually, I'm curious to know what he finds out. Tell him this when you meet him. Tell him I told you all this. And let him be warned! If he has enough spine, let him be prepared to face the things I'm going to write about *his* family history!'

Nagappa was surprised at the hatred and bitterness in his words. An unintended crudeness had crept into his voice.

Appa Nayak's eyes suddenly widened with vulgar curiosity. His mouth hung loose, salivating at the prospect of another piece of gossip. He waited, ready to lap up with relish all the titbits of a new scandal. Nagappa was revolted. 'And another thing, Nayaka! My novel isn't just about Shrinivasa. It's also about all of you who looked the other way and supported his misdeeds. There's plenty about the community . . . about the "eminent" members of the community . . . the head priest, too. Thanks for warning me about Shrinivasa. Thanks for your concern!'

As Nayak sat speechless, Nagappa stomped downstairs with the bill the waiter had just brought, paid it at the counter and stepped on to the street.

With this, I've broken my connection with Santosh Bhavan, he thought.

15

Nagappa knew that his utter sense of loneliness was the cause of his many sorrows. But he was unable to do anything about it, because he was by nature reclusive. All his life, he had been wary of any reference to his childhood, his parents, his caste, his brother and sister or the burning secret he held close to his chest. He snapped ties with anyone who made even an indirect allusion to it. Deciding to snap his ties with Santosh Bhavan was the latest in a series of broken relationships. But paradoxically, Nagappa valued friendship and was ready to do anything for friends. He knew it came from his intense nature. He was sentimental and implicitly trusted people and sought to resonate with their feelings. But whenever this was not reciprocated or when he realized he was being used, he felt a deep sense of betrayal. He had come to the sad conclusion that all bonds were based on selfishness, and had lost faith in human relationships. He often felt he was alone in this plight and grieved inwardly. Take for instance this Shrinivasa, Nagappa thought. Just five days back, when he begged me to spend my month's leave at his place, I readily agreed, forgetting all that had happened between us. I trusted him despite my past experiences. I trusted the honesty and genuine warmth reflected in his face. Let alone his words, even his facial expression was fake! How easily I get cheated! I think I'm incapable of reading people.

Nagappa was angry with himself for being so gullible. He also felt sorry for himself. He wanted to speak to someone. Should I call Mary? he wondered again. But he gave up the idea once more. If it was Mary who had sent the note, then there must be a reason for asking me to call her at eight at night. It must be something she can't tell over the office phone. If I called her now, it would have to be on her office number.

Nagappa visualized her face. What had first drawn him towards her were her sparkling, yet compassionate eyes. He thought her rich black hair cascading down her shoulders added to her attractiveness. But now, more than her beauty, her concern for him, when he was so vulnerable and needed a friend, filled him with gratitude. There was nothing to do but wait till eight in the evening.

What if I go and meet someone? he thought, but knew he had no real friends. The thought depressed him. A few faces floated before him. Even Rani's. But he didn't feel like meeting any of them. At this decisive moment, when his fate hung between life and death, human company seemed unbearable.

By now, Nagappa had reached Prarthana Samaj. He walked to the main road, crossed to the other side and found himself in front of the newspaper stall. He smiled remembering his earlier plan of opening a newspaper agency. He pulled a stool and sat down, nodding at Tukaram, the owner. Tukaram was touched by Nagappa's humility. 'Shall I order tea, sahib?' he asked.

'No, I just had coffee and breakfast at Nayak's restaurant,' he replied. He couldn't bring himself to utter the name

Santosh Bhavan. Tukaram's presence was comforting. Nagappa opened the newspaper he had bought earlier to glance at the headlines.

'Tender coconut water?' Tukaram hesitated.

'Okay, but in glasses so we can share,' Nagappa said.

Tukaram gestured to the boy to fetch two tender coconuts and gave him some money. The boy ran to Benham Hall Lane.

After matriculation, Nagappa had spent his college days in Khetwadi's two-room chawl in Khemraj Bhavan. And later, after graduating in chemical technology, he had roamed the streets of Bombay in search of a job. Those days, Shrinivasa was his only close friend. Tukaram's newspaper stall and Santosh Bhavan were familiar haunts. Sher-e-Punjab which served non-vegetarian fare and Light of Asia hair-cutting salon nearby were old landmarks. Those days, many people in the area had become friendly with Shrinivasa. Nagappa would watch amazed as he laughed and chatted for hours with the shopkeepers. His easy familiarity and utter lack of self-consciousness thrilled him. Even now, the bylanes of Khetwadi, Prarthana Samaj, Thakurdwar, Charni Road, Grant Road, Chowpatty and Dhobi Talao were intimate parts of Nagappa's inner territory. But he could never go beyond nodding acquaintance with the people who lived there.

He wanted to speak to Tukaram, open his heart to him and lighten his burden, but was tongue-tied. It's not in my nature to nurture relationships through spoken words, he thought. I express the affection I feel for all these people I've known for years in my writing. They inhabit my stories. But I can't show what I feel when I come face-to-face with them. Also, earlier, language was an obstacle. Shrinivasa could nonchalantly speak in his broken Marathi, mixing it with Kannada, creating an illusion of fluency. But I remained quiet, though I could actually string sentences together. More than Shrinivasa's knowledge, what impressed everyone was his supreme confidence to go on despite making mistakes. Though he was boastful, it wasn't an empty boast most of the time. He had the guts to do what he said he would.

Why am I thinking of the person I've come here to forget? Nagappa wondered, surprised by how his mind had wandered off in another direction. It also made him uneasy. One day, I must write about this Khetwadi-Girgaum area, where I've spent the most significant part of my life, Nagappa thought. But why do I feel this way? Maybe as I sit here, the feeling that this place has triggered in me—which could be called some kind of affection, for want of a better word—has made me want to write about it. Maybe because I can't articulate this emotion in front of anybody.

The boy came back with two tender coconuts, offered one to Tukaram and another to Nagappa, and went away under the pretext of a tea break, sensing Nagappa's awkwardness. Nagappa haltingly started asking Tukaram about his business in his Konkani-accented Marathi. A passing thought in the morning was now taking the shape of a serious decision.

When he left Tukaram's shop and walked home, he thought he would be able to spend the rest of his life in anonymity, running a small newspaper stall or a circulating library in one of the innumerable bylanes of Khetwadi, if he lost his job: I'll learn to live like a nobody without the crutch of my lineage, my professional status, my money, why even without the fear of losing the position I've earned in society because of my knowledge and talent.

He reached home, closed the door and sat down for a long time, thinking about it. As time passed, the seemingly dispassionate decision acquired such an emotional undertone that for a moment, Nagappa debated quitting his job: What if I chuck this bloody job on my own? What if I walk out of it all? What if I send in my resignation before they send the ticket to Hyderabad? When the present MD retires, Phiroz will take his place. It would be impossible to work with him in a toxic environment for the rest of my career. Why perpetuate this relationship of mutual hostility? And for how long? But, on the other hand, the thought of becoming a newspaper vendor must have come to me at a vulnerable moment that shook the very depths of my being. Maybe I needn't go to such extremes. Probably I'm unnecessarily panicking. Even if I lose this job, aren't there other companies I can join?

The thought that no matter what happened, he was in control and knew the way out of this tortuous maze was comforting. He felt at peace with himself.

But the feeling didn't last long. His mind was once again in turmoil: What reason can I give for quitting this company, where I've worked for so long and earned respect in my field, and joining another company? Do I need to give any reasons? Do I really owe an explanation to anyone? Doesn't explaining one's actions to others imply ceding one's will power to others? Isn't it a sign of fear—fear of something beyond my control? Also, in reality, isn't wanting to give up everything and walk away a camouflage to hide the fear of something else—facing the unknown? Again, it could be triggered by a familiar fear . . . something already experienced. In this unasked for, unwanted life that's given to us, perhaps the only achievement we're capable of is to remain ourselves in the face of all that the world throws at us. If this is true, should I be running away from the gauntlet Phiroz and Shrinivasa have thrown? Should I turn my back and flee like a coward? I have not sought this battle. But if these evil forces have challenged me to it, should I refuse to accept it and vegetate in one of the sordid backstreets of Khetwadi, selling newspapers or, worse still, sitting in a dusty *raddi* shop among discarded old stuff? Maybe, in the end, I'll do just that. But only after giving a fitting reply to these wily bastards. I might lose this battle, but I shouldn't give up the fight. No, I have not given up my right to fight my own battles. No, handing in my resignation is out of the question. And maybe, that's precisely the reason they're putting tremendous psychological pressure on me so that I'll succumb and quit. Yes, *that's* their evil scheme—to force me to lay down my arms and leave. It's a battle of attrition. Maybe Phiroz wants me to make way for his sidekick, Jalal, and send him to America instead. And Shrinivasa has his own axe to grind in all this. I should be prepared.

Nagappa decided that after lunch, he would write down all that he knew about the fire accident in the factory, as it would come in handy during the inquiry. He began planning his day ahead: Let me have a bath first. From today, Santosh Bhavan is out of bounds for me. But there's Sher-e-Punjab. After lunch, I need to take a nap. I must call Mary. But, before that, after my nap, I should get some writing done. How about visiting Rani tonight? But the desire for physical pleasure has dried up. I want nothing now. No distractions. Everything after I come back from Hyderabad. Let everything be decided first, once and for all, one way or the other.

16

Nagappa's 'home' in Khetwadi's dilapidated sixty-year-old chawl comprised a sitting room in the front and an adjoining room with a bed. The narrow passageway connecting the two had a makeshift bathroom with a sink. Nagappa was eligible for a car and a spacious two-bedroom apartment in one of Bombay's upmarket suburbs. The first three months after he was transferred to Bombay, he could get hotel accommodation. But Nagappa had not claimed any of this, and had chosen to live in his old coop, for which he paid a pittance, preferring his usual simple way of life. He also hoped that his transfer to Bombay was temporary, and once Phiroz's anger cooled down, he would be sent back to the Hyderabad factory. Nagappa was aware that this hope was also based on his secret pride that no one else but he was qualified for the post of the R&D manager. He felt extremely depressed whenever this pride was wounded.

He had turned a major part of the front room into his personal library—a simple bookshelf he had put together with a bamboo framework—with hundreds of rare books he had collected over the years from second-hand bookshops in the city. He had been collecting books ever since he started working. Old booksellers in Grant Road, Mohammad Ali Road and Dhobi Talao knew Nagappa well. Whenever he came from Hyderabad to Bombay on office work, he would spend a lot of money on books. He had arranged them in neat rows and dusted them regularly. He loved the heady smell of books.

Though he had got up to have a bath, on a sudden impulse, he climbed the tall stool in front of the shelf, picked up a book, opened its pages and inhaled its musty smell. It jolted him. It took him back years to Netravati's tragic death—the death Shrinivasa feared Nagappa was writing about in his novel. He got down, collapsed on the easy chair and closed his eyes.

Netravati: She was just twenty-one then. She couldn't be called pretty, but oozed youthful sensuality. Her swaying hips, blazing eyes and provocative smile were open invitations. Nagappa didn't like her the first time they met. It was probably because of the rumours he had heard about her elder sister, Anasuya. It was well-known that she was the keep of a rich businessman in Bombay. Nagappa had heard from Shrinivasa that Anasuya belonged to a Saraswat Brahmin family from Dhareshwar. When she was eighteen, her parents had forced her to marry an old man, and she had run away in protest to Bombay on the day of her wedding. The rest was like any other story on the inside page of a newspaper: She fell into the clutches of pimps in Bombay's red-light area, but finally managed to escape and become friendly with the businessman whose wife had been bedridden for years with an incurable ailment. He had set up another house for her. Though he couldn't legally marry her, he made her feel she was no less than a lawfully wedded wife, and that he was a decent 'family man'. The couple had even performed the Satyanarayana pooja with the blessings of the Brahmins from the community, and invited married women for a feast. Jealous of her dazzling jewellery and brazen disregard for 'family values' the women had sniggered behind her back. Anasuya, who could not get rid of the label of a 'keep', no matter how hard she tried, had one wish—to see her sister, Netravati, marry a decent man from her community and lead a normal domestic life like other women around. Tied to this wish was the craving of childless Anasuya to give Netravati away in marriage in a grand ceremony, along with the husband she could never marry, and invite eminent members of the Saraswat clan. In preparation for this, she had brought Netravati from the village to live with her. She treated her more like a daughter than a sister. Shrinivasa had told Nagappa a lot more. He had also gone around telling everyone that he was in love with Netravati and wanted to marry her. This had given him the licence to have a torrid affair with her. She would even drop in at Nagappa's place at all times and spend hours with Shrinivasa in the bedroom. Shrinivasa began introducing her to the neighbours as his fiancée and praised her many virtues. Nagappa's attitude towards her gradually softened after this, as now she was not only his friend's lover but also his future wife. He had even visited her house a couple of times with Shrinivasa and met her sister's presumptive husband. Anasuya was delighted that her dream of getting her sister married was about to come true.

Those days, Shrinivasa, who had come forward to fulfil Anasuya's wishes and had the courage to marry Netravati, was a hero in everyone's eyes. He went around boasting about his 'broad-mindedness'. No one could deny the enormous social significance of what he had decided to do. And then, the same Shrinivasa, who had romanced her in public and pleasured her in private for nine months, had gone back on his promise just three months before the wedding, and pretended to have forgotten the entire episode.

Nagappa thought about the way Shrinivasa had become the cause of her tragic and horrifying death. He clearly remembered that morning: He and another roommate, Gopala, were in this very room, studying. It had been a few weeks since Shrinivasa had broken his promise and cut off his ties with Netravati. There was a knock on the door. Nagappa opened it. It was Netravati. Her face was calm and expressionless as she stepped in, and bore no signs of her mental state. There was a hint of a smile on her lips as she glanced briefly at him and Gopala. If it was indeed a smile, that was her last smile. The thought that she had smiled made Nagappa's hair stand on end now. She wordlessly walked into the other room, confident she would find Shrinivasa there. But she didn't close the door behind her this time. In that brief moment, Nagappa observed that she was wearing a deep blue transparent georgette sari. He suddenly remembered it now. He had not seen her in that sari before. Because she looked more attractive than usual or, for no reason at all, he felt for a fleeting moment that she could be pregnant. Some corner of his mind must have unconsciously registered that her body exuded a special radiance not seen before. Though he and Gopala had no idea what was happening inside, they felt uneasy. They knew this was no ordinary visit. Netravati had come to tell Shrinivasa something. They heard the sound of running water. It must be Shrinivasa bathing. The sound of water splashing was louder than usual. This must have been on purpose. Netravati must be speaking to him as he bathed. They didn't know what exactly took place between her and Shrinivasa. But within minutes, she appeared near the doorway, looked at Nagappa and Gopala and said, 'Take care of your sisters. Don't let even the shadow of this man ever fall on them.' She darted inside and they heard women screaming from the chawl opposite. Netravati had jumped from the third floor window.

Nagappa was drenched in sweat. Did the musty smell of the book trigger this memory? Or was it a coincidence that his mind was forming some unknown connections at the very moment he smelt the book? He couldn't tell. But two images were etched in his mind: Netravati lying in a heap on the ground with her limbs flailing seconds before her body went still, and Shrinivasa, his body dripping, running with a towel around his waist to Arjunrao's house to call the police. Netravati had been declared brought dead at the hospital.

Later, at the coroner's court, Nagappa was the prime witness. Netravati's grieving family had accused Shrinivasa of pushing her to her death. But this did not influence Nagappa's statement. Two women had seen Netravati jumping from the window. But Netravati must have told Shrinivasa she had decided to commit suicide. He could have prevented it. But from Shrinivasa's behaviour, it was clear he wanted her out of the way. That was why he didn't do anything to stop her from falling to her death. Also, his immediate act was to inform the police that someone had jumped out of his window. His first thought was to establish it was a suicide and not murder. Nagappa's evidence entirely

hinged on these two points. According to him, legally and
technically, it may have been a suicide. But Shrinivasa was
morally responsible for Netravati's death. Nagappa was
trembling when he said this and was about to burst into tears.
This did have an impact on those in the courtroom. The only
two people who appeared unaffected were the coroner, who
had grown immune to such outbursts, and Shrinivasa, who
sat immobile. Nagappa himself was taken aback by his next
words. They had flowed in a rush, as he stood at the witness
box. They had raised many eyebrows, including Shrinivasa's
and the coroner's.

'I always suspected that Shrinivasa didn't really love
Netravati. At first, I didn't have any basis for this suspicion.
But as my suspicion grew stronger, it struck me suddenly
one day: It was not love but some kind of fear that prompted
Shrinivasa to indulge in a relationship with Netravati.
Shrinivasa always had doubts about his virility. He had
indirectly hinted this to me once. I understood his fears
from the kind of books he read. He had even secretly met
a doctor near Charni Road, who treated such cases. The
desire to test his potency was so strong that he had even
thought of visiting prostitutes. I know this for a fact. The
only thing that had stopped him from doing so was the fear
of contracting venereal diseases. Oh, god! It's all becoming
clear now! He used Netravati only to test his masculinity. He
had no intention of marrying her. Also, I think Netravati was
pregnant when she died. Something in her body language
made me suspect this. He used this girl. Such a crime should
not go unpunished . . .'

Nagappa had almost blacked out when he finished. The
post-mortem report stated that Netravati was three months

pregnant when she died. It proved Shrinivasa had had a physical relationship with her. But more importantly, it threw new light on Nagappa's evidence. But the court acquitted Shrinivasa. The only question before it was: Is it a murder or a case of suicide? The irrefutable eyewitness evidence was that Netravati had jumped to her death. No one had pushed her. But the reasons leading to her death were something society had to find solutions for. What was needed was social correction. The court expressed its helplessness in the matter. It did not consider hearsay evidence on Shrinivasa aiding and abetting Netravati's suicide. The rest was routine procedure. The coroner gave the verdict that Shrinivasa was not guilty, signed the papers and proceeded to hear the next case. Shrinivasa had quietly fled the courtroom by then.

Within six months of this, he had married Sharada, the seventh daughter of Shesh Kamath, the owner of four small and large restaurants in Bombay, in a lavish wedding ceremony. His father-in-law had bought him a flat and a printing press, and laid the foundation for Shrinivasa's prosperity. Shrinivasa had quit his government job and moved from Khetwadi. Ironically, this was the punishment society had meted out to him for his heinous crime. Nagappa shook his head vehemently at the thought of Sharada being condemned to live with this cheat. He had been smitten by her beauty.

Why such a wealthy man like Shesh Kamath chose someone like Shrinivasa for his lovely young daughter, was a question raised in the community circles. But it didn't remain a mystery for long. The story flying around was that a neighbour had experimented with seventeen-year-old Sharada, brimming with youth, the same way Shrinivasa had with Netravati, and left her in the lurch. She had given birth to a baby girl—a full-term child—within eight months of marrying Shrinivasa.

Nagappa's blood boiled at all the ugly rumours when he thought of Sharada's pristine beauty. He went to the washbasin, spat loudly and decided that he should quickly have a bath and get out of this hovel. He began lathering his face with the shaving cream. But he couldn't get Shrinivasa out of his head. Over the years, with Shrinivasa's expanding business and increasing clout in his community, the Netravati scandal had receded to the background, assuming the form of a long-forgotten lore. Nagappa felt disgusted at the thought of how Shrinivasa had paraded around as a hero for marrying a pregnant girl.

One day, Shrinivasa himself had told Nagappa the reason for rejecting Netravati: He came to know that the man who had 'kept' Netravati's sister didn't belong to their community, but was from the lowly barber's caste from Ankola, and had made his money by smuggling illicit liquor. But Shrinivasa had decided to go ahead with the marriage, as he didn't want to break his promise to Netravati. But when she insisted they marry in March instead of May, he grew suspicious. It was her bootlegger 'brother-in-law' who had actually got her pregnant. When Shrinivasa realized his relationship with her was based on a lie, he was heartbroken and wanted to commit suicide even before Netravati could think of it. But later, he had decided not to take the extreme step because of some worthless people, and had gone and surrendered himself to Lord Siddhi Vinayak for solace.

Shrinivasa had cleverly shifted the entire onus of Netravati's pregnancy and suicide on the man who kept

Anasuya. People had lapped up the new piece of gossip with lip-smacking relish. How easily Shrinivasa had shrugged off his moral responsibility with his tale of deceit, Nagappa thought.

Memories unleashed by the musty smell of a book must be the mind's way of preparing me for something else, he reasoned. He recalled Nayak's words, which threw new light on this: 'Shrinivasa has sworn to expose your entire family background in front of our community with solid proof. He's going to Goa to find out things about your family.'

Nagappa had never been bothered about his caste. What really troubled him was people accusing his parents of hiding their antecedents, insinuating they had tried to deceive everyone by saying they belonged to a caste they did not. He realized that Shrinivasa had accused Netravati's brother-in-law of exactly this. Maybe nudging him to remember it now was his mind's way of warning him to brace himself for the coming onslaught!

As Nagappa poured cold water over his head, he realized the time had come for him to finally know the truth about himself. If Shrinivasa is going to unearth my past, so be it, he thought.

17

As he bathed, the reason for Shrinivasa joining the conspiracy began to become clear to Nagappa. Or so he thought: Shrinivasa's ego was obviously badly bruised by what I said in the coroner's court, and he has nursed the hurt all these years, biding his time to take revenge on me. Our aggressive nature must've come to us from our primordial necessity to hunt. But we hunted for our survival. Then what's the driving force behind Shrinivasa and Phiroz's vicious attack against me? What's its relevance in the ongoing process of evolution? Twenty years ago, I'd taken a moral stand when I gave my evidence. Shrinivasa has vowed to destroy me because of a standpoint I expressed. This trait of vengefulness and waiting for years to get even with someone is not found in pre-human history. Man is perhaps the only animal who gets gratification in destroying a fellow human being. Also, we're probably the only creatures arrogant about our mental prowess. This Phiroz, who has never in any way helped my career growth, has set out to destroy it and is deriving obvious pleasure in doing so. What does it imply? We have nurtured and perpetuated the aggressiveness needed for survival during our hunting days. But we haven't been able to develop strategies to curb our instinct to destroy our own species. It seems the animal kingdom has been able to achieve it. The complete eradication of this trait of mutual destruction is probably possible only in the social context. But maybe human society has not evolved in this direction.

Nagappa was aware that all this was a mere cerebral exercise. It was the mind's way of assuaging some mortal fear that had shaken him. It had set off a chain of thought to suppress an uncontrollable dread that had physically manifested itself. He knew that even this clever reasoning he was now indulging in was another defence mechanism. He was impatient with his own cowardice.

I must go see Sitaram, he thought. It's been such a long time. I must meet Doshi, who had shown such warmth towards me. But he gave up the idea. No, let me not get into this bad habit of constantly overanalysing and verbalizing everything and escaping reality through some twisted logic. And what will I gain by meeting anyone? Some more analysis, some more talk to mask my fears. But one thing is certain: It doesn't matter if I'm destroyed, but I'll not accept defeat. Fighting against injustice and not surrendering before it is, perhaps, the last sign of humanity—the last shred of human dignity. I'll fight!

Nagappa cringed at the way his resolve had begun to sound like an incantation.

He got out of the bathroom, dressed and went to Sher-e-Punjab for lunch. Sheikh Anwar sitting at the counter gave his usual friendly smile and said, 'Been a long time, sir. In fact, I told the same thing to the boy who left an envelope for you yesterday. Waited a long time. It seems someone told him that you come here regularly. He didn't give his name.'

Nagappa quietly took the envelope Sheikh Anwar gave him, sat at a corner table, ordered lunch and clumsily tore open the envelope. The note inside was a copy of the earlier one. Nagappa was now sure it was from Mary. She was desperately trying to reach him. He was deeply touched by her concern. But overriding the feeling of gratitude was the question: What is Mary trying to warn me about so urgently? What could be the terrible news awaiting me? Pressure began to build inside him. The thought of waiting till eight was unbearable.

Nagappa hardly noticed what he ate, paid the bill and walked along the familiar Lamington Road. He had never felt so alone in his life. He suddenly realized something and stood stock-still in the middle of the pavement: In the last six days he hadn't been to work, not one colleague had called to inquire about him. No one from his office had visited—not his peers and not his assistants, whose affection and respect he thought he had earned. Were these feelings then merely based on ulterior motives? The thought was so revolting that he was worried he might throw up what he had just eaten. Realizing he was still standing on the pavement, he somehow controlled himself, bought a Banarasi masala paan from the corner shop and started walking hurriedly towards his house, chewing the paan. No, he thought, as he walked. *Someone* must have come to see me. Maybe I wasn't at home. Someone must've come when I was in Shrinivasa's house and must've gone back seeing the locked door. The neighbours must've forgotten to tell me . . . Nagappa knew the truth, but his mind hesitated to accept it: By now the news that I've been suspended must've spread through the office, and the reason for it. That's why everyone's trying to avoid me.

Mary must've found out from my colleagues that I ate either at Santosh Bhavan or at Sher-e-Punjab . . .

As he climbed the stairs, he sensed the curious glances of the women of the chawl. He was at home when all the menfolk in the neighbourhood were at work. From a respectable person, he had now become a nonentity. He suspected that, ironically, this had made him an object of interest. They now had something to talk about, and were trying to extract some excitement from his suffering. He was a momentary source of entertainment in their mundane lives. 'Are you unwell?' the tailor's wife next door asked him, as he unlocked the door. Her tone was sneering rather than sympathetic, as if to say, 'We all know why you aren't going to work.' Her tone, and the obvious pleasure she derived from his discomfort, both nauseated and annoyed Nagappa. 'Yes, I'm unwell, but you don't have the cure for my ailment,' Nagappa said, without attempting to hide his annoyance. Her face fell. Nagappa was pleased by his own audacity. He closed the door behind him, changed and lay on the bed, still smiling, as he remembered the two other women whispering and giggling at how he had shut up the woman next door. He was surprised how something like this could make him happy. He instantly fell asleep.

When he woke up, he thought he had heard a strange noise. He rubbed his eyes and looked at the clock. It was three in the afternoon—another five hours of wait before he could call Mary. He splashed water on his face and decided to have tea at Shrikrishna Vilas downstairs, instead of making it himself. As he stood combing his hair in front of the mirror, he trembled at the thought that came to him for no apparent reason. Netravati's death must have once again stirred something in his subconscious mind: Netravati had jumped to her death from the third floor. Appa had drowned in a well. How someone chooses to die differs from person to person. Does choosing how to die reflect their personality? It probably does, or why should there be so many ways of committing suicide? And what if I decide to commit suicide? (His hair stood on end.) I'll probably take sleeping pills. But I'll definitely not choose two methods: hanging myself and setting myself on . . . He couldn't complete the thought.

To shake off such morbid thoughts, he quickly opened the door to go out, and found Prabhakar, the company peon, standing outside. He folded his hands respectfully and handed Nagappa an envelope. He seemed to be in a hurry to leave. Nagappa knew it must be the Hyderabad ticket and kept it on the bookshelf and signalled Prabhakar to wait. 'I was about to go out for tea. Join me,' he invited. Prabhakar fidgeted awkwardly at this unexpected courtesy. Nagappa locked the door.

'It's my flight ticket, right? Which day?' he asked, as they walked along the corridor.

Prabhakar hesitated. He didn't know whether or not to let Nagappa know that he knew about it.

'Must be for tomorrow?' Nagappa prodded.

'Maybe tomorrow evening. I heard Miss D'Souza telling someone . . .'

Miss D'Souza was the personnel manager's secretary, who deliberately ignored Nagappa.

Nagappa and Prabhakar didn't speak for a while. Prabhakar walked behind Nagappa with his head lowered, maintaining a respectful distance between them. As they climbed down the stairs, Nagappa wanted to ask about

Mary but controlled himself. He knew Prabhakar wouldn't volunteer any information. He was alarmed at the very thought of having tea with someone as senior in position as Nagappa. His mouth had gone dry. He didn't know what to make of the rumours circulating in the office about Nagappa. He was surprised at the way even those who had shown great respect for him till recently, had turned against him after the news of the charges had spread. It was disgusting to see that they were the ones who relished every bit of gossip that was being whispered around.

Nagappa and Prabhakar entered Shrikrishna Vilas, and Nagappa invited Prabhakar to sit with him. Touched by this gesture, he blurted out, 'Sir, don't be scared . . . all this is happening because MD sir has gone out. He wouldn't have allowed it. All this has been hatched in Hyderabad by the DMD and Khambata, his *chela*.'

Nagappa had no idea the MD was not in Bombay. That changed everything. He ordered tea.

Prabhakar shook his head when Nagappa asked him if he would like to eat something.

'Where has the MD gone to?' Nagappa asked, trying to sound casual.

'Sir, didn't you know he has gone to America?' Prabhakar asked. 'It seems he had to leave on some urgent work. He has some idea of what's happening here, but maybe he doesn't want to get directly involved in it. It seems he has told his secretary that you have nothing to fear.'

'How do you know all this . . .?'

'His secretary has slipped a note in the envelope I gave you. She arranged for me to bring the ticket to you, as she doesn't trust the others . . . she's really concerned about you . . .'

Prabhakar stopped, realizing he had probably said too much.

Nagappa was eager to read the note Mary had sent. He quickly finished his tea, paid the bill, thanked Prabhakar for bringing the ticket, and hurried upstairs, forgetting to ask for more information from him. When he tore open the cover and pulled out the ticket, the note he was now familiar with slipped out. The message was identical to the earlier ones, but 'Love' had been added with a pen. Though Nagappa smiled at the anticlimax on seeing the same old message after the heart-pounding anxiety, he read it again. He held it to his lips. He felt immense gratitude and affection for Mary. His eyes moistened even before he knew it. At a time when he felt alone and friendless, and when the mind was surreptitiously making other morbid plans, the note had brought some hope and made life worth living. He was ashamed of his cowardice, his wanting to find an easy way out. No, I'll never run away from the situation when it demands that I fight. I'll never think of quitting the battlefield, Nagappa told himself. I'll not turn my back on life.

As Prabhakar had said, the ticket was for tomorrow. I must write down all I know about the fire accident in the factory. I must work on it tonight and tomorrow morning, Nagappa thought. I *must* be battle-ready, he repeated for the nth time.

18

Finally, it was almost eight. Nagappa was once again filled with anguish. Each passing minute seemed unbearable. He had decided to call Mary from the restaurant below. As he stepped out, he was filled with doubt: Can I trust Mary? Why am I reading meanings into her kindness? Oh, god, why am I losing faith in humanity?

When he came to the public phone at the restaurant, there was already a girl before him. He began to observe her keenly to suppress his anguish: She was a willowy young woman. She was wearing a dark blue georgette sari, which accentuated her figure. Even Mary had a sexy figure. Except for a slightly prominent nose, she was an attractive girl. As he realized that this was probably the first time he was thinking of Mary's physical beauty, the young woman had finished her conversation.

'Sorry to have kept you waiting for so long,' she said with a charming smile and left. Nagappa could hear his heart pounding as he dialled the number Mary had given. As soon as he heard a female voice say 'Hello' at the other end, he dropped the coins he had kept ready into the slot, with trembling fingers, and said, 'Hello, Mary?' in a croaking voice, forcing the words out. Mary wouldn't have recognized the voice. But, fortunately, it was her friend who had answered the call.

Mary came on the line. 'Is that Nagnath?' she asked.

Nagappa's voice shook when he said, 'Yes.'

'Listen, Nagnath, before the MD left for the States, he asked me to tell you to be very careful and patient and not do anything impulsively . . . not to get provoked by anything Mr Bandookwala says or does. Everything will be all right. I know what you're going through, but don't lose hope. Don't lose courage.'

Nagappa was overcome with emotion. 'Thank you, darling!' he said, and was surprised by the endearment he had never used before. Even Mary was taken aback. But gauging his state of mind, she reciprocated the warmth. 'Listen, my dear friend, things have changed drastically in the office after the MD left. If you ask me, his sudden trip to the States was not as unexpected or unplanned as it's made out to be. The DMD must've known about it. The news in the office is that the MD is going either to New York or Hong Kong on a big promotion. That's why he has been called to New York. It's supposed to be top secret. Bandookwala . . . the DMD is planning to take his position. But it seems he has been caught in something big . . . his name has appeared in some scandal, and he's looking for a scapegoat. That's why all this drama of an inquiry against you. In fact, it was the assistant admin manager who asked me to tell this to you. He's a good guy. You know how he and Khambata can't stand each other. Anyway, no one knows who all are involved in this mess. It seems there's a huge misappropriation of funds. Though right from Bandookwala to all his chelas are involved in it, no one has the guts to name them directly. Everyone's trying to save their own skins. Though many people respect you and are on your side, I don't think anyone will come forward to openly support you . . . not even the assistant admin manager. And you know how it is . . . there are many who want to take advantage of the situation . . . side with those who have more clout. Even people in your department. It's really disgusting.'

Nagappa tried to say something but the words choked him and came out as a sob.

'Are you all right, sweetheart? Take it easy,' Mary said kindly. 'Actually, I wanted to personally come and explain all this to you. But to be honest, even I don't have the guts. You know how Bandookwala is. He can be very spiteful. And I'm not sure what kind of trouble he's got into. Seeing how he's plotting all this the moment MD's back was turned, it must be something serious. All I can say is, be very, very careful. Don't think this's an ordinary inq . . .'

Nagappa heard the doorbell ring at the other end.

'Hold on,' Mary whispered. Her friend must have opened the door. 'Oh, it's you . . . good evening, Mr Khambata. What a pleasant surprise!' Mary said loudly, for Nagappa's benefit. 'Bye, Anette. Thanks for calling. All the best!' she said to Nagappa and cut the call.

Nagappa put the receiver down. He was sweating all over. But he didn't have the courage to think how terrified he was. He thought his legs would give way and he wanted to sit somewhere. He dragged himself to the Irani tea shop nearby and ordered a strong cup of tea.

Mary had handled the situation well. But what was Khambata doing in Mary's house at this time? And Khambata knew where she lived! And he himself had never bothered to find out. Nagappa gave up his futile attempt to focus on something trivial to avoid thinking of what Mary had told him: So Phiroz is trying to implicate me in something he has been caught in. Oh, god! Why me of all people, who runs scared of such things? I'd never have come in the way of this bastard's great ambition to become the MD. Why this fight against me, when I'm not even his match in this vicious game? I don't know what twisted rules it's played by. I've never asked for too much from this job. I don't even know what I really wish for professionally. Whatever it is, it's not to climb to any rung higher than this. 'Be very, very careful. Don't think this's an ordinary inquiry,' Mary had warned. The nature of such pure evil was beyond Nagappa's understanding. Despite the steaming hot tea, his innards froze at the thought.

Though it was nearly nine, he didn't feel like eating anything. He got out of the tea shop and started walking aimlessly along one of the bylanes. The shops had started downing their shutters one by one. The all-pervading stench of Khetwadi was stronger than usual. Though the filth couldn't be seen in the dull halo of the half-broken municipal street lights, he could sense the slime underfoot sticking to his soles—cow dung, slush from overflowing sewers, garbage spilling over from bins and rotten vegetables discarded by the vendors who had left for the day. A constant, chaotic buzz emanated from the overcrowded chawls on both sides, bathed in pale yellow light—an indistinguishable amalgamation of radios blaring, children crying, people cooking, quarrelling, praying. Nagappa knew he was deliberately paying attention to the smells and sounds around him to desperately suppress his fright. He imagined they too, had joined the conspiracy against him.

He had reached the end of the lane. Ahead of him, to the right, was Banavali Medical Stores, at the corner of Grant Road. He knew Banavali, the owner, and hoped he could get some sedatives without a prescription. He walked up to the counter, wrote 'barbiturates' on a piece of paper, folded it and gave it to Banavali. 'It's too late to go to a doctor and get a prescription. Please oblige,' Nagappa pleaded.

'Haven't seen you for a long time. Aren't you feeling well? You seem to have lost a lot of weight,' Banavali said, and raised an eyebrow as he looked at what Nagappa had written. He nodded in understanding, handed him a bottle wrapped in paper. 'Take it easy. Shrinivas Rao told me everything when he was here the other day. My sympathies.'

Nagappa was so taken aback that he was about to leave without paying, when Banavali said, 'It's ten rupees. Sorry, I won't be able to give you a receipt for it.'

He hurriedly paid and left. The only thought in his mind was, Oh, god, let me not swallow the entire bottle. Please stop me from doing it.

He suspected that when Banavali gave him the bottle without a fuss and said, 'Take it easy. Shrinivas Rao has told me everything,' more than concern, his voice had a hint of cruel pleasure in it. Nagappa didn't know if he could spend the night alone. He dragged himself home, as if propelled by the bottle of barbiturates in his pocket.

As he neared Khemraj Bhavan, he had the strange feeling that the clump of ugly, overcrowded buildings in the lane were standing in eerie silence, with all the noise blanked out. The long, aimless walk, Banavali's snide remark, Mary's

warning, the reason why Khambata could be visiting her and
the turmoil the bottle of barbiturates he was carrying had
kicked off had made him numb with fear. He couldn't hear or
feel anything, except for a sickening churning in the pit of his
stomach. As he climbed the stairs, he felt he was entering a
pestilence-stricken ghost town, which everyone had deserted,
leaving him alone. The thought triggered an emotion he
couldn't name. But in the throes of that unnamed emotion,
he did something he had never done before, knowing it was
juvenile—he began counting each step as he climbed. When
he reached the first-floor landing, he said 'thirteen' just loud
enough for him to hear, 'twenty-six' and 'thirty-nine' when
he reached the second and third floors. 'Thirty-nine' came
out so loud that neighbours on either side of the corridor
must have heard it. Fortunately, no one was curious enough
to find out who had shouted out the number. In a chawl full
of so many people, such strange things happened every day.

But Arjunrao lay waiting for him with his door open.
As soon as he saw Nagappa, he grinned and blurted out
without any preamble, 'It seems you're going to Hyderabad
tomorrow . . . heh, heh . . .'

'Happened to meet Shrinivas Rao, and he told me,'
Nagappa completed the sentence without looking up at a
surprised Arjunrao, walked up to his door, unlocked it, and
went in, still mumbling something to himself. He closed the
door, flopped down on the bed and fell asleep.

It was past eleven when he woke up next morning. He
tried to get out of bed, but couldn't. He lay there for some
time. He began to vaguely recall what had happened after
buying the pills: He had opened the bottle and swallowed
about five of them in the middle of the road, knowing it was

over the limit. Was it five or more? He wasn't sure now. What if the root of my misery is my acute awareness of my misery itself? What if dying in deep sleep, unaware of the misery is the way to end it? Nagappa wondered. Was Netravati falling to her death symbolic of her moral downfall?

Nagappa drifted off to sleep.

When he woke up, he suddenly recalled screaming his age out loud to someone: 'Thirty-nine!' Whom did I tell it to? Nagappa asked himself. Was it to Mary? How old is Mary . . . twenty-six? I should ask her. When Appa committed suicide, I was thirteen! Maybe it wasn't the steps I was counting. I must count them again when I go down.

The illogical, bizarre coincidence of the steps hit Nagappa so hard that he was wide awake, despite the heavy dose of sedatives. He suddenly remembered his trip to Hyderabad and jumped out of bed.

PART III

19

Nagappa sensed the first signs of the noose tightening around him when he landed at the Hyderabad airport.

It was Sunday. Sher-e-Punjab was crowded. The chicken biriyani they served was famous in the area. Of late, they also sold chilled beer. Nagappa's colleagues came there for lunch sometimes. But he didn't want to meet anyone. So he decided to go to Darbar on Grant Road. It was right opposite Banavali Medical Stores. It was closed on Sundays, but brought back raw memories of last night. He felt embarrassed. He vaguely realized that, somewhere deep down, he feared failure and wanted to flee from the battlefield—the arena where his trial by fire was to take place. He knew why he had succumbed to the temporary respite barbiturates offered. When he sat at the table, he warned himself that now more than ever, he needed to be mentally alert. Though he knew he didn't possess the cunning needed to fight the lethal political cabal of Phiroz–Shrinivas–Jalal, he had truth on his side. That gave him courage. But soon, the thought that the MD, who liked him, was not there to protect him, and no one else in the company cared or had the guts to defend him, nagged him.

He once again realized that everyone was concerned about safeguarding their own positions and personal interests. For them, earning a livelihood was more important than fighting for the cause of truth and righteousness. It was a depressing thought. Whether knowingly or unknowingly, willingly or not, everyone had joined this conspiracy and lined up behind Phiroz's hunting pack. They were now circling him, beating their drums and tom-toms, nudging him towards Phiroz, who stood with his gun trained on him, waiting for him to come in its crosshairs. Nagappa's fear was so palpable that he could actually visualize the image. He shook. His eyes filled with tears.

'Tea or coffee, please?' the air hostess asked him, jolting Nagappa back to reality. He could barely see her pretty face through the tears. 'Tea, please,' he said, after a long pause. She placed the teacup on the tray table, and as she bent to pour milk into it, she whispered, 'Please come to the back seat when you've finished your tea. We can talk there', and quickly moved towards the seat behind him. Strange things are happening to me, he thought. Things that didn't happen in the last twenty years are waiting to tumble out in twenty days. But who *is* she? And what does she want to talk to me about?

Nagappa finished his tea and looked behind. She was still busy serving the passengers at the rear end of the plane. She looked very attractive in the Indian Airlines uniform—a peacock blue Mysore silk sari that suited her figure and fair complexion. Her glossy hair was tied up in a bun. Her unadorned charm reminded him of Mary. He noticed that the last two rows were empty. He started walking towards them with a sudden spurt of courage and enthusiasm. But he stopped midway, got back to his seat, took out his notebook from his briefcase and walked to the empty seats. The air hostess had finished serving everyone, and as she wheeled the trolley back, she asked Nagappa with a smile, 'Care for another cup of tea?'

'No, thanks,' Nagappa replied.

'I'm Mary's friend. I'll join you soon,' she said and disappeared into the galley area.

Though the mystery was at an end, the question of how she had recognized him troubled him. But he was relieved that he now had a question to start the conversation with, instead of groping for words. Just then, 'May I?' she asked politely, and sat next to Nagappa. 'I'm pleased to meet you Mr Nagnath. My name is Diana Driver. I'm Mary's neighbour,' she introduced herself, flashing a smile.

'Miss Driver . . .' Nagappa began.

'Please call me Diana,' she said, smiling again.

'Okay, Diana, how did you recognize me?' he asked.

'Your sweet, sad face,' she replied, throwing Nagappa off balance.

'Actually, I was there when you called Mary last night. It was I who answered the call. Mary told me you'd be on this flight, and asked me to speak to you, and described you.'

Nagappa wondered what could Mary have told Diana about him for her to spot him from among the passengers.

'She told me you have the habit of touching the right side of your chest with your left hand.'

'No!' Nagappa exclaimed, shocked. He had no idea he did this. It came out louder than he intended and Diana gestured to him to lower his voice. Was this typical mannerism of his so obvious that a stranger could recognize him?

'I knew who you were right away, when I stood at the entrance to welcome the passengers. You touched your chest at least four times before you entered the plane,' she whispered. 'But shall I tell you the truth? I knew it was you from your brilliant eyes that Mary admires so much, reflecting your intelligence and the deep sadness in them! And even I fell for your eyes.'

She gently pressed Nagappa's hand on the armrest and quickly let go of it.

So, all this is Mary's doing, Nagappa thought. She has asked her friend to look after me, knowing I needed some reassurance. What kind of bond is this? Certainly going back to some other lifetime! Otherwise, when those who are supposed to be my own people were out to get me . . .

'Don't keep brooding all the time, Mr Nagnath,' Diana said gently.

Nagappa emerged from his thoughts. For a moment, he had forgotten Diana's presence.

'Thanks, for your kindness, Diana. I used to call air hostesses "air hostiles". You're an exception to it,' Nagappa said.

Diana smiled. 'You're very naughty!' She laughed softly, and got up as she heard an announcement from the cockpit. 'Excuse, me,' she said and left.

Nagappa opened his notebook and began to write: Mary and Diana's compassion towards me has renewed my faith in humanity. Diana's reassuring smile has made me wonder whether I'm needlessly exaggerating what awaits me in Hyderabad. What's intriguing is how or when did Phiroz and Shrinivasa join hands?

Nagappa had stopped writing. The notebook lay open and the pen was poised between his fingers. But the images before him were those he couldn't capture in words: Hanehalli, the hostel in Kumta, the well Appa jumped into, the slum near Shrinivasa's apartment building, Saraswati with her fugitive eyes, Vomu and Sitaram, Doshi, who had shown such warmth in a chance meeting, Chetana with her dimpled smile, Achyuta, who furtively stared at him, making him wonder if he was the brother he had never seen, his long-lost sister, Shrinivasa's wife, Sharada, who had shaken him in an unfathomable way with her forlorn glance when he left the house that day, Mary, who made him believe in bonds from a previous birth, Diana, who had spoken to him kindly a few minutes back . . .

'Hey, what are you dreaming about?' Diana's melodious voice woke him to his surroundings. A voice over the intercom was announcing that they were about to land at the Hyderabad airport and that passengers were requested to return to their seats. As Nagappa fastened his seatbelt, Diana sat next to him, held his hand in hers and, as if overcome with emotion, said, 'Don't lose courage. Mary has told me everything. She has great regard for you . . . she loves you.' She quickly got up and left.

The plane landed. Nagappa went to his seat, picked up his small suitcase and walked to the door, where Diana stood with folded hands, bidding goodbye to passengers. 'Goodbye, Diana. I'll never forget this journey,' he said and left. As he got down the steps, he realized he was smiling and that he had not smiled like this for days—a genuinely happy smile.

As his feet finally touched the ground, a chill ran down his spine. Earlier, every time he travelled from Bombay to Hyderabad, someone from the personnel department would be waiting with a chauffeur-driven car. He had assumed somebody would be there today too. But he wasn't sure now. His legs gave way at the possibility.

When he reached the terminal building, no one had come to receive him—not even a company car with a driver, not even his faithful Sardar driver, who Nagappa was sure would be there. Yes, Phiroz had sounded the first war bugle. It was loud and clear. The battle was to begin.

When he stood waiting for the car in the sweltering heat, he saw all the airport taxis leave one by one. There were only autorickshaws left. He hailed one. As he got in, he saw Diana climbing on to the Indian Airlines station wagon. He was sure she saw him. But she looked away, not seeming to notice him. He gave the company guest house address to the driver. The driver started the autorickshaw and honked the horn for no reason. It sounded like something else to Nagappa. The hair on his body stood still.

20

A four-bedroom bungalow atop Banjara Hills served as the company guest house. The path leading to it was lined with huge, withered old rocks, their sharp edges smoothed by the elements. Nagappa had never seen such bald, round rocks anywhere. He liked the guest house because of the ruggedness they lent to it. As if to challenge their grey austerity, a profusion of bright bougainvillea tumbled down the compound walls from the hedges. Tall champak trees stood around randomly, wafting a heady scent. Jasmine creepers in full bloom adorned the entrance, with deodars on either side creating a canopy of branches. Behind the backyard, a brook flowed down to the valley below, accentuating the steep drop and the rocky ledge on which the bungalow stood. Beyond the valley rose a hill, dotted with boulders. In the last eight months since his transfer to Bombay, he had visited Hyderabad about four times, and enjoyed his stay there.

Nagappa looked forward to relaxing in a cane chair on the terraced roof, with his feet stretched on the teapoy, sipping chilled beer, gazing at the star-studded night sky, and momentarily forgot the humiliating 'welcome' he had received at the airport. But when the autorickshaw neared Banjara Hills, it struck him that probably no one had bothered to inform the staff at the guest house he would be coming. His body tensed at the thought. The housekeeper, Krishna, and his assistant, Muthuswamy, always took good care of him. Muthuswamy was also a wonderful cook. Nagappa always tipped them generously. On occasions, when he asked them to get a bottle of whisky, they helped themselves to a peg on the sly. That SOB 2, Krishna, had discretely asked if he wanted girls, the first time Nagappa stayed at the guest house. It had made him extremely angry. Krishna had not dared to bring it up again. Nagappa smiled, despite his troubled state of mind, thinking about it.

When the autorickshaw reached the narrow path leading up to the bungalow, 'Is this the 8th Cross?' the driver asked, before turning into it. Nagappa wasn't sure. He had always come here in a chauffeur-driven car. 'Ask the petrol bunk guy at the corner,' he said. The driver got out, ran to the bunk and came back nodding his head. Within a few minutes, the autorickshaw had climbed the winding path and stood in front of the guest house gate. A dog barked loudly somewhere, probably from another bungalow nearby, which echoed loudly, ricocheting against the rocks. Krishna opened the gate and smiled with folded hands, looking a bit surprised as the autorickshaw entered the compound. Nagappa's suspicion had been proven right. No one had informed the guest house of his arrival. Since there were no guests that day, Muthuswamy was on leave.

Nagappa couldn't control his temper. He asked Krishna to get his suitcase, and ran to the hall to call the personnel

manager. He found his residence number from a list on the
table. His hand was trembling with rage when he dialled the
number, but he controlled himself when he heard a female
voice at the other end, and asked for Ramakrishna. She told
him that he had left for Bombay with Bandookwala by the
evening flight, and would be away for three days. His anger
gave way to confusion. If Phiroz had left by the evening flight,
he must have taken the one Nagappa had arrived on. Why
had he left suddenly after summoning him to Hyderabad?

Nagappa had earlier thought of taking the autorickshaw
that still stood waiting, to a restaurant nearby, but he had
suddenly lost his appetite. He paid the driver who was already
getting impatient, and asked Krishna if he could rustle up an
omelette.

'Sure, sir,' he replied. 'We have eggs. I'll go get a loaf of
bread. What about beer, sir?'

'Yes, two bottles of beer.'

Nagappa knew he needed something to help him sleep
that night. He gave Krishna extra money and said, 'Keep the
change.'

Krishna got on to his cycle enthusiastically. Since there
were no other guests, he wondered if he could suggest
bringing a girl, but didn't, remembering how angry Nagappa
had been the last time.

After Krishna left, Nagappa went to the room that was
always kept reserved for him, took off his shoes and lay
down on the bed. For a moment, his mind felt emptied of
all thoughts. But soon, it began to buzz as usual: This is
no ordinary inquiry. And it's not an inquiry set up merely
to take revenge on me. It goes beyond vengeance. It's a
vicious political game. Its tentacles have spread deep into

the organization. Could it be true that Phiroz is making me a fall guy to extricate himself from something serious he has got himself into? Why did he leave by the same plane I came in, after asking me to come all the way here? I'm sure there was no emergency in Bombay. This's a good old fascist subterfuge: The plan is to confuse me, tire me out, break my resolve to fight and finally break my spirit. This is a battle of attrition. Nagappa felt drained. As weariness washed over him, he was about to fall into a fatigued stupor. He suddenly sat up, prodding himself to stay awake. No, I mustn't give up. I mustn't give in to their ploy of weakening me, he told himself. What's the worst that could happen? Anyway, I've steeled myself to the possibility of quitting my job if things come to such a situation. So why fear Phiroz? Let me not indulge in these impotent apprehensions. He got out of bed and walked to the window.

What sapped his energy now was not the fear of losing his job. Nor was it the realization that a man could so easily be mentally broken, and that he was actually verbalizing it: What I really dread is, when falsely accused, I might not be able to prove my innocence in front of others and clear my name, despite not being guilty, despite the truth being on my side. I dread failing to prove I've done no wrong, just because I might not be able to explain my innocence to others. I fear the inadequacy of words. I fear not being able to prove that some evil powers have robbed me of justice that's rightfully mine. Though I believe in the power of truth, I'm not sure if truth can finally prevail against the diabolical scheme that Phiroz has unleashed. Yes, this is it! *This* is my deepest, strongest, mind-numbing fear—the fear of my inability to prove my innocence before the dark forces that can so easily prove me guilty and show me as a criminal. Yes, I'm losing my strength. My courage is deserting me. I'm completely, incurably exhausted, unable to grasp, to describe this despair. Yes, this's the anguish that's beyond words that's breaking me. I'm trembling with fear like this because I'm no longer certain that truth is enough to defeat deceit, because someone like Phiroz has changed the very discourse of truth . . .

As Nagappa stood staring out of the window, he thought it might be a good idea to call Hyder. He got the number from the telephone book and dialled it. A familiar voice said, 'Hello!' at the other end. 'Hyder saab, Nagnath here,' he said with an urgency in his voice he didn't know he felt.

'Hello, hello, Professor,' Hyder responded with his usual enthusiasm, but suddenly lowered his voice and asked, 'When did you come? Does anybody in the factory know you're here? Why didn't Ramakrishna tell me anything?'

Nagappa didn't know what to say. Something made him cautious: Who knows who's on whose side now? And what if there was no inquiry, and Phiroz wanted to secretly discuss something with me but had to go to Bombay urgently? Maybe I've misunderstood his motives . . . Nagappa realized how absurd this thought was. Noticing the long pause, Hyder asked, 'Where're you calling from, Nagnath? The guest house? I hope no one else's around?'

'No. And Krishna has gone to get bread.'

'You shouldn't have come here now. Has no one told you all that has happened here? I've taken a week off just to be away from this mess. I heard big names are involved in this factory *lafda*. It seems material worth lakhs of rupees has gone missing . . . unaccounted for. And it looks like they're trying to somehow connect it with the fire accident. Please be very careful, Nagnath. I think you need to tread with caution . . .'

This scared Nagappa so much that he was unable to think clearly for a moment.

'Hyder saab, I didn't come here on my own. I was summoned by the DMD. But I just learnt that he himself has now gone to Bombay . . .'

A sense of despair had crept into Nagappa's voice, which made Hyder, who was already scared, panic. He was now worried he might get dragged unwittingly into the trouble brewing in the factory by speaking to Nagappa. Picking his words carefully, he said, 'Actually, I really don't know anything about what's happening. I'm the wrong person to ask. Don't misunderstand me, but please don't tell anyone you spoke to me. As I told you, I'm on leave because I didn't want to get involved. When bigwigs are trying to save their own skins, what about small fry like me? Actually, DMD's Bombay trip had been planned four days back. Don't know why you weren't informed. Now you'll have to wait till he's back. Why don't you call Khambata and find out? That dimwit must've forgotten to tell you. Anyway, you must be tired. Take rest. Try not to worry too much. Something has gone wrong somewhere. I'm sure the facts will finally come out. Good night.'

Hyder seemed to be in a hurry to disconnect the call. His fear was palpable. If this harmless soul is so scared, the stakes must be high, Nagappa thought. Hyder had spoken of big names being involved. But one consolation—it looks like the news of my suspension has not yet reached here. Or did Hyder know but pretended he didn't? But why? Oh, god, is there no end to this suspicion?

Nagappa stood, unable to decide whether or not to call Khambata. He was relieved when Krishna came in with the bread and bottles of beer. 'Thanks, Krishna, open a bottle and get a glass,' he ordered. Let Phiroz, Khambata, Ramakrishna and this harmless coward Hyder go to hell, he thought. Tonight, I'm going to forget about all of them and relax.

He sat sipping the beer. As he felt its mild intoxication rising, he pictured Mary with her provocative figure and Diana's sweet face. He felt that the last few days had brought Mary and him closer. It was a nice feeling. He asked Krishna to open the second bottle. He had never had two straight bottles of beer alone before. He remembered thinking of the barbiturates when he got off the plane. Beer appeared to be a better option than sedatives.

As he emptied the second bottle, Vomu and Saraswati stood before him smiling. He realized this was the first time he had seen them smile. He smiled back.

21

Nagappa woke up, filled with a strange sensation. He had no idea what time it was. The thick curtains had kept the sunlight away. He knew it was late in the morning and that he needed to get up, but couldn't. Either because of the beer or the uncertainty he faced, he was confused about what he had to do next: It's strange that Phiroz, who has triggered all this has remained elusive. I've not had direct contact with him since this sordid saga began. And I don't have any definite proof that Shrinivasa is part of this conspiracy against me. Could it be that I've fallen prey to my own thoughts? I'm the child of disaster. I grew up under the dark shadow of doubt that Appa wanted to kill me and my sister, and end his own life. I'm the survivor of that tragic plot. Has my mind, haunted by this, succumbed under its own weight in a weak moment and is now showing its innards? And again, the pride I've nursed that I'm responsible for the company's R&D department's excellent reputation—is that sheer arrogance?

Unfortunately, Nagappa had not realized that others had benefited from his work in the R&D department. He enjoyed his work and focused on improving his department's standard, rather than how to manipulate it to his advantage. He had not bothered about public recognition, winning awards and climbing the corporate ladder. This innate lack of ambition, this holding himself back from the limelight, was probably the reason for being caught in this present situation. Apart from his work, Nagappa had immersed himself in his writing. He had started writing poems and stories from his school days. Though he could have made a name for himself in the short story genre, he was indifferent to fame. He had invested all his creative genius into a volume of short stories, and had asked a friend, who was already well-known in the field, to write the foreword to it. The friend had written back: *Since we are both Brahmins, it might be misconstrued if I write a foreword to your book. It might do it more harm than good. Also, since your stories have already earned a place for themselves in the field, why do they need a foreword?*

Nagappa didn't know how to respond to it, and had left it at that. But later, after the volume was published, a few people whom he considered his friends, had severely criticized it under the pretext of analysing it. Instead of the stories, the 'Brahmin sensibility' and the 'Brahmin consciousness' the stories purportedly portrayed had come under heavy assault. It had become the subject of bitter debate. The comments his work elicited threw Nagappa off guard. When the criticism reached its crescendo with a cry of 'Works of such people should be burnt!' Nagappa had lost interest in writing. But he didn't protest against being falsely accused of parochialism. He didn't raise his voice against the cruelty he had been subjected to. After that, though he continued to write occasionally, as he couldn't give it up altogether, he stopped sending his writing to any publication. He now

wrote because of certain inner compulsions, but had not yet
found a rational answer or explanation to the question, 'Why
publish?' He often thought that though writing was a solitary
vocation, it was, perhaps, only human to want to share the
joy of creation and the creative process, and crave the sense
of gratification that appreciation brought. There were times
when Nagappa wished he could translate into creative writing
all the hurt and pain he had experienced. And if it could reach
others, then, probably it would give me the courage to deal
with what I've gone through, and am still going through,
he would think. But then, he would smile to himself at its
absurdity: If the caste of my parents alone was an obstacle
to my creativity, I could've written under a pseudonym.
But would the critics, who pretended to have taken upon
themselves the responsibility for all social concerns of the
world, leave me alone? Wouldn't they track me down and
target me with their barbs again? Many of them are poets
and short story writers themselves. But the only thing is,
when the village is burning, they won't write about the rising
moon or the rose bush, but will directly respond to the fire
. . . will write about the conflagration. Yes, I swear these
creative bastards . . . these brave heroes of social justice will
write poetry when the village is burning! All they are capable
of are mere words! And yes, I'm jealous of them. And will I
ever get justice from these bloodthirsty hunters? But then,
the awareness that 'this is unjust' is the root cause of misery.
Where's the question of misery if there's no awareness? But
one cannot unlearn awareness after one has become aware
of something. It cannot simply be erased at will. But still,
I must write. I need to verbalize and give shape to all this
amorphous pain and suffering I'm going through because of

all the Shrinivasas and Phirozes. I must write to touch a heart capable of pulsating to what I write. I must write with the full awareness of the meaning and implications of what I write. And I must write under my own name.

Nagappa was surprised by this courage born of a strange state of mind. He wanted to hold on to it. His heart beat fast. But, as usual, he felt elated at one moment and defeated the next. He was acutely aware that unless he found a way to change his fundamental nature and his attitude towards life, he would have no reprieve from this constant inner turmoil. He was thrilled at the thought that, perhaps, the emotional upheaval, the very experience he was going through itself, could have hidden within itself the tremendous power to bring about a complete transformation in him. The tenuous assurance the possibility offered momentarily calmed him.

What if I grew a beard and wore my hair long, or completely shaved my head like Yul Brynner—a total image change? Nagappa laughed at his own wild imagination.

Rubbing his groggy eyes, he pressed the switch next to the bed. A bell rang somewhere and Krishna came running. 'A cup of tea please, Krishna. And what time is it?' he asked.

'It's past nine, sir. There was a call from Bombay. I think you were in deep sleep then. I knocked the door many times, but maybe you didn't hear it. The person didn't give his name. When I asked him if he'd call again, he asked me in what way I was concerned, and said, "Tell him to get as much sleep as possible now when there's time . . ." It looked like he didn't know Hindi well. Sounded short-tempered . . .'

Realizing he had spoken too much, Krishna said, 'Sorry, sir, I'll get your tea.'

Nagappa didn't worry much about what Krishna had just reported. Instead, he was pleased there were already signs of a transformation taking place within him. That sisterfucker Phiroz or his sidekick Khambata must've called, he told himself. Let them call. I don't need any of them now. I don't! I don't! I don't! Nagappa chanted it like a mantra, hoping to strengthen his resolve to stay calm and brave.

In reality, he didn't need such verbal incantations. Some unknown force deep within him that had gagged his voice had given way. The floodgates had opened. His long-suppressed voice was raring to be heard—effortlessly, without any coercion. His mind was gathering courage to rise against injustice. It was an inflection point. Nagappa thought: The thread binding me to the company has now snapped. I should free myself from all these false ties and fake people—people who are gearing themselves to prove me wrong. I should break one by one all the bonds that have tied me up and made me pledge some false allegiance in the name of an illusory sense of honour and loyalty. Maybe only then are real relationships and new bonds possible. Maybe only when we aren't driven by ulterior motives and the compulsion to protect vested interests can we escape from the tyranny of such unwanted ties that weigh us down. Maybe only in a state where we are free of these will Man cease to inflict cruelty on Man . . .

Nagappa laughed at his own futile attempt to capture in words what was now shaking the very foundations of his being. He quickly got out of bed, filled with self-disgust at his verbose philosophizing, and briskly drew aside the curtains. It was a bright morning and the valley below was ablaze under the sun. He wondered how many eons ago had lava burst out from the bowels of the earth, cooled down and turned into these boulders. For how long had they been standing, exposed to the elements? Nagappa stood gazing at them as if he was seeing them for the first time. How beautiful the world looks when we stop being obsessed by our pain and suffering, and step out of our cocoons! he thought. He stood staring at the still life before him for a long time. When he turned away, he vaguely remembered Krishna bringing in the tea tray and trying to draw his attention. The teapot had grown cold. He asked for another cup and lay on the bed waiting. It was nearly ten, but he was in no hurry to get up and start the day. He was aware that the resolution he had made today was different from the several others he had made earlier. He was pleased with himself.

From where he lay, he could see the valley. He felt there was some kind of connection between his present becalmed state of mind and the gigantic weather-beaten boulders bleached smooth. The next moment, he shook free of the facile comparison. No, let me not get emotional, he decided. If Phiroz calls again, I'll tell him, 'I've nothing to do with you or your bloody inquiry, you son of a bitch! Get lost!' Nagappa realized that he hadn't bitten his lip hard with suppressed rage or held his breath tight as usual, when he said this. As he sipped the fresh cup of tea Krishna had brought, he thought of the few moments of companionship he had experienced with Diana yesterday. He smiled at how she had recognized him among the passengers. Do I keep touching my chest to assure myself that the secret I hold close to me is real and not something I've imagined? he wondered. But he realized it was an obsessive habit only after Diana told him about it. Another nagging thought he had been avoiding crossed his

mind again: Diana had looked away as she sat in the station
wagon when he got into the autorickshaw. She's a Parsi, like
Phiroz and Khambata. Are they in some way connected? But
he brushed it away, rationalizing that it didn't matter even if
there was some sort of connection, as he wasn't going to use
Diana for his own selfish end, anyway. Nagappa knew he was
deliberately distracting himself with such superficial worries,
while his mind was grappling with something else deep within:
What were the compelling circumstances that drove Appa to
want to kill his own children? If only I knew what pushed Appa
to commit the unmitigated, horrendous act. One day I must
really find out. In fact, from now on, I must involve myself in
pursuits like going back to my roots . . . my origins—guilt-free
activities that are pure and sinless, untouched by malice of any
kind. I must learn the limits of my being, my personality, and
embrace them unhesitatingly, unconditionally.

The telephone rang. Could it be from Bombay? Nagappa
wondered. But his heart didn't race uncontrollably. He didn't
mentally rehearse what he was going to say if it was Phiroz.
I'll respond as the situation demands, he thought, and waited
for Krishna to tell him who it was.

His guess was right. It was from Bombay. But his hand
didn't shake when he picked up the receiver. This surprised
him. It was Khambata at the other end. Nagappa pretended
not to recognize his voice, and said, 'What a pleasure to hear
from you, Phiroz!'

Khambata at the other end screamed breathlessly, 'Hello,
hello, it's me . . . me, Noshir Khambata, not Phiroz.' It was a
long-distance call and he wanted to give his message quickly.

'Relax, Noshir, what's the hurry? Good you called. Let's
have a nice long chat. You see, I was getting bored with

no one to talk to here,' Nagappa drawled with deliberate laziness. 'It's so good to hear your voice at last. Oh, I almost forgot. Thanks for organizing such a great reception for me at the airport . . . and the arrangements at the guest house. Wonderful! Noshir, I don't have words enough to thank you. Only you could've done it . . .'

'Hello, hello, Nag, the matter is serious . . .'

'Who's serious? What's wrong? Which hospital?'

'Hello, Nag, listen, Phiroz . . .'

'My god! Don't tell me! What happened? I was wondering why he called me to Hyderabad and he himself rushed to Bombay. Must be an emergency. What's the diagnosis? Is there something I can do to help?'

'Listen, Nag, please LISTEN!'

'Oh, you can't hear me clearly, is it? These terrible telephone lines . . . long-distance calls are always a problem. The operator's indicating that the three minutes are over. Operator, extend the call, please. Yes, Noshir, as I was saying . . .'

'Nag, this's an urgent PP call . . .'

'Okay, continue please,' the operator interrupted.

'Now, listen, Nag, I'll send you a telex to the factory . . .'

'What? Are you asking me to go the factory? Whom should I meet there? I came to know only when I got here that there are rumours of some swindling . . . huge misappropriation of . . .'

The line was abruptly cut. Nagappa put the receiver down, laughing. He had no idea why he had this sudden urge to pull Khambata's leg. He was surprised by it himself. He was also surprised that he had derived some kind of pleasure from it. He was sure Khambata wouldn't have the nerve to report this to Phiroz. Maybe this SOB 1 will tell his boss he couldn't get through to me or the line got cut, he thought, picturing Khambata with his sad, comical face, trying to wriggle out of the situation. Nagappa felt like laughing again.

All these SOB 1s have managed to get into the company by licking Phiroz's boots. No self-respect! And Phiroz has used his influence to fill the company with these good-for-nothing SOB 2s with no qualifications! All his own people! Nagappa stopped midway through his mental rant, remembering Khambata cutting the line suddenly at the mention of swindling. This was serious. But he wanted to get the anger and bitterness out of his system. And this arrogant, egotistical maniac Phiroz has surrounded himself with incompetent yes-men, just to hide his own incompetence. Who knows what trouble he has got himself into because of these stupid buffoons! And maybe this SOB 1 is trying to scare me with this 'inquiry' because he needs my help badly to come out of this mess! He stopped. Hey, why didn't I think of this possibility before?! Yes, there could be another side to this entire affair! Nagappa felt relieved that instead of feeling scared, he was now curious to know what really was the 'serious' matter Khambata wanted to talk to him about, and Hyder had hinted at.

Nagappa called Krishna and asked if Muthuswamy had come. As it happened, he had just come, and hearing his name, stood before Nagappa with folded hands, asking to be forgiven for yesterday's leave. 'The only penalty for your leave of absence is preparing a fantastic lunch today,' Nagappa smiled.

'Don't worry, sir, today's menu is chicken biryani, mutton cutlet . . .'

Krishna, feeling left out, added, 'If you aren't going to the factory today, shall I get beer, sir? I told the shop guy our sahib has come and he wants chilled beer, but I think it wasn't very cold yesterday. I'll make sure he gives absolutely chilled beer today.'

Nagappa knew Krishna was ingratiating himself in the hope of getting a huge tip like yesterday. But he was not in the mood for beer. But he felt he should celebrate his first victory over Phiroz and Khambata, and it would also go well with the lunch Muthuswamy had planned. 'All right, Krishna, two bottles of beer. But, before that, for breakfast, a single fried egg, a couple of pieces of toast and a hot cup of tea. I'll have a quick shower by the time it's ready. And when you go to get the beer, bring whatever is needed for lunch.'

Nagappa was in a good mood as he went to shower. He was tempted to mentally list the reasons for his good mood, but dismissed it as an absurd idea. He remembered snatches of Dale Carnegie's tips he had read somewhere long ago, though he couldn't recall the exact words: When you are faced with a challenging situation, analyse the situation fearlessly and honestly. Figure out what is the worst thing that can possibly happen. When you have pictured this, gather the courage to face it. When we force ourselves to accept the worst outcome, we have nothing more to lose. Then the challenge before us automatically loses its power to cause anxiety . . .

What could be the worst-case scenario? Nagappa thought. At the most, I might lose my job. But it's not a life-threatening situation. So why worry about it? As already decided, I could open a newspaper shop, in one of the alleyways of Khetwadi.

Though he felt some mental clarity, Nagappa wasn't fully aware that the decision he had taken at some unexpected moment had now solidified and strengthened like the giant rocks of Banjara Hills standing like sentinels for centuries.

22

The telephone rang as Nagappa was reading the newspaper after breakfast. He heard Muthuswamy answering it. It was for Nagappa. He said 'Hello,' into the receiver without getting agitated. It was from Murthy, Ramakrishna's assistant.

'Is that Mr Nag?' he asked, instead of addressing him as sir, as he always did.

'Who's that?' Nagappa asked, still in a mood for a bit of fun. He thought it would serve as an appetizer before lunch.

'I'm Murthy here,' he replied with a tinge of arrogance in his voice.

'Hello, *Mister* Murthy!' Nagappa said sarcastically. 'What's wrong with your voice? It sounds strange.'

Murthy's voice had lost its earlier confidence. He mumbled something incoherent.

'Did you say something, *Mister* Murthy?' Nagappa stressed on mister even more.

Murthy, completely deflated by now, said, 'Sorry, sir, there's a telex for you from Bombay.'

'Would you mind sending it to the guest house, *Mister* Murthy?' Nagappa didn't want to loosen his hold.

'May I read it to you on the phone, sir?'

'Yes, you may read it over the phone now. But it's absolutely necessary that you send it to the guest house later. Firstly, it's imperative that I get the telex that's addressed to me. Secondly, I cannot take any action based on an oral message. And thirdly, how can I check the authenticity of the person conveying the message over the phone? How can I be sure it's you? Anyway, read out the telex message for now.'

Murthy realized he was not dealing with the soft-spoken, mild-mannered Nagappa he knew. He obediently read out the text: *The DMD requires your presence in Bombay immediately. Return by the evening flight or latest by tomorrow morning's flight.—Khambata.*

'Thanks, Mister Murthy. I need you to do three things: Firstly, send the telex to the guest house immediately. Secondly arrange a ticket to Bombay. And thirdly, arrange for a car to take me to the airport accordingly.'

Nagappa was surprised by the confidence in his voice. 'Did you hear me, Mister Murthy?' Nagappa asked sternly.

Murthy was unable to respond because his boss, Ramakrishna, had already ordered him not to do any of the things Nagappa had demanded. He had told him that he could arrange for the ticket if Nagappa insisted, but under no circumstance should he send a chauffeur-driven car for him. 'Let him take a cab to the airport if he wants. Tell him both the company cars have gone for servicing,' Ramakrishna had instructed. The last thing Ramakrishna had told him was something Murthy was sure he wouldn't be able to tell Nagappa: 'Ask him to take a train if he can't get a flight ticket.'

Noticing the long pause at the other end, 'Look, Mister Murthy . . .' Nagappa began.

'Please sir, don't call me Mister,' Murthy pleaded. 'I'm the same old Murthy, but I don't have the courage to go against Ramakrishna and lose my job. Sir, I'll send the car and the ticket. But please don't tell Ramakrishna. Sir, he's not the same Ramakrishna . . . sir, he keeps taking DMD's advice for everything. He takes direct orders from him and goes around boasting that he's going to be the next DMD . . . sir . . .'

'Don't worry, Murthy. I'll take the responsibility if you're questioned about not following his orders. Do one thing. Please call Ramakrishna right now and tell him what I told you earlier. Also, tell him that I won't go to the airport if I'm not sent a car, and I'm not responsible if the ticket is wasted or if my departure to Bombay is delayed. Not only that, if my departure is delayed beyond tomorrow, I'll start coming to the factory from the day after. And if you aren't able to tell Ramakrishna all this, ask him to call me directly, and I'll speak to him.'

Krishna came with the beer, just as Nagappa finished the call. The aroma of biryani was wafting from the kitchen. 'Touch the bottle and see, sir, it's absolutely cold . . . really chilled beer. Better than yesterday,' Krishna smiled. Nagappa touched the bottles to humour him and said, 'Very good! Open one now and put the other in the fridge.'

Seeing Krishna making a pretence of taking out the change from his pocket, Nagappa said, 'Keep the change,' as he patted him on the back.

Krishna had never seen Nagappa in such a good mood before. He wondered if he could cadge a few more rupees of commission by suggesting Farida Banu's name to make the evening colourful. He had heard she was back from Calcutta. But seeing no trace of lechery in Nagappa's smile, and remembering the dressing down he had got the last time, he didn't suggest bringing a girl. 'Thanks, sir,' he mumbled. Though Nagappa outwardly looked his simple self as usual, Krishna found something intimidating in his brilliant eyes that stopped him from taking liberties with him. He quietly went to the kitchen with the beer bottles.

As Nagappa sipped the beer, the mild intoxication coursing through him felt different. Today, he was not drinking to drown his sorrow. He was on a rare emotional high. The noon had spread across the veranda. The rocks around were radiating heat. In the far sky, a plane flashed under the sun once in a while, as it descended towards the airport. Nagappa could hear its distant drone. In the corner, the neem tree was shimmering as the leaves quivered in the gentle breeze. He sat gazing serenely through the French windows separating the drawing room from the balcony. When his eyes got tired of the dazzling light, he asked Krishna to pull the curtains close. Now the room was filled with a deep, shadowy cosiness, with the light softly filtering through the dense green drapery. Nagappa closed his eyes with pleasure, feeling mellow.

The MD going to America suddenly . . . No, let me not think of all those things. Let me, for once, be free from doubts, conjectures, suspicion and anxiety. Let me respond only to this moment—live from one moment to the other. Let me react to the present as it unfolds. And let me not think about my work or office, now that I've decided to cut myself off from everyone and everything. I need to sever all ties, all things that bind me. I shouldn't wander away from the present, which is the reality that I'm living and experiencing . . .

Nagappa heard a car pull up in front of the bungalow, someone opening the door and getting down and walk in. The Sardar driver saluted and stood before him.

'How are you, Sardar?' Nagappa asked him with the old familiarity.

Answering an unasked question, the driver replied, 'Sir, no one told me you were coming yesterday. I got to know only when Murthy sir told me. Sir, he gave the ticket for the evening flight and this envelope.'

He handed them to Nagappa.

'Did Murthy say anything else . . . any message?' Nagappa asked.

'No, sir. He has asked me to take you to the airport in the evening. It looks like he's not well. He took half day's leave and went home. I left him home and came here.' He paused. 'Sir, the flight is at 7.50. I'll be here at 6.30 in the evening to take you to the airport. If you need the car before that for going anywhere, please let me know. I'll come, sir.' He saluted and left.

As Nagappa had guessed, the telex was in the envelope. It had been addressed to Murthy and not him, with the instruction: *Please read the following message to Nag on phone.*

Ramakrishna must've shouted at Murthy for messing things up. No wonder he took half day's leave and went home, Nagappa thought. He felt bad that Murthy had got into trouble because of him.

After lunch, Nagappa praised Muthuswamy for an excellent meal and Krishna for the beer, told them not to disturb him till four, and went to the bedroom. He fell asleep almost immediately.

When he came awake, he wondered if Diana would be on the flight. Thrilled by the possibility, he got out of bed and began to get ready.

23

The airport was only fifteen minutes from the guest house. But because there was a railway crossing on the way, Nagappa was ready and waiting so they could start as soon as the car arrived. Sardar was there exactly at 6.30. Nagappa realized this might be the last time he would be visiting the guest house, and probably even Hyderabad. He tipped Muthuswamy and Krishna generously. They thanked him and waved goodbye. Nagappa sat in the car with a heavy heart. Though he had decided to sever all ties, it was not easy to completely detach himself from relationships built over eighteen years. As Sardar started the car, Nagappa resolved not to brood over things and forced himself to look outside—at the setting sun, the rocks bathed in the twilight glow, the blazing gulmohar trees, the tall deodars, the hedges and compound walls of bungalows with a profusion of flowers, and the pond, as they took a slight detour to avoid roadwork. Once again, he was acutely aware that this was the last time he would be looking at these things.

Since the railway crossing gate was open, it was only quarter to seven when they reached the airport. Nagappa gave Sardar a handsome tip, shook his hand and said, 'Thanks, Sardar,' as he bid him goodbye. The driver was deeply touched by this unexpected gesture.

The check-in counter was not yet open. So Nagappa thought of going to the handicraft shop nearby. Just then, a man in dark glasses, who appeared to be waiting for him, approached him.

'Good evening, Mr Nagnath, I need to speak to you confidentially about something,' he said.

Nagappa was taken aback. 'Sorry, I didn't recognize you,' he said hesitantly.

'No, not here. There are too many people. Please meet me at the restaurant upstairs as soon as you check in. I'll be waiting for you at the corner table,' the man said, and began to climb the stairs towards the restaurant with the air of someone who was sure Nagappa would meet him there. Nagappa stared after him. He was wearing a dazzling white starched and ironed pair of pyjamas, an open-collared Hyderabad-style kurta, revealing dense chest hair. A thick, well-trimmed moustache on a shining dark face oozed arrogance, which accentuated his rippling masculinity. Hair worn fashionably long and the confident stride added to his imperious personality. As Nagappa was in a quandary whether to meet this stranger or not, the Bombay counter opened. Since he was first in the queue, it was only seven when he checked in. There was still some time for the security check. He was certain that the man wanted to speak to him about something related to the factory. What do I have to fear, now that I've decided to quit the company? he thought.

He went to the restaurant and cast his eyes around. The man stood up to show where he was. Nagappa walked to the corner table. The man was still wearing dark glasses, probably to hide his identity. Nagappa decided he wouldn't speak to him if he refused to reveal his name.

The man pulled a chair for him and politely asked Nagappa to sit. 'Anything to drink . . .?'

Nagappa shook his head.

'I understand, sir. There isn't much time. My apologies for approaching you like this without introducing myself. But I'm sure you'll realize why I need to be careful, when I finish. All I can say is, I'm a worker at the Hyderabad factory, and have great regard for you,' he said in Hindi, with a strong local Urdu flavour. What he said, and his deep masculine voice made Nagappa's hair stand on end. He leaned forward, eager to listen to the stranger, without insisting on knowing his name.

'Sir, I'm a clerk in the stores section, and I'm shocked by what's been happening there for the last few months. I'm new to the department. I was transferred here ten months back . . . used to be in packing. But from what I've gathered, these things . . . these dealings haven't started recently. Sir, I'm not saying this just to please you, but everyone in the factory has a very high opinion of you. Sir, all the workers are angry . . . frustrated about what's going on. But they're really scared of the DMD and his right-hand man, Ramakrishna, and their reign of terror. The workers dare not complain. Sir, they tried to ignore everything and decided not to open their mouths. But now things have become so bad that everyone, from the watchmen to the factory manager, is scared that finally they'll all be caught, while the big bosses will get away. So, three months back, ten of us secretly got together and wrote a letter giving details about what has come to our notice in the last few months, got it typed and signed, and sent it to the MD, requesting him to order an urgent probe. We also made a request for you to be transferred back to Hyderabad . . . to your original position. Though you were the R&D manager, we've all been impressed by you, sir . . .'

Just then they heard the call for the security check for the Bombay flight. Nagappa, who had been listening intently, barely able to breathe, was a bit flustered.

'I won't take more of your time, sir. It's over three months now, and it looks like the MD hasn't taken our letter seriously, because, let alone order an inquiry, he hasn't even visited Hyderabad after that. Maybe he hasn't received our letter at all. We're really disappointed. Sir, the rumour floating around the factory is that the DMD has more influence over the Board of Directors than the MD. Since most of them are from Hyderabad or the south, it seems the DMD has got really close to them and managed to get all of them on his side. We heard he gives these big parties and invites them and has kept them happy. The rumour is that the DMD's side has become very strong and the MD is powerless in front of them. These people are very ambitious, sir . . . ready to do anything for power. The latest news is that the DMD has suggested in the board meeting that from now on, he'll take complete charge of the entire factory and run it himself, and that the MD will handle the other things, especially marketing. It looks like the MD has no authority left to overrule it. It seems all he could do was bang the table angrily at the meeting. He lost his cool . . . couldn't utter a word. But the DMD remained calm and explained to the board members why he should take charge. It seems the board members were really impressed by him and praised

him for working with dedication and expertise for the last
twenty years to bring the company to the present level.
Inside information is that the members have decided that the
company should make use of the DMD's vast experience and
technical knowledge, and have recommended that he should
assume charge of things at least informally for now. The MD
was so agitated by this that all he said was, "It won't work!"
He wasn't able to put any arguments forward. We heard
they're now questioning the MD's ability. Is all this true, sir?
One thing we must admit, sir, no one can beat the DMD's
style . . . his way of speaking . . . the way he can attract people
. . . Isn't it, sir?'

There was another announcement asking passengers to
proceed for the security check. Nagappa looked at his watch.
It was nearly 7.25.

'Don't worry, sir, you still have ten more minutes,'
the man said, and without allowing Nagappa to respond,
continued, 'A few days back, we realized that even if our
letter has reached the MD, he won't be able to take any
action. So we made copies of it and sent them anonymously
to all the directors, even those in America. It looks like this
has had an immediate effect. Yesterday, suddenly, the DMD
flew to Bombay with Ramakrishna. As soon as we came to
know you were in Hyderabad and taking the evening flight
back to Bombay, I hurried here to give you a copy.'

The man took out a blue envelope from his pocket and
handed it carefully to Nagappa, indicating its importance.
Nagappa put it in his briefcase.

'Sir, if we had known your home address, we would've
posted it to you. We didn't want to risk sending it to the
office address because of that *bavaji* . . . Sir, all the workers in

the factory are looking to you for direction. We're ready to go on strike if needed. Not just the labourers, but even the supervisors and managers . . . everybody. We're all behind you . . .'

The last call for security check was announced. 'Don't worry, I'll do what I can. Thank you very much for the trust you and your friends have placed in me.'

Nagappa shook the stranger's hand, bid him goodbye and walked briskly towards the security gate.

24

As Nagappa climbed the steps of the aircraft, he remembered what Diana had said and shifted the briefcase from his right hand to his left and smiled to himself. He wondered if she would be at the entrance to welcome the passengers, and looked up. No, it was someone else. As he entered the plane, 'Is Diana Driver on duty today?' he asked her softly.

'No, sir,' she answered tersely, without smiling.

As he made his way towards his seat, another air hostess walked up to him and asked, 'May I help you, sir?' She took his boarding pass and indicated, 'This is 13 C, sir.'

The entire row was empty. Nagappa thought number thirteen had been unlucky at least for him. Appa died when I was thirteen, he repeated to himself. He was trying hard not to dwell on the past and thought he could perhaps chat with the air hostess who had shown him to his seat if the seat next to him remained unoccupied. She didn't appear as serious as the one at the door. He fastened his seatbelt and glanced around. Many seats were empty. He craned his neck to see if he could spot the friendly flight attendant, and wondered if he was trying to distract himself from something else that was troubling him. He knew that the letter inside the envelope that the stranger had secretly passed to him at the restaurant, lying in his briefcase, was the reason for his present state of nervousness. Should I open it and read it? he wondered. He didn't want to shake his resolve and disturb the fragile peace of mind he had managed to achieve after a week of unbearable uncertainty and turmoil. He didn't have the courage to once again subject himself to the anguish that he was sure the letter would cause. Having gone through days of mind-numbing dilemma, he knew the agony of changing his mind once again after arriving at a difficult decision. He didn't want to step into a new minefield now. What he wanted to do now was disentangle himself from his ties one by one, based on selfish ends, and spend the rest of his days forging genuine bonds, though he was not yet sure what it really meant. He knew his writing could help him in this objective, but felt he was being deprived of it because of reasons he no longer had control over. The thought depressed him. He began to think of Mary to cheer himself up. Was he hesitating to name something that he was deeply aware of but didn't want to articulate? Was his mind refusing to accept a fledgling bond? The possibility of such a bond brought a smile to his lips, which lingered when the air hostess held a tray of sweets before him.

'Thank you,' he said, making eye contact with her, as he picked a couple of toffees.

'You're welcome,' she replied.

'I know it,' Nagappa told himself, with a mischievous smile.

It prompted him to decide he should visit Mary at her Bandra flat once he reached Bombay.

The flight was about to take off. A voice welcomed
everyone on board and wished them a pleasant trip.
Nagappa liked the voice and the command the announcer
had over Hindi. She was the grim-faced girl at the entrance.
He thought he should speak to her if possible.

When she later came with the tea trolley, he said with
genuine appreciation, 'You have a marvellous voice and by
far the best announcing style I've ever had the pleasure of
listening to.'

She shed her serious expression, smiled and said, 'Thank
you so much!'

She looked lovely when she smiled, which surprised
Nagappa.

As time passed, the stranger at the airport—Nagappa
named him Reddy—invaded his mind, despite his efforts not
to think of him. As he recalled everything the man had said,
he began to have a strong suspicion that the whole thing
was a part of Phiroz's conspiracy. Or was he part of a gang
that had benefited from Phiroz swindling the company, but
was trying to use him to get out of the mess, now that they
knew they would be caught? One thing Nagappa was sure
of was that Reddy belonged to the typical breed of small-
time politicians found in every organization. His swagger,
his style of speaking, the self-assured arrogance in his words
and the confidence about the effect they were having on
others, the suaveness with which he ran a finger over his
well-groomed moustache, that look of being pleased with
himself, the crooked, cocky smile that could mask deceit,
his exposed hairy chest accentuating his masculinity, the
calculated casualness with which he kept rolling up his
sleeves to reveal his muscular hands and the fake modesty

with which he attempted to cover them, the way he picked his words delicately to express his humility and his machismo that belied it—Nagappa knew all the signs.

It seems everyone has a good opinion of me in the factory. Indeed! It seems I've impressed them even though I'm only an R&D manager. You SOB 1s! SOB 2s! I know what I've gone through in the last one week . . . what I've been silently going through these last eighteen years at the hands of Phiroz . . . the sheer psychological torture I've endured. Nagappa thought the long-suppressed anguish and anger held under check with stupendous patience and self-control would explode, demolishing everything in its wake. He feared even chanting aloud all the swear words and obscenities learnt from Koligiriyanna wouldn't be able to staunch this sudden emotional outburst. Phiroz, Shrinivasa, Jalal, Khambata, Ramakrishna, the directors who had praised Phiroz's technical knowledge and the wily politician who tried to hide his identity behind dark glasses at the airport—Nagappa had an irrepressible, irrational urge to shriek loudly, to scream out all their names one by one, shouting out all their misdeeds, their viciousness. Suddenly realising where he was, he controlled himself with superhuman effort. He had bitten his lower lip so hard in the process that blood oozed out. He thought he would go insane if he was forced to endure this agony any longer. Before he realized it, droplets of blood had fallen on his shirt and the blot began to spread. 'Here, take this ice. You must've cut your lip,' the air hostess who had served tea earlier said, handing him a napkin with an ice cube in it.

Nagappa held it to his lips. The air hostess lingered, wanting to speak to him. He looked at her with gratitude.

When the cut stopped bleeding, 'Thanks,' he said in a choked voice.

'How did you manage to do that?!' she asked, pointing to his cut lip. 'And now you've spoilt your shirt.'

'Would you have come to me if I hadn't?' Nagappa was tempted to ask, feeling calmer. But stopped himself, recalling a similar scene from a mushy film.

'I think I was angry with someone,' he said casually—in fact, more casually than he thought possible. She slid into the empty seat next to him. The professional smile she was wearing disappeared and her face became serious. She stared at Nagappa.

'Why do you look at me like this? Don't you believe me?' Nagappa began speaking, his usual guard down. 'They asked me to take the evening flight to Hyderabad, and I took it. They've now asked me to take the flight back to Bombay, and I'm taking it. Ask your colleague Miss Diana Driver. She was on yesterday's flight.'

'Are you . . .?'

'Nagnath,' he completed her question, before she could ask it.

She nodded and smiled, as if her suspicion had been confirmed.

From the way she looked at him, he realized Diana had told her something about him.

'Do I have a sweet, sad face?' he asked.

'And brilliant eyes!' she laughed. 'I'll see you soon.' She got up to leave.

'You didn't tell me your name?'

'I'm Miss Irani . . . Thrity Irani,' she said and left.

Oh, another one of Phiroz's tribe, Nagappa thought.

He remembered something Reddy had said: Phiroz impressing the members with his calm and composed demeanour at the board meeting, while the MD was shown in a poor light only because he had lost his temper and banged the table. Perhaps all you need for surviving is the art of impressing others, Nagappa thought. And Phiroz was a master of the art. He also knew how to throw others off-balance and force them to trip up, while pretending to remain unruffled. And what had Reddy said about Phiroz's technical knowledge and expertise? Nagappa didn't want to think about it. He knew he might end up biting his lip again, trying to control himself from exploding with helpless rage. His face flushed with controlled anger. He felt suddenly hot. He got up and adjusted the air vent above. Whatever the reasons for him not reaching a higher position in the organization, those who were aware of his innovative genius couldn't deny his immense contribution to his company. He was now aware that genius alone was not enough. You also had to know how to fight for what was rightfully yours and have the courage to demand and get your due credit. If truth had to triumph, a person who valued truth had to wage a relentless war to protect it, to ensure its victory. Not that Nagappa was unaware of all this all along. It was one of the principles he had always believed in. But when it came to actually practising it, something in his basic nature stopped him from entering the arena. He also knew that he supported his inaction by pretending to be indifferent to fame—apathetic to reaping the fruits of his innovations. And, by extension, when he realized someone else was benefiting by them, he would simmer with impotent anger. Therefore, when he came to know from Reddy that the directors had given all the credit for the company's progress and its present position to, of all the people, Phiroz, his endurance had reached the breaking point. His cut lip was the physical evidence of his explosive rage. Its intensity had startled him. The rage had subsided. But it had left him deeply agitated.

In the last eighteen years . . . No! Nagappa thought. Let me not dwell on the past. Let me not succumb to the temptation of looking back. I've already decided to quit my job and open a newspaper stall or a second-hand shop in an alleyway of Khetwadi. Maybe I could open something like the Strand Book Stall and be among books and spend my spare time doing what I love most—writing. But I've been gagged. I simply cannot write what or how others want me to write—for causes others feel strongly about. It's impossible for me to create something that has not emerged out of my own experience. And its's equally difficult for me to keep waiting till I reach *that* moment of climactic intensity, when I must express in words what I experience. I feel stifled when my creativity is unable to find an outlet and dies inside me. The awareness makes me feel sorry for myself . . . .

'What are you brooding about?' Thrity asked, placing her hand casually on the armrest. Her voice startled Nagappa. Emerging from his thoughts, he gently pressed her soft, warm hand impulsively and said, 'Thank you, my friend.'

Touched by the sincerity in his voice, 'Thanks for what?' she asked.

Nagappa was unable to speak for a moment. Then he managed to say, 'For everything, especially for your kindness, which restores one's faith in life.'

'Nonsense! Why should you lose faith in life and in living? You're young, talented, well-placed in life . . .'

Nagappa was surprised by her last remark. Suspecting she was flattering him to merely while away her time, he looked at her. As if waiting for this moment, she said softly, 'Diana has told me everything.'

Nagappa was confused. Why are people I meet accidentally, showing so much concern towards me? Is it because we'll probably never meet again? Is it because they have no stakes in this brief emotional encounter? Are they sympathetic because there's no chance of them getting entangled in this web I'm caught in? Has this sympathy stemmed from the liberating knowledge that someone else is suffering, and they are not? Are we losing our ability to become spontaneously emotional, because we refuse to empathize with other people in their suffering? For these air hostesses, is it part of their professional training to be able to smile intimately and speak to everyone in such a way that each one of us feels special, and that they're attentive only to us? Is it something that comes mechanically to them, like second nature? Nagappa suddenly remembered Doshi, who had shown genuine warmth and sympathy towards him during a chance meeting. He didn't seem to have any ulterior motive, Nagappa thought. Why didn't he meet me as promised again? Was his concern for me only momentary?

'Hey, have you forgotten I'm sitting next to you? This is an insult to me,' Thrity said.

'Sorry, Thrity, I'm touched by your kindness. It has made me so emotional that . . . Perhaps, it's only in such accidental meetings that we can express our genuine emotions honestly. Maybe long-term relationships are based merely on day-to-day interactions, or end up being false because of the need to

guard our own self-interests . . .' Nagappa mumbled almost
to himself.

'It looks like you take everything too seriously, and
overthink everything. Just because I go around with a smile
on my face doesn't mean I've no worries or things to be sad
about. And do you think it was a mere coincidence that of
all the passengers, I spoke to you? Granted that I may not
have noticed you if Diana hadn't spoken to me about you,
but why not accept that what we shared for a few moments
was significant? I heard that you're a big writer. I may not
have the ability to capture feelings in words like you do. But
I've majored in English literature. I graduated from Wilson
College in Bombay. Hemmingway's my favourite author.
Shall I tell you why his descriptions of bullfights, war and
death touch me? It's the way he captures the experiences of
the transitoriness of life! I feel our genuine feelings have got
corrupted because we look for permanence in everything.
Fear of death is our greatest malady today. If fear of a plane
crash makes my mother anxious, I feel elated that I'm in a
job where I need to fly. One thing we both need to accept
honestly is that we two may never meet again. Perhaps,
that's what's making this meeting so special . . . so intensely
beautiful. Don't go on analysing the reason for its intensity.
I call that vulgar.' Realizing that she had perhaps spoken too
much, she suddenly stopped. Nagappa didn't know what to
say. The main lights had been switched off and a dull glow
from the rear end filled the cabin. He unconsciously, but
without any false sense of intimacy, sat with his hand on
Thrity's. In this new-found awareness about the transitoriness
of human relationships, the brief companionship gave him
an indefinable sense of solace.

As the plane approached Bombay, all the cabin lights came back on. Thrity got up. 'Don't worry, everything'll be okay. I'll pray for you,' she said.

'Goodbye, my transient friend,' Nagappa said softly. She gave a knowing smile and left.

He wanted to act upon something he had made up his mind about when he was sitting quietly with Thrity. He opened the briefcase, took out the envelope Reddy had given him, tore it to bits and stuffed it into the seat pocket. Go to hell, you SOB 1s! I've nothing to do with any of you any more! he screamed silently.

If all ties with my company could be severed by tearing up the letter, I could've read it before tearing it, Nagappa thought. Did I destroy it before knowing its contents because I didn't have the courage to face the truth it might have revealed? Was I scared of the challenge it could pose? A new scenario I'd have to deal with? This filled Nagappa with a new kind of anxiety. Just then, Thrity's voice announced that they would soon be landing in Bombay. He looked out of the window at the city twinkling with millions of lights. He could make out the fire-spewing chimneys of Trombay Refineries. And there was the airport control tower standing tall like a taciturn giant, with its beaming searchlights knifing the darkness. As the plane touched down and moved along the serpentine runway lights, Nagappa's mind came slowly back to reality and what awaited him. As he stepped off the aircraft, he broke into a sweat, despite the cool breeze, and shook slightly.

The one thought that forced itself through the labyrinth of worries was: It was cowardly to tear the letter given to him before reading it. It was a mistake.

25

Entering room number fifty-one of Khemraj Bhavan was like entering another world. Nagappa put his suitcase down. The snacks served on the flight had killed his appetite. He decided to skip dinner and have a glass of hot milk at the dairy downstairs instead. As he climbed down the stairs, apart from the feeling of loneliness, he was also aware of everything that had happened in the last eight days. He realized how laughably, utterly absurd and unreal it all seemed. His confidence in his creativity that had spontaneously, albeit momentarily, stirred within him in the company of Diana and Thrity had now dried up, giving way to a sense of helplessness. The building was teeming with hundreds of people, but he felt totally detached from everyone, each person was isolated from the other, amidst this sea of humanity.

He looked at his watch. It was past ten. What if I call Mary now? he thought. The idea thrilled him. But is it right to call her so late at night? What if she or the family she lives with misunderstands me, he wondered. I don't even know if she lives in somebody's house or, for that matter, where she lives. I guessed it might be somewhere in Khar or Bandra from the phone number she had given me. No, not now. Better to call her in the morning, maybe by seven, before she leaves for work. He drank the milk without tasting it, went upstairs, changed and lay wide awake on his bed. He knew Reddy's letter wouldn't let him sleep. 'Damn it!' he muttered. And before he knew what he was doing, he downed two barbiturate pills with a glass of water.

His head felt heavy when he woke up. He looked at his watch. It was past eight in the morning. He had thought of inviting Mary for dinner. 'Oh, hell!' he cursed, angry with himself. She would've left for work by now. I can now call her only after 8.30 at night. What if I call her at her office number? No, she might not like it . . .

He heard a knock on the door. He got up, still feeling groggy. His walk was unsteady. He couldn't believe his eyes when he opened the door—it was Khambata!

'Hello, Noshir, come in . . . what a surprise early in the morning!' Nagappa indicated a chair.

'Just a moment.'

He went in, splashed some water on his face and came back, wiping it with a towel. Khambata was looking at the bookshelf. A new-found arrogance and a kind of disdain for the grimy surroundings was trying to mask the permanently stupid expression on his face. Nagappa felt like having a bit of fun at his expense again. 'Don't tell me you're seeing books for the first time in your life!' he sneered. 'Sorry, Noshir, the way you were gaping at them made me wonder. Anyway, they're beyond your reach.'

Khambata appeared to have rehearsed what he had to say before coming to meet Nagappa. 'Call me Khambata.

Don't forget that you are still under suspension orders!' he blurted out.

Nagappa began to laugh. This flustered Khambata. He forgot his lines. Nagappa stopped laughing. 'Thank you, Mr Khambata. Sorry, I totally forgot you had suspended me. Good you reminded me. Now, listen carefully. I'm going to take you to court. I'll sue you for damages. My lawyer will send you the notice directly. Keep a pile of cash ready as compensation for suspending me under false pretext, for defamation and for causing me emotional trauma. Don't worry, your lawyers will explain everything. Anyway, the amount isn't big for you. What Phiroz, you and your gang have made in Hyderabad by swindling the company must be ten times more than this, isn't it?'

Khambata looked nervous. He sat holding the sides of the chair tightly, afraid he would begin to stutter if he spoke. Regaining his confidence after a while, 'Please, Nag . . .' he began.

'Call me Mr Nagnath,' Nagappa interrupted.

'Okay, okay . . . Mr Nagnath. The matter is serious. The inquiry will begin tomorrow. Two directors are flying in from Hyderabad especially for the inquiry.'

'Oh, is it? I'd be delighted to meet them and expose the dealings of Phiroz's entire gang to them. Do you know the names of the directors?'

'N . . . n . . . no, no, I haven't met them,' Khambata stuttered. 'They're staying at the Taj . . . I . . . I got to know from Phiroz. I don't know anything else.'

'Why do you bluff, Mr Khambata? You were the one who informed me about the inquiry. If you don't know the details, who else will? Anyway, don't worry. Tell Phiroz I'll not answer any of their questions unless I know their names. And surely *you* know what this inquiry is all about, don't you? It seems you're the company's admin manager? Tell me, do you know what it means, Noshir? I mean *Mr* Khambata?'

Khambata had never heard Nagappa speak like this before. He wondered what had happened in the last one week that had brought about this transformation. Did being away from work give him this courage? He sat staring in amazement at Nagappa's new avatar, trying to size him up. The transformation within him had been wrought because he had emotionally cut himself off from the work he had been deeply involved in. Free from the lure of any aspiration his profession offered, he had gained a philosophical detachment. But Nagappa knew Khambata wasn't astute enough to understand this. Khambata kept staring at Nagappa, which made Nagappa want to provoke him. 'Why? What happened, Mr Khambata? Surprised how much I've changed? You'll get to see its real face during the inquiry. You'll see how I'll expose all the underhand dealings all of you have been involved in . . . I'll expose all your fraud. I'll reveal the serious mess you and Phiroz have got yourselves into by your sheer cunning and arrogance. I'll unmask all of your true nature!'

Khambata's face had lost its colour. He realized he would forget why he had come to see Nagappa if he stayed there any longer. 'Look, Nagnath . . .'

'Mr Nagnath.'

'Okay, Mr Nagnath, let me give you the information I came to give: You have been asked to present yourself before the inquiry commission at 10 a.m. sharp in room number 717 at the Taj Mahal Hotel. I'll personally be waiting for you at ten minutes to ten at the reception desk. All right?'

'Have you brought any official letter regarding this?'

'Isn't it enough that I've personally come to inform you as the company's administration manager?'

'No, it's not enough, Mr Khambata. My lawyers have advised me so. They've told me to get everything in writing. Forget about the legal issue. It's also a matter of principle and protocol. I cannot appear before any inquiry commission based on a verbal message from a Mr Khambata. Please convey this to the DMD in no uncertain terms. Also, make arrangement for a car to be sent to take me to the Taj Mahal Hotel. Please don't presume I'll take a cab.'

The determination in Nagappa's voice surprised Khambata. He had planned to take revenge for his earlier humiliation over the phone. But now he wasn't sure how to respond. But he didn't want to accept defeat either. 'Listen, Nagnath . . .'

'Look, Mr Khambata, I can't keep reminding you again and again how to address me.'

'Okay, I . . .'

'Mere okay isn't enough.'

'Okay, Mr Nagnath, you'll realize the gravity of the situation when you appear before the inquiry commission . . .'

'Are you trying to threaten me, Mr Khambata? "Gravity!" Somehow the word doesn't sound right coming from you. And this role doesn't suit you either. The job of a circus clown might fit you perfectly—you and your godfather, Mr Bandookwala. So, say whatever you have to say in simple, plain English, instead of this high-sounding officialese. I'll understand. And don't please use words to threaten me. Tell me, will you send the official letter and the car?'

'I'm not sure it'd be possible. I'll personally come . . .'

'I don't trust you. And don't try to force out of me what I plan to say about you during the inquiry. It won't work. Let's not waste time. I'll not appear before any inquiry commission till I get an official letter addressed to me, conveying the information about the reason for the inquiry and the date, time and the exact place where it'll be held. Remember this! The whole office knows about your absent-mindedness. So, I'm underlining it!'

'This entire endeavour on our part is for your own good. That's the reason why we cannot reveal the objective of the inquiry. We need to maintain utmost confidentiality. All over the company . . .'

'Oh! Your entire endeavour is to help me, is it? I told you to drop the bureaucratic blubber. Leave the responsibility of maintaining the secrecy regarding the inquiry to me. And another thing, if you don't send the letter and the car, please don't think I'll tell them I didn't appear before the commission because I was not given the official summons and conveyance. I'll tell them that Khambata . . . sorry, Mr Khambata didn't inform me about it at all. I'll say no information reached me . . . that you didn't come here . . .'

'Oh, no! You aren't serious, are you?'

'I'm very serious indeed! Even if I receive the letter, but if it doesn't contain all the information I've specified, or even if the letter is as I have specified, but if no vehicle is sent to take me to the inquiry, I'll directly hold you responsible for I not appearing before the inquiry commission. I'll make it known that Mr Khambata agreed to all my terms and conditions, but failed to . . .'

'This's pure blackmail!' Khambata screamed.

'Don't lose your temper, Mr Khambata. This bluster doesn't suit you. And I didn't know there are pure and impure varieties of blackmail. May I know which category this drama of "inquiry" you're going to hold belongs to—pure theatrics or pure blackmail? Please don't forget to tell Phiroz this: The whole thing will backfire on him and his tribe. And if you happen to meet Ramakrishna, tell him that I've vowed to make him shed his Hyderabadi airs. I'm not *that* stupid that I don't understand why the inquiry was suddenly moved from Hyderabad to Bombay. Probably even you don't know why it was shifted here. Okay, Mr Khambata, I now need to prepare myself for this investigation . . . this inquiry. I might have to meet my lawyers, if necessary. Even you must be in a hurry to go to the office. I know, you're never in a hurry about anything. But anyway, goodbye.'

Khambata kept sitting on the chair. Nagappa wanted to get rid of him quickly. He held out his hand. Confused, and not knowing what else to do, Khambata got up and shook Nagappa's hand.

'Goodbye, Mr Khambata. It was a great pleasure to see your face first thing in the morning. I'm looking forward to meeting the members of the inquiry commission. Don't forget about the letter and the vehicle!'

Nagappa saw Khambata out and closed the door behind him. It banged shut louder than he had intended it to, which made him smile. Nagappa suddenly felt liberated from years of oppressive, suffocating self-imposed constraints he had shackled himself to. His growth as a person, stunted for decades, was now beginning to gain its full stature. And with it came tremendous courage—an awareness of fearlessness that was greater than courage—a sense of doors that had been closed shut for long opening one by one.

That he shouldn't have torn the letter Reddy had given him before reading it was still nagging him, as it could have helped during the inquiry. But he didn't regret it. He decided he shouldn't rely on hearsay evidence and dubious information fed by others. He now needed to go to the very roots of Phiroz's years of irrational, inexplicable hatred and needless cruelty towards him. For this, he had to dredge deep within his own psyche and his own experiences.

He felt elated that he was actually looking forward to meeting the members of the inquiry commission. It made him decide to call Mary in the evening: It'd be nice to hear her soothing voice once again, and I can tell her about meeting Diana and Thrity, and about today's encounter with Khambata. I'm sure she'll be proud of the way I handled him.

It now seemed the most natural thing in the world for him to unhesitatingly accept to himself that he was in love with Mary. He felt light-hearted. He walked to the window and stood gazing at his favourite banyan tree, as the morning sun filled him with warmth.

PART IV

26

It was at last eight. Nagappa hurried downstairs and went to the Irani restaurant to call Mary. His heart was pounding and his ears felt hot. Should he just call her Mary or darling or sweetheart? He was confused. The phone outside the Irani shop was out of order. The other public booth was at the end of the 6th Lane. He had called Mary the first time from there. He walked towards it, trying not to feel disappointed or anxious. As he took out the coins to make the call, he wondered what if someone else answered the call, but remained calm. He picked up the receiver and was relieved to hear the dial tone. The phone was working. He kept the coins ready near the slot and dialled the number. A female voice said, 'Hello' at the other end. He quickly dropped the coins into the slot and asked, 'Hello, is that Mary?'

'Mary's not at home. She's gone to a party.'

Nagappa was flustered. 'Is that Diana?' he asked.

'No, it's her younger sister. Sir, may I know who's calling?'

Nagappa liked the courteous tone. 'It's Nagnath here.'

'Good evening, Mr Nagnath,' she said, indicating she knew who he was. 'Mary and Diana have gone for a dinner party. They may be late getting back. When did you get back from Hyderabad? Diana spoke a lot about you the other day.'

'All good things I hope. May I know your name?'

'I'm Zarin.'

'Sweet name. Zarin, please tell Mary I'd called. Would you know where the party is?'

'I think it's at Hotel Taj . . . Taj Mahal.'

Nagappa's heart skipped a beat. Could Phiroz be hosting the party?

'I think someone from Mary's office is hosting the party. She has taken Diana for company.'

Nagappa thought his legs would give way.

'Bye,' he said in a faint voice, which Zarin wouldn't have recognized. The rest was hazy. He vaguely remembered walking to Sher-e-Punjab, but not what he ate. He recalled staggering home and meeting Arjunrao as he opened his door but had no memory of what they spoke. He had a faint recollection of swallowing the barbiturate pills, but not how many. He knew it must have been a heavy dose when he tried to get up from his bed in the morning, but couldn't. He had no idea what made him take so many. He couldn't open his eyes, but could sense it was past noon. He could feel the blazing heat. He lay in bed for some time. After a while, he somehow prised his eyes open and looked at his watch. It was past noon. He couldn't believe it. Had the watch stopped? He held it to his ear. It was ticking. He realized with a jolt that something had shocked him senseless—something so terrible and painful that he wanted to be numb to any feeling, pass out and lie dead to the world. He got out of bed with a start, lost his balance, pressed his hand hard on the wall to stop his head from hitting against it and somehow steadied himself. His hand hurt from the impact. He was wide awake now.

He brushed his teeth, washed his face and drank a glass of cold water from the earthen pitcher. He quickly put on a pair of pants and a shirt, and ran to the end of the corridor to Arjunrao's house.

Arjunrao didn't usually come home for lunch. His mother was standing at the door. 'What happened? Aren't you well?' she asked, looking at his dishevelled hair, unshaven face, bloodshot eyes and drawn face. 'Come in, come in . . . sit for a while,' she invited.

Nagappa was alarmed by the look in her eyes.

'No, *Ajji*, it's okay. Actually, someone from the office had to come and meet me at nine. I was awake till late at night writing, and fell asleep early in the morning . . . just woke up. Maybe I didn't hear them knock. If you could ask the lady next door if someone had come asking for me . . .'

The old woman knew Nagappa was hesitant to speak to the tailor's wife. Her lips twisted into a smile and she was about to make a snide remark, but changed her mind. 'Lakshmeee!' she called out. Her daughter-in-law, who had been listening behind the door, stepped out as if on cue, nodded, walked briskly to the tailor's house and knocked. Nagappa followed her, eager to get the information first-hand. Still smarting under his earlier jibe, she said brusquely, 'No, nobody had come.' Nagappa was so relieved and overcome with emotion that he folded his hands gratefully, and said, 'Thank you,' his voice barely audible. Still under the after-effects of the sedatives, he felt vulnerable. He thought he would burst into tears if he stood there much longer, and quickly stepped into his house, closed the door and flopped down on a chair. His mother's face floated before him and he began to sob inconsolably.

This time, the scene that unravelled before him was one he didn't remember seeing before. It was a series of grainy images superimposed one over the other in a random sequence: It was dusk. Amma was going to Koligiriyanna's house through the backdoor. She returned, climbing down the steps of Koligiriyanna's backyard and climbed up the steps of our house, her face sad, her eyes fearful and furtive, worried if somebody had seen her. She tripped as she ran up the steps in a hurry. I must've been about six then. The reason Amma had stealthily stepped into the alley of low-caste people must be to beg for some rice from Koligiriyanna's wife. Amma usually sought her help in times of need, rather than from our own upper-caste people. But it was always like this—through the backdoor, as it got dark. Then there was Appa's sorrowful face. And there was this image of he and Amma speaking in hushed tones about something, out of my earshot, while Amma drew water from the well. That day, Appa had come running from his tea shop. Seeing Amma near the well, he had rushed there, panting. He was telling her something urgently, despair and worry etched on his face. I had a vague feeling it must be about my elder brother I had never seen. They looked anxious as they came in . . . Images buried deep in my psyche, that had never been translated into words, are now surfacing. The emotions they wrenched out of me still remain beyond the reach of words . . . beyond the realm of articulation.

Nagappa realized he was hungry. But he didn't feel like going out for lunch. He didn't have the will to shave and bathe. So Khambata had not sent the letter or the car, which meant he had not taken Nagappa's threat seriously. Or . . . There was a knock on the door. Nagappa opened it. It was the tailor—the next-door woman's husband. The couple had moved in recently. Nagappa had seen but never spoken to the man who was always in a loose white pyjama–kurta and a black cap a size small for his head. He must have just taken it off. It had left a mark on his forehead. He now stood with folded hands and a stupid grin on his face. 'I'm Dhondoba Shimpi, your neighbour. I heard you aren't well. I don't think you've eaten anything. Please join us for lunch.' Nagappa was taken aback.

'Everything is ready . . . my wife suggested I should invite you . . .'

'I don't want to trouble you . . .' Nagappa was subdued.

'It's no trouble at all,' Dhondoba's wife standing outside interrupted. 'The lunch's ready. We're inviting you to share it with us, that's all. What trouble can there be?' Nagappa couldn't see her.

'All right, please start, I'll join you,' Nagappa said, changed into fresh clothes and went to their house.

As Dhondoba's wife served lunch, he looked at her properly for the first time. Their eyes met, and Nagappa was unnerved by the open invitation in them. He wondered if she was throwing a challenge at him in reply to his audacious 'You don't have the cure for my ailment' remark. Or was there an invitation in her eyes even that day, when she tried to make conversation? Her every stance and gesture oozed raw sensuality. 'She's not the kind of woman who can easily be satisfied by her simpleton husband,' Nagappa thought. Her earlier question now seemed to insinuate something else. He decided to be on his guard. He quickly finished his meal, thanked the couple and was about to leave, when she said, 'It was all very simple today. I hadn't made anything special for you. Please come again.' She smiled provocatively and winked at him. Now there was no doubt in his mind that she was deliberately trying to tease him. Though he had seen her a few times before these last few months, he had not really paid attention to her. These damned memories! he thought. They constantly keep tugging me towards the past. They've changed the way I look at things around me.

As he lay down, he felt emotionally exhausted by the scenario that had played out in front of him before he went to Dhondoba's house. More than his wife's provocative glances and the clear signals they were sending him, he was still in the throes of the anguish he felt, remembering the faces of his father and mother. Though he had been haunted by his childhood memories all his life, this was the first time he had broken down like this and wept like a child. It's all because of those damn barbiturates, Nagappa thought. They've played havoc with my ability to think clearly . . . made me emotionally vulnerable . . . He got up, went to the window and emptied the entire bottle on to the street. The pills lay scattered near the sewer below his house. He tossed the empty bottle into the garbage bin. Now, no more emotional crutches . . . no more drowning my sorrow with intoxicants. I must learn to look my memories in the eye . . . have the courage to face them squarely and experience and accept them for what they are. Yes, I realize that even the feelings I thought Mary had towards me were fake. The very thought that she had gone to Phiroz's party ripped me apart. The pangs of jealousy were so intense that they made me completely forget about the inquiry! Look at Phiroz's audacity! He arrives in Bombay and next day invites her to a party! And she sidles up to him. Have they grown so close in such a short time? The very idea is revolting! This SOB can impress anyone with his sweet talk. And he has the looks to match! What a physique! What style! It can make anyone fall for him.

Phiroz's face loomed in front of Nagappa with all its details. He saw the chiselled face as he had never seen it before. His nostrils flared in unbearable rage. There was a tightening in Nagappa's throat. He felt suffocated. Society appreciates the outer appearance, not the person within, he rationalized bitterly.

With the thought of the 'person within', he felt deeply disturbed once again. Unable to calm himself, he got up and started pacing the floor: As the MD or someone else had told me once, mine is a one-track mind. Mary, Diana and Thrity conjured up a unique moment in time, filling me with self-confidence that urged me to believe I could sever all ties with my company. The same bravado made me take a tough stand and behave obstinately with Khambata. But, now that Phiroz has struck a blow to the very root of that self-confidence, I'm filled with a new kind of dread I've never known before. I'm filled with a crushing despair. Maybe I need this job more than I realized. Only when we establish ourselves firmly in a particular field . . . Was there a knock on the door?' Nagappa opened it. It was Dhondoba's wife. She was standing with a cup of tea. She stretched her hand forward to give it to him. As Nagappa took it, she let slip the fold of her sari, and in the pretext of pulling it back into place, drew attention to her firm, youthful breasts bursting through her tight blouse, gave him a quick wide-eyed glance and left.

Nagappa sat on the chair drinking tea, and felt the last traces of the barbiturate-induced grogginess completely drain out. He thought of the tailor's wife and smiled. She was openly tempting him. Silly girl, she's still very young, he thought. I need to be careful and not let matters go out of hand.

He got up. He wanted to shake off his lethargic mood. He quickly shaved, and as he bathed, he felt the reason for suspecting Mary was his jealousy towards Phiroz. But things need to be resolved either way, once and for all, he thought. And more than anything, I shouldn't lose the fragile maturity I've gained in the last eight days. I should call and ask Mary in the evening about the party. And if it's true that it was Phiroz's party she had gone to, I must not be under any illusion, and let go of this fledgling relationship. I must break away from it too. His eyes filled up. Mary, whose compassion had made him believe in rebirth and bonds spanning lifetimes, Mary, who had warned him against Phiroz—had the same Mary changed so much overnight that she had gone to the same Phiroz's party?

As he scrubbed his chest, he mentally placed Phiroz next to Mary, then Diana and then Thrity, who had lectured him on the transitoriness of human relationships. His heart shrank in self-disgust. He had felt the same way when he sat tongue-tied in front of Reddy at the Hyderabad airport, listening to his deep, masculine voice. Nagappa pictured Reddy's broad shoulders, the arrogant way he carried himself, his hairy chest and arms, his rippling biceps, his physique exuding virility that could make any woman want him. And his style of speaking—the self-assured stance that could make people agree with him even without listening to what he said! Nagappa had felt small and insignificant in front of him. Was some hidden envy also a reason for tearing up the letter Reddy had given him, without reading it? When Nagappa had briefly held Thrity's hand, he had wondered what if it was Reddy's hand instead of his, holding hers. It was after visualizing this that he had felt like tearing up the letter. He now imagined Phiroz flirting brazenly with Mary and Diana at the party. He felt himself shrinking further. This SOB has crossed 50, but still chases skirts! Sisterfucker! Though he was thinking of Phiroz, his anger was directed at his father. He cursed him as he wiped his chest and stomach. What an inheritance he's left behind! he thought, his bile rising in his throat. Not only did he leave me with this disfigured body, but also bestowed upon me the morbid benediction of, 'Die! Die!' He branded me forever. A crazy idea came to him in the wake of this anger: I must ask Dhondoba's wife her name the next time I see her. I must show her my bare chest and see her reaction. He was stunned by his own thoughts. He began to laugh, imagining the scene, but stopped when he visualized baring himself before Mary, Diana or Thrity. Suddenly, without warning, even my past has gone and joined Phiroz and his hunting pack, he thought. It has succumbed to his bait, and is now out to get me. He felt a burning sensation all over his body. He wanted to bathe again to douse it. But the tap had run dry and there was no water left in the bucket.

He knew he would never be able to have a lasting relationship with either Mary, Diana or Thrity. He wouldn't be able to take it to its culmination. He felt unworthy of such a relationship. All he could hope for was a 'hello' from Mary as he went to the MD's office once in a while, or elicit compassion for his sweet, sad face from Diana and, perhaps, a transient friendship with Thrity. That's all he was ordained to have. But Rani was different. She had never shown revulsion towards his naked body. He had longed to see her these last few days, but something had stopped him from meeting her. I must send her some money from the post office tomorrow, he decided. I should check how much I have in the bank. I must call the finance department and find out the amount accumulated in my provident fund. I'm also eligible for a gratuity after eighteen years of service . . . Nagappa stopped. He realized where this was leading to. Khambata not sending the letter and the car meant only one thing— Phiroz's ego had come in the way. And this clearly meant he had taken a decision: *Nagappa, alias Nagnath Santayya Mapsekar, aged thirty-nine, has been terminated from his service. He joined the company in 1950 as Research Chemist and went on to become the R&D manager. His present designation is manager, special assignment. In his eighteen years of service, he has shown unstinting dedication towards his work and has been responsible for the company reaching its present stature and position of pre-eminence due to the dint of his merit and his innovative abilities. He has contributed immensely to the organization through his hard work and commitment. The reason for terminating his services is his total lack of ability and skill to reap the benefits of his talent and potential, which is needed in a professional environment.*

Signed, Phiroz Sorabjee Bandookwala, acting managing director. Date . . .

As time passed, the mock termination letter became so real in Nagappa's mind that he was unable to shake off the feeling that he had been languishing at home these last eight days without a job. He blamed himself for not planning what to do next, despite being out of work for over a week. He grew anxious: Should I look for work? It wouldn't be very difficult to get a job, since the company's customers and competitors know of my achievements. The papers I have presented at various seminars have earned me a good reputation in the chemical industry. More than anything, what has given me great pride and satisfaction is that I have six patents registered in my name. I know they are no ordinary patents. They involve pioneering research and are acknowledged to be of a very high calibre. In fact, one of them had been entered for the National Invention Award. The MD himself had recommended sending it and had personally signed the entry form. Another of my big contributions is the major role I've played in the company's diversification programme. But then, there's no point looking for another job because all companies are the same, and the people in them are the same—human nature's the same everywhere. There'll be the same old politics and cut-throat competition. In fact, when it comes to job satisfaction, this company is better than others. It's sheer bad luck that Phiroz has this irrational hatred towards me. He has spewed venom at me for no reason. What about a bookshop? But it isn't easy to find space in a city like Bombay, and I can't afford the down payment. Can I live on my writing alone? What if I get a salesman's job at Strand Book Stall and join a political party or an NGO as a volunteer in my spare time? What if I do social work . . .? Nagappa smiled sadly. Social work, indeed! I didn't even have the guts to visit Cheshire Home Gilbert spoke so much about. I finally sent a cheque for five hundred rupees to assuage my guilt. And politics isn't suited to my nature. In fact, the ambit of my abilities itself isn't very wide. I can only walk this narrow path I've chosen for myself. The only thing I've been able to achieve within my limits are inventions in chemistry. And apart from that, occasional dabbling in writing. Nothing else . . .

Nagappa shook his head and stood up: No, I shouldn't give in to such impotent thoughts. I should look ahead, think of my future and plan my next move. What I told Khambata yesterday shouldn't become an empty threat. Also, it's not easy to throw out someone who has worked sincerely for so long in a managerial position. And that too, when I have the support of the MD himself. There must be a simple explanation for Khambata not coming with the letter today. My mind feels numb and empty thinking about the same thing again and again. I must stop thinking about myself like this all the time. It isn't healthy. I must get out of the house . . . walk to Chowpatty. I must call Mary exactly at eight. I should go to Gaylord in Churchgate for dinner. I should have some beer . . .

As Nagappa combed his hair, he saw the cup and saucer below the washbasin. He thought of returning them on the way out and rinsed them carefully, but changed his mind. He decided he would do it after the tailor returned home. When he opened the door, the tailor's wife was standing, as if waiting for him. 'Cup and saucer,' she said softly. 'Just a second,' he said and hurried inside. She must've heard me washing them, he thought. When she took them from him, he wasn't sure if her fingers lightly brushing against his was an accident. She was still lingering near the door as he locked it. 'Going out?' she asked, opening her eyes wide. 'Yes,' Nagappa replied, confused. He stood for a few moments, not knowing what do. He thought it might be rude to walk away, especially after having lunch at her place. All the doors on the floor were closed and there was no one else in the corridor.

'You must be bored alone at home . . .' he said, trying to be courteous.

'My husband comes home late at night . . . it's usually past ten. He has to come all the way from Colaba.' She looked at him suggestively.

Nagappa looked back, mesmerized. 'May I know your name?' he asked. His mouth felt dry and his voice sounded strange.

She was aware of the effect she was having on him. 'Janaki' she replied, bit her finger and laughed seductively like a *tamasha* dancer.

He heard Arjunrao's door open at the other end of the corridor. 'I'm going for a walk,' he said and hurried downstairs. Did he hear her say, 'Come back soon' or did he imagine it?

A new kind of relationship was evolving at an unexpected moment in an unimaginable manner and dragging him in a totally unpredictable direction. Nagappa missed a step and held on to the railing to stop himself from falling. What was happening was raw and unpretentious, primeval, wordless and mindless.

27

Nagappa didn't remember when he had come to Chowpatty beach last. Maybe years ago. He sat on the sand, gazing blankly. Despite the lulling rhythm of the waves and the people around, he couldn't come out of the dispirited mood he was in. Everything was blotted out, leaving him with his own thoughts: The slow and endless wait is breaking me from within. Why is all this happening to me? Why am I being targeted? Of all people, why a harmless creature like me? And why *now*? When will this reach its culmination? And what kind of culmination? And in these eight days, not one person has come to meet me, except that SOB 1 Khambata! Even Mary has spoken to me only over the phone. Cut off from everyone, my mind keeps wandering back to the painful past or racing ahead towards a frightening future. I'm mentally exhausted. And why am I thinking of Janaki now? It's a relationship—if it could be called that—which has suddenly come into being without any past or future. It's born of a present and immediate need. The only yardstick to measure it is physical gratification or the lack of it. It's free of my stature, my achievements and intellect. It's neither woven around compassion elicited by my sweet, sad face and brilliant eyes, nor predicated to any orchestrated art of enticement. It's elemental and primeval, going back to the beginning of life itself. It's a strong animal attraction, where questions of why and why not don't arise. It's beyond and above any questions, untouched by morality. But here I am, whose life is inextricably entwined with the fundamental question of why—why should I live? Why ever should I live? Even the question 'Was the path Appa chose really wrong?' is a recent one, an analytical one, asked by those on this side, not the other, measured by the criterion of their own philosophical coordinates. As Albert Camus said, there's only one philosophical question—suicide. It's true at least in my case—I, who grew up with the decree of death. I've lived with the decree all my life. The only way to carry it out is to ask what relevance the act will have . . . what relevance my life has. I can end it all by submerging myself in this vast and boundless sea before me. It'll affect no one. Nothing will change. But then, even this thought belongs to this side of death. On the other side of the brink lies death. The question of dying itself is rooted in life. And the root cause of all my problems lies exactly in this—in constantly questioning myself, in asking myself these fundamental questions about life and death—in this awareness of questioning them, in this relentless cerebral centre of my being! And Janaki? She's bound by no questions. She demands only answers from life. Her spirit cannot be held captive within the dilapidated walls of Khemraj Bhavan and the anonymous people who live in it.

When Nagappa's mind was contemplating death, this woman—as if symbolizing the life force itself—lingering near doorways, was holding him back from crossing over to the other side with her seductive glances, asking unthinkingly, openly, to be satiated. Her wide eyes seemed to stare into his now. Perhaps the words to express what they were saying had not yet been invented. Let me not defile it by capturing it in words, Nagappa thought. He sat for a long time, cleansed of all desires and expectations, gazing at the ancient waters before him.

He was awakened from his entombed silence by the clock tower striking eight in the distance. How was it that I heard the sound amidst all the noise around? he thought and, becoming aware of the answer, got up and started walking briskly towards an Irani tea shop across the street, hoping there would be a pay phone there. His heart didn't begin to pound as usual. He didn't make wild guesses about what he would ask Mary and what she would answer or if she would be home.

The Irani shop-cum-restaurant had a phone, but not the kind where you dropped coins in the slot. There were already three people waiting before him. They looked like college students. Nagappa got into the queue. From where he stood, he could see the Irani owner at the counter with his prominent nose, which reminded him of Phiroz with his flared nostrils. Nagappa smiled. The Irani thought Nagappa was smiling at him and smiled back. Nagappa gave him a genuine smile and asked how much a call cost. He said it was fifty paise. He wondered why, of all things, these Iranis had opened tea shops in this country. And all the shops looked the same inside: They had round, marble-topped tables, polished black wooden chairs with round hands to match the tables, pillars with full-length mirrors, glass-fronted cupboards lining the walls, with delicate jars filled with a variety of biscuits and toffees, boxes of cigarettes, bottles of Brylcreem and hair oil. There were not many people in the restaurant. A few were drinking tea, while others had a plate of wafer-thin *khari* biscuits on the side. Each table had an array of biscuit jars, from which customers could select what they wanted. The waiter would serve them on a plate. The sole waiter here was dressed in long, Pathani-style kurta and loose, flared trousers. He looked impressive in his thick but well-groomed moustache. When he was busy serving a customer, the owner himself got up to serve others. Nagappa didn't know any of the customers.

When it was his turn at the phone, the owner signalled to him. He was relieved he was the last one in the queue. He dialled the number. 'Is that Zarin?' he asked the voice which answered the phone.

'Oh, good evening, Mr Nagnath! Please wait, I'll call Mary,' she said. He heard her call Mary and tell her he was on the line. He felt no anxiety during the brief seconds he waited for Mary to come to the phone, but this didn't surprise him. He told himself, yes, she went to my deadly enemy Phiroz's party, and I'm now calling her to dispel any misunderstanding I have about the incident, that's all. There was nothing more to it.

'Hello, Nag, how're you? Zarin told me you'd called yesterday. Thought you'd call again. I didn't go to work today . . . really tired. Zarin must've told you Diana and I went to this party Phiroz hosted. Do you know what time we returned? Make a guess . . . at one in the morning! Phiroz himself dropped us back home in his car. He was in a great mood. He was so sweet to us girls throughout the evening. The party was at Taj's Crystal Room! He'd invited about forty people. Most of them were his friends it seems, and a few customers. A couple of them asked about you. All very sophisticated crowd, you see. I'd no idea Phiroz had so many friends in Bombay. And what a charming host he was! Though I'm the MD's secretary, he's never invited me to a single party. I felt really angry with him yesterday! And Phiroz had the courtesy to personally call me. Don't be jealous, but I almost fell in love with Phiroz for the most enchanting way he invited me. Can you believe I was the only one from the Bombay office, among the junior staff, that is? Khambata and his wife had come. Shireen was her sweet old self. She asked about you, by the way. But that dirty rogue, Ramakrishna, behaved badly. Nasty guy! Must've had too much to drink. Ah, yes, it was cocktails and dinner. It was great! I think I had misunderstood Phiroz because of what the MD had told me about him. But after yesterday's party, I've really changed my opinion of him. He's really charming! And he looked so attractive in cream-coloured trousers and a dark blue shirt. I can't believe he's fifty! Diana was all praise for him. She fell head over heels for him . . . you see what I mean? In the beginning, we were a bit hesitant to mix with such a posh crowd. But can you believe it? Phiroz came to where we were sitting and said, "What are you charming girls doing here? Come, let's go and meet the others." He held our hands . . . and he has such large firm hands . . . and introduced us around! "Call me Phiroz," he said. "It's an insult to me if you call me Mr Bandookwala." You should've been there. Even you'd have changed your opinion of him if you'd seen him yesterday. Our MD lacks his personal charm . . . his sophistication. You really need these qualities for a person in such a high post, don't you agree? What's the use of mere intelligence? Hello, hello, Nag, are you listening? Hello . . .?'

Nagappa had stopped listening long back. He wasn't sure if the receiver had slipped from his hand or if he had placed it back.

'Sahib, did you get some bad news?' the Irani shop owner asked. Nagappa realized his eyes were filled with tears. He quickly took out his handkerchief from his pocket and dabbed them. Two other people who had queued up behind him looked at him sympathetically. They had watched Nagappa's face change from shock to pain and anguish, as he listened over the phone for nearly ten minutes without uttering a word. Thinking it was news of a death or accident, they had waited patiently for their turn. Even the Irani owner had not tried to hurry him.

Nagappa placed a rupee on the counter and mumbled 'Thanks' with great difficulty. He walked to a corner table and sat down. Not wanting to break down in public, he tried to control himself. When the waiter came to take his order, 'Do you have beer?' he asked in a low voice The waiter looked at the owner, who came up to Nagappa and asked him gently what he wanted. 'We don't have the permit to sell it, but if you could please step this way.' He ushered Nagappa to an anteroom behind the curtain. There were a few tables there, but they were all empty. Nagappa ordered an omelette and bun and butter along with the beer. He waited for the beer to arrive.

28

Nagappa got up before dawn and settled down to write. He recalled fragments of what had happened after he left the Irani restaurant, but decided not to give in to the temptation of regurgitating the emotions that followed. For a moment, he wondered why he was writing about Koligiriyanna, of all people. But he rationalized that this was a trivial matter compared to the question of why he should continue to live, about which he hadn't been able to reach a definite view.

Koligiriyanna's house was adjacent to Nagappa's backyard. And beyond that was Maasti Honnappa's house. Both families belonged to Nadkarni Appooraya's clan. Honnappa's wife, Parameshwari, and Koligiriyanna's wife, Devi, were sworn enemies. Parameshwari's three daughters were dark like Honnappa, while Devi's two children—a boy and a girl—were fair-complexioned. The two women found something to quarrel about every evening, and exchanged abuses, standing on either side of the fence. In the heat of the argument, they often let their tongues loose and flung unspeakable obscenities at each other, with matching gestures. These generally alluded to their physical attributes, sex lives and prowess in bed. When the squabble reached a crescendo, the women hitched their saris thigh-high, screaming, 'Slut! Whore!' until one of them spat out, 'If *you* can't satisfy your husband's itch, send him to *me!*' When this daily ritual was going on, oblivious to it, Koligiriyanna lay on his back on the cool red-tiled floor worn smooth, dandling his granddaughter on his knee, singing a silly rhyme. Only on rare occasions when the ruckus became unbearable, he would scream, 'Shut your mouths, you bitches! Give your filthy tongues a rest!'

Nagappa smiled at the memory. He stopped writing, scared his father, mother, brother and sister would invariably enter the narrative. No matter how hard he tried, he had never been able to continue after a point, as his mind withdrew from describing the exact scene of his father trying to burn him alive. Though his mind kept constantly revisiting the past, it recoiled when it sensed it was inching towards that particular moment. Though he could vividly recall several incidents from his childhood, this was one area that was always shrouded in darkness, refusing to face the glare of daylight. If only I had the courage to write about it or tell someone about it, he thought. But whom? Janaki? He suddenly remembered that last night he had deliberately returned home after ten. Janaki's door was closed. Her husband was probably home.

Nagappa found it impossible to continue. He closed the notebook and stood near the window. A soft breeze blew from the banyan tree. But it was still dark and he couldn't see the tree. The devotee in the chawl opposite had not yet woken up, but the oil lamp, lit last night in front of the shrine, was still burning, creating a small, flickering halo around it. In the silence before daybreak, Nagappa once again became aware of his loneliness. No one was awake. On the rope-strung beds lined up on the pavement below, bhaiyya from the dairy, *kolsewala* from the coal mart, the sugarcane juice shop's Maratha owner and a few others were deep in sleep, covered in their white dhotis from head to toe. A dog lay curled up under one of the makeshift beds, probably the bhaiyya's. Nagappa felt a twinge of envy: If only I could sleep like them! What if I hadn't got educated? What if I had stayed back in Hanehalli, tilling a patch of land? Maybe I could've married someone like Koligiriyanna's daughter or someone like Janaki, who, when in heat, with her insatiable, irrepressible libido, brazenly, invitingly, even innocently looked at a male body with her provocative eyes. And maybe I'd have continued to eke out a living, running Appa's crumbling tea shop . . .

There was Amma, who managed with just two cheap saris, and Appa, who sat in his tea shop all day, wearing nothing but a piece of cloth around his waist, another flung over his shoulder and the sacred thread across his bare chest. Yes, it was there as a proof of his caste. And I wore a pair of frayed old shorts, a shirt and a white cap only when going to school. Otherwise, like all the Christian and low-caste kids in the neighbourhood, I ran around in a dhoti. I got a pair of slippers only after finishing high school. I now remember once again Phiroz's deliberately probing question about my father's profession, and my hesitation to answer it, and Phiroz's derisive 'Oh', when I finally answered.

To challenge that dismissive sneer, Nagappa rewound his childhood which had shaped his personality, and Hanehalli, in which he was still rooted: Koligiriyanna, Honnappa, Yenku from the salt pans, and Murkundi . . . and there was Sheikh Fareed from the next lane, who polished old iron pots, Saavera, who ran the oil press, Ganapayya Shetty, who owned the sweet stall, Devu, the cobbler, Madeva, the washerman, Santana, the village midwife, Yeera, the barber, Rayashetty, the goldsmith, the prostitutes Uttami, Beeramma, Nagamma . . . the fields, the hedges, haystacks, pastures, vegetable patches, pumpkin creepers, rows of watermelon, mounds of jaggery, harvested cashew nuts, the colourful festoons strung around the chariot during the temple fair, the drumbeats, the bustle of festivals, the narrow alleyways that held me close to their heart and filled me with snug warmth, the dusty lanes . . . Amidst this collage, an image I hadn't recalled before: It was a Sunday during the auspicious monsoon season. Amma was worshipping the sun. There were different kinds of flowers, tender blades of grass and leaves of plants that grew only during the rains along the ridges of the alleys, with names describing their shapes—tiger's paw, cow's ear, horseshoe . . . I plucked them for Amma, running in an old hitched-up dhoti, with the boys and girls of the neighbourhood in knee-high water, splashing, whooping and laughing . . . Rising above this sound was Mary's voice, saying, 'All very sophisticated crowd, you see.' Nagappa was filled with uncontrollable rage. Bullshit! he thought. To hell with you and your sophisticated crowd! He felt the entire lot of them bound to his professional life—Phiroz, Mary, Diana, Thrity—were mocking him, laughing at him and making fun of his beloved, rustic Hanehalli.

The image was deeply disturbing. Their artificial world seemed alien to Nagappa. But it was now impossible to return to his old life in his village. He felt like a trapped animal, scurrying to find an escape route from the claustrophobic confines of his cage. He moved away from the window.

He wanted to go somewhere far away from the familiar places he usually went to. He bathed and got ready. He thought of having breakfast, and going to the bank on his way back to update his passbook and sending money to Rani. It's Friday, he reminded himself. If there's no news from Khambata, then I'm not likely to hear from him till Monday. I should meet a few of my old friends over the weekend, especially Sitaram and Vomu, and maybe visit Cheshire Home with Sitaram, which Gilbert has spoken so much about. If possible, I must go to the Strand Book Stall and meet Shanbhag and ask him for a job. He'll definitely offer at least a salesman's job for five hundred rupees. That was my salary eighteen years ago, when I first started working in this company. Now it's many times more. But no, let me not compete for such things any more. I should stop running after the mirage of false hopes and fake ambitions. I should free myself from all those old entanglements.

It was past eleven when Nagappa got back home. All the men in the chawl were away at work. Janaki's door was locked. Nagappa smiled at his own sense of relief. Maybe I'm reading too much into her natural body language and misinterpreting her youthful eagerness, he thought.

There were two envelopes lying on the floor when he opened the door. They didn't have any postmarks. One was from the office, perhaps dropped off by Prabhakar or Khambata's driver. He opened the second one, which bore no address. It was a note from Shrinivasa: *Tomorrow is a day off for the press. Come home for lunch. I have something important to discuss with you.*

As Nagappa wondered what Shrinivasa could possibly want to discuss with him, he remembered what Nayak from Santosh Bhavan had told him. So, this SOB 1 is planning to conduct his own personal inquiry before the official one by Phiroz, he thought. Okay, let me see how deep Shrinivasa has dug his dirty hands into my past to unearth my roots. But is it a coincidence that all this is happening at the same time? Nagappa was scared he had begun to believe in horoscopes and predictions, despite arguing with Arjunrao that it was all utter nonsense.

He tore open the second envelope, wondering why he was hesitant to find out what was inside. As expected, it was a letter from Khambata: *My dear Nagnath, The inquiry has been postponed to Monday due to unavoidable circumstances. It will be held at 10.30 a.m. at Taj Mahal Hotel in room no. 717. Apart from the DMD, two of the company's directors will be present to conduct the inquiry. You will know their names at the time of the inquiry. All precautions have been taken to make sure that your interests are safeguarded. The DMD has personally instructed me to inform you that the purpose of the inquiry is to obtain some vital information from you, and is in no way aimed at subjecting you to any kind of psychological pressure.*

As per your wish, I will be sending a car to pick you up. Driver Abdul will come to your place at 9.30 a.m. sharp. I request you to be ready by then.

With kindest regards,
Noshir Khambata

His inscrutable signature had been scrawled below in blue. The rest of the letter had been typed.

The tone of the letter indicated that the firmness with which he had dealt with Khambata the last time had had an impact. Nagappa sensed that Phiroz had apprehensions about the inquiry being conducted in the MD's absence backfiring. Khambata would've made a copy of the letter to save his own skin, he thought. Let him frame the letter for posterity after the inquiry! I shouldn't have torn Reddy's letter without reading it. It would've at least revealed Phiroz's underhand dealings.

Despite this niggling irritation, Nagappa felt at ease, either because everything would be resolved once and for all, or because of the assurance Phiroz had given that the purpose of the inquiry was merely to gather information from him. In this upbeat mood, he decided to go to Sher-e-Punjab for lunch. I'll have chicken biryani with chilled beer, he planned, and a long siesta after that. And if Janaki invites me for dinner, I'll go.

29

It was four in the evening when Nagappa woke up. The beer had soothed his nerves and he felt rested. He sat on the bed in the strange silence that enveloped the building. The menfolk were still at work, children had not yet returned from school and the women were indoors. He sprang to his feet before the thought that he had been forced to waste away his life at home like a bed-ridden patient brought a fresh bout of self-pity and anguish. Not wanting to disturb the present state of fragile calm, he went to the washbasin and splashed handfuls of water on his face to keep himself from thinking. As the beer-induced intoxication wore away, he felt like having a hot cup of tea. With it came the thought of Janaki. Has she affected me more profoundly than I'm willing to accept, he wondered. My mind has wandered towards her several times since last night. Sexy girl! But where's she? Her house was still locked when I got back from lunch. It looks like she's gone away somewhere.

Nagappa didn't feel like making tea, and decided to go to the restaurant below. It struck him that he had become lazy from the time he stopped going to work. What if I get married? he thought. If I have to quit my job, I'll marry a village girl—someone like Janaki, exuding life force. What if I marry Rani? He laughed. He knew he was trying to distract himself to keep the mental torture he was going through at bay. 'Hey, you SOB 1, I know what you're up to!' he said in mock rebuke.

Though he was only going downstairs, he pulled out his favourite blue shirt and cream-coloured trousers from the trunk. As he wore them, he wondered if this was a reaction to Mary's gushing description of how Phiroz had dressed at the party. He brushed it aside with the excuse that maybe he was trying to impress Janaki. As he stood in front of the mirror, admiring his own reflection, he remembered Mary once saying, 'It really looks good on you!' when he had worn the same set of clothes. Particularly complimenting his shirt, she had advised, 'Leave the top two buttons open when you wear a half-sleeved shirt. You have a broad chest and a firm neck. Show them off! Don't you know, girls actually like a glimpse of the hairy chest peeping through the open collar?'

Nagappa didn't remember how he had reacted then. But now, when he buttoned his shirt, even the top button, as he always did, he was aware of the sad reality of why it had become a habit. 'Hairy chest, my foot!' he said out aloud, moving away from the mirror.

Instead of slippers, he felt like wearing shoes to go with the shirt and trousers. He sat on the stool near the door, pulled them out from underneath and wiped them with a piece of cloth. As he wore one shoe and sock, and was about to wear the other, he had the crazy idea of checking if Janaki's door was still locked. Just as he hobbled out with one shoe on and stood outside Janaki's door, Arjunrao's mother came out of her house. 'Why're you standing there? Were you looking for Janaki?' she asked, giving him a strange look. 'She isn't there . . . gone to Kalyan to her mother's place. Her husband left her there in the morning.'

At first, Nagappa couldn't understand why her face had contorted into something akin to disgust as she spoke. 'I was actually . . . I wanted to find out . . .' he stuttered and grinned stupidly, unable to explain why he was standing in front of Janaki's door with one shoe on.

'Where are you going at this time? To the cinema? Isn't your leave over yet? When'll you start going to work?'

He was irritated by her tone and her prying. At any other time, he would have given a curt reply and walked away. But he had been caught in an awkward situation, for which there was no logical explanation. Trying not to lose his cool, he laboriously began, 'I had my lunch there . . . at their place yesterday, and they also offered me tea. The door was locked from morning, so I got a bit worried and came to check . . . I'll start going back to work from Tuesday. Even I'm getting bored, staying at home all day. The novel I'm writing's almost done.'

She didn't look convinced. Nagappa gave up, stepped back into his house and began to wear the other shoe, hoping she would leave him alone. But she stood outside, peeped into his house, screwed up her nose and finally walked away, muttering. 'Meddlesome old woman!' Nagappa cursed. He didn't feel like having tea. He had also lost his desire to look smart, but decided to go downstairs anyway, trying not to let what had happened depress him. He had always found Arjunrao's mother irritating. She had lost her husband when she was young, and was forced to shave her head as was the custom. Now, in her old age, she was obscenely inquisitive about all relationships. He knew she would spread the news of seeing him outside Janaki's door. He wondered what meaning she would ascribe to his presence at her door. He was worried Janaki could get into trouble because of his foolishness. Maybe her husband has noticed the way she looks at me and become suspicious. I'd better be on my guard, he thought.

Thinking about all this, instead of going to Shrikrishna Vilas downstairs, he had walked towards Santosh Bhavan, which he had vowed never to step into. As he crossed Benham Hall Lane, he automatically slowed down to soak in the fresh aroma of flowers, fruits and vegetables that reminded him of Hanehalli: The scent of jasmine took him back to the shrine at home, heavy with the scent of flowers, shrouded in darkness. With the memory came things he had experienced even before he had learnt to speak properly. He was thrilled that his mind was now trying to articulate them in words he didn't know then. He looked among the flower-sellers for the girl who had called him dada, and sold him a string of jasmine last time. She wasn't there today. He suppressed the desire to buy flowers (and Janaki's memory that came unbidden with it) and walked briskly towards the restaurant.

Nayak was not there. His brother-in-law Shridhar Kamath was sitting at the counter in his crisp white dhoti, kurta and Gandhi cap. Flashing on his fingers were three heavy gold rings on each hand. His lips glistened red with betel juice. A colourful lot, all these hotel owners, Nagappa thought, resentfully.

At one end of the counter, a bunch of incense sticks stuck in a silver bowl filled with grains of rice spewed heady rings of smoke. If anyone asked, Shridhar was sure to boast he had got them all the way from Mysore. Next to it was a platter of betel-leaf *beedas*, artistically folded and arranged in neat rows. In an alcove behind the counter stood framed images of Lakshmi, Saraswati and Ganapati, with garlands of *jaji* flowers. At the other end of the counter was a large framed photograph of a godman, perhaps the swami of the matha, with a thick garland around it and the forehead smeared with *kumkum*. Nagappa had never seen the swami in person. Silver oil lamps had been lit in front of the frame.

'Oh! Oh! Oh! Professor . . . after a long time! Welcome! Welcome!' Shridhar gushed, flashing his fake smile, showing his betel juice-stained teeth.

'You weren't there last time I came,' Nagappa said brusquely, without looking at him, went upstairs, sat at his usual table and ordered uttappa and coffee. When the waiter said the vadas were hot, he asked him to get a plate of those and a newspaper. The waiter brought *Prajamata* and *Samyukta Karnataka*.

It's been so long since I've read a paper, in fact, read anything, Nagappa thought. He flipped through the pages without registering anything. There were the usual ads—a doctor guaranteeing to cure venereal diseases, an astrologer screaming: 'Know your future now!' and the regular weekly horoscope. Out of curiosity, he read the prediction under Leo: *You might fall prey to enemies conspiring against you. Be careful of colleagues and those pretending to be your friends. 5th and 6th are unlucky days. 8th, 9th and 10th could be lucky.* The waiter brought the uttappa and vadas. Nagappa tried to focus on the food, telling himself the prediction was a pure coincidence and was merely feeding his fears, and someone like him with a scientific temperament shouldn't take such things seriously.

He ate in a hurry, had his coffee and paid the bill. When the waiter brought the change, he tipped him, quickly climbed down the stairs and walked out of the restaurant without glancing at the counter. He turned towards Portuguese Church and took the road going to the Opera House. Road repair work was on. Labourers pouring tar over dug-up patches reminded him of one of the things he had patented. If adopted, it would help the municipality save lakhs of rupees. Even his company could make a huge profit. It reminded him that it was almost a year since he had lost touch with the research lab.

Running across Sandhurst Road, leading to Chowpatty, was the Kennedy Bridge. If he climbed down and took the middle lane, he would reach a chawl where Rani lived. She was his office building watchman's distant cousin. Poor girl! She must be so worried about me, Nagappa thought. In the last few months I've known her, she has grown really fond of me. He wondered if he had moved away from Rani from the time he had become friendly with Mary. His relationship with Rani was one which needed no language. She spoke broken Hindi. But she giggled more than she spoke. One day, she had expressed through gestures that she belonged to no one but him, and had slowly taken him to the crescendo of pleasure.

He now stood at the crossroads of Sandhurst Road, Queens Road and Girgaum Road. He looked up and saw giant movie posters staring at him. But they didn't make any sense, like disjointed fragments of a story. His mind was in disarray. 'Saab, please.' A cobbler on the roadside gestured Nagappa to move, as he was obstructing his business.

Nagappa was jolted from his thoughts. Making up his mind about something, he quickly crossed the road and ran and caught a bus standing at the Opera House bus stop. He climbed to the upper deck and sat down with a feeling of having disentangled himself from something. Only when he bought a ticket to Bengal Chemicals at Worli and got the change back from the conductor did he realize he was going to Sitaram's house. He felt he had triumphed over the earlier temptation to visit Rani. But along with it came the question of why he was trying to stay away from her. Though this bothered him, he tried to tell himself that even otherwise, he visited her only once in a while. And by now, her cousin must've told her I haven't been coming to work. Maybe she'll think I've gone out of Bombay, he reasoned. But he had lost the peace of mind he had momentarily gained.

30

Nagappa woke up reminding himself it was Saturday and Shrinivasa had invited him home for lunch. He had premonitions about it. His mind was being pulled in different directions. Yesterday, when he went to Sitaram's house after somehow managing to get into the bus, Sitaram's door was locked. 'Damn you, you SOB 2!' he had cursed, and stuck a note to the lock telling Sitaram he would meet him on Tuesday morning at his office. On his way back home, again via the Opera House, the agonizingly familiar view from the bus—sights and landmarks he saw every day on his way to and back from work—had filled him with both a strange kind of hope and desolation. They now seemed like an old friend who refused to recognize him. His heart had felt heavy. A few months back, a friend of his had written an article in an English weekly about Kannada short stories. But there wasn't even a mention of his name in it. It had deeply hurt him. He kept buying the magazine for weeks, hoping someone would write about this glaring omission. But not one person had reacted. A few of his colleagues had asked him pointedly about it. Maybe no one remembered his short stories. As far as Kannada literature was concerned, he had ceased to exist three years ago.

The series of huge buildings of the Glaxo Laboratories, Poddar Hospital, the Japanese Buddha temple, Haji Ali in the distance, the Forjett Hill beyond and the new skyscrapers that had recently sprung up around it—all, all of them seemed to have turned their backs on him, refusing to acknowledge his existence. He had got down at the Flora Fountain stop, feeling like a dead man walking among the living—invisible to others. A deathlike pall seemed to hang over the city. Even the water gushing from the ornate fountain had failed to rejuvenate him. He walked mechanically with the milling crowd towards the Churchgate Station and reached the Asiatic Restaurant he had been planning to visit these last couple of days, ate something there and reached home late. Arjunrao was standing in the corridor, waiting for him. 'If you aren't too tired . . .' he began.

'Can't it wait till morning? I'm really sleepy. And I must tell you I've started believing in these weekly predictions,' Nagappa had replied, unlocking his door. Arjunrao had lingered for a bit and finally said, 'Have your tea with us in the morning.' Remembering it, Nagappa got up and quickly brushed his teeth and got ready. Just then, Arjunrao knocked. Nagappa followed him to his house, and was relieved to know that the old woman had gone to her younger son's house in Dadar's Hindu Colony. Arjunrao's wife served tea and *batate pohe*. He praised the pohe and asked for a second helping. Arjunrao's wife looked pleased. 'How long are you on leave?' she asked. Before he could reply, Arjunrao interrupted, 'What about your novel? Have you finished it?' Nagappa wanted to say: 'I've not even begun to write it. The mess in my office itself has become a long and complicated story. I need to deal with it first. I'll probably go back to work in a couple of days.' But sensing their questions were not as innocent as they sounded, and inviting him for breakfast had some ulterior motive, instead, he said: 'I'm afraid the novel is turning out to be twice as long as I'd expected. Let me see. I may have to extend my leave . . .' He was surprised by his own lies.

He got back home. Janaki's door was still locked. He began to get ready to go to Shrinivasa's house. While shaving, he wondered about the locked door, but didn't want to read too much into it. As he bathed, he decided to wear the same cream-coloured trousers and the dark blue shirt he had worn the other day. For no reason, he recalled Chetana, with her dimpled cheeks and dazzling smile and Saraswati's fugitive eyes. He thought of taking two packets of chocolate—one for Chetana and another for Saraswati, if he happened to see her. After his bath, as he was combing his hair, he remembered Shrinivasa's wife, Sharada. It struck him that Diana's description of him—the sweet, sad face— suited Sharada more. The few times he had briefly glanced at her, he had seen a shadow of pain and regret in her eyes.

As always, he had already worn his sleeved baniyan. The bath towel was still around his waist. In all these years, he hadn't yet gathered the courage to look at his chest in the mirror.

It was not even ten by the time he was ready. He still had another hour to kill. He pulled out a book from his shelf. It was Bernard Malamud's *The Fixer*—a book he had read long back—where, like him, Yakov Bok, the protagonist, is tormented by his captors and subjected to needless suffering.

It scared Nagappa. Of all the books, he had picked this one. Was it a mere coincidence? There you go again! Started your usual morbid litany. Hey, Nagappa, you SOB 1, the great student of science! The firm believer in the Theory of Evolution! Terrified, aren't you? You coward, why do you keep reading meanings into every little thing, and then start shivering in your pants? Nagappa scolded himself.

He knew where this was going. It was a trap. He didn't want to get into another bout of self-defeating arguments. He stepped out, locked the door and resolutely started climbing down the stairs, telling himself it didn't matter if he went to Shrinivasa's house a bit early. Anyway, Shrinivasa hadn't specified a time in his note. He had just said, come home for lunch.

Though he had thought of going to the Opera House stop and taking a bus from there, when he reached the Khetwadi main road, he hailed a cab parked at the kerb. 'Cadel Road, Shivaji Park,' he told the driver as he got in, and started looking out of the window to avoid getting engrossed in his own thoughts. 'Should we go via Nana Chowk or Kemp's Corner?' the cabbie asked, using the usual ploy to find out if the passenger was new to the city. The Nana Chowk route was a shorter one, but it would go via Kennedy Bridge, from where he could see Rani's house. So he asked the driver to take the Kemp's Corner route. The cab passed Prarthana Samaj, the Opera House and Sandhurst Bridge, and turned towards Peddar Road. It was a posh area with tall gulmohar trees with the Malabar Hill on one side. The cab sped along, passing Kemp's Corner—the call girls' haunt—Cadbury-Fry, the Haji Ali Dargah standing on the left on a small island amidst the breaking waters of the sea. The narrow path leading to the dargah was half-submerged in water. The image of the distant shrine and the narrow path with the sea on either side stayed with Nagappa till he reached Shrinivasa's house. 'I should visit the dargah one day, when it's high tide and the pathway is completely under water,' he thought. He had recently heard that two people who had ventured there during high tide had slipped and fallen into the sea, and drowned.

As the cab reached Cadel Road, the driver asked him, 'Where to now?' forcing Nagappa's thoughts away from Haji Ali. He told him to drive ahead and turn left and stop at the hutments near the garage. As he paid and got down, he was shocked to find the entire cluster of huts razed to the ground. He asked the people at the garage what had happened to them. They looked at Nagappa suspiciously. A mechanic covered in grease said, 'Saab, give me your address, I'll arrange it.' Nagappa realized the mechanic thought he was looking for illicit hooch. This made him so angry that he wanted to punch his greasy face, but controlled himself and walked away. He would never be able to see Saraswati again. The space where the huts once stood had left behind marks of coal stoves. He wondered where the uprooted families had gone to and about Saraswati's fate. The thought troubled him.

He didn't recognize the sari-clad young woman who opened the door when he rang the bell. 'Shrinivasa . . .?' he asked, confused. Hearing his voice, Chetana came to the door, flashing her dimpled smile. 'Come in, Kaka, this's my elder sister, Asha, and this little brat's my brother, Kiran,' she introduced. 'They came back from our village yesterday.'

Nagappa couldn't believe his eyes. Asha, who was about seventeen, was a younger version of her mother—the same flawless complexion and long, glistening, wavy hair, which she had left loose to dry. The uncombed thick strands swirled down her graceful back. A faint fragrance of shampoo wafted from her. She was wearing a deep green sari with a matching sleeveless blouse. Nagappa stared, mesmerized. He was prodded back to reality when she blushed a deep pink under his gaze. 'Hello, Asha, hello, Kiran,' he said, pinching their cheeks affectionately. 'And how are you, my naughty one?' he asked Chetana, giving her the packets of chocolate. 'For all of you,' he smiled, including all three in his glance.

He took his shoes off, went into the living room and sat on one of the sofas. Sharada appeared at the kitchen door, smiled and went back. Nagappa was thrilled at the way the three children sat around him, looking at him with genuine affection. 'Appa's taking a shower and Ajji has come from the village,' Chetana said.

Ajji! Nagappa was surprised—Paddakka from his story! Is this why Shrinivasa has invited me? He was uneasy about meeting Shrinivasa's mother after all these years. He hoped Shrinivasa wouldn't say anything to provoke him in front of the children.

Shrinivasa, realizing Nagappa had come, called out to Chetana to show him to a room. 'Ask Kaka to change into a lungi and get comfortable,' he shouted from the bathroom.

Chetana gave him a lungi and showed him to one of the rooms. 'Kaka, you look smart today!' she smiled, indicating his clothes.

'Really? Then let me not change,' he said, but went into the room. He slipped out of his trousers and wound the lungi around his waist. He decided he would take his shirt off only if Shrinivasa insisted. He was wearing a banyan with sleeves anyway. He had never worn a sleeveless one in his life. And Shrinivasa's conversations usually began with such trivial matters—clothes, cuisine, furniture. This SOB 1 can hold forth like an expert for hours on saris and jewellery. And he literally drools obscenely when discussing food, lecturing on the relative merits of *sambar poha* and *ambode*. Pig! Nagappa vented his irritation. Shrinivasa looked like one, too, with his short, podgy body, a heavy paunch, a thick neck on which sat an oversized head. A flat nose with flared nostrils, small eyes and thick lips completed the picture. Sometimes, when he was in a mood, he would shave off his rotund head and leave a small pigtail behind. Thankfully, he had grown his hair now. And his clothes? He usually wore a faded pair of khaki shorts which refused to go up his waist, and an old-fashioned shirt. But on rare occasions, he surprised everybody by sporting the latest trend. But they looked absurd on him.

Nagappa stood at the window. This was a different room. It didn't have a view of the sea, but overlooked the garage and the adjacent space cleared of hutments. From above, he could see signs of activity. Parts of the vacant space had been dug up. It looked like a building was coming up there. So much had happened within a week! He would never see Saraswati again. He recalled the fear in her eyes when they looked straight into his, and once again felt deeply disturbed. He was suddenly struck by another, seemingly unrelated thought that came in its wake: Asha was not Sharada's first child—born out of wedlock. It was nearly twenty years since Shrinivasa's marriage. Asha was not more than seventeen. What had happened to *that* child? Was she given away? Weren't there rumours that the child had died within a few months of birth? Had he really heard it or was he imagining it? Why this amnesia? Was it because he had been bewitched by Sharada's untarnished beauty and the shadow of despair in her eyes, that prevented him from remembering anything sordid about her past life? Oh, god, how many more doors am I going to bang shut like this? he asked himself. How many doors have I not quietly closed, not wanting to remember things, or forced to forget, bound in knots by one thing or another?

Nagappa didn't know how long he stood there. Shrinivasa pushed the door left slightly ajar, came in and placed his heavy hand on Nagappa's shoulder. 'What're you staring at?' he asked, and laughed for no reason. As if to cover his hollow laughter, he began to speak fast: 'There was a slum the last time you were here. Gave 5000 rupees each to those bastards and evicted them . . . spent 50,000 to get rid of them . . . peanuts for this kind of land. We're planning to build a five-storey building like this one there under the same cooperative society. Six months from now, you won't be able to recognize the place. I'm the president of the managing committee of the society. It took six months just to get all the gutless bastards on the committee on board for this project. Otherwise, a building would already be standing there by now. By the way, your company has booked three big apartments in it! So, I have a business relationship with your company now. And your Bandookwala . . . have yet to come across a thorough gentleman like him! Really large-hearted guy! All business dealings clean and above board. Will tell you everything in detail later. There's still time for lunch. Amma has come, or we could've had some first-class beer. No alcohol was allowed in the house when our old cook was here, too. Remember Achyuta, our cook? Very strict! We were a bit scared of him the few months he was here. Strange fellow. Don't know what happened . . . the very next day after you left, he went away without telling anyone. He must've left early in the morning. Doesn't stick to one place for more than a month, it seems. Has travelled across the country . . . lived in remote villages. Looks like you made an impression on him . . . kept asking about you the day you went back, and then vanished in the morning. Didn't seem to know how to read and write. Anyway, Amma's waiting to see you . . . after all these years. All the kids are at home today. Sharada has made *ambode* for starters. Come, let's go to the hall.' Shrinivasa led Nagappa out of the room.

Is this man, who speaks with such warmth and easy familiarity with me, plotting something behind my back? Nagappa wondered. He wasn't sure. It was always like this with Shrinivasa. But Nagappa was thinking of Achyuta. The suspicion he had about him earlier was solidifying into certainty. He wanted to ask Shrinivasa something more about him, but changed his mind.

'Let me meet Paddakka!' he said, trying to show an eagerness he didn't feel.

'Aren't you feeling warm in that shirt? Change into a kurta if you want,' Shrinivasa suggested.

'Chetana said I look smart in this shirt, so I'll keep it on,' Nagappa smiled, as they went into the living room.

Chetana and Kiran, who were waiting for Nagappa, ran towards him, 'Kaka, let's go downstairs . . . the roses in our garden . . .'

'Wait, let Kaka have some tea first,' Shrinivasa said brusquely. As if on cue, they ran to the kitchen. Asha must be helping her mother with lunch. But where *was* Paddakka? Nagappa had begun to feel uneasy at the prospect of coming face to face with her.

'Sit,' Shrinivasa said, handing him a few magazines. 'Haven't said my prayers yet after bath . . . will be back by the time tea's ready.' He too, disappeared inside.

Nagappa sat alone, looking around the expensively decorated living room. Feeling uncomfortable under the fan, he moved to another sofa. Unable to understand the rising uneasiness within, he flipped through one of the magazines Shrinivasa had given him, without really registering anything. A door opened behind him. Subconsciously aware that that was the door he had expected to open, he looked around and saw a shrunken figure, which said, 'Who, Nagappaaa?'

Nagappa stood bolt upright, shivering slightly. He had goosebumps all over him, and barely managed to say, 'Paddakka?' He couldn't believe his eyes. Was it a human figure walking towards him, he wondered. Suddenly, a wizened old creature beyond description, that no student of evolution could ever have imagined, stood before him. What sent a shiver down his spine was not that Paddakka had turned into this ghoulish creature, but the recognition that the creature he faced was, indeed, Paddakka. The stick-like figure wound haphazardly in a red sari could probably be called human only because of the gnarled, spindly hands and feet sticking out from the red blob. The round, hairless head and ears had been completely covered with one end of the sari. The small exposed space had remnants of a nose and hollowed-out eyes and a gash of a mouth from which jutted out a few blackened stumps of fangs. From this gash emerged some sounds: 'Did you recognize meee? Sit. Not seen you in years . . . told Shrinivasa to call you home . . .'

Nagappa slumped down on the sofa. He found it impossible to stand. He felt the breakfast he had had at Arjunrao's house suddenly coming to his mouth at the sight of this grotesque reality in all its vivid ugliness. The figure collapsed on the floor at the edge of the carpet, forming a misshapen lump, and stared at him unblinkingly with beady eyes, or something that resembled eyes, as the black stumps of teeth clamped on the loosely hanging lower lip in intense scrutiny.

'Everyone in Gokarna keeps talking about the palatial house our Shrinivasa lives in. Thought I'll see it once before I die . . .' Nagappa couldn't bear to see her as the half-coherent words slid out of her slobbery mouth. He suspected that Shrinivasa had deliberately left him and the old lady alone together for some reason. It couldn't be a coincidence. He looked around helplessly. Just then, the two girls brought trays of tea and snacks and started arranging them on the dining table.

'Kaka, please come and have the ambode when they're still hot. Appa will join you,' Asha invited. It was the first time she had spoken to him directly. She had a sweet voice. Like Chetana, she had a dazzling smile and her eyes sparkled when she spoke. Though the two sisters resembled each other in this regard, Asha had inherited her mother's beauty. A girl on the threshold of womanhood, and aware of her charms, she looked all the more attractive.

'Come, Kaka,' Chetana insisted.

'Go ahead, get started. Shrinivasa must be finishing his prayers,' the old woman lisped. Nagappa got up and sat on the chair Chetana had pulled out for him. From where he sat, he couldn't avoid looking at the old woman. She was still sizing him up with her beady eyes. He couldn't move elsewhere, as the girls stood leaning against chairs on either side. He found it difficult to swallow even a morsel. Just then, Shrinivasa came and sat opposite him, partially shielding him from her gaze. Even then, as he bit into the ambode and sipped his tea, he found the girls looking at him affectionately and felt suffocated. What he had just experienced when he first saw Paddakka was still sinking in. Shrinivasa had begun to babble, 'It must be years since you saw Amma.' The fan overhead creaked on. From the garage came the monotonous clang of a hammer hitting an iron rod. There was incessant traffic outside. The grating sounds assaulted his senses and obliterated the soothing rhythm of the sea.

Nagappa broke into a sweat, either because of the spicy chutney or the steaming hot tea. He wiped his neck with a napkin on the table. 'Kaka, why don't you take your shirt off if you're feeling hot?' Chetana asked, and added mischievously, 'Just now in the kitchen, Asha was praising your broad chest . . .' Asha blushed and twisted Chetana's ear.

'Really?!' Nagappa asked, trying not to look flustered. 'But you said you liked my shirt. So I won't take it off.'

'Also, his doctor has advised him not to expose his chest under the fan as he catches cold easily,' Shrinivasa butted in.

Nagappa couldn't understand the reason for Shrinivasa repeating the explanation he had given him last week.

As he got up from the table, he prayed he wouldn't have to sit in front of Paddakka again. But Shrinivasa said, 'The girls have planned to play rummy with you after lunch. I'll join you. For now, you chat with Amma. I'm sure you two have lots to talk about. Who knows, you might find some raw material for another story. Amazing how many things from the past are lying locked up in Amma's memory!'

The girls began to clear the table. Sharada peeped out of the kitchen, asking, 'Where's Kiran? Hasn't he finished his bath yet?' and disappeared. Nagappa felt this was an excuse, and she had actually come to get a glimpse of him. He thought their eyes met briefly, which unsettled him.

'Sit,' said Shrinivasa, indicating the sofa near Paddakka. 'Her eyesight is still good, she's a bit hard of hearing, though. Amma, you've been saying you've lots to talk to Nagappa. Go on. Meanwhile, I'll finish some work.' He sat on a chair at the other end of the room and picked up some files from the corner table.

Now there was no doubt in Nagappa's mind that this act of bringing him face-to-face with Paddakka was a pre-planned ruse. And she hadn't come on her own. Shrinivasa had deliberately got this ripe old woman all the way to Bombay for a specific purpose. Something had been set in motion, though what it was wasn't yet apparent. There were wheels within grinding wheels. The very past I've been trying to run away from all my life is confronting me now in the form of this old woman—this wizened old lump of flesh on the threshold of death, Nagappa thought. He shuddered when he saw the same old cruel streak of vengeance in her skeletal eyes he remembered from long ago. He was startled by the brutal frenzy to kill in someone about to die.

31

Nagappa sat in front of Paddakka, prepared for the onslaught. No one spoke for a while. Shrinivasa had buried himself in a file, pretending to be busy. Paddakka stared at Nagappa with unblinking eyes. Nagappa tried to bring himself to believe it was a human being that was regarding him with such intense interest. Probably because of his inability to do so, he suddenly had a strange feeling that this inscrutable, penetrating gaze, incomprehensible to his conscious mind, was reaching down to the very roots of his being. He instinctively wrapped his arms tightly around his chest. 'Why don't you switch the fan off if you're feeling cold?' the figure in front asked. Nagappa jumped at the sudden sound that shattered the fraught silence. 'Oh, sorry, I forgot the fan isn't good for you,' Shrinivasa said, feigning to be momentarily distracted, got up and switched it off and went back to his files. Everything was quiet again.

Nagappa's nerves were taut. He decided to break the tension. 'How old is Paddakka now? Crossed seventy, right?' he asked, irked by his unsteady voice.

Paddakka, who was waiting to be prodded, began to lisp, spewing spit, 'You must be joking! Do I look seventy to you?'

'Amma's nearly ninety,' Shrinivasa interrupted. (The SOB's attention was here all the time!)

'In six months, I'll be ninety and running ninety-one. But why're you bothered about *my* age? I've been thinking about *yours*. You aren't getting younger. Don't you have plans to get married? Is there a shortage of pretty girls in *your* caste?'

The strange, savage beast has begun to gnash its teeth, Nagappa thought. After sitting quietly on its haunches in wait, it's finally preparing to pounce. Despite the mid-noon heat and the airless room, Nagappa shivered. But steadied himself, relieved that Paddakka had come straight to the crux of the matter. Before Nagappa could respond, 'Amma! Why all this now?' Shrinivasa said, pretending to be alarmed. 'Is it right to speak of his caste after inviting him home for lunch? And who's bothered about such things in this day and age?'

What infuriated Nagappa more than Shrinivasa's hypocrisy was his shrill, self-righteous voice that cracked, as he tried to take a high moral ground. 'Is something wrong with your throat, Shrinivasa? Shall I ask Chetana to get a glass of water (You, son of a whore!)? Was the chutney too spicy for you?' he asked, not attempting to hide his anger.

Nagappa's impertinence had touched a raw nerve. Shedding all pretence, Shrinivasa stood up, violently tossing the files to the floor. The pen flew across the room. 'Chetanaaa! Water!' he shouted angrily, gasping for breath. Probably forewarned of such a face-off, the children had disappeared somewhere. Sharada, who must have been listening from the kitchen, came out running. Shrinivasa glared at her, and forgetting he had asked for water, bellowed,

'Who asked you to come here with your ill-fated face? Get out of my sight!' Though it began as a loud scream, it ended in a soft screech, as his voice shook with rage. Sharada quietly went back. The deep anguish on her face didn't escape Nagappa. Though he had decided to finally confront Shrinivasa, no matter what the consequence, it made him momentarily hold himself back.

Shrinivasa was pacing the floor, unable to control himself enough to say something coherent. Probably, he couldn't find words harsh enough to voice his anger, which had sprung from some bestial depths that Nagappa had tapped. Nagappa looked at Paddakka. She too, seemed to be searching for words, as she rocked back and forth, her sunken eyes spewing a lifetime of rage and bitterness. The scenario in front of him, though disgusting, looked so absurdly preposterous that Nagappa wanted to laugh out loud. Unable to control himself, he walked to the kitchen, unaware of what he was doing. Sharada looked at him with frightened eyes. Nagappa suddenly realized that it was the first time they were standing like this, facing each other alone. She spoke first: 'The children have gone downstairs. I think he wants some water . . .' She poured a glass of water from a jug, handed it to him and said, 'Lunch will be ready in about half an hour.'

Shrinivasa was sitting on the sofa, huffing, when Nagappa came out. 'Drink some water; it might help,' Nagappa said, placing the glass on the teapoy. He picked up the pen still lying on the floor and gave it to Shrinivasa. 'I know the reason for inviting me today is neither for lunch nor to meet your mother. But what I don't know is why you hate me so much. I've never come in the way of your success. But I've come here prepared for everything. And Paddakka, as for the question of my caste . . .'

Shrinivasa's nostrils flared. He started to say something, but collapsed back on the sofa, unsure if the words would come out, paused, and began, 'Before pointing fingers at others' character, look at your own . . .' His voice was gruff.

'Leave my character alone. What about *yours* . . .?'

'Ha! I know where you come from, you son of a whore, even if *you* don't! Ask Amma, she knows everything about you . . . your entire family . . .'

'I certainly will. That's why I'm here. Not for the feast you've invited me for! But beware! If you get down to gutter language, I'll knock your teeth out! Don't think I'm joking. I repeat—I've come prepared for everything. Don't think I don't know you've joined hands with my company to conspire against me. I was anyway coming here to get the truth out of you. Good you invited me instead.'

Shrinivasa turned pale.

'Who are you to threaten my son like this? Knock his teeth out, indeed!' Paddakka screamed. 'Are you man enough to even lay your finger on him? He has come up on his own by sheer hard work. Today, he has earned a name and position for himself in our community, not just in Bombay, but even back home. He's a big man even in the Partagaali Matha . . . Gokarna Matha . . . knows the high priests there. And you can't bear to see his success . . . the respect he commands, his beautiful family . . . his wife and children. You who visit cheap prostitutes and wander the streets like a bull on the loose, what do you know of family life? What reputation do *you* have? What position? But what's the use of blaming you? It's in your blood! Born to lowly scum! Maybe you don't know this—your mother was nothing but a Kalavanta girl . . . not from our caste . . . used to dance at the Mangesh temple in Goa for money, and maybe even offer other favours . . . she, her mother, grandmother . . . two-penny prostitutes . . . the whole lot!'

As Paddakka spat out each word through her slobbery mouth, her tongue darting in and out, Shrinivasa sat, his face buried in his hands, afraid to look at the effect they were having on Nagappa. The words did impact Nagappa, but not the way Shrinivasa had imagined. Nagappa was listening to her with rapt attention, with a smile on his face. 'Why did you stop, Paddakka? Go on, spill some more juicy details. Shrinivasa must've told you—I'm writing a novel . . . a *big* one about the wonderful, spotless history of all the bigwigs of our community (with big asses). What you just told me can be a side story. It'll spice things up! Yes, go on, spew some more venom on my mother, her mother and her mother's mother. And since you know so much about them, I'm beginning to wonder if you too, were somewhere in the neighbourhood . . .'

'You, shameless fellow . . . making fun of me! Don't pretend what I've said doesn't bother you. Joking about it won't wipe out the truth . . . the past . . .'

'How can I say it doesn't affect me, Paddakka, especially when you're telling me all this just to hurt me? But not the way you and Shrinivasa imagine—not for the reasons you think. Yes, my mother was from a Kalavanta family. And my father, who married her despite this, wasn't from one of the respectable Saraswat Brahmin families, as the people of Hanehalli believed. He belonged to some other caste . . . sect . . .'

'Did you *know* this?' Shrinivasa screamed, unable to contain himself. His voice was no longer high-pitched.

'No, I didn't. Santosh Bhavan's Nayak told me you were doing some great research on me and my family.'

Both Shrinivasa and Paddakka were staring at him intently. But Nagappa went on, as if to himself, 'My parents' caste is not important to me. It never was. And especially now, at this age. But what I can't understand is why all of you are trying to use this against me . . . to torment me . . . sinking so low. Anyway, what I was frightened of facing all these days sounds trivial now, even laughable. Everything seems unreal now . . .'

Nagappa realized that Paddakka and Shrinivasa had fallen silent.

'Paddakka, it isn't important that you know which family my mother came from or which caste my father belonged to. It doesn't matter how, where or when you found this out. But what's intriguing is why Shrinivasa has brought you all the way to make you tell this to me. What could be the reason behind it? Why this morbid desire in your ripe old age to reveal all this to me, just to hurt me? As I told you, these matters have no significance. To me they're matters of mere academic curiosity . . .'

No, Nagappa didn't say any of these things. They remained in his head. He saw no need to articulate them. They seemed too trivial. He was surprised by his sudden and complete lack of interest in something he had feared facing all his life. If I have no faith in any of these things, if I no longer attach any importance to them, then what meaning does my enmity with Shrinivasa all these years have? he asked himself. Is my total lack of interest in my lineage, my complete detachment from it, the result of what I had to go through all my life? Is the mental exhaustion I experienced because of it suddenly coming to an end? Or is it because I feel completely drained from it all? Or, more than my parents' caste (it's undebatable that it no longer troubles me), what I'm really terrified of is that this old woman might suddenly put her finger on what has tormented me all my life—that particular raw, vulnerable spot of hurt. I'm petrified that she might know about the fire incident. Does she know about my father torching my shirt? Will she spout it out now? And about my sister getting lost . . . let loose in a crowd? That I had an elder brother? What really happened to him? What's happened *of* him? Will she tell if I provoke her . . . goad her? What if she suddenly did?

What Nagappa did say was not what was on his mind. And when he finally uttered those words, the tone appeared to belong to a Nagappa he was not aware existed till then. 'Look, Shrinivasa, even I don't believe in caste and creed, just as you yourself said you didn't a little earlier. But when I look at it from my father's point of view, from the point of view of the perception that prevailed at the time in a small village like Hanehalli, I feel terribly proud of him. It can't have been easy for a Brahmin to marry a Kalavanta girl. It needed immense courage. Otherwise, it was so easy to promise to marry a girl and get her pregnant and then blame it on her brother-in-law or someone else.'

Shrinivasa's face had turned ashen. He was trembling from head to toe. Unable to utter a word, he let out puffs of air through his flared nostrils. Nagappa realized that when the time came and the situation demanded, even he could turn from the hunted to the hunter. The realization amused him.

Finally, Shrinivasa found his voice. 'Son of a whore! You, son of a bitch!' he bellowed. 'Why do you keep raking up the past and harass me like this? What do you get out of it? Tell me! Tell me, what's your intention? And that Sitaram . . . he's another bloody bastard . . . has no other job but spreading stories about others. He's gone around blabbering to everyone that you're writing a book about me . . . telling *everything*. It seems you've finished half of it. Even Arjunrao said the same thing! When you wrote about Amma, I let it go. You'd written about how poor we were. Yes, we were dirt poor. But what's wrong with that? I've come up the hard way and reached this level! What do you get by dragging me down . . . ruining my life? Yes, I slipped once in life. One mistake, and you keep digging up the muck. I've regretted it . . . made up for it. Don't I deserve a second chance? Why're you hell-bent on spoiling my name like this when the dead girl's sister herself has forgotten about it and moved on? Why do you persist on punishing me? Why so much of hatred towards me? And you don't know the real truth. Don't make me open my mouth. I'm not a writer like you. If I was, I'd have shown what kind of character *you* have. Nagappaaa, I'd have really shown you . . .'

Shrinivasa's voice tapered off. It had grown from an angry outburst to a poignant snivel, almost a whine. Paddakka was incensed. Unable to get up without help, she slithered close to Nagappa, scraping her bottom on the floor, threw a pitiful look at her son and began her tirade. But her gaze was fixed elsewhere: 'Shrinivasaaaa, don't act like a bloody wimp! Have you lost your manhood? Don't become spineless . . . don't become impotent . . . don't become like your father! Shrinivasa, tell him everything. Let me see if he has the guts to hear the truth . . . about his father, his mother, his shameless aunt, his brother, his sister. Why should *we* be afraid of anything? This ill-begotten bastard can't stand you coming up in life! Spreading false stories about you, is he? Don't you have the guts to shut his worm-infested mouth? You made me tell you this third-rate fellow's history all night, and when the time has come to throw all the dirt back at him, you're whimpering like a coward! Was it for this you brought this old woman all the way from the village? Bundled me into a cab and dragged me here for nothing? Did I come here with my rattling old bones at this age to see you like this?'

Nagappa couldn't bear to listen to her any longer. Though she was speaking a human language, it appeared beyond human comprehension. Her words had stopped affecting him the way she hoped they would. He got up and walked quickly to the room where he had left his trousers. As he entered the room, he didn't recognize his own feelings. Was it anger? Derision? Loathing? Revulsion? Horror? Perhaps he had become too numb to resonate with any emotions. He felt drained and was left with something unnamed and unnameable.

He was about to change back into his trousers when Shrinivasa came in, bolting the door behind him. He looked pale and frightened. Though Nagappa knew something unforeseen would unfold when he came here in the morning, he hadn't expected Shrinivasa to react like this under pressure. He looked a wreck. Nagappa was taken aback. He realized that though Shrinivasa had used his old mother to reveal the sordid past he had feared facing all his life, in the very moment of that revelation, he appeared to have been unwittingly forced to confront something frightening about himself. It struck Nagappa that for some mysterious reason, he was a living symbol of all that Shrinivasa had feared all along. The Shrinivasa who stands before me now is not the same Shrinivasa I'd seen twelve days back. In fact, he's not even the same man I saw this morning. This SOB 1, who threatened to expose my past and smear my name, is himself scared of something, Nagappa thought, looking at Shrinivasa's cadaverous face. Even as I look at him now, I can see life draining out of him! He's collapsing.

This was an unexpected turn of events for Nagappa—that *he* personified his adversary's deep-rooted fears and inner demons he had been running away from! He slipped out of the lungi. As he wore his trousers, it suddenly struck him: Could it be that the reason for Shrinivasa's intense suffering and his inexplicable fear is his inability to capture them in words? Is it his inadequacy to articulate what he's going through that makes his suffering all the more unbearable? Nagappa remembered Eric Berne: 'Our experiences are formed as a series of images before we learn any language.' What if they remain as images without getting translated into words? Is it possible that these images, unable to find an escape through a linguistic expression, are still haunting Shrinivasa? Though the realization of such a possibility made Nagappa feel a pang of sympathy for Shrinivasa, who stood staring at him, it died when he thought of what he had been going through these last few days.

Nagappa didn't break his silence. He took his comb out of his pocket and began combing his hair with a kind of detachment. This slow, casual movement, this nonchalance and this obvious intention to walk away from the battlefield without a word unnerved Shrinivasa. He slowly began, 'What about lunch . . .?' He couldn't continue. And before Nagappa realized it, Shrinivasa went down on his knees and held his feet tight. 'Nagappaaa, I'm falling at your feet. Don't be so ruthless. Don't destroy all that I've built for years.' It took a moment for Nagappa to realize that this wasn't play-acting, and that Shrinivasa was genuinely frightened. He was mortally scared of something. And the fear was making him behave in this absurdly irrational manner. Shrinivasa's face was white and sweaty. His hands, which now held on to Nagappa's bare ankles were clammy. He was trying to look straight into Nagappa's eyes to draw his attention.

Nagappa managed to free himself from Shrinivasa's clutches and walked to the window and began to look out. His eyes registered the images, but his brain refused to recognize them.

He heard a noise behind him. The SOB must be saying something or speaking to himself, Nagappa thought. They appeared to be incoherent sounds that didn't resemble any human language. Nagappa's hair stood on end. He tried to focus: 'I've suffered so much in life . . . worked so hard for my success. But I've never grovelled in front of anybody . . . never fallen at anyone's feet. But I've done it today. Yes, I agree, you think our lot and I are vindictive, obstinately holding on to old grudges, adamantly going after what we want. But, in many ways, I don't have your courage, Nagappa. I cannot bear to hear anything bad about my family, my lineage, my character . . . the abject poverty of my childhood. You need to know why. I haven't studied psychology like you. I had no respect for my father. When he committed suicide . . . drowned himself at Kotiteertha, I was relieved . . . thought it was good riddance. I've no hesitation in admitting this. But when I read it in your story, you've no idea how frightened I was. Stumbling upon a part of my life in cold print was unbearable torture. I alone know what I went through. You gave all the minute details of his death without even changing my father's name. You analysed it threadbare. My father, who belonged to some Brahmin community ghetto in an unknown, anonymous village in the backwaters . . . and I feared a minor incident like his suicide becoming common knowledge. I feared the truth. I don't know why, but I've always been scared of you. I don't have the guts to open up about my secrets in front of others. I bury them deep within me. I can do any damn thing as long as I'm sure no one'll find out. I know that you know many things I've hidden from others. But what about things I think you don't know? What if you know those too? What if you already know everything? What if there's a possibility of you finding out everything? I'm petrified at the thought. This monstrous suspicion of what if you know everything has been troubling me from the time I heard you're writing a story about me. I don't know why it's tormenting me like this. Yes, it's true that Appa drowned in Kotiteertha. But do you know why? Do you know how? Do you even know if it was suicide? Do you believe so? I think you know something about Sharada's past. But what about her firstborn child? About its father? I'm not so much scared of what you know about my past. What I'm *really* scared of is your terrible habit of raking it up. I was extremely upset when you wrote about Amma. But now it seems you're writing about Netravati's death . . . It seems you've already finished half the book. Sitaram told me you'd come from Hyderabad to Bombay only to write this book. And that's

the reason why you're still living in that dirty old chawl in
Khetwadi . . . in that same old room! Even Arjunrao told
me the same thing. Even Santosh Bhavan's Nayak. All these
bastards are jealous of me. They deliberately scare me by
telling me all sorts of things. That bastard Sitaram described
Khemraj Bhavan where I lived with you . . . the Golpitha and
Khetwadi area in front of my rich guests when he had come
here for Satyanarayana pooja . . . gave all the spicy details,
smacking his lips. It seems you haven't even changed the
names in your book. Is it true? Nagappaaa, why this hatred
towards me? Why so much hostility? Why this novel after all
these years? Why're you bent on destroying me? Why now,
Nagappa, when I'm rising high in society. Today, I have a
position among the people of my community. I'm going to
be the president of the Saraswat Brahmin League. I've stood
for the local municipal election, and, god-willing, I will stand
for the assembly election. I've earned a lot of money by my
own hard work. I've also started a transport business two
years ago. That's how I have business dealings with your
company. I went to your office saying I'm your friend. I
used your reference. That's when I met Khambata . . . total
fraud guy . . . all fraud business. His wife and your DMD's
wife are partners in my company. I don't know how many
people know about this in your office. But that's how we
got a three-year contract for transporting all the company's
goods . . . all through personal influence. The person who
signed the contract is your Hyderabad factory manager. But
it also has your DMD Bandookwala's initials. He has now
been caught in some deep shit! He's been caught smuggling
out ten tonnes of raw material from the factory to a big
businessman in Bombay. There was an acute shortage of

this stuff for a while because of some technical snag in the
factory manufacturing it. Its market value rose ten times
its real price. Did you know Bandookwala and his chelas
reported that the raw material got destroyed in a fire in the
factory just to cover up the missing inventory? But their plan
went horribly wrong when the fire got out of control and
three workers were killed. Somehow, someone got to know
of all this and sent copies of an anonymous letter revealing
the facts to the Indian and foreign directors and company
shareholders. Bandookwala thinks you're the brain behind it.
And this fake inquiry is their evil game plan to shut you up.
Don't think your MD suddenly going to America has nothing
to do with all this. If pushed against the wall, they're even
ready to make you the fall guy. Beware, you could be the
sacrificial goat! If their cover-up job fails, you're their prime
target! Only I know to whom they've sold the smuggled
consignment. That's why your company has booked three
flats in the cooperative housing society I've started. They've
paid me hard cash for all three flats and promised to make
me your company's director some day . . .'

Shrinivasa found it difficult to capture in a few minutes
all that he had gone through in weeks, months and years
on end. When he opened his mouth to say all this, his lips
moved soundlessly. Even when some scraps of sound came
out, they were in the form of grunts and snarls and moans
that resembled some indecipherable private language.

Nagappa tried to make sense of the noises coming
from Shrinivasa's contorted face. 'Say something, you son
of a bitch! How long do I keep waiting for you to disgorge
everything! Why are you whimpering like a hurt dog?'
Nagappa screamed inwardly. Unable to bear the sight in

front of him, and to hide his own shaking hands, he held the window grille tightly and looked out. He didn't know how long he stood like this, but as the whining behind him grew louder, he knew that he couldn't take it any more. Stepping into the living room too was impossible. It had lost its familiar air and become the scene of an ugly confrontation with an old woman whose toxic innards had been laid bare before him. Not knowing how to escape from the situation, he turned around. Shrinivasa was sitting on the edge of the bed. He looked like someone who had suddenly lost all his youth and turned into a wizened old man. He stood up unsteadily and once again fell at Nagappa's feet in a heap. 'Please don't write a story about me, Nagappaaa,' he begged. 'For god's sake, don't write that novel. Name your price . . . whatever you want . . . if you want . . . if you want . . .' The next few words sounded garbled, which the speaker himself couldn't fathom. But Nagappa heard and understood every word clearly. He pulled himself away from Shrinivasa's clutches, opened the door, ran down the stairs and out of the building.

He stumbled a few times, but wanted to flee from the place as far away as he possibly could. Fear and revulsion were the two compelling and competing forces propelling him forward. He didn't realize he was running barefoot. His mind hadn't given him time to pick up his shoes and socks as he fled.

He was still running like someone in mortal danger, chased by something monstrous, as he reached Cadel Road, unmindful of people stopping and staring at him. When he finally came to a halt, panting for breath, he was dripping with sweat, his hair was dishevelled and his feet were bruised. The sun was overhead. He forgot he was hungry.

The only thing he was aware of was that he had to reach home as quickly as possible. The urge was so strong that when a cab appeared suddenly before him, it took him a few seconds to recognize what it was. 'Saab, do you need a cab?' the driver asked. Nagappa nodded mechanically, opened the door, flung himself on the seat and closed his eyes. Fearing they would open on their own, he closed them tight with his palm.

'Where to, saab?' the driver asked, turning the metre down. He somehow managed to say, 'Khetwadi 7th Lane.' Shrinivasa's stuttered words kept coming back to him. Did he actually say what I thought he said? Nagappa wondered. Did he utter those words? Yes, he really did. There was no doubt about it. As the realization hit him, his stomach began to churn. He asked the driver to quickly park the cab near the kerb, and even before the cab stopped, leaned out of the window and began retching uncontrollably. Fortunately, there were no vehicles on the left side at the time. People standing at the bus stop nearby thought he was drunk and looked away in disgust. Even the driver suspected Nagappa had had too much to drink. Since he had been waiting for long for a passenger, and had finally got someone, he parked the car at a vacant lot on the side of the pavement without complaining. Nagappa's stomach, which had temporarily settled down, heaved when the cab stopped. He flung the door open and threw up violently again. The nausea brought out the vadas he had eaten at Shrinivasa's house, the undigested breakfast, and something resembling tea. Though he thought he had emptied out everything, something bitter and bilious kept rising inside him till he finally felt purged and sat bent over, gasping.

There was no doubt in the driver's mind now that Nagappa had had illicit hooch he couldn't stomach. His messy hair and bloodshot eyes confirmed it. And he had found the man wandering the streets barefoot! 'Bastard! Drunk in the middle of the day! Thoo!' he cursed softly, holding his hand to his nose. Nagappa closed the cab door, took out his kerchief and wiped his face and said, 'Let's go,' in a weak voice. The driver sat motionless, his hand still covering his nose. Realizing the driver hadn't heard him, Nagappa signalled him to go.

'The stuff mustn't have been good,' the driver said, starting the cab.

Though his impertinence both irritated and amused Nagappa, he was too weak to respond, and stretched his legs and closed his eyes. As all that had happened threatened to rewind before him, he opened his eyes and sat upright. He had no courage left in him to think about anything. He was scared that even if he picked a random thread, it would wind back to the price Shrinivasa had offered to stop him from writing the novel. And regurgitating it could lead to another bout of retching. He had to somehow stop himself. Nagappa held the edges of the seat tight. He bit his lower lip hard, clamped his mouth shut and opened his eyes wide. The driver observed these antics from the rear-view mirror. Their eyes met for a brief moment. Nagappa smiled sheepishly.

The driver smiled back. 'Which place?' Nagappa asked.

'I'm from near Mangalore.'

'Oh, really? Kannada or Konkani?'

'Tulu,' he replied. 'But I can speak both Kannada and Konkani.'

Nagappa introduced himself and told him he was a Kannada writer from North Kannada district. The driver didn't know the names of any writers, but nodded respectfully at Nagappa.

'The vomiting wasn't because of liquor . . .' Nagappa tried to explain.

'Sorry, sir, forget it,' the driver said, blushing.

Nagappa was about to tell him what he had written, when his stomach began to heave and churn again. Since there was nothing left inside, he ended up making empty belching and puking noises.

'Maybe food poisoning, sir,' the driver said sympathetically.

Nagappa shook his head. He tried to tell him what had happened, but his lips began to twitch uncontrollably. What could he tell the driver? What possible explanation could he give for this overpowering nausea that had shaken his very being? Could he say his innards had turned inside out because of undigested truth? The thought of it made him want to throw up again. He signalled the driver to pull the cab over to the side again. Nagappa held his sides and bent over. Nothing came out. He felt spasms of pain inside. His throat was hurting. He thought it might be better to take antispasmodic medication. He looked at his watch. It was half past one. By now he would have had his lunch and taken a nap. But when the thought of why he had missed lunch hit him, he threw up, unable to tell the driver to stop. Nagappa felt gallons of liquid come out. When did I drink so much water? he wondered. The cab driver stopped the vehicle, now really worried about his passenger. Since he was from his home state, the driver felt a sense of closeness towards him. 'Sir, if you don't mind, I know a doctor here, near Worli Naka . . . Dr Shetty, from my native place . . .'

Nagappa nodded weakly and collapsed on the seat, shivering.

Dr Shetty was still at the clinic. The driver ran inside and quickly reported about the patient he had brought and helped Nagappa out of the cab and into the consulting room.

'There's nothing wrong with me, doctor. Just psychosomatic complaint,' Nagappa said, worried the reason for it might incite his intestines. 'It looks like my stomach is trying to express things that I cannot in words. Any antispasmodic . . .'

'When you began your self diagnosis, I thought you were a psychologist. But it looks like you dabble in medicine too,' the doctor laughed, and quickly finished his routine examination.

'It seems he's a big writer in Kannada,' the cab driver said.

'Oh, really? What do you write?' the doctor asked, getting a syringe ready. Seeing Nagappa's face twist in pain, the compounder brought an aluminium pan. The doctor quickly gave him the injection and handed him a couple of tablets. 'Have these and take a long nap. If you still don't feel better, come and see me in the evening,' he said brusquely.

Nagappa thanked the doctor and left.

As the injection began to work, his stomach settled a bit and his eyes began to close with exhaustion. He woke up only when the cab entered Khetwadi's 7th Lane. He asked the driver to stop in front of Khemraj Bhavan.

He remembered getting out of the cab, paying the driver, thanking him and going up the stairs. But the rest was like a vague dream seen long ago. Though sapped of all energy, how did I climb the stairs—all thirty-nine steps—that I had counted at some strange moment in the past? Nagappa asked himself. Did anyone see me walking barefoot along the corridor to my room? Did they wonder why I looked like that? Nagappa didn't remember unlocking the door and flopping on the bed.

When he woke up from deep sleep and looked at his watch, it was five in the evening. The first sensation he had was one of acute hunger. His legs were shaking when he stood up. He stumbled to the shelf, took out a tin and found three biscuits still left inside. He devoured them. There was a blackened over-ripe banana in the fruit basket. He ate that too. The water pitcher was empty. He drank straight from the tap. The growl in his stomach quietened down a bit. He thought he would go to the restaurant downstairs after a while, and lay back on the bed, feeling spent.

As if waiting for this moment of pause, the thought he had been avoiding hit him with such force that it shook him physically: This son of a bitch, Shrinivasa—born of the itch that Nadoo Mhaaskeri's Padmanabha Narayana Keni felt in that thing hanging between his thighs, when his weak loins had nothing to do—this bastard born by sheer chance, the son of the vengeful, spiteful Paddakka, who's now a heap of bones, this Shrinivasa, who has inherited her nature of nurturing grudges for long, who now lives as if he has never known poverty, the Shrinivasa, who is valiantly waging a battle to forget where he has come from, the same Shrinivasa, who, while performing the last rites of his father, joked with the priest that he and his lot were born because of his father's insomniac boredom, that same foul-mouthed bastard who sacrificed Netravati's life to test his manhood, who married a pregnant girl to climb up the social ladder and posed as a noble hero, and who now sits on the top rung of that ladder, and has joined hands with Phiroz against me, the Shrinivasa, who is now hunting me down, he who has set out to be the most eminent member of the Saraswat community, who, overnight, has shed his past, or is attempting to, the self-same Shrinivasa who whimpered like a cornered animal, who begged me not to write a novel about him, and tempted me with money, the Shrinivasa who said, 'Name your price, ask whatever you want . . . even Sharada . . .'

Nagappa ran to the sink, scared he would retch again.

32

Nagappa didn't know if he had woken up from deep sleep or if he had passed out. He sat on the chair, his mind completely blank, unable to think, remember or focus on anything. His limbs were weak, like someone who had been ailing for months. He couldn't gauge what time it was from the faint light in the room. He looked at his watch, but couldn't see the dial clearly.

As time passed, he began to recall things: He had swallowed one of the tablets the doctor had given him before lying down. It must have also contained some sedative. It had dulled his mind along with the feeling of nausea. The power to react to anything had drained out of him. With the memory of the tablet came the reason for taking it, and of Shrinivasa, on whom he had heaped a litany of curses, and what had prompted it—the entire chain of events. Though his mind registered all this, it didn't respond with the intensity it earlier had. Nor did his body. The only sensation he had was of hunger. The immediate urge was to eat something.

This spurred him to get up. He wanted to get out of the house before his mind and body gave way. He washed his face, changed, wore his slippers, stepped out, locked the door and quickly climbed down the stairs. He was sweating profusely, exhausted by the minor exertion. Without thinking, he turned to the 6th Lane. The setting sun made him look at his watch in the pale yellow light. It was half past six. He walked like an automaton to the main road, turned towards Prarthana Samaj, and, as if guided by the hand of fate, of all places, walked to Santosh Bhavan. Though he was aware of this, he had lost the will to change the direction of his stride.

He entered Benham Hall Lane. It seemed to wear a mournful look that permeated his senses, and filled him with a nameless angst.

The first thing he did when he sat at his usual table at Santosh Bhavan was to ask the waiter to remove the incense sticks stuck to the window sill behind him. He felt that the strong scent they exuded was the reason for the air of desolation that hung heavy in the fading evening. Though the waiter found this request rather strange, he obeyed out of the respect he had for Nagappa. He came back and asked, 'Uttappa, vadas and upma?'

Nagappa smiled and nodded. 'Bring the upma first, and then uttappa and vadas with coffee. But before that, a fresh lime sharbat with soda. A bit of stomach upset . . .'

'Looking at your face, I thought sir wasn't well,' he said and went to the kitchen.

He came back with a glass of sharbat, that week's *Prajamata* and yesterday's *Samyukta Karnataka*. Nagappa picked up the newspaper and glanced through it, sipping the chilled sharbat. It soothed his nerves and gave him a spurt of energy. He finished all the dishes one by one and the steaming cup of coffee. Though he had been having the same fare at Santosh Bhavan for years, he didn't remember relishing it so much. When he stepped out, leaving a big tip, he felt like going to Chowpatty. The taste of the dishes he had just savoured, his satiated stomach and the prospect of enjoying the cool sea breeze had momentarily mellowed him so much that he didn't notice Nayak sitting at the counter. Nayak, surprised to see Nagappa briskly walking out, asked the waiter to make sure it was him.

It was dusk when he stretched on the sand and gazed at the sea with a sense of quietude. He was oblivious of the bustle around him—*champiwala* with his massage oils, *kulfiwala*, *bhelpuriwala*, *nariyalpaniwala*, raising a din, vending their wares. None of this affected his inner peace. Even the occasional pimps from the nearby red-light area didn't irritate him. His mind was strangely calm. Nagappa did not know whether it was the eerie stillness that descends at the end of a battle or the one that signals its beginning.

The long-drawn-out torment I've undergone will come to an end tomorrow, he thought, impassively, because *I* have decided to end it. I feel no anxiety, no inner turmoil about the final confrontation. Even this—that I'm not filled with apprehension of its outcome—doesn't worry or surprise me. Though what happened in Shrinivasa's house today, despite its intensity, has brought about this calm, I don't even want to ponder over it, for it has lost its urgency, its significance. What this has helped me tap is reserves of my inner strength. What pervades my mind is fearlessness—the supreme confidence that comes from focusing all my energies entirely on this present moment, instead of looking over my shoulder at my past or stretching my hand towards an unseen future and tormenting myself needlessly. I've now decided to give up that futile obsession. And I should never ever loosen my resolve. The way my body violently reacted was not only to Shrinivasa's unthinkable, obscene offer that had opened my eyes to a sordid, horrifying reality, but it was also a rejection of all that which had caused me so much of anguish, held me captive, shackled me to some unnamed fear of the past and the lure of an elusive future . . .

Nagappa lay on his back on the cool sand, gazing at the cloudless sky. His mind refused to dwell on anything. He felt one with the vast universe and the sky above, as if he had submerged himself into it.

What jolted him back to the present was the familiar sound of the distant clock striking eight. He got up and walked homewards.

As he wasn't hungry enough for dinner, he had a glass of hot milk at the dairy downstairs and climbed up the steps. As he unlocked his door, he noticed that the house next door was still locked, and recalled it had been locked when he had left in the evening. He ignored Arjunrao's mother, who lingered at the end of the corridor, trying to draw his attention. It struck him that when he was going down the stairs earlier, she had stood nearby, wanting to engage him in conversation. He had ignored her even then.

When he pushed the door open and switched on the light, he found an envelope on the floor. It was Sunday—no postal delivery. He tore open the envelope and read the note inside. It said that the inquiry had been postponed from Monday to Tuesday. 'Oh, hell!' he cursed. He knew the reason for postponing the inquiry was to break him from inside. Another weapon in this long battle of attrition, he thought, not allowing his resolve to weaken. One more day will not make a difference. Let me see how this trial by fire they're putting me through will finally end. Anyway, truth is on my side. Why not start that long-planned novel on Shrinivasa from tomorrow? Why does Shrinivasa fear me writing the novel *so* much—to the point that even the mere rumour of it has paralysed him? Trying to understand the true face of this irrational fear should become the subject matter of the novel. Nagappa was thrilled at the way his scattered thoughts about it had at last begun to effortlessly coalesce and crystallize. He had found his central theme. He was amused at how the enticement Shrinivasa had offered him to not write the novel was goading him on to write it.

Though he woke up at five in the morning with the intention to start writing, as he lay with his eyes open, his mind had already begun to replay yesterday's chain of events. He knew he was breaking the promise he had made to himself last evening, that he would never look over his shoulder at his past. But then, he also knew this was another one in the long list of innumerable promises and resolutions he had made and broken all his life, under different circumstances. He sighed: If only our resolutions could transform into actions!

Nagappa thought it was strange that more than his mind, it was his body that had reacted violently to the bait Shrinivasa had dangled before him to stop him from writing about his past. Shrinivasa's ambition to rise in life, the fierce contest to climb ladders, had begun to manifest itself as a malady. It had the symptoms of a deep-rooted sickness that had infected his basic sense of morality and decency, where even his wife's honour could be pawned. He was ready to use her as a mere stepping stone. Nagappa had heard that even Khambata had come up in life the same way. It was a mystery how he had managed to marry someone as attractive and ultra-modern as Shireen. It was rumoured that both the MD and the DMD had 'kept' her. Nagappa's mind refused to follow this thread, as Sharada, Asha and Chetana's faces floated before him. His eyes welled up.

To divert his thoughts away from the revulsion he felt at this quagmire of self-aggrandizement and sexual favours, he tried to think of something else. His mind wandered to Janaki. He was acutely aware that no other woman had physically affected him the way she had. So strong was the impact and so intense was his reaction to it that it had taken him to a state beyond the realm of rational and cerebral consciousness. His body had admitted it without any hesitation, inhibition or shame. Nagappa now felt ashamed of himself at the thought of it. Maybe I'm no different from the Shrinivasas, the Patels, the Khambatas and Bandookwalas of this world, he thought. He hurriedly got up to finish his morning ablutions.

If I get cooped up in this hellhole like this without human contact, my mind might sink further to any abysmal depths, he warned himself. I must get out and go somewhere far away from this dingy room, from this filth that foments filthy thoughts, to where the sun shines clean and bright, where the breeze blows, among trees, among greenery, amidst God's creation. I must spend some time outside amidst nature. Maybe we human beings with this big brain imprisoned in a frail body become aware of our humanity only in such rare moments. It doesn't matter if I don't write. I don't even want to read anything. Let me wander aimlessly in the open!

The desire to go adrift spurred Nagappa to get ready. He was filled with enthusiasm.

PART V

33

Finally, the day Nagappa had been waiting for arrived. When he woke up, he felt no sense of anxiety or nervousness. He felt no interest in the inquiry any more. Even this didn't worry him. His only thought was: I had waited for this day, and it's here. There was a sense of stillness in him.

When the car arrived, he got into it looking and feeling unruffled. He had not paid extra attention to his appearance. He was dressed in a sky blue, full-sleeved shirt and black trousers. He had picked up a tie from the stand, but put it back, deciding against it, and left the topmost button open. However, he was in a bit of a quandary while wearing his shoes. He had left his black pair in Shrinivasa's house. He remembered why. But after a moment's pause, he pulled out the brown pair he hadn't worn for a long time and slipped into them, observing with a sense of detachment that they didn't match his trousers. He had combed his hair mechanically, looking at his reflection in the washbasin mirror as though it was someone else's. He felt the man who was sitting in the car going towards the Taj Mahal Hotel was someone else.

He recalled the reflection of his face. Its guileless innocence disturbed him.

When he came out of his ruminations and looked out, they were speeding along Marine Drive with the familiar sight of the sea. On the left, at a distance, were railway tracks with huge playgrounds adjacent to them. There was incessant traffic on both sides. The driver sat in sedate silence, his gaze intently trained on the road ahead, his expression serious, perhaps aware of the gravity of the situation. Nagappa thought of breaking the silence, but didn't know what to say. Tears blurred his eyes. No matter how much he had primed himself to be brave and take the high moral ground, as the destination neared, his courage began to give way to fear and something beyond words. What had been mental torment all these days was actually going to be played out before him. In the very moment of reaching its high point, his long career was in danger of being destroyed. The reason: The innate human instinct to hunt. Reason: Fear becoming second nature. Nagappa, Nagappaaa, you son of a bitch, started the same old rant, haven't you? Stop badgering yourself this way. Stop this nagging habit! You're shit-scared, whether you admit it or not. You know where all this will lead to: What if Phiroz hadn't harboured this hatred against me, what if Shrinivasa hadn't joined hands with Phiroz— nothing but endless, futile 'what if' scenarios. Snap out of it! Get ready!

Nagappa sat straight. The car reached Nariman Point and turned towards Sachivalaya. All around were stately skyscrapers that seemed to have suddenly sprung to their feet and were standing stiff with craning necks. People were hurrying to their work amidst the weaving traffic. Nothing made an impression on him. Feeble resolutions like joining Strand Book Stall as a salesman, opening a newspaper stand in Khetwadi, becoming a village schoolmaster, seemed to be mere daydreams that faded even as they appeared.

The car crossed Regal Cinema and turned towards the Gateway of India on the edge of the waters. It had been ages since he had come here. He could see a few ships in the distance. He jumped when one of them sounded a loud siren. He must have dozed off. He opened his eyes wide to wake himself up.

The car stopped in front of the elegant Taj Mahal Hotel. The driver quickly got out and politely held the door open for Nagappa. As he got down, he noticed that it was not a company car. It was a sleek Mercedes Benz. The driver's face too, was unfamiliar. He was smartly dressed in a spotlessly white uniform, complete with a hat with black trimmings, and shiny black shoes. Nagappa wondered why he was making a mental note of such trivial details.

He emerged from this trance-like state only when Khambata materialized before him, grinning. 'Come, come,' he said effusively, with an outstretched hand. 'Did the car pick you up on time?' he asked, trying to make conversation. Realizing Nagappa hadn't noticed his proffered hand, he thrust it quickly into his trouser pocket, looking abashed.

Nagappa realized there was a tremendous transformation in the way he was reacting to what was about to unfold, when Khambata suddenly appeared dwarfed before him, and when it struck him that he had not been awed by the opulence around him—the red carpet, the richly carved ceiling. 'Has everybody arrived?' he asked casually. It thrilled him that Khambata was confused by the nonchalance in his voice. Nagappa himself was confused by it.

As they walked to the elevator, he looked at himself in the tall, ornate mirror. Is this transformation, which is clearly discernible to me, only an inner one? he wondered, and stared at his reflection to see if there were any external signs. No, there was no outer change. He had not metamorphosed into something else—his head hadn't sprung a horn or his forehead a third eye. He smiled, remembering Kafka's Gregor Samsa. And yes, Khambata was within the ambit of his consciousness. However, when he looked at himself in the mirror again, and at others waiting for the elevator, he felt he should have worn his suit or at least a tie. But he glanced at Khambata and couldn't help smiling. He was bulging out of his ill-fitting, faded old suit. The shirt was not meant to be worn with a tie and the trousers were a few inches short. He looked goofy. He saw Nagappa staring at him and was puzzled by his expression. In fact, he was so puzzled that he forgot to get off at the seventh floor, and got off at the eighth, instead. As they waited for another elevator to take them to the floor below, he began to stutter, which was something of an apology and an explanation. When it took some time for the elevator to arrive, he led Nagappa down the stairs.

Nagappa admired the blood-red carpet with its white floral pattern covering the floor and the broad staircase, the wall-to-wall mirrors along the corridor that reflected the dazzling chandeliers and decorative lamps, and the gilded windows to the east that offered a majestic view of the sea. Nagappa walked unhurriedly, taking all this in, pausing to look at flower arrangements and other intricate showpieces, giving the impression that the sole purpose of his visit was to enjoy the luxurious ambiance of the hotel. This made Khambata uneasy. When Nagappa stood staring at the seascape from one of the windows, he didn't know how to tell Nagappa to hurry along, as the others were already waiting for them. Nervously rubbing his palms, he said, a bit ashamed of his beseeching tone, 'Please, we're getting late . . .'

'Late for what?' Nagappa asked.

This made Khambata angry. 'You'll know for what, you sisterfucker!' he wanted to scream out, but controlled himself and mumbled, 'They're waiting for us.'

'Why *us*? You poor thing! Have they also implicated you in something along with me?' Nagappa asked, without taking his eyes off the window. He felt no urgency to move away from the view before him, which he kept gazing at with a kind of wonder. Slowly, the awareness dawned on him that his mind was steadying itself, bracing itself to face something beyond his control that was going to take place inside one of the rooms. He was amazed at the realization that behind the seemingly innocent, unmotivated act of observing his surroundings with keen interest, his mind was surreptitiously busy at work, calming him.

For Khambata, Nagappa's deliberate, slow movement appeared impertinent. He fidgeted behind Nagappa, not knowing how to prod him to be quick. Nagappa, seeing this, finally decided to put him out of his misery. Looking at his watch, he asked, 'Isn't it time? Do you know which room it is?'

'Yes, we're already late by ten minutes. Please hurry up!' he said, sweating profusely despite the air conditioning. He stopped in front of a suite of rooms, rang the bell and wiped his face with his handkerchief, as they waited for the door to open. Though Nagappa enjoyed seeing Khambata's discomfiture, he also felt bad for him. He tried to put him at ease: 'I know what you must be going through because of this inquiry. Don't worry, I won't be too harsh on you. But I won't spare Phiroz . . .' Exactly at that moment, the door opened and Phiroz stood before him. Khambata, who was already a nervous wreck, was about to collapse. Phiroz signalled him to leave, rescuing him from further agony, turned to Nagappa, and offering his hand, said, 'Hello, Nag, come in, come in!'

'Hello, Phiroz,' Nagappa said quietly. He walked into the room, ignoring Phiroz's offer of a handshake, letting him know with his body language that he was in control of himself. He glanced at the two men sitting on the sofa, and stood admiring the lavish decor of the room. Phiroz closed the door and joined them. Though he was surprised by Nagappa's calm demeanour, trying to hide it, he said, 'Come, Nag, let me introduce you to two of our friends. This is Mr Dastur, managing director of Dastur & Company Private Limited. He'll be joining our board soon.'

'Pleasure to meet you, Mr Dastur,' Nagappa said, shaking his hand.

Phiroz turned to the other person. 'This is Mr Patel, director of . . .'

'Of Patel & Company Private Limited, and he too, is going to be on our board soon.'

Though Phiroz didn't like the way Nagappa had interrupted him, he smiled and said, 'Your guess is right.'

Nagappa shook Patel's hand. 'And you must be a Parsi Patel?'

Patel, not knowing how to respond, merely smiled. Phiroz's face had lost colour. Sitting on the sofa facing Patel,

Nagappa said, 'Patel is a common surname among both Parsis and Gujaratis. Our MD, for example, is a Gujarati Patel.'

Patel, realizing the import of Nagappa's earlier question, looked relieved. However, Nagappa's next words made all of them squirm: 'When I came to know there would be two more gentlemen in the inquiry commission, I asked Khambata for their names. He told me it would be revealed at the time of the inquiry. The letter sent to me said the same thing. I was sure then that the two gentlemen must be Parsis.'

The three looked at each other, wondering what to say. 'Don't get me wrong, gentlemen,' Nagappa smiled. 'I'm extremely pleased and relieved to know that you are indeed Parsis! That's because I have great faith in the sense of justice and fair play of the Parsi people.'

Realizing that the situation was going completely out of their hands, Dastur quickly winked at Phiroz, flared his nostrils, urbanely straightened his already straight tie, cleared his throat and said, 'Thanks, young man, for the compliment. Justice you will certainly have from us. So relax.'

Nagappa gave a pleasant smile. 'I too, wanted to tell you gentlemen the same thing—to relax. And one more thing, I hope you'll forgive me my rather informal clothes, the decor of the place and the status of its occupants notwithstanding.'

Before Phiroz or Dastur could react, Patel, who had been looking at Nagappa with interest, suddenly got up and said, 'I don't know how you two feel, but I think I agree with this young man. Why be so formal?' Taking off his coat and tie, he grumbled, 'It's stuffy, and the AC isn't working properly.'

Even Dastur took off his coat, but kept his tie on. Sensing that Dastur and Patel had begun to like Nagappa for his forthrightness bordering on insolence, Phiroz looked mutinous, but took off his coat to prove he had no personal grudge against Nagappa, and was prepared to go with the flow and give him a fair chance. 'Nag, what'll you have?' he asked.

'Gentlemen, I'm game for anything,' Nagappa shrugged. Patel and Dastur nodded at him approvingly. Phiroz felt a twinge of jealousy at their open admiration for Nagappa.

'Beer won't be a bad idea,' Dastur suggested. Nagappa looked at his watch. 'Early for the day, but ideal for the season,' he smiled.

Phiroz got up and called room service and ordered four bottles of beer, along with plates of cashew nuts and potato chips.

When he sat back on the sofa, he glanced nervously at Dastur, worried things were not going exactly as planned. Dastur winked at him again, signalling he shouldn't worry and should leave everything to him. This didn't escape Nagappa. The moment he had seen Dastur, he had realized that this affable-looking old man was as dangerous as Phiroz. He was the kind of beast that had the tenacity and patience to lie in wait for hours to pounce on its prey at the right moment. He also knew that Dastur was the master puppeteer who held all the strings. This SOB 1 is biding his time to give the signal for the curtain to rise at the opportune moment to start the show, Nagappa thought, with a smile, as he stared at his prominent Parsi nose and flared nostrils. A bit disconcerted by the stare, and unable to fathom the meaning of the smile, Dastur ran his hand over his face. Sitting up straight, he said, 'I'd like to clarify one thing—this is *not* an investigation but an interview.' Though the voice sounded grave, Nagappa couldn't help noticing that there was something comical about his face.

Nagappa looked at Phiroz and quipped, 'I think we should educate our personnel department about the difference between the two.'

Phiroz, worried about the totally unexpected and complete transformation in Nagappa's personality, testily added, 'This is an investigation, too.' Phiroz, who had mastered the art of masking his temper behind his smooth talk when the situation demanded, had slipped up. It was evident he was simmering with rage.

'You mean, this is an investigation through an interview,' Nagappa said, smiling, further inciting Phiroz.

Patel, realizing that they were not dealing with the meek creature that Phiroz had described, brusquely said, 'Enough of these preliminaries. Let's come straight to the business at hand.'

Just then, there was a knock on the door, and a liveried waiter bearing a tray pushed the door open and entered. Coincidentally, the waiter placed the tray with the beer and snacks at the exact moment when Patel said, 'Straight to the business at hand.' Nagappa smiled, but stopped himself from joking about it, and said in a serious tone, 'I'm ready!' implying he had been eagerly waiting for it for long.

The waiter opened the bottles and began to pour the beer into four mugs. Nagappa inhaled the inviting aroma of chilled beer. Phiroz and Dastur excused themselves and went to the adjacent room via a communicating door. This SOB 1 is enjoying himself in this luxury suite at the company's expense, Nagappa thought. Wonder how many girls he has brought here: Diana, Thrity . . . Mary . . . He remembered Mary's gushing description of the party Phiroz had hosted in this very hotel. But he didn't feel the unbearably intense jealously he had felt then. He was pleased. As he began to vow that he would never again allow himself to suffer the way he relentlessly had these last several days, that had almost cost him his sanity, the waiter handed the glasses of beer to Nagappa and Patel, and lingered to get Phiroz's signature on the voucher. Patel asked him to come back later. When he left, closing the door behind him, Patel said, 'Come on, young man, let's not waste time.' He raised his mug and said, 'Cheers!'

'Cheers!' Nagappa reciprocated. They took the first sip. As he felt the cool liquid slip down his throat, he felt his nerves ease. His spirits rose.

'I'm sorry to have upset some of your strategy,' he said, looking at the room where Phiroz and Dastur were still holed up. Patel didn't seem to be particularly interested in the mess Phiroz had been caught in. 'Rubbish! What strategy?' he thundered. 'Phiroz's a coward by nature. And he's become a nervous wreck ever since you and your friends have circulated that anonymous complaint. He's terrified! But my advice to you is, be practical and accept the offer that's being made to you.' He proceeded to enjoy the beer, letting Nagappa reflect on what he had said.

You SOB! Nagappa fumed inside. You want my scalp for something I haven't done! And you expect me to hand it to you on a platter! All this elaborate 'inquiry' is to find out if I've written that anonymous letter; in fact, to prove that I've written it—make me the fall guy. Sisterfucker! You're no less a bastard, you with your genial face! You're trying to soften me up when your two accomplices have gone inside to hobnob. Don't think I don't know that they being holed up there when you work on me is part of your grand strategy!

Nagappa, feigning to look confused, and implying it wasn't right for them to discuss the proceedings without the others, said, 'I'm sure Phiroz won't be pleased if he comes to know you've exposed him like this. It looks like you've taken a liking to me in the few minutes we've known each other. While I'm grateful to you for it, what I'm really curious about is, how you and Phiroz know each other. You don't seem to belong to the same ilk, of course, apart from the fact that both of you are Parsis . . .'

Patel literally jumped out of the sofa, screaming, 'Of course not, of course not! This has nothing to do with us being Parsis.' It was more of a protest than a justification. Feeling a bit edgy at being left alone to deal with Nagappa like this, he shouted, 'Come on, fellows, your beer's getting warm.'

As if on cue, the two men emerged from the room, apologized for taking too long to confer, picked up their mugs and said, 'Cheers.'

'Good that you gentlemen came to the rescue of Mr Patel quickly. He was getting a bit uncomfortable with my questions,' Nagappa said, with a glint of mischief in his eyes. Patel was gazing at the ceiling.

Nagappa didn't want to let go of the upper hand he now obviously had. Before they could react, he said, 'The moment your backs were turned, our Patel saab got down to business and tried to kill two birds with one stone—softening me up with beer and the task you had entrusted him with. To sum up what he told me in a nutshell—or what I gathered—is: There's some big offer awaiting me if I admit I wrote that anonymous letter sent to the board members. Therefore, it's in my interest to keep my mouth shut. That seems to be the gist of the advice Mr Patel gave me. Isn't that so, Mr Patel?'

Even before Nagappa could finish, Patel got up and went looking for the toilet.

Dastur and Phiroz were left speechless. They didn't know what had brought about this complete transformation in Nagappa's personality in the last few days. Whatever it was that had caused it, it was certain that he had changed. Dastur was annoyed with Phiroz for painting a different picture of him earlier, based on which they had planned their strategy. He sat back sipping the beer slowly, looking at Nagappa with curiosity, letting Phiroz dig himself out of the hole he had got himself into. Dastur's attitude scared Phiroz even more. Sensing this, Nagappa obstinately persisted: 'I didn't write that letter. In fact, I don't even know what it contains. But I do have a lot of information that the letter may have possibly revealed about the wrongdoings of certain people. I'm willing to place the information I have before the inquiry commission, in case it can help the inquiry in any way.'

Phiroz couldn't contain himself any longer. Without trying to hide his anger, he shouted, 'Don't be impertinent! The inquiry is to investigate *you*! Don't act as if you're conducting the inquiry.'

Nagappa turned to Phiroz, smiling at this new possibility: 'I'm aware of it, Phiroz. And I haven't said anything to take away from the reality, unless, of course, we're prompted by our subconscious to hear things that were not said.'

This incensed Phiroz further. Dastur realized it was time to step in and nudge the proceedings in the pre-planned direction. He suddenly asked, 'Okay, Mr Nagnath, tell me: How many children are you for your parents? How many siblings do you have?'

Nagappa was unable to answer: Of all the things, why did the inquiry begin with this question—the one I cannot answer? Why should a question that appeared absolutely routine have this effect on me? Or, is the question as routine as it really sounds? Has Shrinivasa given them information about my past to take revenge on me?

Had they started the inquiry with any other question, he had decided to say: 'Please let me know what the real purpose of this inquiry is. Who has given you the right to conduct it? These things need to be made clear at the very outset. Otherwise, it'll not be possible for me to answer any of your questions.' But Nagappa was unable to grapple with the question thrown at him. While steeling himself for this final standoff, he had made up his mind not to buckle under pressure, no matter how strong. He had gathered all his reserves of inner strength and energy to face his tormentors. But the very first salvo fired at him had him on his knees. Courage deserted him when he needed it the most. His heart sank.

Phiroz, not wanting to let go of this opportunity, prodded, 'Come on, Nag, don't let your subconscious read meanings that aren't there in so simple a question.' This had the desired effect on Dastur. He also realized that it had a profound impact on Nagappa. The sarcasm in Phiroz's tone provoked Nagappa into responding: 'My apologies, Mr Dastur. I must confess that your question touched a raw nerve. I'm afraid you might not understand if I put it this way, and there isn't time to put it in a way you'll understand. But since it's a question of my career, please tell me: What is the real purpose of this inquiry? Who has appointed you to conduct it? Who gave you the authority to conduct it?

What really are the charges against me? Who framed those charges? I won't be able to answer any of your questions without getting answers to mine.'

Nagappa said this looking straight into Dastur's eyes, in a steady voice. Though he felt relieved that he was able to do so, he was neither curious to assess its effect on the others nor interested in knowing the answers, because that was not the objective of his questions.

It appeared that on his part, Dastur too, had decided to maintain the sobriety the proceedings demanded, while still maintaining an air of informality. He placed his beer mug on the table, picked up the file he had requested to be brought from the other room, and sat deep in thought for a few minutes, tapping a sharpened pencil on it. A faint smile played on his lips.

This wily old SOB 1 is getting ready to make his first move. He's searching for the right words to frame the question, Nagappa thought, and remained alert and ready to answer it. I shouldn't lose courage. I shouldn't get emotional, he told himself. But suddenly, a question began to nag him: Has Shrinivasa passed on information about my past to Phiroz that he was planning to throw at me the other day? Was that why the inquiry was postponed by a day—because Phiroz got some information dug up from my past at the last minute? But this did not deplete Nagappa's courage. Instead, it made him eager to hear Dastur's next question. He looked at Dastur expectantly.

The time Dastur was taking made Phiroz and Patel uneasy. They fidgeted and shifted in their seats. It became clear to Nagappa that after being put on the defensive by his series of questions, Dastur was mulling over what to say next, looking at an array of possibilities, and the response they might elicit: This shrewd SOB 2 is getting the bait ready. He's thinking of the best technique to cast it. He's wondering how to begin. 'Begin whichever way you want, you bastard!' Nagappa silently screamed. 'The outcome of this inquiry doesn't depend on how *you* begin it, but the way *I* am going to end it. And I know how I'm going to end it. And you too, will, soon. Very soon. I haven't come here to beg for justice, but to expose your injustices, malpractices. Come on, come out of your hiding. I've been waiting for all of you to come out into the open these last two weeks.'

Everyone waited.

Nagappa took a long draught of beer. It felt good. Phiroz was pretending to be busy cleaning his pipe. Patel took quick gulps from the mug to take the edge off the tension, as he waited impatiently for Dastur's next move.

Finally, Dastur cleared his throat and began with an air of supreme dignity. But the facade of fake gravitas did not match Dastur's personality. This irritated Nagappa. But he forced himself to remain calm.

'I can imagine the extent of pain and anxiety you've had to suffer these last two weeks. However . . .'

Nagappa found this blatant lie unbearable. He wondered how he had tolerated such lies for the past eighteen years, working under Phiroz.

'Please don't take my suffering to heart, Mr Dastur. Besides, you can never imagine the extent of my suffering, because you are not in the predicament I'm in. However, I'm grateful for your concern.'

The tone of rebellion in Nagappa's voice didn't escape the three men seated before him. Dastur realized that he

would have to use all the negotiating skills he had mastered
in the thirty years of his professional life to defuse the spark
of revolt waiting to explode in this seemingly mild-mannered
man. But his face remained impassive. 'I know, I know,'
he began in a placating tone. 'Please don't take my words
literally. I was trying to break the ice, so we could begin
the proceedings, that's all. Don't you agree that we all have
our own way of attempting to enter a stranger's world and
letting a stranger enter ours? We don't know each other.
But we're trying to get to know each other. Mr Nagnath,
please consider me your friend and well-wisher without any
hesitation. I urge you, for the moment, to please keep aside
any misconceptions you may have. In fact, let's together do
so. Let's suspend for the time being all mutual suspicions and
preconceived notions, and let's listen to what each of us has
to say with an open mind.'

The words that were as soothing as the beer Nagappa was
sipping, didn't fail to have the effect Dastur had expected. The
beer too, had helped calm his nerves. Patel, who looked dim-
witted, but who was actually the most dangerous of the three,
sensing this, quickly filled Nagappa's mug. Though Phiroz and
Patel had been alarmed by Dastur's words, when he began,
realized they had made the desired impact. The three men
sensed that Nagappa, who had made any headway in talks
impossible so far, was willing to listen, at least for now. All
three picked up their mugs in relief, by coincidence, at the
same time, and immediately felt awkward. Nagappa, who was
mildly intoxicated, didn't pay attention to them. He waited for
Dastur's next words. Dastur began all over again: 'Remember,
I called this meeting both an interview and an investigation?
Do you know why I called it an interview? There's a strong

possibility of you being moved to a new position—with a new designation—that you can't have imagined. Can you believe that the proposed post you could take charge of will be in Hong Kong? The only reason it was called an investigation was because there was a mala fide complaint that you had a hand in the fire that broke out in the factory a few months back. *That* has come in the way of your promotion. We need to go to the bottom of this vicious witch hunt.'

Phiroz sat on the edge of the sofa, looking at Nagappa anxiously, aware that the outcome of the inquiry hinged entirely on his reaction to the preamble Dastur had so cleverly and skilfully presented. Phiroz didn't have to wait for long. But the response didn't come from the Nagappa that Phiroz thought he knew. In fact, it came from a facet of his personality Nagappa himself didn't know existed. That was because, he had never stood like this, exactly at the crosshairs of a hunter's rifle, with the hunter intently looking through its barrel aiming directly at that fatal spot in his heart to mortally wound him. His natural instinct for self-preservation suddenly surfaced, alert and ready to fend off any danger.

'It's very interesting, Mr Dastur . . .' Nagappa began. 'I agree that I need to immediately endeavour to remove any suspicion against me. (That's why I'm enduring this misfortune of having to drink beer staring at your stupid faces). Yes, I must clear my name before being considered for a promotion. So, let's start with the investigation.'

Dastur appeared pleased. 'I'm glad you think so. There's nothing greater than one's own name, one's prestige, one's image. What do you say?'

You SOBs are under the impression that I've consented to the investigation. Watch me make mincemeat of you bastards! Nagappa thought, as he sat staring at Dastur's oversized nose. Dirty pig! He cursed. The more he stared at Dastur, the more porcine his face appeared. Fearing he would burst out laughing, he pressed his lips hard.

'You have nothing to fear, Mr Nagnath,' Dastur finally said, when Nagappa didn't respond. Finding it difficult to control himself, Nagappa pretended to wipe his face with his handkerchief and stifled his laughter.

'Thank you, Mr Dastur. I rely on your wisdom. I'm innocent.' He drank some more beer, fearing another bout of laughter.

'We know, Mr Nagnath, but in the vicious world we live in, it's not enough to be innocent. We have to be perceived to be innocent. We need to prove we're innocent. And we're here to help you.'

'I'm sure you are, Mr Dastur. I've no words to thank you.'

Nagappa couldn't believe his own words. Hey, Nagappa, you SOB, that's an utter lie! Nagappaaa of Koligiriyanna's ghetto, the soft-spoken Nagappaaa, you've at last learnt to lie. You've learnt to be clever! You've grown up! Toughened up! And who's filled your mug with beer again, Nagappaaa?!

His innards had become cool and mellow, but his blood seemed to be raging hot. Like the slow opening up of his inner self, laying bare the deepest truths of his being, his knotted-up body began to loosen and the strictures began to open up. He felt a sudden surge of bravado rising from the depths that had never been tapped before. 'Four more bottles of beer, please.' Whose voice was that? Wasn't it Phiroz's? Sisterfucker! Are they trying to drown me in beer? Break me? Is that part of the strategy . . . the subterfuge— to numb my faculties? Go ahead, get me drunk. I know how to be a villain among you gang of villains—devious like you scoundrels. I can attack you as viciously as you have attacked me! And don't think it's the beer talking . . .

A pleasant sensation swirled down his throat. But he felt a bit unsteady. He leaned forward eagerly to hear what Dastur had to say.

'There's no need to thank me, Mr Nagnath. Now, let's begin from the beginning . . .'

Begin, you son of a whoring widow! Enough of your hemming and hawing and dodging and sniffing around me. Come out in the open and spit out your words. Bark! And if you want, begin at the beginning—from your grandfather's origin. Isn't that at the root of all this?

'About a part of the factory catching fire . . .'

'It didn't catch fire—if you want me to speak the truth, that is. It was set on fire.'

'We want you to tell us the truth. We are here to know the truth. When did you first suspect that it wasn't an accident . . . that the division was actually set on fire?'

'From the beginning.'

'Why?'

'Phiroz knows very well that I'd been protesting about the mismanagement and malpractices in the department for a long time. No precautionary measures were taken with regard to the manufacturing of peroxide. I took the initiative and wrote to leading international chemical companies and gathered information regarding all the safety measures to be taken relating to it. I collated the information and sent it to the MD. All that I got by way of gratitude was to be reprimanded by Phiroz.'

'It must have hurt you deeply—it would have hurt anyone with self-respect.'

'Phiroz knows about my feelings.'

'Did you express your hurt in front of anybody?'

'Of course! I expressed what I felt directly in front of Phiroz himself. He didn't like me for it.'

It wasn't easy for Nagappa to decipher Phiroz's expression. And he didn't feel the need to decipher it. Phiroz sat silently smoking his pipe. The waiter came in, putting a temporary pause to Dastur's interrogation. The waiter set down the tray with bottles of beer and plates of snacks, took Phiroz's signature on the voucher and left. The sight of an array of snacks made Nagappa realize he was hungry. Chilled beer to go with them seemed welcome.

Phiroz, looking at Dastur, said, 'You continue, Bomi. Dassu and I will take care of these.' Evidently happy with Dastur's line of questioning, he focused on opening the bottles of beer, while Patel started fussing over the snacks.

'It's, indeed, laudable that you had the courage to communicate how you felt directly to your boss,' Dastur continued. 'Did you express it in front of anyone else?'

'Many people in the factory knew my views on safety measures or the lack thereof. They knew my concerns . . .'

'Exactly! How did they know about them? You didn't go telling this to everyone.'

Nagappa didn't answer. He didn't know whether it was because he was feeling a bit lightheaded, or torn between what to choose from the plate of snacks that Phiroz held in front of him— chicken tikka, mutton kebab and fish fingers— or because of a voice warning him: 'Nagappa, you country bumpkin from Koligiriyanna's ghetto, be very, very, careful!

This is a question from the world of skyscrapers!' Confused and irritated by the warning signal from within, instead of answering Dastur, he picked up a kebab and bit into it, and took a sip of beer.

'Did you share your dissatisfaction, rather your misgivings, elaborating the reasons, with anyone close to you? For example, things like, "I won't be surprised if the factory gets burnt down one of these days?"'

This salvo didn't seem to have the impact on Nagappa that Dastur had expected or desired. 'This is too general a statement to have been made to any particular person,' he responded casually. However, from the drift of the questioning, Nagappa sensed that the name of someone in particular was about to crop up.

'What I'm going to say might help you jog your memory. Did you tell someone: "Just to teach these blokes what chemical fires are like, I feel like changing the formulation and cause one"?'

'Oh, no! It was only my way of expressing my anger.'

'But it's true that you said this in front of someone. Do you remember who it was, now?'

Nagappa had no doubt in his mind who it was: The only person who always showed great respect and sympathy for him in the entire factory (which could even be interpreted as love in some emotional moments), whom Nagappa went to the extent of believing was the only such person in the entire world—Reena. Even Reena in Phiroz's conspiracy?! Nagappa couldn't believe it. He didn't have the courage to accept it, because if it was true, if someone like Reena, whom he trusted so much, in whom he had so much faith, could join hands with Phiroz against him, then there was no point protesting that he had not made the statement. In fact, there was no point in continuing this inquiry. Oh, god, let this not be true! Let this *one* thing not be true, he prayed.

Nagappa's face lost colour. Alarmed all the beer he had downed would come out, he ran to the next room in search of the toilet. Instead of throwing up, he urinated and felt his stomach ease a bit. He splashed water on his face and washed his eyes. His brain seemed less clouded. The sensation to vomit had subsided, at least for now.

So, the line of questioning is unwittingly dragging me to areas I had least expected it would, Nagappa thought. Despite my innocence, the evidence against me is growing stronger . . . rock solid. They've lined up irrefutable proof to incriminate me. A world I thought was familiar is slowly turning into an uncharted territory, turning its back on me.

There was a knock on the door, startling him out of his thoughts. 'Are you all right, Mr Nagnath?' Patel asked from the other side. Not getting any response, he knocked again, shouting, 'Mr Nagnath!' To Nagappa, it sounded like the hollering and screaming of a pack of hunters to frighten their prey out of its hiding—a reconnaissance mission. He shook his head vigorously, as if to shed the illusion. 'I'm okay. I'll be out in a minute,' he said in a voice barely audible to himself. Patel, who was listening with his ear to the door for every little sound Nagappa made, to gauge his ability to fight back, was elated. Judging from Nagappa's voice, they had managed to intimidate their prey. Nagappa had no way of knowing this then. When he came out, Patel, who was waiting, feigned concern, and, leaning towards him, said in a conspiratorial tone, 'Don't worry, Mr Nagnath, we're all there for your support.' Nagappa knew this was Patel's way of getting even with him for his earlier humiliation. He felt like punching Patel's face. He would probably have done it at any other time, but now, he had no strength left to react to anything.

Maybe I shouldn't have drunk so much beer. Or else, I'd surely have made life hell for these three crooks, Nagappa thought. They have discussed their next move behind my back, and they're now looking at me watchfully, waiting for me to trip up. And who are these three men, really? Who are these inquisitors? Do I know them? Have I seen them before? The suspicion that suddenly came from nowhere, kept growing. As seconds ticked by, he felt that like the skyscrapers of Nariman Point, something that stood outside his ambit, barring him from entering its realm and its emotional sphere, and refusing to enter his, had turned its back on him and stood sniggering contemptuously at him and the world of Koligiriyanna. He found it difficult to get rid of this feeling, to escape from its vice-like grip. He stared at the three men—the men who kept growing in front of him to gigantic proportions, who had slowly become inscrutable, hiding some dark, deep secret within them, who had suddenly fallen silent, who had made it impossible for him to utter a word, who were now waiting for him to blunder, waiting to force an error out of him by their sheer silence.

Nagappa wondered why he had come back to the room. He wasn't even sure why he was here in the first place. Everything seemed hazy. He had vowed to expose their sins, but now found himself forced to prove his own innocence. The onus had shifted on to him. He felt the burden too heavy to carry.

Astutely guessing what was going on in Nagappa's mind, Dastur broke the silence and said, deliberately making it sound grave, 'Sorry to be personal. But we can't help it. The matter is so serious that we can't afford to take chances.'

Though someone had refilled his mug, Nagappa didn't pick it up. Something in Dastur's face made his insides knot up. He suspected that for some reason, Dastur didn't believe he was innocent. Nagappa silently appealed to the man intently looking at him to trust him. He wanted to say out loud, 'I'm innocent. Please believe me . . .' Dastur asked him abruptly, 'What's your relationship with Reena?'

Nagappa was taken aback by this totally unexpected question. More than the question, what hit him was the naked, irrefutable proof of Reena joining his enemies. She had exposed him! She had revealed to them what he had told her in a moment of utter frustration about wanting to set the factory on fire. But then, what right did Dastur have to intrude into his personal life? Wasn't it because he was an employee of this company? But he had already decided to quit his job. He had come prepared to kick it. *That's* why he was here—to throw it in their faces. But now, proving his innocence seemed more important than getting back at his tormentors. He waited with a kind of disinterested curiosity for Dastur to elaborate.

'Did you have a physical relationship with her?'

Nagappa wanted say, 'It's entirely a personal matter, and you have no right to ask me such questions.' But he couldn't muster enough anger needed to respond. The anger had died in him. No one except Reena could have told his inquisitors about their relationship. Or were they pretending to know more than they did to expose his vulnerability? Worse still, was this a play being enacted to force a confession out of him?

His doubts were confirmed by Dastur's next question: 'Is there any wound or scar on your body that causes you to be paranoid about fire? Do you have a neurotic fear of fire?'

Nagappa was not even interested in knowing how they had found out his innermost secret. He knew the answer. The many nights he had spent in Reena's company were the most pleasurable, the most memorable in his life. A married woman and a mother of two, she had begged him to keep their relationship a secret. Respecting it, he had hidden it, buried deep within him, not allowing to acknowledge its intensity even to himself. It was an act of faith. What surprised him was his lack of rancour at Reena's betrayal. He felt he no longer had the strength or power to comprehend the truth about human relationships. The composure and detachment with which he accepted this probably made him pick up the mug of beer he had left untouched for a while and take two quick gulps.

He looked at Dastur as if he was seeing him for the first time, and said with a tinge of curiosity, 'Go on, Mr Dastur, don't stop. What you are saying's really fascinating. You've aroused my interest.'

But his voice betrayed a total lack of interest. He sounded too fatigued and exhausted to care. Unable to provoke any reaction from Nagappa, Dastur did not know how to go on. But clearing his throat afresh to indicate that the inquiry had taken a serious turn, and to flaunt his brilliance in front of Phiroz and Patel, he began in a deep baritone: 'Please pay attention to the question I'm about to ask, as it has serious implications . . .'

'Is that a veiled threat that my future in the company could be in jeopardy if I don't toe the line?' Nagappa asked.

To let Nagappa know he wasn't stupid enough not to grasp the import of his words, Dastur said with a hint of a smile, 'If the matter was as simple as that, then our worry would have been unfounded, and this inquiry would have been a futile exercise, for we certainly need people like you with stupendous talent and technical expertise. But the roadblock we are facing is of a very serious nature. May I say that it has criminal implications that might involve the entire management?'

Nagappa was embarrassed at the way his hand holding the mug shook. By the time he placed it back on the teapoy, he could feel beads of perspiration forming on his forehead. He took out his handkerchief. He realized what Dastur had said had taken even Patel and Phiroz by surprise. Dastur was recalibrating the war strategy to get a little more wriggle room. Nagappa felt cornered. Phiroz gave a slight nod of appreciation at this masterstroke and focused on his pipe to hide his elation. But Patel slapped his thigh impulsively at the first round of hard-won victory, and immediately looked sheepish.

Nagappa had closed his eyes, oblivious to all this. The two words—criminal implications—and the way they had been enounced, touched some unplumbed depths within him, bringing to surface the kind of panic he had never experienced before.

Dastur himself seemed pleased with what he said next: 'You alone can vouch for what I'm going to say. And it'll become amply clear to you that we're not here to falsely implicate you for anything. Also, you'll perhaps appreciate our deep concern regarding certain things that have come to our notice.' He paused for effect, and said by way of highlighting the issue, 'We did not go after facts. They came to our notice.'

Looking at others, 'This beer's damn good!' he said in a self-congratulatory tone. He took a sip and looked at Phiroz, smiling. But Nagappa had no patience to parse the statement Dastur had cleverly tossed at him.

Dastur took a long swig from his mug and looked at the others to signal he was about to deploy a very potent weapon. He leaned forward and said: 'Some terrible incident in your childhood made you grow up under the suspicion that you were part of a suicide pact made by your parents . . .'

Oh, Reena! Why this treachery? Why this heinous betrayal? It was unbearable to even recall the circumstances under which he had revealed the most painful secret of his life to her. The moment of intense pleasure had also been a moment of unbearable pain. In the throes of an orgasm, Reena had confessed amidst moans that no man had ever given her so much fulfilment. Lying in his arms, she had wondered why he had shyly refused to take his shirt off while undressing. Completely sated, and still under the intoxicating euphoria of the pleasure her body had given him, Nagappa had said with immense sadness, 'I hide there a great secret of my childhood, both painful and shameful.' But he hadn't told her what it was. Again, in the heat of foreplay, when her hand had tried to sneak under his shirt, he had gently removed it.

'Was it the plan to kill you by torching your shirt?'

The question had come suddenly like a sniper's shot from an unexpected direction, but aimed straight at him. Dastur momentarily panicked, seeing Nagappa's state.

'Yours seems to be the practised hand of an assassin, Mr Dastur. You've mastered the art. I had heard of such psychological techniques being used to draw out a confession, but this is the first time I'm its target. Please don't think I'm *that* gullible. Give up this blackmail. Come straight to the point. Tell me how I can save your friend Phiroz.'

Phiroz, who had been listening intently, was enraged by the way Nagappa had made the statement casually. Masking his anger, but unable to control his shaking voice, he said, 'This isn't a question of saving me, Nag. It's a question of saving the company. In the capacity of the DMD of the company, and as in-charge of the factory, while I admit that I'm, in a sense, morally responsible . . .'

'What exactly are you responsible for, Phiroz?'

'That such things . . . incidents don't occur in the factory . . .'

'What kind of incidents? It isn't fair to assume that I can second-guess what you have in mind. Please make it clear what kind of incidents you're referring to.'

Phiroz looked at Dastur and Patel and got nods of permission from them. Nagappa, warming to the situation, quickly drank some more beer. He was eager to grill Phiroz, who, though responsible for what was happening, pretended to be outside the ambit of the inquiry.

'Nag, you know about the pilferage . . .'

'It's probably better to believe I don't know.'

'Okay, about ten tonnes of chemical number 389 . . .'

'I don't think only 389 was pilfered.'

Both Dastur and Patel didn't appear to know this. They anxiously looked at Phiroz.

'Yes, and a large quantity of 387 . . .' he reluctantly admitted.

'How much?' Dastur asked, looking alarmed, and before Phiroz could reply, looked at Nagappa and said, 'You didn't mention this in your letter.'

'I was not the one who wrote that letter, Mr Dastur. In fact, I haven't even read it. But that's not the point here. The most important thing you really need to worry about is that it was a chemical imported from abroad under the "387 actual users' licence". I hope you are aware of the fact that according to the stringent rules of its import, let alone selling it in the black market, the sale of it itself is prohibited. It amounts to a criminal activity!'

Dastur looked at Phiroz inquiringly. The fear on Phiroz's face confirmed what Nagappa had said was true. Dastur didn't attempt to hide his dismay. 'Excuse me,' he said and went to the toilet. Before leaving, 'Please read this; I'll be back soon,' he said, placing a neatly typed report on the teapoy. Nagappa was excited by this new turn of events. He realized he was extremely hungry and looked at his watch. It was nearly twelve. He picked up a kebab that had gone cold and raised an eyebrow at Phiroz. Phiroz did what he always did in such situations—pretended to be busy filling his pipe.

Patel, not sure what to do, picked up Dastur's file. Two photographs slipped out and fell down. Phiroz quickly grabbed the file from Patel's hand, pushed the photographs in and put the file back on the teapoy, hissing, 'For heaven's sake!' He looked at Nagappa from the corner of his eye to see if he had noticed anything. But Nagappa was in no mood to pay attention to such things. Pleased at the prospect of at last exposing Phiroz, he waited for Dastur to return.

Dastur came back and sat down, and realized his file had been moved. He gave Patel a stern look, sure it must be his handiwork.

Unaware that it was going to provide the background for the intimidating questions that were to follow, Nagappa sat back and slowly began to read the report Dastur had given him. As he read through the pages, first, casually, then slightly shaking with terror, he prayed, Oh, god, if I come back out of this alive, and if I don't have the guts to buy barbiturates from Banavali's shop, and even if I buy them, if I don't have the nerve to take them, I'll become a salesman at Strand Book Stall or rent a place in Khetwadi and open a newspaper stand. I'll become a schoolmaster in Koligiriyanna's neighbourhood school. But please, save me from this!'

'What do you want me to do with this report, Mr Dastur?' he asked, aware of his beseeching tone, but helpless to do anything about it. Dastur, a seasoned manipulator, looked unflappable. Nagappa knew what was happening was an attempt to gradually break him, including the ruse of pretending to win a round, and unexpectedly losing another, letting Nagappa think he had put his opponents on the defensive. It was a carefully choreographed act guided by a diabolical mastermind, being played out on an elaborately set stage. Dastur had written the script and knew how exactly it was going to unfold. Everyone had practised their lines. They had come prepared to completely destroy him.

Nagappa cautiously looked at Dastur and knew he was looking at a pro. He was dangerous. Dastur was staring directly at Nagappa. There was an animal-like alertness in his eyes Nagappa hadn't seen earlier. His gaze was sharp, intense and unwavering. It was hypnotic. Nagappa vaguely recalled something he had barely registered—was it Reddy in the photos that had fallen out of the file? It was someone in dark glasses.

As the eyes looking into his grew wide with terror, Dastur quietly said, 'Sign the report, Mr Nagnath. Here's the pen.'

Though Dastur's command was what Nagappa expected it would be, the tone was chilling. Its finality hit him with an unexpected force. He suddenly sprang to his feet. 'No, Mr Dastur,' he said. 'Let's not make this theatrical. I won't sign the report. I won't sign it at any cost. My erudition . . . the vast technical knowledge I have in the field . . . will not allow me to sign such nonsense! And never when you threaten me like this with dire consequences! However, if you are amenable to reason and willing to have a discussion on the subject, I'm prepared to consider other methods of saving Phiroz . . .'

'Stop that nonsense!' Phiroz shouted. 'I've heard enough! First try to save your own skin! And, Bomi, don't forget that we have a lunch appointment at one.'

It had been a long time since Nagappa had heard Phiroz yelling at him like this. He had goosebumps. He quietly sat down, feeling listless.

'Why do you think it's suicidal to sign this report?' Dastur asked.

'It's obvious. Even Phiroz knows why. Chemical 387 is an unsaturated acid. And it's totally useless in the manufacture of the product you have indicated in the report. Phthalates plasticizers are needed for the manufacture of peroxide catalyst. And 387 is not used in this process. There can be absolutely no connection between the division that was destroyed in the fire and this chemical. Therefore, it's impossible that a large consignment of this chemical was destroyed in the fire. And the report is attempting to prove exactly that! The brain behind such a suggestion is, indeed, diabolical! But it's a brain that knows nothing about the basics of chemistry. In fact, 387 was not imported for this purpose at all. Its use has been explained in great detail in a project report my two companions and I have prepared—research work that I'm very proud of. I'm not sure if Phiroz has a copy of it. If he has, he would know what a project report detailing the manufacture of a completely new product looks like or needs to look like. Mr Dastur, it's impossible for me to put my stamp of approval on the shoddy report you have just shown me. However, I must admit that it's only now I have realized why work hasn't started on my polyester project till date, despite being accepted by the board of directors.'

Though sarcasm was evident in Nagappa's words, his voice still had a tinge of his earlier panic.

Dastur looked as if there was nothing new or unexpected in what Nagappa had said. 'It's not that we haven't thought about all this, Mr Nagnath,' he said. 'But firstly, please do not lose your temper without knowing the entire contents of the report you are about to sign. We haven't claimed you have written the report. We have only indicated that it was prepared eight years ago. You probably didn't notice that the date of the report has been changed. Therefore, it's not surprising that you didn't have the experience or expertise to write such a report back then, as the date is endeavouring to prove. Also, changing the date of the report establishes that it was written much before the report you referred to earlier—the one you said you took great pride in. Secondly, the objective of this report is not as significant as you think. It has a very limited scope and is somewhat ad hoc in nature. And it's certainly not aimed at scientists in the field of chemistry. Its purpose is merely to dispel or address certain objections raised by the audit report, which is the main cause of the knotty situation that has arisen at present. It's just to satisfy the auditors, that's all. No, don't look surprised. In fact, it was the auditors themselves who advised that such a report be prepared and even suggested its title. When those who raised the objections themselves have no problem with the solution, then why should we bother about it? It's they who indicated that it would be better if the report carried your signature. Thirdly, I'm saying this for your satisfaction: Numbers like 387, 389 are not names of specific chemicals, right? They are just code numbers or labels that companies have created to maintain secrecy related to their production. Is there any rule that the numbers cannot be changed once in a while? And even if there's such a rule, there's always a possibility that they could be inadvertently interchanged for . . .'

'My god!' Nagappa exclaimed, even before he realized it, leaving Dastur's sentence incomplete. He trembled at the very thought of what Dastur was suggesting. He looked at him, unable to control the tremor that had started from somewhere deep within him.

Dastur picked up his file and placed it on his lap, with an air of determination to show that he was about to add a totally different dimension to the inquiry. He opened it, glanced at it, closed it again and began gravely, 'Look here, young man, I can appreciate your predicament. But as a student of human psychology, let me tell you a few things.'

He quickly pulled his business card out of his pocket, and giving it to Nagappa with a flourish, said, 'Not to impress you, but to introduce myself properly, I have a postgraduate degree from the School of Sociology, UK. I've majored in Industrial Psychology. I later got my PhD in Business Management from Harvard. Since my doctoral degree was not relevant to our discussion so far, I'd asked Phiroz to introduce me as Mr Dastur and not Dr Dastur. By the way, your MD and I are contemporaries. We even spent a few years in England together. I'm now fifty-five and have over a quarter century of experience in a wide range of disciplines. I've seen your biodata, Mr Nagnath, and am impressed by it. (Nagappa: Utter lies, you, sisterfucker!) Your achievements are, indeed, laudable—ones you can be proud of. However, it's not enough to have erudition and expertise. (Nagappa: Yes, along with that, you need to develop thick skins and prominent noses and big assess to occupy big positions, or else, you should have awards imported either from America or England, and if possible from both countries to dangle before others at every available opportunity! These're the only kinds of people you get to deal with professionally.) Along with knowledge of your subject, you need to know how to deal with people—different kinds of people with different temperaments and interests, varied pace of professional growth and motivation towards their profession. (Nagappa: And the ability to pontificate like this! What an amazing range of masks these SOBs can wear!) I have been carefully and keenly observing you from the time I have come here. (Nagappa: Like a vulture.) I have identified various facets of your personality. I have recognized the creative artiste in you. I hear that apart from your brilliance in your field, you are also a writer. (Nagappa: Congrats! You're well-informed!) That endows you with the ability to immediately sense what others are thinking and feeling. (Nagappa: Thanks for the compliment!) However, you have tapped this potential only in the creative sphere, but not in the professional arena and in your day-to-day dealings with people. Moreover, the creative streak in you has made you oversensitive and sentimental. (Nagappa: Oh, shut up!) Importantly, you appear to repose great faith in certain fundamental values and principles, and think that others share this faith. In fact, you obstinately insist that others adhere to such a value system. But things don't work quite that way. Your attitude and demeanour towards us today indicates that you have unshakable faith in the power of truth. You believe truth is on your side and that truth will finally win. You are still hanging on to this age-old myth. You therefore think that it's enough to present the facts before us, and that facts are self-evident and self-explanatory. You think you don't need to prove anything beyond that, as you believe it is as axiomatic and indisputable as night following day. You want the facts at your command to act as eye-openers to provide insights into complex situations. You are arrogant and confident in the knowledge that you are right and others are wrong. Because of your blind faith in the moral power of truth and incontrovertible facts, you are angry and impatient whenever you perceive any injustice. You speak out against it. You have been doing exactly that today—you have been protesting against perceived injustice. Yes, Mr Nagnath, truth may offer great moral insights. Facts may act as eye-openers. But you are absolutely unaware that what the eye sees—even when you force it open—is purely subjective. It depends upon the viewer's point of view, and is influenced by selfish motives. I have great regard for the artiste in you, the writer in you. But in matters that concern us professionals, I'm afraid you are too naive and immature. Pardon me for being blunt. The professional world is not a world of truth and values—at least not in the way you imagine it should be. It's a world of self-interests. Of course, there are organizational "visions" and objectives, and an organizational structure that evolves in the process of interlocking the individuals working for these objectives into a network of interpersonal relationships and all that bullshit. Excuse my language. But I'm sure you will agree with me when I say that the prime mover of an organization—the motive working behind the facade of its evolving structure and all that four-letter jargon—is the ambition of the individuals to climb its ladder. You are unable to understand why I'm saying all this, isn't it? You look cynical and bored. But your boredom and cynicism will vanish . . . will be wiped off your face when I prove to you that you are no exception to this cut-throat competition. Like all others, you too, want to climb the corporate ladder. But the method you have adopted to climb it . . . to fulfil your ambition is rather naive, and, if I may add, downright stupid. In fact, that's what has been responsible for all that has transpired now. It's not enough to have great ambition to rise in your profession, Mr Nagnath. Also, merit alone will not take you there, as you seem to think. You need all the strategies you can marshal, along with skill and dexterity to climb up. And that requires a political mind, which you don't have. Not that you are any less ambitious than others, but that . . . Please don't try to interrupt me. Let me come straight to the point. The reason for this long preface is to assure you

that our intention is certainly not to frame you for a crime
you have not committed. Also, it was important to highlight
the fundamental difference between the way we both view
crime—or what we regard as criminal. We have constructed
your profile, based on information gathered about you and
our interpretation of it. What we are driving at will become
amply clear to you when you look at this profile. You will
also understand why we are confident you will sign the
report. We are not only confident you will sign the report,
but that you will also put the date we ask you to. Do you
know why? When you look at the persona we have created,
you will voluntarily confess that you are responsible for
everything. You will also realize the definition of truth in the
real world—that the new discourse of truth is different from
what you imagine it to be. The two don't match. Truth is not
self-evident, nor does it automatically prove itself based on
reality, as you think it does. Truth is not an abstract concept.
It has meaning only when it becomes relevant in the real
world and is seen within a context. It gives a new meaning in
relation to real-life events. For example, what meaning do
individual pieces of glass have in a kaleidoscope? But give it a
slight tilt, and the same meaningless pieces arrange
themselves into a pattern in relation to one another. Another
tilt, even accidental, and the pattern and the meaning change,
based on the relationship of the individual pieces. Therefore,
even an unintended touch has the power to capture our
attention by creating potentially endless configurations
through permutations and combinations of the otherwise
intrinsically meaningless glass pieces. The same glass pieces,
but different patterns and different viewpoints! If you agree
that the tilt of the hand and the pattern thus created are

accidental and unintended, then you will understand what I
have been trying to illustrate about the real world, in the
human context, all this while. It all depends upon who is
tilting the kaleidoscope of reality and how much. Do you
think history is the enduring, eternal truth? No. It depends
upon who writes it and the power the writer wields and what
he chooses to highlight. Even when a murder takes place in
broad daylight, it's possible for a person to prove through
clever arguments that the alleged murderer was not even
born, let alone murder someone. You can imagine what
could happen to truth in the hands of such a person! The
entire secret of politics and politicking lies in this. Now,
coming to you, Mr Nagnath, you, in your own ivory tower,
rather in your self-exiled world, caused something to happen
in the real world—triggered something by a slight tilt of
hand—that upset the status quo and hurt the interests of
certain people. And, in the process, you set in motion a whole
set of counterforces. Knowingly or unknowingly, you
antagonized a group of extremely powerful people—a squad
with unmatched experience and prowess in wielding the
right kind weapons with the right force. To put it simply and
bluntly, and ironically, what they set out to prove was exactly
what you had so categorically asserted with chest-thumping
confidence—the fire did not break out in the factory; it was
set on fire. And *you* had set it on fire . . . Please take it easy,
Mr Nagnath, don't get provoked like this. We are not going
to heap all sorts of accusations upon you. All that we will
offer you is proof. Please don't lose your faith so quickly in
the Parsi sense of justice and fair play you yourself had
endorsed earlier in the morning. First and foremost, please
listen patiently to what I have to say. After that, you are free

to accept or reject it. This is my request to you. No, we are not stating that it was an act of arson on your part—that you deliberately threw petrol over a part of the factory and struck a match to set it on fire. Mr Nagnath, even we agree that the fire was not caused by a burning match. As you said in front of your lady friend, it was a chemical fire—caused by a series of chemical reactions. It was caused by your own new peroxide catalyst formulation. We have enough evidence to prove this. So please don't think that this is a wild allegation based entirely or only on the information your lady friend has shared with us. There was a sudden spurt in demand from customers for a stronger catalyst than what we were manufacturing. As a result, we entrusted you with the responsibility of finding a way of manufacturing it at our factory. These are widely known facts. Our informed conjecture is that the idea of causing a chemical fire came to you while working on manufacturing the new catalyst. According to us, the motive behind such an idea was your intense paranoia of fire. You told your lady friend angrily, "Just to teach these blokes what chemical fires are like, I feel like changing the formulation and cause one." The reason for your anger was not your concern for the safety of the workers and inadequate safety measures taken. It was, in fact, your neurotic fear of fire, which, in recent months, had grown into an obsession. And once that happens, the forces in the unconscious take charge of your thoughts and actions. And we know the reason for your fear of fire, Mr Nagnath. You have our full sympathies. Based on the information we have gathered, we have prepared a brief note. You can read it later. Since it was not intended to defame you, we have been careful not to name you. We have struck your name off

wherever it has appeared inadvertently. There is enough
material in it to support the portrait we have drawn of your
psychological make-up—about your parentage, your
childhood, the incident of the fire where you sustained burns,
the struggles, trials and humiliations you had to face during
your student days, the imprisonment of your brother by the
Goa government at a young age . . . please don't look at me
like this. You are surprised, right? But we do know that your
knowledge of your own childhood is rather sketchy. And he
who is ignorant about his past is confused in his thoughts and
actions, because his ignorance is a mask to hide deep-rooted
fears. In such a situation, it's easy for others to scare you, as
you are vulnerable. You'll be shocked to know who all have
come together to provide us information about you. And
please don't think all of them have something personal
against you or are your enemies. As I described earlier, they
are mere pieces of glass in your kaleidoscope. They have no
significance by themselves, including your friend Shrinivas
Rao—an obnoxious person who stops at nothing . . . scum of
the lowest order. We know that a large part of the information
he has provided is false. But still, we have used them
judiciously only where needed. Coming back to your new
chemical formulation, no matter what the original reasons
behind coming up with it were, once it was ready, it's no
coincidence that it went into production after you moved to
Bombay—within a few weeks, in fact. It was motivated and
pre-planned. This is where the legal angle for your act comes
in. It's a police case. Don't be alarmed, Mr Nagnath, *we* know
better than you do why you've started trembling at the mere
mention of legality and police case. Please see the analysis of
your brother's profile in the note, and you will understand

what I mean. The reason I alluded to legality was, according to criminal law, what is more important is not the motivating factor behind the act but its intention. Its prime concern is the intention behind the act and not its motive. When a new formulation is ready, the general practice is to send it to the production division only after ascertaining that both its production and its use pose no hazard. There is absolutely no record in your laboratory logbook of such precautionary tests being conducted. Also, the proof to support your recommendation that this formulation is safe and suitable for production is not found in your notebook . . . Please don't protest so vehemently that it's not true. You know my definition of truth. Now, please listen to what I have to say without interrupting. There's no dearth of brilliant and learned scientists like you who try to decide something is not hazardous without backing it with proof. In our opinion, such a practice is not as harmless as it may appear. We believe that it was part of a premeditated plot. You saw it as a way out of a difficult situation in your career you suddenly found yourself in. Your idea was to incriminate Jalal in this heinous crime, as you thought he was responsible for the tight spot you were in. Also, you wanted to take revenge on Phiroz, whom you have hated from the beginning. That was the real intention behind your plan. The amazing thing was, your plan succeeded beyond your expectation in achieving their twin goals, albeit in an extremely deadly manner. Firstly, you succeeded in proving that Jalal was not competent to take your position. Please don't shout. Don't forget we are in a place like the Taj Mahal Hotel. We know you suspected Jalal was behind your sudden transfer to Bombay and your trip to America getting indefinitely postponed. We also know that

you believed Phiroz wanted to trample you and give a leg up
to Jalal by promoting him. Predictably, Jalal moved to your
position after you came to Bombay. You wanted Jalal to
initiate the production of the new formulation. Please first
try to understand the pattern we saw through our
kaleidoscope—or the truth, as per your lingo. You will
certainly be given an opportunity to speak later. That's
exactly what happened. We have now come to know that it
was, indeed, Jalal who sent the new formulation for
production. He was in a hurry to claim credit for a formulation
he did not develop. And he paid the price. Through his haste,
he proved he was not fit to occupy such a big position. Even
Phiroz now concedes this. This might, perhaps, make you
feel vindicated at some level. Jalal was dealing with the
process of manufacturing a new formulation he was not fully
familiar with. Before giving his nod for its production, he
should have conducted certain precautionary tests that you
had failed to conduct. Or he should've at least tried a pilot-
scale production to test the waters as per normal practice,
instead of sending it for full-scale production. Phiroz agrees
this should have been done. But it wasn't. It was a major
lapse on Jalal's part. But poor Jalal, he relied entirely upon
the genius of an experienced and senior colleague like you.
That was your calculation too, Mr Nagnath. It was an astute
calculation! After you moved to Bombay, instead of looking
for an apartment befitting your status and position, you
decided to stay in your old dilapidated chawl in Khetwadi.
Please do not deny that this was also part of your malicious
calculation. You had assumed that it was impossible for the
company not to send you back to your R&D position in
Hyderabad. You had taken this for granted. Your arrogance

about your indispensability in the factory was the reason for it. That was why you thought of your transfer to Bombay as a brief stint. Don't look so scared, Mr Nagnath. The only way to prove what I've said so far isn't true is to find loopholes in my arguments. And you will get a chance to do so. I will now ask you a question: When we asked you to go on leave, you did. When we asked you to go to Hyderabad, you went. When we asked you to return, you returned. Do you think all this has no meaning or implications? Do you seriously want us to believe this is the behaviour of an innocent person? Will you believe me when I tell you that if you hadn't committed the blunder of sending copies of the anonymous complaint to the board members, you would have been in Hyderabad by now, occupying your original position? Don't protest. We have absolutely no doubt that you were the brain behind that anonymous complaint. That's because it would not have been possible for anyone else but you to know certain details and be privy to certain information contained in it. We have proof that this information reached the hands a few people in the factory. This is evident from the fact that the mail originated from Bombay. It's a different matter that none of the people who got the information knew you had provided it. The person who met you at the Hyderabad airport . . . Don't be so shocked. The real moment of shock—the manner in which we got to know of this meeting—is coming up soon. So save all your emotions for that. Anyway, coming to the meeting, we don't exactly know the identity of the person who met you at the airport. Our informant, who was sitting at the same restaurant having tea, doesn't know him. But we can make a guess. You can later take a look at his photographs that are in our possession. But what is important is that the envelope the stranger gave you contained a copy of the anonymous complaint. And here's the proof!'

With the air of a person who is about to perform a stupendous feat, Dastur took out an envelope with a flourish, opened it and emptied the contents carefully on the teapoy, as if they were precious gemstones. 'Oh! No!' Nagappa exclaimed. It was a loud scream that emerged breaking all barriers of self-control. Nagappa stared as if it was some awe-inspiring magic trick that had just been achieved with a quick sleight of hand. Even Phiroz and Patel looked incredulous. The envelope Reddy had given Nagappa that he had torn to bits without opening and stuffed into the seat pocket lay in a heap on the teapoy. 'Oh, Thrity! Why did you do this?' Nagappa said aloud.

'What Thrity did was just out of curiosity,' said Dastur. 'But just see how it fits into the pattern in the kaleidoscope! The person who gave you the anonymous complaint had no idea that you knew each and every detail it contained. That is why you tore it to pieces without reading it . . . without even taking it out of the envelope . . .'

Nagappa was not in a state to listen any further. He saw Thrity's face. Fearing his eyes were welling up, he rushed to the toilet. He locked the door, stood before the washbasin, thrust a finger into his throat and retched his gut out.

PART VI

34

Nagappa walked out of the Taj Mahal Hotel. He felt the person who crossed the road and walked on the pavement by the waterfront was not him at all, but someone else wearing his body like a cloak and wandering aimlessly. A little later, he had the strange feeling that the figure shuffling along wasn't even a human figure.

Nagappa had decided to quit his job, but with dignity, after exposing the conspiracy to implicate him in some serious underhand dealings, and after clearing his name. He had now submitted his resignation, but not as a human being exercising his free will and on his own terms. It was a cowardly, impotent act. He felt disgusted with himself. He was nothing but a sewer rat, hiding in a hole clawed out in Koligiriyanna's backyard under a stack of rotting hay. No, he thought, I've gone beyond even feeing disgusted with myself. Look at the way the world of skyscrapers has so easily, so cleverly, so completely demolished Koligiriyanna's backwater ghetto and shaken its very foundations.

Nagappa's life lay scattered haphazard around him. Strangely, the thought of suicide that had come to him, albeit momentarily, several times in the past, had not even crossed his mind today.

His long ties with his professional life had finally been severed. Unknowingly, he had invested all his ambitions and expectations in it. It had become the focal point of his life—the reason for his existence. That which had been an inextricable part of him now lay in tatters.

Breaking the bond with his work was no longer a possibility or an option or even a resolve. The event had actually happened before him, and was concrete and real. From this moment, he had no job. Whether he had given it up or lost it depended upon how much he wanted to preserve his pride and self-respect, and what his mind was ready to concede and how much. The only saving grace was that he had refused to sign the report that the inquiry commission wanted him to. Nagappa wasn't even sure if that was the real aim of the inquiry. All that they probably wanted was to get his resignation. That was the purpose behind the theatrics. The rest was nothing but an elaborate backdrop. They just wanted him out of the way. The fleeting suspicion that had come to him when he was writing the letter of resignation, now took root in his mind. It robbed him of any vestige of dignity left in him that he had decided to walk out on his job, rather than succumbing to their pressure tactics. The resignation had now become meaningless, not a symbolic gesture of the moral stand he thought he had taken.

Without realizing it, he had crossed the Gateway of India and turned to the road going towards Regal Cinema. He was startled when a horse-drawn tonga stopped and the tongawala invited, 'Come, saab, take a ride.' Such carriages were a rarity now, with just a few left in the Girgaum and

Kalbadevi area and here. As an unemployed man, a cab would now be beyond his reach. He thought of taking the carriage, but where to? Certainly not to Khetwadi. He suddenly felt he wanted to go far away from all the places that stood as monuments of his pain and suffering. He wanted to go somewhere where he knew no one and no one knew him, and nothing reminded him of his past. 'Come, saab,' the tongawala persisted. Nagappa realized that he had been standing stock-still before the carriage for a while. He mechanically got into it, as if obeying a command. 'VT, Times of India,' he replied, surprising himself, when the tongawala asked, 'Where to, saab?' He then remembered leaving a note at Sitaram's place that he would be meeting him at his office on Tuesday.

He looked at his watch. It was half-past one. By the time he reached Sitaram's office, Sitaram would have finished his lunch. Nagappa became aware that he was extremely hungry. The bastards! They filled me up with beer and snacks. Good I threw it all up!

As the tonga wound through the familiar route, all that had occurred began to slowly sink in. His mind was surprisingly calm. When they reached The Times of India building, he paid the driver, got off and walked straight into Sitaram's office.

Sitaram had just finished lunch and sat smoking, with his feet stretched out on the table. Nagappa felt a twinge of jealousy at Sitaram's carefree manner. 'Oh, the boss is relaxing!' Nagappa said. Sitaram pulled back his legs from the table and tried to recognize Nagappa through the rings of smoke swirling around him. 'Oh, Nagappa! My god, this must be telepathy! I've been thinking of you! In fact, I've been thinking of you these last three days.'

Nagappa was thrilled his friend had addressed him by his real name and not as Nag. 'Why? Didn't you get the note I'd stuck to your lock?' he asked.

'Don't tell me you'd come to my room!'

'Of course, I had. I needed you so badly to save me from . . .'

Nagappa was unable to finish the sentence. He was about to say, 'from possible suicide', but couldn't. Touched by Sitaram's anxious face, he decided to come straight to the point. 'I quit my job,' he said in a flat voice.

'Don't tell me!' Sitaram screamed, surprised at Nagappa's expressionless face. But as he saw pain slowly permeating it, 'Shall I order tea?' he asked softly.

'I haven't had lunch. So, something to go along with tea . . .?'

Sitaram quickly stubbed the cigarette into the ashtray. 'Come, let's go to the canteen,' he said, looking concerned. 'You can have something to eat there, and we can talk.'

When they were about to leave, Sitaram's colleague, Ranjana Bhoopetkar, pushed the cabin door open and came in with a few letters. 'Oh, Professor is visiting his friend after a long time!' she said smiling. 'And, by the way, my hearty congratulations! I heard you're going to the States . . . Sitaram told me . . .'

Nagappa didn't shake her outstretched hand. 'Not so lucky, Ranjana. Thank you all the same,' he said, without any trace of emotion. 'Sitaram will tell you about it later.'

'Yes,' said Sitaram. 'We were about to go to the canteen.'

The two walked out before Ranjana could respond.

Nagappa knew it would be impossible to tell his friend all that he had gone through in the last two weeks. But just walking with him was so reassuring that he wondered why he hadn't come to him earlier. Though he had gone to Sitaram's room, there was no sense of urgency then.

They didn't speak till they reached the canteen on the first floor. Sitaram was unable to imagine what could possibly have happened for Nagappa to quit his job when he was eagerly waiting to go to America. For Sitaram, who breezed through life with an air of someone asserting his birth right, untouched by the sordidness around him, his friend walking out on his job seemed like a revolutionary step. But he knew from Nagappa's face that something terrible had happened. However, Nagappa himself wasn't aware of all that his face expressed.

When they sat at the table, though Sitaram was anxious to know the details, he knew that could wait. What was important was that his friend was hungry and needed to eat. 'Gajanana!' he called the waiter. The waiter came running. He knew Nagappa. He bowed and smiled and said politely, 'Saab is here after a long time.'

Gajanana's greeting and the surroundings gave Nagappa a sense of normalcy, after the bizarre turn of events of the morning. The contrast between the two was heart-wrenching. He felt a sob caught somewhere inside, unable to escape. He forced a smile in response to Gajanana's.

'Saab has not had lunch,' Sitaram said.

'Lunch service is over, saab, but how about a spicy hot omelette with bread?'

'Great!' Nagappa said. 'And two cups of tea,' he added, looking at Sitaram.

'Okay, I'll join you,' Sitaram nodded.

Not quite sure how to begin, Sitaram lit a cigarette and said, 'You won't believe all that I'm about to say, but you must. I swear by . . .'

Knowing Sitaram's incurable habit of swearing by someone or the other, Nagappa said, 'I believe you. You don't have to swear by your dead ancestors.'

Sitaram smiled. But aware of the gravity of what he was about to say, paused, took two quick puffs and began again: 'For the last two months, I've been telling several members of our league about you going to America. In fact, a felicitation ceremony before you left . . .'

Nagappa's eyes widened with surprise. Just then, Gajanana brought the omelette, bread and butter and placed them on the table. 'Should I serve tea now, sir?' he asked.

'Yes, please,' Nagappa said, and nodded at Sitaram to continue, as he began to eat.

Unable to muster enough courage to ask about the events leading to Nagappa's sudden resignation, Sitaram started gossiping about Shrinivasa: 'I knew you'd protest if I told you about the felicitation ceremony. The league is filled with people who've made money by crooked means. It's disgusting how they show it off by parading their wives decked in gold during community events! Bastards! Full of false prestige and giant-sized egos! I don't want to name names, but Shrinivasa with his printing press, the Udupi restaurant Nayak, building contractor Kamath, Pandurangabhatta, who has moved up from being a two-bit priest to a big-time marriage contractor—all of them are the same! Can you believe, Shrinivasa was the first to raise objections when I put forward the idea of felicitating you? Do you know why? Make a wild guess! The book you're writing! Rather, the book you've *not* written! It all started as a practical joke. I swear by my mother! Remember, long back you wanted to write a novel about Netravati? I think I must've casually mentioned it to Shrinivasa. I don't know why I let the thing slip out. It was probably for the fun of . . . you know . . . scaring him a bit. But I didn't realize this son of a whore got shit-scared! Much later, when you got transferred and moved to Bombay, and your name happened to come up during a conversation, Shrinivasa asked why you'd suddenly come here when you were well-settled in Hyderabad. Somehow his tone irritated me—you know, that prying tone of his. On a sudden whim, I said you'd asked for a transfer to Bombay to write that novel. I added for effect that you were staying in your old Khetwadi home, as you wanted to write it at the scene of the tragedy, and that I'd promised you we'd get a few sections translated and serialized in our *Illustrated Weekly*. I guess I got carried away, seeing his frightened face. I swear by my father, this son of a whore believed it . . . swallowed it whole! He felt extremely insecure. So he tried to consolidate his position in the league by getting a few powerful members on his side. He must've bribed them one way or the other, but managed to get their backing. And then he started a rumour that you were writing a novel about a few of the league members . . .'

Nagappa could hear Sitaram's words. His eyes indicated he was listening. But Sitaram did not know that Nagappa had moved far away from the world where all this mattered. As he tried to grasp what Sitaram was saying with an impersonal, disinterested curiosity, what Dastur had said was acting as a filter through which he heard everything: 'Mr Nagnath, you, in your own ivory tower, rather in your self-exiled world, caused something to happen in the real world—triggered something by a slight tilt of hand—that upset the status quo and hurt the interests of certain people. And, in the process, you set in motion a whole set of counterforces. Knowingly or unknowingly, you antagonized a group of extremely powerful people . . .' So, what was a mere prank or a game for Sitaram, was seen as an invasion into their world by certain powerful people. They perceived it as an assault on their status and position they so jealously guarded. It aggravated the long-festering hatred Shrinivasa had against me. Did a careless comment by Sitaram start this? Nagappa wondered.

In his hurry to unburden himself, Sitaram appeared to have forgotten why Nagappa was there. He was venting his old bitterness against Shrinivasa and the members of the league. By the time Nagappa finished the omelette and bread and picked up his cup of tea, Sitaram had revealed new damning secrets about Shrinivasa. He expected Nagappa to be shocked. But nothing Sitaram said affected him. By way of explanation, Nagappa said calmly, 'Those SOBs pumped me with beer by the time the inquiry started . . . it looks like you don't know about the inquiry held against me today. Wonder why Shrinivasa didn't tell you about it. He played a big part in it.'

'That rascal!' Sitaram exploded. 'Oh, now I understand! "Just wait. There's going to be a big felicitation ceremony for your friend," he said last week. Oh, my god! Don't worry. We'll fight him! We'll fight him to the finish!'

Not even this had an impact on Nagappa. All the anger, all the fight had drained out of him. The omelette and bread had sated his empty stomach. The mild intoxication of the beer still lingered, and his eyes were heavy with sleep. 'I've a lot to say . . . so much to tell you about all this. But not now, Sitaram,' Nagappa said. 'All I want to do now is go home and sleep. I'll meet you in the evening. Meanwhile, read this— the confidential report prepared by the inquiry commission.

But don't lose your cool. A few things mentioned there are facts, and correct in themselves. I don't know about the rest. But, on the whole, the profile they've created . . . the case made against me is a bunch of lies. Don't underestimate the brain behind the report, though. He's brilliant! He can dress utter lies and parade them as the absolute truth. And he has a fascinating theory to support it—about perceived truths and patterns that can be viewed differently from different angles. He based the entire inquiry on this self-propounded theory . . . lectured me about it. You'll find it interesting. Let's talk about it in the evening. Read the report and you'll know what I've resigned from.'

Nagappa handed the report to Sitaram. 'Be careful. It's the only copy I have. Let's have dinner at Flora. My treat. Thanks for the lunch.'

As he waved and left, a fleeting expression on Sitaram's face shook Nagappa.

35

The real implications of the disastrous way his fourteen-day-long torment had ended struck Nagappa only after he woke up.

He looked at his watch. It was nearly six. He was completely drained of the beer-infused courage. He gazed at the chawl opposite through the grille-less window. The familiar structure stood veiled behind the anaemic yellow light of the setting sun, like an old and worn out friendship, bereft of all warmth and intimacy. The neighbourhood lay still, covered in a shroud. Or was it a mask? The moment the extremely dangerous situation he had been dragged into hit him, he became aware of his complete isolation. Loneliness gnawed at him. He had never experienced such loneliness and with such intensity before. He wanted to scream out loud. He wanted to cry his heart out. He began to tremble uncontrollably in absolute dread. He imagined that the pale sunlight on the chawl opposite was the reason for his present state of mind. He got up, closed the window and switched on the light. But his fear grew more acute. No, I mustn't sit huddled here like a fugitive, he thought. He opened the window. He wanted to go out. He thought of something that quickened his movements. He washed his face, pulled whatever clothes he could lay his hands on and changed. He had no patience to wear his shoes. He wore his slippers, pulled out his wallet from the trousers he had worn in the morning, stepped out and locked the door behind him, focusing on the familiar tasks to stop himself from thinking beyond them. He hurriedly climbed down the stairs, his eyes intently fixed on the steps. He felt he knew no one. He went to the restaurant below. The phone was not working there. He walked to the other telephone booth in the 6th Lane. There was already a girl there. She looked like the one he had seen before. She looked up, gave a smile of recognition and indicated with her eyes that she was about to hang up. Her smile made him feel better. He remembered Rani. He needed her badly today. But first, he had to call Sitaram. The girl hung up and said with a mischievous smile, 'It's all yours, sir.' Spunky girl! he thought, thanking her.

He dialled Sitaram's number. The operator came on the line and said, 'Please hold on.' I hope this SOB is still in the office, Nagappa prayed. I hope he hasn't already left. Sitaram finally came on the line, and when he realized it was Nagappa at the other end, began, 'My god! I've really started believing in telepathy! You've got to believe me. I just thought of you, and here you are!' Nagappa sensed that Sitaram didn't sound like his usual self. Something in his tone was different. Something was missing. Nagappa wasn't sure what it was. He didn't feel like confessing to him why he had really called. He wanted to say, 'I don't know why, but after I got up from my nap, I felt terribly alone. I felt something was out to get me. It was frightening. I'll come to your office right away. I'll take a cab.

I have lots to discuss . . . need to talk to you . . .' But he didn't.
He didn't feel like talking. In fact, Sitaram didn't give him a
chance. Presuming Nagappa had called for the same reason
why he had thought about him, he said, 'I just can't believe it!'

'What's it that you can't believe?' Nagappa asked, now
sure he was not the same Sitaram he had spoken to a few
hours back.

'I read the report,' he said.

'That's right, Sitaram, it's really unbelievable! Does the
persona they've created in the report resemble me? That's
why I wanted to come and see you . . . to talk to you about
. . . to tell you what I found out today—that there exists a
parallel universe in this city that looks at everyone and
everything from a bizarre viewpoint . . .'

'Come on, Nagappa,' Sitaram shouted impatiently. 'A
point of view can interpret facts; it cannot *create* them. Do
you deny that your parents weren't Brahmins? Though you
knew the truth, you tried to . . .'

'No, Sitaram, not true. It was all very vague. I didn't
know it for sure. And I don't give a damn whether they were
Brahmins or not. That's not the issue here . . .'

'Really? Don't pretend to be a great revolutionary.
Shrinivasa has a lot of documents to prove that neither your
father nor your mother was a Brahmin. In fact, this report is
based on a lot of information he has provided. Shrinivasa was
here. He left just before you called. An emergency meeting
of the league's Scholarship Working Committee has been
called at seven today . . .'

'What's that got to do with me?'

'We need to urgently discuss ways to prevent the kind
of fraud you've committed from happening again in future.'

Nagappa was outraged. 'What fraud have I committed? All this is Shrinivasa's mischief . . . just to take revenge on me, I don't know for what.'

'It seems you've admitted before the inquiry commission that your parents weren't Brahmins. And it seems you knew about it when you were eighteen. Surprised how I know it? Shrinivasa himself told me. He had lunch at the Taj with the members of the commission after the inquiry was over.'

Nagappa was taken aback. He had wanted to tell Dastur of his decision to resign when he stepped out of the toilet. But before he could do that, the issue of his parents' caste was raised suddenly, without any context. Nagappa had retorted angrily, in fact, sarcastically. And it had already reached Shrinivasa! Dastur must have deliberately raised the issue and taunted him on Shrinivasa's behest, just to provoke him into responding. It was true that he had blurted out something. He realized there was no point explaining all this to Sitaram now. Sitaram mistook his silence for agreement and said, 'So you aren't a Brahmin by your own admission. Yet, you applied for and availed of the special scholarship set up exclusively for needy Saraswat Brahmin students. What it implies is that you *knew* you weren't a Brahmin when you applied for it.'

'I'm not sure even now. Also, I was only twelve when I applied for the scholarship. Actually, it wasn't even a scholarship. It was a student loan. And I repaid every rupee of it.'

'But that's beside the point. The point is, you and your father were capable of misrepresenting facts if it . . .'

'Careful, Sitaram! Mind your words. I know you and your dirty tribe! And from the way you speak, it's evident

which caste *you* belong to. I'd never thought you'd sink so
low. You've forgotten our years of friendship just because
of some absolutely baseless report put together by a bunch
of unscrupulous people to malign me. I didn't expect this
from you. I thought you'd know better than that. I gave you
the report only because I thought you were the one person
who'd understand . . . that you'd look at all the crap written
about me for what it really was . . . that you'd know the truth,
because you know me. But now . . .'

     'Are you trying to threaten me, you worthless bastard?
What's the level of a person like you who doesn't even know
about his parents? Don't think I don't know all your dirty
secrets . . . all the things you've tried to hide from everyone.
Don't think I don't know the real reason you quit your job.
It was all just bravado to save your face. You didn't quit.
They forced you to resign. Thank your stars they ended the
matter there and let you go. You gave me the confidential
report because of your faith in our friendship, right? But you
remembered you had a friend called Sitaram only when you
were thrown out of your job. But you went to Shrinivasa's
house, licking his boots when you were suspended. That
reminds me, it seems you'd gone there the other day to fall at
his feet to get you out of the mess. Shrinivasa told me you ran
out of his house barefoot, without even wearing your shoes.
It seems the neighbours are still gossiping about it. Shrinivasa
was decent enough not tell me the details. Poor man, what
can he say? But I can imagine what must've happened. And
about the report . . . don't think you did me a big favour by
giving it to me. I'd have got it anyway. Shrinivasa has given
me a copy, that too, with your name on it, unlike your copy,
where it's been struck off. It's all there in big, bold capital

letters—Nagnath, alias Nagappa Santayya Mapsekar. Yes, Mapsekar! The proof is right there for all to see. Thoo! Son of a bitch! And as for your brother . . . that's another story . . .'

'Sitaram, listen! Listen very carefully. You gutless bastard, you're saying all this only because I'm not in front of you. If I was, I'd have knocked your teeth out! I can understand my colleagues conspiring against me. It was to save their own skins . . . to protect their own interests. I can even understand Shrinivasa joining them. I don't know why, but he's always hated me, and it has grown over the years. But you? What's *your* excuse? All these days, you spoke against Shrinivasa in front of me. You just couldn't stand him! And now you've suddenly changed sides. But why?! What have I done to you that you spew such venom at me? You call yourself a journalist? You, who have no convictions. You're like a cancer cell that multiplies and kills without any reason . . . at random. Anyway, the line behind me is growing. Others are waiting. Let me come straight to the point. I've decided something. I made up my mind just now as I was speaking to you: There's no use hating the Sitarams, the Shrinivasas, the Bandookwalas and Dasturs of this world. I've no personal hatred against any of you. What I need to do is expose this world built on deceit and lies—the world all of you have built and nurtured—this ugly underworld and organizations like the league that whitewash your black deeds for petty personal gains. I was wondering what to do after I quit my job. But now I've resolved to dedicate the rest of my life to this—to dig up all the muck. And not to turn them into novels like you think. No more fiction. Only, cold, hard truth. I'll reveal your true colours through a new brand of journalism . . .'

Nagappa stumbled out of the telephone booth and lost his balance. It was only when he opened his eyes that he realized he had fainted. He was squatting on the pavement and a small crowd had gathered around him. Embarrassed, he got up and mumbled, 'I'm sorry.' An elderly man bent over him, his kind eyes full of concern. He was wearing white trousers, a long coat and a round cap. 'Do you live nearby?' he asked softly, looking at Nagappa through metal-rimmed glasses perched on a prominent nose. That, his typical nasal twang and his clothes revealed he was a Parsi. He gently held Nagappa's hand, which Nagappa found comforting. The crowd began to disperse. 'I'm okay, now . . . I'm all right,' Nagappa said, trying to free himself. 'Of course, you are. Of course, you're all right,' the man said, like someone coaxing a child, and slowly walked Nagappa to Khemraj Bhavan. As they stood at the bottom of the stairs, the old man patted Nagappa's back. 'I don't know why I'm telling you this, but I feel like telling you anyway,' he said. 'I watched you when you were speaking over the phone. From the way you were trembling and gesticulating, you appeared to be angry with someone. It struck me that you were not just angry with the person at the other end, but with many others . . . many things. So much of anger isn't good for your health. Think about it. But first, get some sleep. Or, if you believe in it, try praying. Forget about everything, close your eyes and pray.'

The old man slowly shuffled back towards the telephone booth, as Nagappa stood staring at him, his mind in disarray. He willed the man to turn and look at him once, but he didn't. Though Nagappa had decided not to give in to any emotions, he was grateful to the stranger.

He climbed the stairs and walked down the corridor. Arjunrao's door was closed. Janaki's house was still locked. When he was about to unlock his door, he saw the pair of shoes he had left at Shrinivasa's house outside. Shrinivasa must have sent someone with them. As he opened the door and went in, he saw two envelopes on the floor. One was from the editor in Hubli. Why has my revolutionary friend thought of writing to me?' Nagappa wondered, picking it up. The other had been hand-delivered and bore *The Times of India* logo. It was thick. The person who brought the shoes must have brought it.

He tore it open. It was the report he had given to Sitaram. A note attached to the report read: *I'm returning the report you gave me. I've received another copy from Shrinivasa. He personally came and gave it to me. Was shocked after reading it. Might take a while to recover from it. Will not be joining you for dinner—S.*

Nagappa eagerly opened the other letter. It had a brief note from the editor, whose name Nagappa couldn't immediately recall, along with a long letter in sloppy handwriting. The editor's note read: *Though the enclosed letter appears to be written by one of your enemies, I'm not naive enough not to realize that you have got it written. The main reason why I am sure this is your handiwork is because the letter provides proof that you are not a Brahmin, and is written to me, who holds avowed anti-Brahmin views. Also, the hallmark of Brahmins is their intelligence and the art of expressing a point of view in a subtle manner, of which the letter is a fine example. However, you have deliberately got it written by someone who can't even spell properly, and in an ungrammatical language, so that the finger of suspicion does not point at you. But you have expressed what you wanted well. My hearty congratulations! The only reason I am sending the letter back to you is because, I do not consider it even worth the matchstick in my box of matches to set it on fire.*

Nagappa knew right away that Shrinivasa was the brain behind the anonymous letter. He felt like laughing. Shrinivasa had sent it to the editor who had published several of Nagappa's stories, including the one about his mother, Paddakka. Shrinivasa had taken out a subscription for the magazine as soon as he had come to know it published Nagappa's stories. This stupid SOB 1 doesn't even know the editor has stopped publishing my work long back, ironically for the opposite reason—because he thinks I'm a Brahmin! And this idiot has gone and written terrible things about me in the letter! He probably doesn't know other publications exist, Nagappa thought. He was about to tear the editor's note and the letter, but stopped, got a box of matches from the kitchen and set them on fire. How would Dastur, the SOB raised to the power of all 10 SOBs, interpret this act? Nagappa wondered. But for him it was significant. It was the first act in his resolve to destroy the roots of evil that sucked the very essence of the soil it got its sustenance from. He watched the fire consuming the pages slowly. Once it was a heap of shrivelled bits of carbon, he scooped it up and threw it in a corner and washed his hands. As he was drying his hands, he noticed that the house hadn't been swept and mopped for days. His unwashed clothes were lying around. The old woman who did these chores hadn't come in for a while. Even the milkman had not delivered the milk. That reminded him that Janaki's house was still locked. He wondered why. Something told him that all these things were somehow interlinked. He thought Arjunrao would have the answer to it and decided to find out, but realized he would not have got back from work yet. He was about to sit down and wait for a while, when there was a knock on the door. He wondered if it was Janaki. His heart began to pound. But it was Arjunrao's wife at the door. 'There's a call for you on our phone,' she said. 'It seems it's very urgent.'

Nagappa hurried to their house, picked up the receiver and said, 'Hello?'

'Hello, Nag, this's Mary.'

Nagappa was first surprised and then angry.

'I'm Mary here, Nag. How are you?' she said, when he didn't respond.

'To hell with you and all that put on sweetness!' he wanted to scream, but couldn't. His eyes filled up against his will. His throat went dry. He wanted to quietly place the receiver back, but Mary guessing he would do that, said urgently, 'Please speak here to Dr Patel.'

It was the MD! 'Oh!' Nagappa exclaimed, without realizing it. He pulled out a chair and sat down. Arjunrao's wife seemed to be alone at home.

Dr Patel cleared his throat at the other end and said, 'Hello, Nag.'

Nagappa, as usual, addressing him by his first name, said, 'Hello, Jeetu, when did you get back?'

'Last night.'

'Well-timed, isn't it?'

'Well-timed for what?'

'Come on, Jeetu, we aren't exactly thumb-sucking infants, are we?'

'Nag, I want you to withdraw your resignation.'

'So, you've already come to know, then?'

'Listen, Nag, let's not discuss this over the phone. Why don't you join me for dinner tonight?'

A sad smile flitted across Nagappa's face, remembering he had planned to have dinner with Sitaram. He wondered why the MD wanted him to take his resignation back, after so much havoc had been wreaked, and after the resignation had put an abrupt and painful end to his torment. Why should I reopen the raw wounds and think about things I've forced myself to forget? he thought. No, I've no courage left in me to go through it all again—succumb to new baits and new snares set up to lure me all over again, just when I have disentangled myself. Why expose myself to new hurts? However tempting it may be, I don't want to walk down that path again—of new aspirations, new possibilities.

'Sorry, Jeetu, I won't be able to make it. Thank you all the same.'

'Listen, Nag, please listen for my sake!' It was Mary again. 'Dr Patel has gone to the next room with Mr Bandookwala. He didn't want Mr Bandookwala to know he was speaking to you. The MD has fabulous plans for you. Believe me, he's extremely upset about what's happened. Please do come for the dinner. It's at the MD's house. It's a small group. I'll be there, too. There'll be a car to drop both of us back home.' Mary's voice was almost a whisper when she said this, as if sharing a secret. The bitch! Nagappa cursed inwardly. I bet Phiroz isn't there. She's lying. The MD is using her to put pressure on me. Yet another strategic move.

'Thank you, Mary, for the most tempting offer,' Nagappa replied calmly. 'But I've no interest left in all these things any more. Please don't think I've become bitter. I'm not even angry. But, yes, I've changed. The truth is, I not only resigned from my job in the company, but from all that my professional life stood for. No one can change my decision now, (Not even the most tantalizing charms of a bitch called Mary). So let's say goodbye to each other. Please thank Dr Patel on my behalf . . .'

'Please, Nag, wait! Please listen to me . . .' Mary continued to plead at the other end.

Nagappa hung up and looked around. He had forgotten where he was. He couldn't even believe all this was happening to *him* of all people—Nagappa, from Koligiriyanna's ghetto, who hadn't asked much from life. I've already given up a lot, he thought. I can probably live without many things. But without love? Without friendship? Without sympathy? Without human compassion? Though he was not ready to admit it to himself, his mind had not yet come to terms with the way his friendship with Sitaram had snapped. Everything seemed to have come to a nought. Trying to fathom how much he had lost in a mere span of fourteen days, he looked up, unable to recognize the figure in front of him through tear-blurred eyes. 'It's too much for anyone . . . for so much to happen in such a short time,' he said. Though he had spoken the words out loud, they sounded like words left unspoken.

Nagappa realized he was still sitting, and it was Arjunrao standing before him, when he felt a hand on his shoulder. Arjunrao said with what appeared to be genuine kindness, 'Take it easy, my young friend. It's just a phase in your life. It'll pass soon.'

He asked his wife standing at the kitchen door to get two cups of tea. 'Where's Amma?' he asked her.

'She has gone to Torate's house on the second floor. Janaki has come there. As soon as you got back from work, they . . .'

Arjunrao nodded as if he understood, signalling her to stop. 'Get the tea first,' he said brusquely. 'Nagappa, sit here, this chair's more comfortable. I'll get changed.' He closed the front door and went into the other room with his files.

Nagappa sat on the chair Arjunrao had indicated, like someone following orders, with no will of his own. He felt he was under a spell and had lost all ability to think. He didn't even remember if he had closed the door behind him when he came here. He had no desire to go and check. All he wanted was to do nothing. Think nothing. Just when I thought I'd closed the door on everything, and was looking for a way ahead, Sitaram and Shrinivasa on one side, and Mary and Patel on the other, are pulling me in different directions—one towards the world I've turned my back on, with the same old vicious dead-end, and another towards new possibilities. Was I too rude to Mary? Too cruel? I didn't want to cast one last glance backward at what I'd left behind. I wanted to snap all ties. I've already snapped . . .

'Did you doze off?' It was Arjunrao's wife, with a cup of tea. As he took it from her, Arjunrao came out, picked up his cup from the tray on the stool and took a noisy sip. 'In a way, it's good that it's all over,' he said.

Nagappa suddenly became alert and looked at him.

'Shrinivas Rao had come to my office. He told me. It seems you were asked to resign? Really felt bad when I heard it.'

The hunters' pack is swelling. They're whooping. The hounds are baying for my blood. The drumbeats are growing unbearably loud. They're circling me. They're closing in on me . . . Nagappa bristled. I thought my resignation would put an end to all this. But it looks like it's only the beginning. Arjunrao

is already baring his poisonous fangs. Let me see how many
hoods of past hatreds he'll fan out. Was his earlier sympathy
genuine? What he said just now was certainly fake. But I no
longer have the strength to ferret out information from him
about me. No more backstabbing, please. I've reached the end
of my patience. I've had enough for a day. You gave me a soft
chair to sit on, and I sat on it. You offered a hot cup of tea, and
I accepted it gratefully. All I want to do now is to go to my
room and sleep—a long, dreamless sleep. I met an old Parsi
gentleman who asked me to pray. I don't think I can bring
myself to do that. Should I go to Banavali's shop and get some
barbiturates? But I'm now scared of sedatives. But why?

'Your tea's getting cold.'

Nagappa started from his chair. He steadied himself
and sipped the lukewarm tea. It had lost its taste. Arjunrao
looked at him. Why am I scared even of this nobody called
Arjunrao? Why is he staring at me like this? This SOB didn't
say, 'It seems you gave your resignation.' He said: 'It seems
you were asked to resign.' Look how he's staring at me with
his hyena-eyes. Did he growl? Did he bare his teeth? Did he
laugh?

'I don't know how Shrinivas Rao got hold of a copy of
the inquiry commission's confidential report. Even I've got a
. . . he gave me a . . .'

Nagappa looked incredulous. Looking at Nagappa's
expression, Arjunrao slunk into the room. He came back
with an envelope. 'Take a look at this,' he said, holding it
out in front of Nagappa. Nagappa didn't dare touch it. He sat
staring at Arjunrao.

Arjunrao had never seen Nagappa like this before. 'There's
no use getting emotional. You must fight this Shrinivas Rao.

Fight him legally if necessary. It looks like he's taking revenge on you because you're writing a novel about him. He wants to defame you before you defame him in front of his community. It seems he has collected a lot of information about your parents . . . even about your brother. And today, at the matha, in front of people of your caste . . .' Seeing Nagappa smile, he stopped midway, confused. But he continued after a pause, gathering courage, 'Please don't mistake me. I know you don't believe in such things. Even *I* don't believe in it. But it's not merely a question of your lineage but about your reputation . . . about the accusation that you've cheated your community. You must clear your name. You must investigate your past and collect facts to refute those presented by Shrinivas Rao. I'll help you if you want. I can understand how ironic the situation is—the necessity of someone like you who doesn't believe in the caste system having to prove you're a Brahmin . . .'

The undertone in what Arjunrao was saying didn't escape Nagappa. He knew there was a catch somewhere. Arjunrao was dangling a bait before him. But Nagappa wasn't sure what he was out to get. The neat logic of the case he was presenting was irrefutable. It was clear Arjunrao was trying to step out of his limited orbit, with an eye on something beyond him. It was unusual and out of character for him to do this. Nagappa was tempted to delve deeper to find out what he was really after.

'There're other interesting things in the report, apart from my parentage and caste,' Nagappa finally said.

'I know. But I don't give them too much importance. Besides, most of the information has to do with your company. To sum it up, what they've done is, studied your mental make-up, spotted criminal tendencies in you, using the fact that your brother went to prison at a very young age for some crime he committed, and created a psychological profile of yours. I think that's rather an audacious thing to do—a bit far-fetched, I daresay. I consider all this a vicious strategy to put psychological pressure on you. But I must admit one thing: The brain behind it is brilliant! Ingenious! Wonder from where they gathered all the information. A really meticulous job! And the way they've linked each piece of information, one leading logically to the other to establish a series of proofs to create a watertight case is a marvel . . .'

There was no doubt in Nagappa's mind now. This slimy creature that usually slithered quietly, wasn't as harmless as it appeared to be. It had suddenly unfurled its many hoods and it waited, hissing, ready to strike.

Nagappa's look must have revealed this. Arjunrao had stopped mid-sentence. Just then, his wife appeared, and as if on cue, he said, pretending to remember something, 'I'd almost forgotten . . . she'd asked me to invite you for dinner . . .'

Nagappa nodded even before Arjunrao had finished, looked at his wife and said, 'Thanks.'

Just then, there was a soft knock on the door. Arjunrao opened it. It was Mary. 'Excuse me, is Mr Nagnath . . .?'

'Hello, Mary,' Nagappa said, unable to believe his eyes. He got up and introduced her to Arjunrao: 'This's Mary, my colleague, or rather, my ex-colleague. I'll see you later. Come, Mary, let me show you my "palace".'

He led Mary along the corridor to his room.

36

Mary was wearing a deep blue georgette sari with a sleeveless matching blouse, which highlighted her flawless, fair complexion. Her hair had been stylishly twisted into a doughnut bun, probably with false hair. The faint scent of an expensive French perfume wafted from her (a gift from the MD?). The high heels she was wearing added inches to her already tall frame.

Nagappa looked at her with admiration, as if he had just realized how beautiful she was. He became suddenly and acutely aware that a lovely and sophisticated woman like her looked out of place in a dingy, dilapidated chawl like Khemraj Bhavan. He was deeply embarrassed. The neighbours saw her as she walked with him into his house. They kept their doors open, curious to know what was going to happen. He led her in, switched on the light, pulled the two chairs away from the window opening into the corridor, offered her one and sat on the other. 'Please close the door,' she said. Nagappa got up and pulled the door shut, but didn't bolt it. She smiled and bolted the door herself. Though the room was small and dirty, the huge shelf lined with books lent it some dignity. Mary sat, staring at the collection. Nagappa felt bad that he had mentally called her a bitch a short while ago. He thought her beauty had the intoxicating power to blunt his ability to think clearly.

Unable to read his expression, she said, 'Let me warn you, Nag! You're going to get ready in the next fifteen minutes. You're coming with me to the MD's house for dinner! The car's waiting downstairs.' Though it sounded like a hypnotist's command, it lacked its mesmerizing power. She realized this when she looked at his face. 'Please, Nag, for my sake . . . please don't throw away such a great opportunity,' she pleaded.

Nagappa looked up as she spoke. Something made him soften his stance. 'Sorry, Mary, I've already told someone I'll eat at their place,' he said, as if coaxing a child. 'I know the MD has sent you here. Tell me, what does he want from me now?'

He sat back, indicating he had nothing more to say but was willing to listen. Even though he was intently gazing at her, he looked aloof and far away. His complete lack of interest, tinged with a deep sense of regret in his eyes, disturbed Mary. She knew she had failed at the task entrusted to her. The realization that the power she had over him was slipping away made her want to cry.

She made one last attempt: 'Please, Nag, look at me! Look, I'm here, sitting in front of you. Please don't withdraw into your shell. Keep an open mind to what I've to say at least for a few minutes. Don't shut the door on everything like this. Listen! I know what you've gone through these last two weeks. I can understand your state of mind. But I've brought news that'll put an end to all your suffering . . . the

most exciting news you can ever imagine! I know it'll make
you very, very happy when I give you the fantastic news.
Don't look at everything with suspicion, Nag. Stop being so
sceptical about everything. Believe me, I've not dressed up
like this to entice you . . . persuade you, but to show you how
happy I feel. I closed the door because I thought I'd burst
into tears when I gave you the news . . . when I'd see a smile
on your face. But I won't be able to speak if you sit like this
as if it's got nothing to do with you. Don't make it difficult
for me, Nag. Please help me give you the news that'll make
you change your mind. Help me fulfil the responsibility the
MD has given me, because of the special friendship you and
I share. I willingly accepted this task, because I'm *so* happy
for you! In fact, the MD himself wanted to personally give
you the news. But he knows how stubborn you are. That's
why he sent me here. What's surprising is, with all your
intelligence, you fell into the trap laid by others. The MD
hasn't accepted your resignation. He never will. Instead, he
has promoted you to a higher position. Do you know which?
Can you make a guess? As the company's technical director,
Nag! Congrats, Nag! Now cheer up! And can you believe
it, Rutter, the vice president of our American company
is planning to recommend your name as a member of the
board of directors. He's personally coming here to attend
the board meeting. And what's more, you'll be travelling to
America as the company's technical director. Cheer up, Nag!
And please stop being so obstinate. Don't bang the door shut
on the opportunity standing at your doorstep. Don't throw
it all away. Don't let the DMD win. Don't let deceit win.
He doesn't know about your promotion. The MD wants to
announce it in front of everyone at the dinner tonight. That's

why he wants you there. Even the DMD is coming. Please cancel the other plan and come with me. You should've seen how angry the MD was when he heard you had resigned. In fact, even the DMD, who's behind the conspiracy, was surprised! He hadn't expected things to go this far. He'd no idea his scheme would backfire so badly and you'd get angry enough to resign. It came as a total shock to him by his own admission to the MD. It seems the inquiry was at Hotel Taj? No one in the office knew. The MD still doesn't know what exactly happened. But it seems someone called Dr Dastur went against you . . . carried things too far and provoked you into resigning. Is it true? In fact, we got to know from the DMD that even Dr Dastur hadn't expected you to resign. The DMD was really upset. You should've seen his face! It seems, as per the original plan, the DMD was to conduct the inquiry himself. The MD is at a loss why or when names of two people who have nothing to do with the company got added to the inquiry commission. Even now he doesn't know what exactly the DMD would gain by all this! But that's all in the past, Nag. That's history. But now the future lies ahead of you . . . a great future. It seems the American director thinks highly of you. I was so happy when the MD told me this. I'm *so* proud of you, Nag! I'm . . .'

Nagappa suddenly felt totally and utterly bored. Anxiety, fear, hope, expectation, desire and several other unnamed emotions churning within him receded, and a kind of ennui settled over him. He tried to suppress a yawn.

'Excuse me, Mary, I've not slept properly for the last one week. All I want is to grab some sleep. My neighbour Arjunrao, whom you met just now, has invited me home. I'll eat there. Also, I just don't have any strength left in me to go anywhere. It's not that I'm not pleased with the news you've brought. Believe me, I'm happy to hear it. But not for the reason you think. I'm not even sure of the reason. Mary, I didn't just quit my job. I resigned from the workaday world—the professional world where people manipulate each other, use each other for their own selfish ends or to hide from their insecurities. I may have walked out of my job in an extremely agitated state of mind, in a weak moment, as you believe. But I realized how strong my resolve was, now, when you gave me the news of my promotion . . . when you told me the American director has a very high opinion of me. I honestly think my decision wasn't based on some kind of false arrogance. Should I call it wisdom that has come to me at long last, at the end of years of torment? Shall I tell you what struck me as I listened to you with a clear mind, without any professional ambition or temptations? Here it is: Mary, this isn't petty politics. It goes deeper and is more sinister than you think. Material worth millions of rupees disappeared . . . was stolen. It would've seriously damaged the company's reputation and its future growth if the shareholders got to know of it. The directors would be in deep trouble if word went out that the company was being mismanaged . . . was in the hands of people who were unaware, or worse still, part of such dealings. As you know, every company needs to safeguard its reputation in the market at any cost. The American director was aware of this more than anyone else. Our MD or DMD weren't bothered about it. They were busy pulling each other down. The MD was urgently called to America to discuss this—not for his promotion as you thought. The real reason for the urgency was that an anonymous complaint had reached the American directors.

They must've wanted the MD to hush up the whole affair. Shall I make another wild guess? The anonymous complaint was based on inside information the MD himself had deliberately placed in the hands of a few people—those who shouldn't have been privy to it. No, Mary, don't look so scared. Wonder how I know this? Simple logic—all actions have their roots in selfish motives! Probably even you don't know what I'm going to tell you now—the MD's hand was behind even the leaking of the classified information contained in the audit report. Or, perhaps, you know this. But you'll be able to confirm if the proof I'm going to give to support my guess is valid or not. Shall I go ahead? It was the MD who got me transferred to Bombay, because he *wanted* me here. Mary, please don't look so frightened. I'm not accusing you of anything . . . that you knew this all along, but didn't tell me. Please relax and enjoy this game of guessing motives: The MD wanted to trap the DMD. He didn't want me in Hyderabad when he began this game. He was worried that if the DMD got into trouble, I'd be naive enough to find a solution to somehow get him out of it. He didn't want to take any chances. He thought it safer to keep me away from the DMD and from Hyderabad. In fact, that's exactly what happened! I think the real reason behind the inquiry commission the DMD set up was to get me to help him out of the serious mess he was caught in. But he didn't ask for my help because he was worried I'd refuse. So he and his gang thought of arm-twisting me into doing it. Also, they suspected I was the brain behind the damaging anonymous complaint sent to the higher-ups. Anyway, their plan was to put fear into me . . . to terrorize me. From the way the inquiry was conducted, it's clear that it had been carefully planned for days. They had come well-prepared. I can understand the reason for that sudden spark in your eyes just now, Mary—that's why the MD has sent you here in such a great hurry. He badly wants to know what happened at the inquiry. That's why you're here, isn't it Mary—to gather information from me? I won't find fault with you. So, relax. It's all part of the game. I've now learnt the ropes, Mary, the twisted rules it's played by. I'll tell you something to show you just how well I've learnt them: They . . . I mean the so-called inquiry commission wanted my signature on a false report to establish some kind of connection between the material smuggled out of the factory and the fire. There was, of course, no connection. The DMD himself was to conduct the inquiry—that's what Khambata had told me. I don't know what reason the DMD had given the MD for conducting the inquiry. The MD is no less a villain. No matter what the reason, he probably calculated that once the inquiry began, it would involve the DMD and his gang, who would then be exposed. After the MD went to America, the DMD must've decided to get in Dastur and Patel, who had advised him about the inquiry. The bundle of lies Dastur presented during the inquiry didn't scare me. It only made me sick to my stomach. Poor man, he thought I didn't know Jalal has not yet taken over as the R&D manager! He also didn't guess I knew that my new formulation, which, by the way, isn't flammable, had not yet gone for production! To tell you the truth, if he had told me, "You not knowing your proper parentage clearly proves that you are behind the fire", I'd have probably believed him. Of course, the MD will be interested to know that I didn't sign that report—if that's what you wanted to know and that's what you're here to find out. However, to come back to the story, the reason I gave my resignation was not what the DMD thought it was. The reason was quite different: It was the strange fear which two girls who had treated me with respect and kindness, who had nothing to do with this inquiry, created in me at a crucial moment during the inquiry! Mary, even I'd got a copy of the anonymous complaint. I had torn it without reading it. Your friend Thrity was on the flight. I thought she didn't notice me stuffing the torn pieces into the seat pocket. But it looks like she had. She must've gathered them out of curiosity and later shown them to you to reassure you she had spoken to me on the flight. I'm now certain the torn complaint reached Phiroz through you. But the mere suspicion that that's what must've happened was enough to make me panic during the inquiry. At that moment, I thought you were on Phiroz's side. That's what you wanted me to believe. But I now know you were working on the MD's behalf—as a decoy. You played that rather well! You went to Phiroz's party and tried to make me believe you liked Phiroz more than the MD. By giving the anonymous complaint I had torn and discarded to Phiroz, you confirmed his suspicion that I was the brain behind it. You're doing a wonderful job for the MD! I hope you're paid well, Mary. Yes, it's true that I loved you. But I didn't have the courage to admit it to you. I thought you had similar feelings for me—that was much before you joined the MD's game of using me as a pawn for his selfish ends. I know the MD will be in trouble if I don't take back my resignation. And if I accept the offer of promotion recommended by the American director himself, then I can be used to reduce the DMD's power and influence in the factory. Anyway, don't worry, I've not signed the report. I refused to sign it. When you tell the MD this, he'll force the DMD to agree to all his conditions. That'll help him sideline the DMD . . . Phiroz, and wrest back power from him. I bet he'll then have no hesitation in accepting my resignation. If the American director questions him about it, he'll personally send a copy of the profile Dastur has prepared about me with a note expressing his deep regret and disappointment at the turn of events and subtly hint at his helplessness in having to accept my resignation. You think the MD doesn't know I'm no match for a scheming villain like Phiroz? Of course, he does! Mary, on my behalf, please tell him this: No matter what others may think or say, I'm extremely happy that at least the American director, from thousands of miles away, recognized my merit and my ability to become the company's technical director. Believe me, Mary, my experience . . . what I've gone through these last two weeks have made me an expert in guessing motives behind human behaviour. Now, take for example, my neighbour Arjunrao. He has talked me into accepting an invitation to have a meal at his house. I had to go there to take your call. He showed me some sympathy and softened me up for the kill. A drama is going to unfold here by tomorrow morning. The woman living next door, whose house has been locked for the last few days, has a major role in it. The motive behind it all? To evict me from this house . . . to make me flee from here. But I can't run any more, Mary. I'm tired. I don't know if you'll ever visit me here again. It's a hellhole in an extremely filthy chawl. And from today, I'm a nonentity—a jobless nobody. Why will you come?'

Nagappa somehow felt he was talking to himself. He opened his eyes. The chair in front of him was empty. The tears that had welled up in his eyes flowed unchecked. He didn't know when Mary had left. The door was open. He got up to close it when Arjunrao appeared. 'Dinner's ready. Your friend didn't stay for long, did she? She left in a hurry . . . almost ran out of the building, it seems. My other neighbour told me,' he said.

37

It was late when Nagappa got up. He had closed all the windows. But the familiar sounds of daily routine from the world beyond had begun to sneak in with the rays of the sun, indicating it must be eight in the morning. Nagappa didn't remember when he had slept like this, without the help of beer or sedatives. He was filled with a saint-like serenity, free of all entanglements. It tempted him to look for its cause. He realized he was lying bare-chested for the first time in his life, as far as he could remember. After more than thirty years, he had at last found the courage to look at his body. He was able to stare without cringing at what had come to symbolize his past, that had needlessly tormented, terrified and lacerated him all his life. After today, I might continue to hide my terrible scar and the ghastly truth it reveals, he thought, not because it frightens me, but because it might frighten others. But I'm now free.

He had told Mary a drama was going to unfold by morning. And his conjecture had proven right. Last night, in an extremely unexpected moment, he had suddenly bared his chest before Arjunrao, his wife, his mother, Janaki, her husband and a few other neighbours. They had screamed in shock. Janaki's husband had almost fainted. The dramatic gesture was in response to an accusation Janaki's husband and the others had made against him. He had realized Janaki's flirtation had been part of a game plan to throw him out of his house. Her husband needed space to open a tailoring shop, and his house next door was perfect for this. It was not surprising that the ploy had Arjunrao and Shrinivasa's support. The allegation fabricated against him was that when all the menfolk of the chawl went out to work, he would lie in wait for Janaki and make all sorts of obscene gestures at her. Terrified of his disgusting behaviour, the poor girl had gone away to her brother's house for a few days. Arjunrao's mother had taken it upon herself to describe his vulgar gestures in graphic detail for the benefit of others, in a manner that belied her age. With a kind of macabre cruelty he was yet to fathom, she had grotesquely gesticulated and spat at him: 'It seems he goes even to the extent of unbuttoning his shirt slowly in front of her to show her his hairy chest! What does he think . . . is this the red-light area of Foras Road or what? Never heard of such shamelessness in my life! If he can't control his itch, let him either get married or leave this place right now!'

Her revolting words, and more than the words, the ugliness within her that she had laid bare, and the morbid relish the others obviously derived from it—the lip-smacking satisfaction in their eyes—had shattered Nagappa. Not one of them had spoken when he left Arjunrao's house, bare-bodied, still holding his shirt and baniyan.

He had come home and thrown himself on the bed. When he lay awake for a long time, what had troubled him was their silence. In the shadowy stillness of his room, when the memory of Janaki's seductive body flitted across his mind, what he felt was a deep sense of regret mixed with fear. And the next moment, he was filled with a kind of gratitude—a sense of deliverance. Last night's incident was the climax of the play that was being enacted these last two weeks—the two weeks that had given him the courage to accept all that he had been running away from all his life. Last night had been the final act.

This place in which I've suffered so much belonged to my aunt, he remembered. Amma died here. We stayed in this very house when we brought her to Bombay for the treatment of an incurable ailment. My sister disappeared forever in the crowds around here. When we went back to the village, Appa torched me and almost killed me. He then killed himself, and then the death of my aunt—everything that happened, I remember all that now. I'm thinking of all that now . . .

Nagappa had fallen into a deep, dreamless sleep, as he felt imbued with the courage to at last see all that had happened in a new light, and gained the perspective to see them for what they were.

He kicked the blanket covering him aside, and felt his chest and stomach with both his hands. His eyes closed. As minutes passed, they slowly welled up with tears. Somewhere in this city was a woman whose heart beat for him, who looked at what he dared not, and touched his disfigured body as if it was the most natural thing to do. She expressed her love and compassion with the touch of her fingers. Rani. It was her thought that made him want to get out of bed. He didn't want to ruin the wordless pleasure the relationship gave him with his verbose analysis. It seemed irrelevant even to question why. He felt like seeing Rani right now. He remembered her dimpled smile and her slanting eyes that grew smaller when she smiled, which seemed like an answer to his terrible habit of demanding reasons for everything and analysing all motives and intents. I haven't seen her lovely face for so long! Nagappa thought. He quickly bathed and wore the cream-coloured trousers and blue shirt that Mary and Chetana said they liked. He got into the pair of black shoes Shrinivasa had sent back yesterday. He looked at himself in the mirror. He was pleased that he was happy. Life's joys are probably found in such momentary states of happiness, he thought. But he didn't feel like delving deep into this awareness. He decided to go to Santosh Bhavan for breakfast and then to Rani's house. He had never gone to Rani's house during the day. But he thought he *had* to see her now.

When he reached Benham Hall Lane, his eyes automatically looked for the girl who called him dada and sold him flowers. He was disappointed when he couldn't find her. But he bought two strings of jasmine from a boy who was sitting at her spot. The thrill that rose in his mind at the question, 'For whom?' made 'Why?' irrelevant. The fragrance of the flowers lifted his already high spirits.

As he entered Santosh Bhavan, Nayak greeted him with a crooked smile. Now this SOB 1 is going to start with, 'Shrinivasa told me everything . . .' Nagappa thought. And that was exactly how Nayak began the conversation.

'Really?' Nagappa smiled. 'That makes my work so much easier.'

He went and sat at his usual table, without stopping to hear Nayak's response. The waiter pretended not to see him and walked towards another customer. So, even he knows, Nagappa thought. Shrinivasa has been going around distributing the report like some flier. Nagappa asked the waiter who came to take his order to send Gopala, who usually served him. Gopala hesitantly came and stood shuffling awkwardly. 'It seems you were thrown out of your job . . . is it true, sir?' he asked, before Nagappa could speak. Nagappa didn't bother to reply. There was no point in trying to explain anything now. And it was not a question that sought an answer. That he was not facing the same plight had given the waiter courage to ask the question. Whether people were crushed in a house collapse, burnt alive in a fire accident or killed by an assassin—it was all the same. People displayed the same sadistic curiosity—an unhealthy appetite to sup on other people's suffering.

'If the idli is hot, bring a plate of that, and piping hot coffee,' Nagappa ordered. The waiter's face fell. Sullen at not getting a response to his question, 'The owner himself told . . .' he said defensively. Nagappa didn't react.

He finished his breakfast, paid the bill and left. As he was leaving, he heard Nayak telling someone about him. Nagappa ignored them and walked in the direction of the Opera House. From there he walked towards Rani's house near Kennedy Bridge with an urgency that surprised him.

He held the packet of jasmine strings tight. His heart was pounding as he neared Rani's building. He was visiting her after a long time. His eyes moistened without his knowledge. He found it difficult to put words together to express what he felt as he climbed up the familiar wrought-iron spiral stairs to the third floor.

He reached her doorstep, still in the throes of his emotions. It was only then did he feel that he shouldn't have come here at this time. Two girls squatting in the corridor disappeared quickly into one of the rooms, scared and embarrassed by their appearance. Nagappa had seen one of them before, but he didn't know her name. She was Rani's friend. Rani's door was locked. Nagappa knew he had wronged her and felt sad he hadn't visited her for so long. As he stood before her door, her friend who had run inside came out. She had combed her hair and changed from a nightie into a sari. 'After a long time . . .' she smiled with genuine warmth. Was she trying to say, 'Rani waited for you for long?' Nagappa wondered. He waited for her to say something. 'Rani doesn't live here any more. Another girl's going to come in her place,' she said. She added after a pause, 'Rani's going to leave Bombay.' Just then, two more girls came and stood near Nagappa. One of them said, 'A rich sethji is going to take her to Ahmadabad . . . in two days. She went to her brother's house yesterday evening. Her brother had come to take her.' The other girl interrupted in a masculine voice, 'It seems you lost your job. So sad! Rani's brother told us.'

Was she trying to imply that Rani wouldn't have otherwise gone from here? Nagappa couldn't make sense of anything. His mind was somewhere beyond the realm of words. He wondered why the girls were looking at him in this strange way and mouthing strange sounds. Am I really here? Why am I here? he asked himself, panicking. He walked towards the stairs like a sleepwalker, his eyes looking blank. Rani's friend walked with him along the corridor. 'Will you come tonight? I'll wait for you,' she said, at the head of the staircase. He mechanically handed the flowers he had brought for Rani, without saying anything. The girl in front of him was not she. It was no one. The space seemed empty.

As he stood on the first step, looking down, 'My name is Vatsala,' the girl said. Did she misunderstand my gesture of giving her the flowers? Nagappa wondered.

The ground below appeared hazy from the third floor when Nagappa looked down with tear-blurred eyes. But as he climbed down, a step at a time, he heard his footfall clearly, as if for the very first time in his life. A resolve that was crystallizing somewhere deep within him was searching for words: Finding my brother whom I've never seen and my lost sister should be my sole aim in life. I should spend the rest of my days searching for them. As he neared the bottom of the stairs, things began to fall into place. It all became clear to him. He paused.

The huge banyan tree in front had cast a long shadow in the blistering sun. Below it sat an old man in a white dhoti, black coat and a red piece of cloth around his head. A pair of green and yellow birds fluttered in the cage that stood before him. He had spread a few cards on a mat to tell the future. Nagappa had seen him on his way up. But he now suddenly assumed the appearance of a magician. As Nagappa stood staring at him, he remembered Vomu. He felt Vomu symbolized the only path that lay ahead that he must now take—alone. He imagined Vomu would appear before him and nudge him to take that path. As he stood hesitating, he felt he did not yet have the courage to take that path. But he was sure he would find the courage one day, when he who had paraded as somebody all these days, would have the courage to live as a nobody.

He thought his days of rigorous imprisonment had just ended, and the years of exile lay ahead. 'I'll find that path, Vomu, on my own,' he said. 'But now, I'm going in search of my brother and sister. Here, I have taken the first step!'

Nagappa ran down the steps with a sense of urgency, as though his brother and sister were waiting for him below. His feet at last hit the ground.